D0888653

THE SPLINTER

A LANCE SPECTOR THRILLER
BOOK 5

SAUL HERZOG

AUTHORCONTACT

1

Valentina Brik eyed the building from across the street. The moon was almost full, and her breath billowed in the ghostly blue light like an apparition. She was surprised by the cold—she'd been expecting Prague to be warmer than Saint Petersburg—and she stamped her feet to stop them from going numb. She was leaning in a doorway, smoking a cigarette, and when it was done, she flicked it in a high arc into the cobbled street.

She knew the apartment was empty. The lights were out, there was no sign of movement, and the tenant, a junior CIA analyst at the nearby American embassy, was still at her desk at work.

Valentina reached into her pocket and felt the cold steel of a PSS silent pistol. She hated the little thing—developed during Soviet times for the express purpose of carrying out assassinations. It was quiet—she'd grant it that much—thanks to its specially designed SP-4 cartridge. The neck of the cartridge sealed when the gun fired, preventing smoke, blast, and sound from escaping the barrel. But that was where the benefits ended, and the weapon never saw widespread use, even within the GRU for whom it had been developed. It certainly wasn't Valentina's weapon of choice. For one thing, its effective range maxed out at fifty feet, and with a muzzle velocity of just six-hundred feet-per-second, it was always at serious risk of being outgunned. The magazine held six of the custom cartridges, and when things went south, as they invariably did, the chance of finding more 7.62x41mm ammo in the field was zero.

In her opinion, the gun was a toy, a novelty. The fact that it was manufactured in Tula, at a factory most famous for having been opened by Tsar Peter I himself in 1712, said it all. It was a curiosity, more suited to display in the State Weapons Museum than actual active use.

The gun had entered production in 1979 and was made available to GRU operatives and certain Spetsnaz units a few years later. It had been standard issue for assassins briefly before a litany of complaints relegated it to Special Order status. To even get her hands on one, Valentina had been obliged to fill out a three-page requisition form, get that approved by her operator in Moscow, and then submit the form in hard copy to the Plant Administration Office in Tula. The process had brought her to the post office in person twice, and as she'd feared, when the gun arrived, it came with just four SP-4 magazines.

It was a lot of hoops to jump through for a measly twenty-four underpowered bullets, especially given that she usually had access to one of the most formidable weapon inventories on the planet—the Prime Directorate's assassin armory in Moscow.

Needless to say, it was not by choice that she'd jumped through those hoops. Her kill order had come from

Direktor Osip Shipenko's office, and he, in his infinite wisdom, had expressly ordered that one of two specific weapons be used for the job—either the PSS silent pistol or the even less practical, and more obscure, NRS-2 Scout Firing Knife. Valentina had to do a double-take when she'd read that. The NRS-2 was another brainchild of the Tula Arms Bureau and was brought into service in 1986, again for assassins. The weapon was a gun-knife hybrid— a gun of sorts that was also a tactical knife with a six-inch retractable blade. The knife's handle contained a built-in, single-shot firing mechanism that used the same impossible SP-4 ammo the PSS did. When it was introduced, it proved even less popular than the PSS, and an extremely limited number were ever produced. Valentina had requested hers directly from the armory at the Kremlin, and it arrived at the Prague embassy in a sealed diplomatic pouch just the day before.

As well as the knife, the pouch had contained a note, handwritten by Shipenko, that said, regardless of whether it was necessary or not, she was to make sure that at least one SP-4 bullet was left at the scene of the murder for investigators to later discover.

That was strange.

Ordinarily, she made a conscious effort not to think about her jobs—after thirty kills, it was the only way to remain sane—but every once in a while, a small detail of a mission would get stuck in her mind. She hated when it happened. She'd lose sleep over it. Her concentration would suffer. She'd lie awake at night obsessing about some random, unimportant detail, such as the way a target had his shoelaces tied.

She knew it was the strain of the job, a symptom of the mental anguish that came from killing on a regular basis, and she suspected it would eventually put her in the asylum. And it was getting worse, to the point she was considering mentioning it to her handler. Surely there was a pill they could give her. But then, the GRU wasn't known for its enlightened HR practices, particularly when it came to the mental health of its operatives. The traditional remedy, vodka to the point of oblivion, was probably the wiser option. It was certainly the option she'd been leaning on, though she was beginning to worry that if she didn't do something more sustainable soon, the voices in her head would consume her.

She lit another cigarette. Her very first job, her first kill, first taste of blood, before she'd graduated to overseas missions and become one of the most formidable killers in Moscow, was a political dissident living in a remote Siberian region near the city of Tomsk. The man was a member of an Orthodox church that had resisted Soviet attempts at assimilation—what was known as an *Old Believer*. Valentina hadn't minded that. She watched him go about his business—pray, buy bread, shovel snow— then carried out the order while he was swimming in the Ket River. The river was cold, naturally, but good Russians liked the cold. Valentina believed that. She prided herself on her ability to withstand it. It was something the GRU took seriously. Something they tested for. So she watched in mild admiration as this Old Believer swam in near-freezing water, alone but for his dog, and only shot him when he was done. Two bullets. One for the man, one for the dog.

It was only after that, when she got up close to the body to check her work, that an image was planted in her mind. It was an image that visited her to this day, an image that could only be banished by another swig of vodka before she passed out for the night. When she got up close to the body, she noticed that the man, the Old Believer, only had three toes on each of his feet. There were no scars. No marks. He hadn't lost the appendages in an accident. His feet had always been that way. The three toes he had were wider than normal, and filled the width of his foot. Like the hoof of a pig, she'd thought. She still dreamt about it. No matter what she took or how much she drank, the image of those deformed feet bubbled to the surface of her mind and stayed with her.

And that was just one of them.

Another time, not long after, she'd been ordered to kill a British diplomat at the European Commission in Brussels. When the job was complete, she'd noticed that, beneath an impeccably tailored Savile Row suit, the target was wearing the most intricate set of women's lingerie she'd ever seen, complete with corset, garter, and black lace thigh-high stockings. It wasn't something Valentina thought she'd been particularly shocked by—what people did in the privacy of their bedrooms was of little interest to her—but for some reason, the thought stuck in her mind. As soon as she got back to Saint Petersburg, she trawled obsessively through the sex classifieds of all the magazines until she found a man who would act out the fetish. She met up with him, a high-powered business executive who wore expensive suits and had the same brown hair as her target in Brussels, and told him what she wanted. After that, they met regularly at a seedy hotel in Tverskoy, where they played out the scenario in her head. The man dressed in lingerie as close to what she'd seen in Brussels as she could find, and then played the role of a submissive female while Valentina played the role of the man.

She got no pleasure from it. She found it ridiculous, repulsive even—the obscene rubber toy strapped to her waist like a codpiece, and the pitiable man practically salivating while awaiting his fix. It was sordid—undignified. If anyone ever found out, she might have killed them to keep the secret. But there was nothing she could do about it. Like an abuse survivor, she felt compelled to play out the scenario, over and over, as if searching for a way to resolve what her mind already knew was unresolvable.

As she sucked on the cigarette, she already had that nagging feeling that this was going to be one of those jobs that left a mark. Shipenko's specification that she use the SP-4 ammo was a thread. A thread that she would later pick at, compulsively, and might never get to the bottom of.

She knew there was a very real possibility that there was no reason behind it at all, that it was nothing more than the whim of a sick man who'd grown accustomed to toying with his victims. But she could also see how it might fit into something more. A plan. An intention. If Shipenko was trying to send a message to the Americans, for example, then using the SP-4 ammo was certainly one way of doing it. It was a perfect calling card, something no one but the GRU had access to, something the Americans were certain to pick up on in an autopsy.

But then, if it was a message, what was it saying? And why was he sending it? One answer simply led to another question. Unless Shipenko decided to let her in on his thinking, the chances of which were vanishingly slim, then she'd simply never know. Unless, that was, the victim herself knew.

Valentina stubbed out her cigarette and crossed the street. A man in a hat was leaving the building, and she caught the door before it shut, then slipped inside and hurried up the stairs to the second floor.

The target's name was Yvette Bunting, and she didn't fit the mold. She was twenty-seven, unmarried, unconnected in Washington, and, apart from four Spring Break trips to the same resort in Cancun during her four years at Ohio State, had never set foot outside the continental United States before leaving for this posting six months ago.

As Valentina picked the lock to the apartment, she wondered what Yvette could possibly have done to attract this kind of attention. The Prime Directorate did not concern itself with minutiae. It did not deal in trivialities. It was a lion. It moved only when it wanted to move—only when there was reason. If Valentina was here, then something was at stake.

Yvette Bunting was scarcely out of the academy. She was at the very beginning of her career. Valentina had been watching her for days and had seen nothing at all to suggest she was anything more than an ordinary CIA rookie. She was a girl in a man's world, underpaid, overworked, laser-focused on proving herself to her superiors, of playing the game, getting ahead, working her way up the ladder. She had no boyfriend, no social life to speak of, no pets, no bad habits. Her only activity, other than work, seemed to be the four-mile run she went on every morning. Valentina had followed the route up to the castle, along the Královská Zahrada, the Royal Garden, and back down the other side past the Franz Kafka museum.

She'd considered making her strike along the route, there was no shortage of possible locations, but the thing that decided in favor of the apartment was the blasted

PSS. It was no good in the open. The range was too short.

The apartment in Malá Strana was the safer bet. It wasn't embassy-owned, the security was nothing out of the ordinary, and it didn't look like Yvette took any special precautions to ensure her safety. She acted like she didn't expect to be targeted, and as far as Valentina could see, she had little reason to fear otherwise.

The apartment was in a quaint neighborhood that was popular with ex-pats. It had narrow, cobbled streets, stunning medieval architecture, and no shortage of trendy bars and restaurants. Not that Yvette took any notice. From what Valentina had seen, she showed up at the office every morning before seven and stayed until well after the rest of the consular staff had clocked off for the evening. She passed dozens of bars, cafés, and nightclubs in the short walk from the embassy back to her apartment each night and never so much as looked at them.

If there was anything important to her other than work, Valentina saw no trace of it. That didn't surprise her. It wasn't suspicious. Didn't raise any red flags. It was a mindset Valentina could relate to. Writing up her pre-op report, she could have been describing her own life. She had no one either—no one to come home to at night, to go out with on weekends, to miss her when she was gone.

If Yvette had worked for the GRU, if they'd been at the same station or reported to the same Direktor, Valentina would have had her on her radar—a rival, a competitor, a potential threat.

And Valentina didn't play nice with rivals. She didn't let people get close to her. That was just how she operated. She didn't have friends. She had contacts, sources, assets. When she spoke to people, when she spent time with them, she analyzed them. She looked for strengths, for weaknesses. If she'd come across Yvette at the Prime Directorate, she would have sought ways to sabotage her, or at least insulate herself from her. She was a loner, a recluse. It was what made her good at her job.

They had a nickname for her at the Directorate. They called her *Volchitsey*, or she-wolf. She had the highest success rate of any assassin in her cohort, and the highest kill count. For her most recent birthday, she'd bought herself a seventeenth-century necklace containing thirty perfectly formed natural Volga river pearls. One for each year of her life. One for each kill.

She heard someone coming down the stairs from the floor above and clicked open the lock to Yvette's door. Cautiously, she pushed it open with her foot and peered in through the gap, the PSS in hand. She slipped inside silently and shut the door behind her. Its latch caught, and then—silence. She stood in the darkness, absolutely still, for a full minute, listening. Then she turned on a flashlight and performed a sweep of the apartment. There wasn't much to it, a kitchenette and living room, a single bedroom with a balcony overlooking the street below, a standard Ikea-issue bathroom. The space was anonymous, lacking in personal touches. She wouldn't have thought someone had already lived there for six months. There were no photos in the frames, no books on the shelves. The refrigerator was almost empty. The cupboards contained stacks of plain white plates and cups, most of them still in their boxes. Nothing was out of place. It almost felt staged. There was a reproduction Rothko on the wall behind the couch, but she thought it probably came with the apartment.

She shone the flashlight around the living room and

stopped on the sideboard next to the TV. There it was—
the one sign of individuality in the apartment, the sole
item that proved the person who lived there had a personality at all. It was a record player, and beneath it on a shelf
built into the sideboard was a thick stack of vinyl records.
She went over and flicked through them—Dexter
Gordon, Cannonball Adderley, Art Blakey. Not a bad
selection. She pulled one out and looked at the notes on
the back. It wasn't a Czech edition, the liner notes were in
English, and she wondered if Yvette had brought it over
from the States.

She slid it back into the stack and went to the
bedroom. She didn't need to search the apartment, it
wasn't part of the mission, but she opened each of Yvette's
drawers methodically, and the closet, and the bedside
tables, carefully examining everything. She searched the
bed, the bathroom, the desk in the corner. There was a
laptop charger plugged into the wall behind the desk, but
the laptop itself wasn't there. She shouldn't have been
searching, she should have been in position, waiting for
Yvette's return, but already, the nagging curiosity was
beginning to get under her skin.

Who was Yvette Bunting?

Why had she been targeted?

What message was Shipenko trying to send with the
SP-4 ammo? And to whom?

She was about to go back to the living room and take
up position, but just as she turned, she heard the click of
the door unlocking. She switched off the flashlight and
reached for the PSS. It wasn't in her pocket. She'd left it by
the record player.

2

Yvette Bunting stopped at the Chinese noodle place near her apartment and ordered her usual, the vegetarian lo mein with two spring rolls and a small soup.

"You like wonton?" the proprietor said in his broken English.

"No wonton tonight," she said, handing him a bill. "Keep the change."

She hurried down the narrow street, pulling her coat tight as icy gusts blew up from the Charles Bridge. Flurries of snow whipped around in the light of the streetlamps like frenetic moths. She got to the door and fumbled in her purse for the key, then hurried inside and climbed the stairs to her apartment. She was tired and hungry, and the walk home had given her a chill. She wanted a bath. When she got inside, she shut the door firmly behind her, as if to shut out the world, and flicked on the light.

She put the takeout on the counter and took off her coat and boots, then turned on the TV, as she did every night, to fill the silence. It was her only company. She'd found that she couldn't stand being alone in the apartment without it on. She'd managed to find a cable plan that had a good offering of English language channels, some British, some American, and she flicked through them until she found the one that showed old sitcom reruns. It was playing an episode of Seinfeld she must have seen half a dozen times in the past six months.

She unpacked the food, mouthing the lines of the show along with the characters, and opened the plastic packets of hot sauce and soy sauce with her teeth. She squeezed the sauce onto the noodles and brought the bowl over to the sofa in front of the TV.

She set it down and went back to the refrigerator for the bottle of chardonnay she'd opened the night before. Then, finally ready, she went back to the sofa and sank into it with a long sigh. She put some noodles in her mouth and looked up at the TV for the first time. There was something on the floor next to it. A gun.

And then a voice.

"Don't move."

She froze. There was a woman standing in the hallway leading to the bedroom. "Who are you?" Yvette stammered, her voice catching in her throat.

The woman was blonde, athletic, dressed from the neck down in black as if she'd just gotten off a motorcycle. In one gloved hand was a tactical knife, held out horizontally in front of her, its steel blade glimmering in the light like a mirror. From her stance, Yvette could see she knew how to use the knife. It would not go well if it came to a fight.

"I'm a messenger," the woman said.

"What?" Yvette said, her mind reeling. She tried to

focus. What was this? *Who* was this? The woman spoke English with a slight Russian accent. Yvette could distinguish it from Czech. "A messenger?" she said. "What does that mean?"

"Your name is Yvette Bunting?" the woman said.

Yvette said nothing.

"Well, Yvette Bunting," the woman continued, "it would appear you've attracted the attention of some very powerful men in Moscow."

Yvette shook her head. She had to force herself to take a breath. She didn't understand what was going on. "Why are you here?"

"I was hoping *you* could tell me that," the woman said.

Yvette's eyes widened. "Me?" she said. She had no idea what the woman was talking about. Powerful men? A messenger? It didn't make sense.

The woman took a step forward, and Yvette felt her pulse quicken.

"Come now," the woman said. "There's an assassin in your living room, and you expect me to believe that you have no idea why?"

"Assassin?" Yvette gasped, the panic beginning to rise in her chest. "Is that what this is?"

The woman shrugged slightly as if she'd just tossed some paper at a trash can and missed.

"Tell me what you're doing here," Yvette said, her voice growing more shrill with each word.

"I already told you," the woman said flatly.

Yvette glanced around the room, her sense of desperation growing. She was on the building's second floor. The thought flitted through her mind that if she jumped, she might survive the fall. She looked at the pistol. It was ten feet away. The woman had made a mistake. The gun wasn't supposed to be there. Of course it wasn't. She'd been in the bedroom, searching for something, and had left it on the floor by accident.

"Don't look at that," the woman snapped, taking another step forward.

"Please," Yvette said, her voice beginning to break. "What's happening? What are you going to do to me?"

"That depends," the woman said.

"On what?"

"You tell me why I'm here, and I make this easy on you."

Tears filled Yvette's eyes. She wasn't going to be walking away from this. She could feel it. With a shiver down her spine, she suddenly realized her death was imminent. It was coming for her like a shadow stretching across a field. "I already told you," she stammered, "I don't know why you're here. I don't know what this is. I swear to God."

The woman shook her head. "You know," she said insistently. "You don't simply pop up on the radar of the Prime Directorate without reason."

Yvette glanced from the woman to the pistol and then to the television. The sitcom was still playing, Kramer had made his entrance, and the audience was giving him a round of applause. It was incongruous now, absurd given what was actually happening. She would die while Jerry Seinfeld complained about how itchy his new sweater was. "This is a mistake," she said again quietly. "Whoever sent you, this is a mistake."

"I assure you," the woman said, and Yvette could hear the sarcasm in her voice, "the Prime Directorate doesn't make mistakes."

"They've made a mistake with me."

The woman shook her head, refusing to believe it. "No," she said. "You've made a name for yourself. The top floor knows who you are. They want you dead. You've got to know the reason."

"I'm sorry," Yvette said, "but it's not possible. I haven't even made a name for myself in my own office."

The woman took another step forward. Yvette could see the doubt on her face now. It didn't add up to her either.

"You shouldn't be here," Yvette said again. "You know this isn't right. Look at me."

"Even if what you're saying is true, it doesn't change anything. I have to carry out the order."

"I don't even have my full clearance," Yvette said. "They have me working dispatches. I'm telling you, this isn't right. You've come for the wrong person."

The woman sighed. She looked troubled.

Yvette glanced at the pistol again. It was just a few feet away. If she could only get to it, she would have a chance. "Who sent you?" she said, trying to distract the woman, stalling for time.

"I assure you, no one you've heard of."

"Try me," Yvette said. "If they want me dead, maybe there's a connection that I didn't put together before."

The woman was hesitant.

"Whoever it is, whoever put my name on your list, I promise you they've made a mistake."

"You know that makes no difference," the woman said. "I can't let you go. Either way, I have to kill you."

Yvette glanced at the gun again. She knew she was being obvious. The woman was taking in everything. Every furtive movement, every shrill word. She was as alert as a hawk.

"Tell me who sent you," Yvette said, "and I'll tell you why you're here."

The woman was quiet for a moment, then said, "His name—"

In the same instant, Yvette leaped toward the pistol. She hadn't even made it off the sofa when she felt the rush of pain. She fell back heavily and clutched her chest. Her shirt was sodden with blood.

"What happened?" she gasped, her voice fading to a weak wheeze. She looked from her blood-soaked hands, to Jerry's face on the television, to the woman.

The woman hadn't moved from her position and was holding the handle of the dagger in front of her like a gun. The blade was gone. "I told you not to move," she said softly as she approached. She pushed a button on the knife handle, and the blade re-emerged.

"Please," Yvette gasped, "you don't have to do this."

The woman put her hand on Yvette's forehead and, almost tenderly, pulled back her head. "If only that were true," she whispered, then ran the blade across Yvette's throat.

3

Nate Gilhofer turned in his bed and swung his arm out over the nightstand, knocking over a lamp and a mug of yesterday morning's coffee. "Damn it," he muttered, grabbing the phone. It was ringing, had been for the last ten minutes, and he rubbed his bleary eyes as he tried to focus on the screen. It was the embassy.

"Gilhofer," he said groggily, glancing at the clock. It was four in the morning.

"This is the night desk. We have an issue."

Gilhofer grabbed his cigarettes from the nightstand and put one in his mouth. "Is that Pritzker?" he said, picturing the kid who'd just shipped in from a town called Pawhuska, Oklahoma. He remembered speaking to him. He was a hockey fan—some godforsaken minor league team from Tulsa.

"It is, sir."

"All right, Pritzker. Might as well spit it out."

"We got a notice from Prague Police. Something involving one of our people."

"Who?"

"A staffer named Yvette Bunting."

"Never heard of her."

"I pulled up her profile," Pritzker said. "She's blonde."

"I see."

"Looks like a younger, hotter Cameron Diaz."

"Oh," Gilhofer said, letting out a wheezy laugh. "I know the one."

"Yes, sir."

"What's she gotten herself into?"

"They didn't say, sir."

"She's new, isn't she?"

"Been here six months."

Gilhofer looked around the nightstand for a lighter. "Well," he said, "I suppose they wouldn't have called if they didn't think it was important."

"No, sir."

He stood up and looked for his pants. The room looked like a crime scene. He found his slacks beneath the bed and checked the pockets. There was a plastic lighter in one of them. "Wait a minute," he said, lighting the cigarette, "You still got her profile open?"

"Yes, sir."

"She's CIA, isn't she?"

"She is, sir."

"Where's the damn station chief? This is her problem."

"I tried her, sir. She's in Washington."

"What's she doing there?"

"I have no idea, sir."

"Did you call the ambassador's office?"

"They said to call you, sir."

Gilhofer sighed. "I bet they did." He went into the

bathroom and rested his cigarette against the side of the sink. "All right, send me her file. Her apartment, you said?"

"Correct, sir."

"I'm on my way."

He glanced at the mirror. After three failed marriages, two adult children who never phoned, and twenty-six years serving at eleven different embassies around the globe, he wasn't exactly aging gracefully. He ran a hand over his gray stubble, then doused his face with cold water. The toothpaste tube was practically empty, but he managed to squeeze out a minuscule amount to brush his teeth with. He ignored the disgraceful state of the bathroom, the towels on the floor that stank of mildew, a bathtub that hadn't been cleaned since the ex left him, and a toilet seat he was scared to look underneath for fear of what he'd find.

He'd given the better part of his life to the Diplomatic Security Service, the federal law enforcement agency responsible for the security of US embassies, and three months ago, after wife number three finally decided she'd had enough, he'd done something that went against every natural fiber of his being and accepted a promotion to RSO. Regional Security Officer was not a title to which he'd ever aspired, even though it was the natural career progression for a man in his position. He didn't like what it entailed—meetings, paperwork, responsibility. It meant he was the senior law enforcement representative for the entire embassy, Security Attaché was the fancy name for it, and it gave him extensive investigatory and arrest powers. While the powers may have been extensive, the jurisdiction was not, which extended exactly as far as the gates of the US embassy compound in Malá Strana. As soon as you passed those gates, his power ended, and he was just another Joe Schmo.

He went back to the bedroom and threw on some well-worn thermal underwear, a creased beige shirt, the slacks he'd fished from beneath the bed, and a brown corduroy jacket that had infuriated his ex every time he so much as looked at it. He took the elevator down to the basement parking lot and, a moment later, was seated behind the wheel of his black government-owned, diplo-matic-plated BMW sedan. The car was the only perk of the promotion he actually appreciated. He took out his phone and pulled up the personnel file that the night desk had sent over. Yvette Bunting's apartment wasn't far, the same district he and most of the other embassy staff lived in, and he made fast progress through the nighttime streets to the address. When he got to Mostecká, the blue and red lights of the emergency vehicles told him imme-diately that this was something more serious than the usual kerfuffles he had to deal with. He counted four squad cars and an ambulance and pulled up next to one of them.

A uniformed police officer came over, and Gilhofer rolled down the window and said in his atrociously bad Czech, "Americký."

"You can't stop here," the officer said, also in Czech. "You're blocking the lane."

Gilhofer pulled out his State Department credentials. "I'm from the embassy."

"I know where you're from, but if you don't move out of the way, I'm going to have you towed."

Gilhofer pulled up onto the sidewalk and got out of the car. "I'll only be a minute."

The officer sighed. "You'll be longer than that."

Gilhofer didn't like the sound of that. "What happened?" he said.

"You'll have to speak to the detective," the officer said. "She's still inside."

Gilhofer pushed open the door and entered the building. He immediately had to make way for the forensics team coming down the stairs. There were four of them in their special blue suits, and one of them was carrying a big lamp, like the kind used on film sets.

"How long were you up there?" Gilhofer said.

The guy looked at his watch and said, "A few hours."

That bothered him—the Czechs were supposed to inform the embassy of incidents involving US personnel immediately—though he couldn't say that he was surprised. Jurisdictional tit-for-tats were the name of the game in the DSS. He couldn't imagine it was much different in DC if someone from the Czech embassy got into trouble.

He went up to the second floor, where another police officer was standing by the open door to one of the apartments. Gilhofer nodded and said, "Can I go on in?"

The man shrugged, and Gilhofer knocked on the open door lightly. "Hello?" he called.

There was a woman in plain clothes standing in the middle of the living room. She was scribbling something in a notepad and didn't look up from it as Gilhofer entered.

Immediately in front of her, splayed out on a white fabric sofa with so much blood on her she looked like a prop from a slasher movie, was the body of Yvette Bunting.

"What in the hell?" Gilhofer said, stepping up next to the woman.

She looked up at him for the first time. "Not good," she said in English. "Not good at all."

"You can say that again," Gilhofer said, leaning in closer. There was no doubt it was her. How was it Pritzker had described her? A young Cameron Diaz? The photo in her personnel file was a perfect match. Her head flopped over the back of the sofa so that her lifeless eyes stared directly at the ceiling. The slash in her neck gaped open. "She was found like this?"

The woman nodded.

"And that's a bullet wound?" he said, nodding at a separate bloodstain on the torso.

She nodded again. "Small caliber by the looks of it. We'll have to wait for the autopsy to find out exactly."

Gilhofer looked around the room. There was Chinese takeout on the counter in the kitchen and a half-empty bottle of white wine on the coffee table in front of the body. On the TV, an episode of Seinfeld was playing on mute. "That was on?" he said.

"No, me and my guys put it on."

"Very funny."

She reached out and switched it off.

"Anything out of place?" Gilhofer said.

"Hard to say."

"Anything that might help with motive?"

"You mean like a note?" the woman said sarcastically.

"I'm just asking."

"Look for yourself. You know her better than we do."

"I don't know her at all."

The woman shrugged. He didn't care. He was used to the attitude. No one wanted a foreign law enforcement officer poking around their investigation.

"Any paperwork or anything?" he said. "Any documents?"

"Nothing in the open."

"You're sure of that?"

The woman looked at him. "Am I *sure* there were no documents out in the open?" she said pointedly.

"You waited long enough to call us."

"We didn't know what we were looking at."

"The slit throat didn't give it away?"

The woman's tone sharpened. "We called you as soon as we realized she was one of yours. It's not like she has an American flag tattooed to her forehead."

Gilhofer had the advantage of knowing what the credentials of embassy staff looked like. If Yvette had come from work, she'd have been carrying hers. He went over to the coat hanging on a hook by the door and searched it. The first pocket he checked contained a large plastic lanyard with a holographic US flag etched clearly into its face, as well as Yvette's name, photo, and department.

He looked at the woman. She shrugged nonchalantly, and he said, "I'm going to need to see an inventory of everything taken from this apartment."

"Which you'll get," she said.

"As well as access to the body to perform our own autopsy."

"Look," she said, "I'm not the enemy here. We're on the same side."

"Sure we are."

"My bosses are as concerned about the optics as yours are."

"The optics?"

"Young, pretty CIA agent, murdered in cold blood in

mysterious European capital. It's not exactly the image our press department is looking for."

"Who said she was a CIA agent?" Gilhofer said.

"She is, isn't she?"

"Not officially."

"If you want to get to the bottom of this, you're going to have to work with me," the woman said. "Neither of us wanted to be here, but here we are."

Gilhofer sighed. He knew she was right. No one was coming out of this looking good, especially if they didn't get to the bottom of it. Unless there'd been some drastic change in the diplomatic stance of one of America's staunchest and most reliable allies in the region, the Czechs had as much reason as he did to want to solve this murder quickly. And discreetly. "Can your people keep it quiet?" he said.

"We'll have to put out something."

"We will, but let the embassy do it. Something innocuous. Maybe we can say she had a medical condition."

The woman raised an eyebrow skeptically but said nothing.

"And listen," Gilhofer said, his tone softening, "I appreciate the heads up. I know you could have kept this to yourselves much longer."

She nodded curtly, as if the change in tone embarrassed her, as if she preferred arguing.

"Gilhofer," he said, extending his hand. "I should have introduced myself sooner."

"I know who you are," she said.

"And you are?"

"Detective Klára Issová. Prague Police."

"Klára," he repeated.

She nodded.

He looked her over. She was everything he wasn't. "You're lead on this?" he said.

"You don't approve?"

"No, no," he said, raising his hands, but it was too late.

"Too female for you?"

"Not at all. Just...."

"Just what?"

"You're young."

"Not that young."

"It's a big case, is all. NATO ally. CIA."

"I can handle it."

"No doubt," Gilhofer said. "No doubt at all."

"Anyway," she said, flipping her notebook shut and stuffing it in her coat pocket, "have a look around. Satisfy yourself that everything's in order. My people will send you a full report of what we found."

"And the body?"

"Paramedics will be up shortly to remove her to the morgue."

"It would be preferable to do that before light."

"You think?"

He shook his head. That sarcasm was going to get old fast. "Well, if I can be of any assistance—"

"I'll let you know," Klára said curtly, then walked past him out of the apartment.

4

---

aurel stepped out of the pool and grabbed a towel. She patted herself dry and looked at her watch. Ninety minutes. She'd lost count of the number of laps, but the watch had recorded it all for her. She had messages too, she'd heard them coming in but refused to look until she was done swimming.

She looked now.

Junior analyst at Prague Station found dead. Local police in possession of scene.

Not the worst news ever to greet her after one of her swims, but concerning nonetheless. She took a quick shower, dressed, and grabbed a coffee from the Starbucks in the lobby before hurrying out to the quadrangle and past the Kryptos sculpture. It was a cold night, late, and there was a stillness that made the campus feel a lot more remote than it was.

After the infiltration of the Saint Royal, she'd made the call to move Group operations back inside the relative safety of Langley's new headquarters building. The move had been fairly painless and, so far, Roth had given her everything she'd asked for. That included the entire sixth floor, hermetically sealed from the rest of the building, with its own access elevator, a state-of-the-art comms system with quantum-based encryption, hardwires to the Pentagon, CIA, and NSA real-time intel streams, and a dedicated relay satellite with Keyhole access. Lest there be any doubt as to where Roth's loyalties lay now that he was Director, he'd lobbied the White House and Pentagon personally for her satellite. He'd even attended the launch, making the trip out to Wallops Flight Facility in Virginia to watch the Minotaur I rocket take off. He'd invited Laurel, telling her the event would be like every orgasm in her life happening simultaneously, but she'd told him if that were true, she wanted to be as far from it as humanly possible.

She flashed her credentials to the guards and made her way to the dedicated elevator. There was a mirror inside, and she touched up her makeup during the ascent. When she stepped out, she was greeted by an empty reception desk, beyond which were rows of workstations, enough for about twenty specialists. They, too, were empty. The Group had been burned too many times, and Laurel had decided to hold off on hiring until she was absolutely certain of what she needed.

For now, it was just the two of them—herself and Tatyana. Tatyana wasted no time getting comfortable, installing herself in the largest conference room they had, her desk facing the floor-to-ceiling windows that commanded one of the best views over the Potomac in the entire building. Built into the sideboard next to the desk was a wet bar and chrome espresso machine, and Tatyana had also taken the liberty of ordering the most impossibly plush, leather-clad office chair money could buy. She was sitting on the chair now, sipping coffee and staring at an array of high-definition computer monitors showing streams from incoming data feeds.

She swiveled around when she heard Laurel.

"I see you've made yourself comfortable," Laurel said as she entered.

"Might as well," Tatyana said. "There's no one else here."

"Got your own little kingdom," Laurel said, taking the decidedly less extravagant seat next to Tatyana and rotating the monitors to get a better view. "So," she said, "what's this message about Prague Station?"

"Just came in from the RSO. The Station Chief is out of country."

"You couldn't have ordered two chairs?" Laurel said.

"I didn't know you wanted one."

Laurel shrugged. "Two people, two chairs," she muttered.

"What was that?"

"Nothing."

"If you don't like it—"

"Let's just get to work, shall we?"

Tatyana straightened herself in her seat and pulled up a live satellite view of central Prague. "Our agent was found at her apartment here." The view switched to photographs of a young woman with her throat slit so deeply that her head threatened to fall off over the back of the sofa she was splayed out on.

"What the hell?" Laurel said.

Tatyana nodded.

"You could have warned me."

Tatyana ignored the comment and proceeded to flip through ever closer and more detailed images of the woman. "We're looking at Yvette Bunting," she said. "Twenty-seven years old. Stationed in Prague six months ago."

"Any idea who did this?"

"Not so far."

"What was she working on?"

"According to the Station Chief, nothing. She was the rookie. They were still babysitting her, had her in comms, writing internal memos, updating procedure documents."

"Not exactly the type of stuff worth killing over."

"No," Tatyana said.

"There's a chance it's not work-related."

"There is," Tatyana said. "There's a chance it was completely random."

Laurel looked at her.

"Not likely, though," Tatyana added.

"Agreed," Laurel said, taking a sip of her coffee.

"We've picked up nothing on the wire," Tatyana continued. "Just the usual static. It's a tough time. A lot of noise. Tensions are high with the Ukraine situation."

"As per usual," Laurel said, getting up and going over to the sideboard. "Do you have sweetener in this thing?"

"The drawer," Tatyana said, "next to the frother."

Laurel pulled open the drawer and found what she was looking for, then took a moment to admire the coffee and bar paraphernalia, all top-notch, top shelf, no expense spared. "All this came out of budget, I suppose."

Tatyana ignored her. "NSA is picking up chatter. The

algorithms definitely think an attack across Ukraine's eastern border is imminent."

"But they have no idea when."

"Of course not."

"And the humans? What do they think?"

"Whatever the algorithms tell them to think."

Laurel sighed. "This is something," she said, nodding at an image of the young analyst. "It's related. I don't how, but it's...."

"A shot across the bow?"

"Exactly. Who have we got on our end dealing with it?"

"The RSO."

"So State Department?"

Tatyana nodded.

"Hardly ideal."

"Not ideal at all," Tatyana said, pulling up a picture of a tired-looking middle-aged man in a cheap suit and unstylish glasses. "Some career guy coasting toward retirement by the looks of it."

"Nate Gilhofer," Laurel said, reading the name on the screen. "Forty-nine years old. Twenty-six on the force. Twelve in Prague. Less than three months RSO." She raised an eyebrow at that.

Tatyana looked at her. "Three times divorced."

"Not exactly ironclad."

"Says here he's waiting for ballistics from the Czech detective, a woman named Klára Issová."

"We're going to have to watch him."

Tatyana nodded.

"Maybe get on the phone with him," Laurel said. "Impress on him the importance of finding out why this happened. If this Yvette Bunting got herself mixed up in something, that's all of our problem."

Tatyana hit some keys on the keyboard, and a picture came up of an attractive, bright-eyed, twenty-seven-year-old with blonde hair and a prim navy blue blazer and white blouse. The picture had been taken by CIA security in the lobby of the building Laurel and Tatyana were in now, six floors below them, on Yvette's first day on the job.

"Looks like a first day of school photo," Laurel said.

"Yes," Tatyana said, hitting more keys.

"How did a girl like that end up in an apartment in Prague with her head nearly chopped off?"

Tatyana hit enter on the keyboard. Yvette's service record popped up, including the contents of her security file and any routine CIA surveillance that had been conducted on her. It was all clean, not so much as an unpaid parking ticket. "There she is," Tatyana said. "Yvette Bunting. Clean as a new whistle."

"There's something here," Laurel said. "We just don't know where to look."

"Yet," Tatyana added, "but whoever killed her, they did it for a reason."

5

G ilhofer sat in his car, the engine running and the heat on full, chain-smoking cigarettes. He'd cracked the window a few inches and blew the smoke toward the opening. He was watching the entrance to the Prague city police morgue. He'd been sitting there for the past thirty minutes, the sun slowly rising to reveal a day as drab and gray as any he'd ever seen, while he waited for Klára Issová to emerge with the autopsy report. The entrance to the morgue was at the top of a set of rather grand steps, more fitting for a courthouse than a morgue, he thought. He was parked at the bottom of them, right behind Klára's vehicle.

He stubbed his cigarette against the outside of the window and let the butt fall to the ground. He was just lighting another when his phone started to ring. He looked at the screen. It was the security desk at the embassy.

"Gilhofer," he said with a sigh.

"It's me, Nate. I've got a call for you from Langley in a few minutes."

He recognized the voice of Arabella Bradwell, the CI, or counter-intelligence liaison, at the embassy. She was the person responsible for the somewhat impossible task of keeping the State Department and the CIA from each other's throats. Technically, she came out of CIA's budget, but Gilhofer thought of her as one of his. She certainly spent more time with him and his crew than she did with the station chief.

"Langley?" he said, his phone lodged in the crook of his neck while he held a lighter to the end of his cigarette. "What do they want with me?"

"They want to make sure you find out what happened to their agent."

"She got her throat slit," Gilhofer said. "Case solved."

"Yeah, well, they're going to want a little bit more than that. You know how they are. There are no coincidences in their world. Everything's part of an intricate plot."

"One dead CIA agent, and it's the opening gambit of World War Three."

"Exactly."

"I'll find out what I can, but my hands are fairly tied. I'm at the mercy of this lady detective the Czechs have working the case."

"They don't say lady detective anymore, Nate."

"That's what she is, isn't she?"

"There's that famous charm," Arabella said. He could picture her shaking her head, her hair falling carelessly in front of her eyes. "You should use that on her. Ten bucks says she finds it a real treat."

"I know, I know," Gilhofer said. "I'm a dinosaur. But this investigation is running on Czech time. Make sure Langley knows that."

"Hold on," Arabella said. "Here they are. I'm patching you through now."

Gilhofer sucked the cigarette as Beethoven's *Für Elise* filled the line, rendered flawlessly in dial tones by the CIA phone system. It was times like this that reminded him why he'd resisted accepting the job of RSO for so many years. He still wasn't quite sure what had possessed him when he'd finally agreed to it. No doubt something his ex had said about avoiding responsibility, living up to his potential. It would be a counseling session one day.

The music stopped, and a stern-sounding voice, female, possibly Russian, said, "Nate Gilhofer? RSO, US Embassy, Prague?"

"This is Gilhofer," he said, his attention drawn to the door of the morgue where someone was just exiting the building. It was a man in a double-breasted suit with a briefcase. Definitely not Klára.

"I'm calling from Langley," the woman said.

"So I hear."

"I wanted to make sure you were aware that Yvette Bunting was one of ours?"

"Oh, I'm well aware," he said. "Your personnel. Your responsibility too."

"Well, we're rather light on the ground over there at the moment."

"No kidding," he said, and then, under his breath, "*conveniently.*"

"I'm sorry. What was that?"

"Oh, nothing."

"It sounded like you said something."

"Nope."

The woman cleared her throat. "Well," she said, "it

says here a local detective's been assigned the case. Her name is Klára Issová."

"I met her. I'm waiting outside the Prague morgue for her right now."

"You need to get as much access to her investigation as possible. She finds anything, I don't care how small it seems...."

"You'll be the first to know," Gilhofer said.

"We understand each other then?"

"Perfectly," Gilhofer said, eager to bring the call to a conclusion.

"In that case, there are just a few other details I want to go over."

Gilhofer rolled his eyes and sighed audibly.

"Yvette was shot in the chest, correct?"

"Among other things."

"Will there be a ballistics report?"

"The Czechs are working on that."

"Good," the woman said. "I want you to stick to Klára Issová like glue. If she gets so much as a whiff of who is behind this...."

"You'll be the first to know," Gilhofer said for the second time, making no effort to hide the impatience in his voice. "Now, if that's all you called to say, I have an investigation to get back to."

There was a moment's pause, then, "Did I say something to upset you, Mr. Gilhofer?"

"No, no," he said. "Everything's peachy. I'm thrilled to be at your service."

"I'm detecting a certain tone."

"A tone?"

"Yes."

"You're aware," Gilhofer said, "that I don't actually work for you people?"

"We're all on the same team here."

"Sure we are," he said. He could tell from her voice that this woman wasn't someone he wanted to get on the wrong side of, but for some reason, he couldn't stop himself from antagonizing her. The way she was talking to him, like he was answerable to her, combined with the four hours of sleep and the fact that he needed to take a leak, and his feet were getting cold, and her accent—it was all coming together in a way that seriously rubbed him the wrong way. "Hello?" he said. She hadn't spoken in a few seconds, and he wasn't sure she was still on the line.

And then the line went dead. She'd hung up on him. He listened to the dial tone for a second, then let out a little laugh.

Insulting anyone from Langley was probably unwise, but he shrugged it off. He didn't care. With his latest breakup, a third marriage down the drain, and a financially crippling settlement that guaranteed him a shitty retirement, he'd decided he'd had enough of women calling the shots. He was done bending over backward. He didn't care how out of tune with the laws of society that made him. From now on, he was calling it as he saw it.

He sucked hard on the cigarette and flicked it toward the crack in the window. It missed, hitting the glass and sending ash and embers onto his lap. "Damn it," he said, raising his ass from the seat to avoid getting burned. He found the butt quickly before it burned a hole in the seat and threw it out the window.

What else was going to go wrong?

His phone vibrated. It was the CIA validator for the call he'd just had. He opened it and took a look.

CIA Call Verification Token
  Date: Classified
  Time: Classified
  Call Duration: Classified
  Department: Classified
  Caller: Classified
  Recipient: Classified
  Memo: Classified

About as useful as a glass hammer, he thought. He reached into his shirt pocket for his cigarettes and was about light another when Klára Issová appeared at the top of the steps. She was holding a document under one arm.

He got out of the car and called out, "Detective!"

She saw him and veered to the right as if she might still be able to avoid him.

"Hey!" he called, hurrying up the steps to intercept her. "I need to see that report."

"You want it, you can submit a request through the embassy."

"Oh, come on! Don't give me that," he said, blocking her path.

"Let me pass."

"Not without seeing that document."

She gave him a withering look. She wasn't giving in. She brushed up against him, and, reluctantly, he stepped aside. She hurried past, and he watched her descend the rest of the steps. He wondered how the woman from the CIA would respond when he told her he hadn't put eyes on that autopsy and needed to submit a request in writing.

"Hey!" he called. "Detective Issová!"

She was just reaching the bottom of the steps and stopped to look back at him.

"I know how I come across," he said.

"You what?"

"People don't like me."

"No!" she gasped in mock disbelief. "That can't be true."

He nodded. "Women *despise* me. Been that way since I was a boy."

"What possibly could be the reason?"

He took a few steps toward her. "Believe me, if I knew...."

"You'd change your ways?"

He shrugged. "Who knows?"

"Right."

"It's my manner, isn't it? You wouldn't be the first to say it was."

"It's something."

He descended the remaining few steps and sighed. "I'm a...."

"An asshole?"

He shrugged. "I mean, if I was at least good at my job, that would be one thing."

"But you're not?"

"I have the distinction of being one of those men whose principal talent is staying out of the way. I get by. I avoid trouble. That's about it."

"That's it?"

"I'm good at nothing."

"Nothing?"

"Ask my ex-wives."

She seemed to soften. "I'd be within my rights to get

you to go through the embassy for everything," she said. "Do it all by the book. Everything by written request."

"I know you would," he said. He still had an unlit cigarette in his hand, and he put it in his mouth.

"But you don't want me to," she said.

He lit his cigarette and exhaled smoke, blowing it over her head as if avoiding her face was all that etiquette required. "I got a call from Langley."

"How did that go?" she said.

"I was an asshole. They hate me already."

Klára shrugged.

"It shouldn't even be me on the case," he said. "I'm a glorified security guard. I'm not qualified for this."

She looked him up and down, then turned and opened the door of her car. "Is that yours?" she said, nodding at his BMW.

He nodded.

"Well," she said, "go park it. You can ride with me."

"Where?"

"You'll see."

He hurried around to the passenger door before she changed her mind.

"What about your car?" she said.

"I'll leave it here."

"You'll get towed."

"Nope," he said. "Diplomatic plates."

She shook her head.

"See," he added. "Asshole to the bone."

They got into the car. She started the engine and said, "I'm guessing neither of us has had breakfast."

They drove to a place near the Legion Bridge called Café Slavia, and he followed her inside. It was very traditional in style, full of linoleum booths and art deco light fixtures that had survived the communist decades completely intact. At the far end of the café, shelves behind a faux-marble bar held hundreds of bottles, every cheap brand of liquor available in that half of Europe. On the walls were old black and white photographs, all signed, of famous Czech actors and celebrities smoking cigars and knocking back Fernet in the café's booths during its heyday.

"Nice place," Gilhofer said.

"Don't speak too soon," Klára said. "You haven't tasted the food."

The restaurant could seat well over a hundred guests, but they were the only two customers. They chose a booth by a window overlooking the car, and Klára said, "What are you having?"

"You order for me."

She beckoned the waitress and ordered two soft-boiled eggs and a plate of Vienna sausage. It arrived with a pot of viscous coffee and a plastic basket of white bread rolls.

Gilhofer watched Klára open her egg carefully with a spoon. Then she cut thin slices from a bread roll and dipped them in the yolk.

"Pass the salt," she said. He did, and she looked up. "What? You're not eating?"

"No, I'm eating," he said and began to do so.

They didn't speak for a few minutes, not until the eggs were gone and some of the sausage, then she picked up the thin report the coroner had given her and put it on the table.

"Have you read it?" Gilhofer said.

She shook her head.

"Is it in English?"

She rolled her eyes and opened it up.

"What does it say?"

"Slit throat, gunshot wound. 7.62x41mm ammunition."

"Say that again?" Gilhofer said.

"Does it mean something to you?"

He nodded slowly. "It will mean something to the CIA."

6

Valentina Brik stared at her phone. She was sitting in the restaurant of her hotel, sipping a small glass of freshly squeezed orange juice, while Prague's Old Town Square gradually came to life outside the window. It was early, and she'd already arranged a cab to the airport for her flight back to Moscow, but it looked now like she wouldn't be needing it.

"Madam," a waiter said, placing a silver tray on the table in front of her. On it was an ornate pot of coffee, a basket of elegant little pastries, and a selection of preserves. "May I?" he said. She nodded, and he poured her coffee.

"Thank you," she said, taking a sip. She looked at the phone again.

What was Shipenko up to?

What game was he playing?

The job last night hadn't sat well with her. Something wasn't right about it. She'd slept badly thinking about it, playing the words she'd exchanged with Yvette Bunting over and over in her mind. It bothered her. "This is a mistake," Yvette had said. "Whoever sent you, this is a mistake."

And she remembered her own response. "The Prime Directorate doesn't make mistakes."

She didn't think Yvette had been concealing anything. She believed that she didn't know why she was being targeted. But she also knew that what she'd said was true too. The Prime Directorate didn't make mistakes. That wasn't to say it was infallible. It was anything but that. But when Osip Shipenko gave her the order to kill Yvette Bunting, there was undoubtedly a reason for it. In Shipenko's mind, it made perfect sense.

And Valentina should have left it at that. It was a loose thread, something that would nag at her, but it wouldn't necessarily keep her up at night.

But now this—a second kill order. Something was definitely off.

Yvette Bunting hadn't felt like a target. She hadn't known why she was a target. She had no access, no power, no value.

The new target gave Valentina that same feeling. She looked at her picture on the phone. She was pretty. She was young. Beneath the picture, the order read:

Identifier: KO_457831

Agency: Prime Directorate

Lead Agent: Osip Shipenko

Assassin: Valentina Brik

Target: Arabella Bradwell

Target Post: US Embassy, Prague

Target Position: CIA Counterintelligence Liaison

Order: Kill target. Leave at least one 7.62x41mm
bullet at the scene.
Prime Directorate Kill Order

It was almost a carbon copy of the previous one—no
stated objective, no order to interrogate, nothing to take
from her. Just kill her and leave behind the Russian-
designed, unique-to-GRU bullet.

She opened the research file. There was nothing there
to provide further enlightenment. Arabella was young,
like Yvette, and while she was slightly more advanced in
her career, she certainly didn't have the kind of résumé
one would expect to get the attention of the Prime Directorate. Technically, she was a CIA staffer, paid for from the
CIA's general service budget, but administratively, she was
more like a Diplomatic Security Service employee. From
what the file said, she worked more closely with the
Prague security attaché and the local consular staff than
anyone at Langley. That wasn't unusual. Prague wasn't the
hotbed of international espionage and intrigue it had
once been. As far as the CIA was concerned, it was a backwater—a distant outpost on the very edge of NATO. The
Agency had nine in-country personnel, the Station Chief,
who was currently in Washington, Yvette Bunting, out of
action for obvious reasons, this woman, Arabella Bradwell, and six specialists, mostly SIGINT, responsible for
monitoring Russian comms in the region and keeping an
eye on the natural gas pipelines.

The personal research was just as unrevealing.
Arabella was an American citizen, born in Kansas, an only
child, no known connections of value, no known domain
expertise of value. In short, she was ordinary.

Valentina spread some butter on a miniature croissant and watched it melt. She was beginning to feel that this woman, and Yvette Bunting before her, weren't being targeted for their specific value but for what they represented. They were American, they worked for the CIA, they were soft targets. She took a bite of the pastry. They were female.

She poured more coffee and finished reading the file. Outside, it began to snow lightly. It was all so picturesque, she thought. The quaint square, the quaint buildings, everything as picture-perfect as if it had been laid out by a set designer.

The waiter left her alone for about thirty minutes, then came over with a fresh pot of coffee.

"That's fine," she said, putting some money on the table. She got up and went from the restaurant to the main desk in the lobby. "I'll be extending my stay," she said to the concierge. "One more night."

7

Tatyana looked at the clock in the corner of her screen. It was well after midnight, and she needed to get home and get some sleep. She looked out the window. She was used to seeing the streams of traffic on the George Washington Memorial Parkway, one red, one white. It was so late now, and traffic so light, that she saw only a single car, its white lights following the contour of the road as it hugged the bank of the Potomac. It was snowing, not heavily, the flakes hardly seeming to fall at all, as if they were hanging, suspended in the stillness of the night air.

She sighed. She wasn't glad to be going home. There wasn't much waiting for her when she left the office—an undecorated apartment in Georgetown, an unmade bed, empty. She'd been thinking of getting a cat. She went to the coffee machine and poured what was left in the pot into a paper takeout cup, and snapped on a lid. She locked the computer, shut off the lights, and was just leaving the conference room when the phone on the table started to ring.

She looked at her cell, which was connected to the landline router, and saw Nate Gilhofer's number on her screen. She'd called him earlier, just after Laurel left for the night, and hadn't been impressed.

She went to the desk and picked up the receiver. "Gilhofer?" she said.

"You're going to want to hear this," he said. "The bullet that was taken out of Yvette's chest. It's a 7.62x41mm."

Tatyana sat down. She knew the caliber well, knew what it meant. "From an SP-4?" she said.

"That's what the Czechs think," Gilhofer said. "That or the SP-16."

"I see," Tatyana said. The SP-16 was an updated version of the SP-4, almost identical in design but with slightly better penetrating power. Both were Russian, both were highly specialized, used only by Spetsnaz and GRU agents for covert operations, and even then, only very rarely.

"We've got an international situation on our hands," Gilhofer said.

"I think you might be right." She took a sip of the coffee. It was lukewarm, but she hardly noticed. "The detective showed you the report?"

"I had breakfast with her. Nice lady."

"And there's no doubt about the bullet's caliber?"

"I don't think so."

"Did they find the cartridge casing?"

"They did not, but a professional wouldn't have left it behind."

"No," Tatyana said.

"And there's no headstamps on that ammo, I understand."

"Correct," Tatyana said. "Did she give you anything else?"

"That's all they have."

"Did she say what their next step would be?"

"Next step?"

"In the investigation."

"She'll go through the motions," Gilhofer said, "but we both know this investigation is going to end at the gates of the Russian embassy."

"Maybe."

"What do you mean, maybe? That bullet came out of a Russian silent pistol. There's not a lot of people using those."

"No," Tatyana said with a sigh. "There's not."

She was about to hang up when Gilhofer said, "Mind me asking you a question?"

"That depends," Tatyana said.

"It's just, you know, I like knowing who I'm dealing with."

"You're dealing with the Central Intelligence Agency."

"All right," Gilhofer said. "Real nice. Enjoy your night."

"Hold on," Tatyana said.

"What?"

"You can call me Tatyana."

"Tatyana?"

"That's as friendly as we're going to get, Gilhofer."

She hung up the phone and pulled up the file she'd just received from him. Photos taken on his phone of the ballistics report. She could see the signs of his breakfast with the detective in the picture. The bullet had been measured carefully. It was in good condition, having entered the chest a few inches off-center, between two ribs. Not exactly the precision marksmanship they taught at the academy, but no less effective for it.

Why the slit throat, she wondered. That was excessive —unprofessional even. Maybe a sign of passion. Had this been personal? It certainly wasn't the usual MO.

And then there was the bullet. Tatyana had done her time in the Main Directorate. Her role had been compartmentalized, siloed, sealed off from the work of other operatives, but she couldn't help crossing paths with them from time to time. It was inevitable, and when it happened, she paid attention. She watched them like she would have watched a scorpion. She knew all too well that, when the time came, it would most likely be at one of their hands that she died.

She thought back to what she knew about the other operatives in the inner circle. Who did she know of that used the SP-4 ammo? It was exceedingly rare. Laurel would confirm it from production statistics in the morning, but she doubted there was a factory in Russia actively producing it. It was an artifact, a relic. She did know of an asset named Genadi Surkov, dead now, who'd carried a PSS in his day. Usually the updated version, which used the SP-16 cartridge, not the SP-4, but it was close. There'd also been Maksim Mironov. She'd heard of him using the OTs-38 Stechkin silent revolver, which was chambered for the SP-4. That was it.

She picked up her coffee cup and called down to the front desk for a car. Then she went down to it.

"You know where to go," she said to the driver when she got inside, then took out her cell and called Laurel. "It's me. Sorry. Did I wake you?"

"No," Laurel said, which Tatyana knew was untrue. "What is it?"

"The RSO in Prague reported. He got eyes on the ballistics. It definitely looks like a Russian job."

"I was hoping you wouldn't say that."

"Sorry to disappoint."

"How do they know?"

"A custom silent ammo type was used."

"Could someone else have gotten their hands on that ammo?"

"It's possible."

"Maybe trying to make it look like a Russian job."

"Who would do that?"

"I don't know," Laurel said. "Take your pick."

"Anything's possible," Tatyana said, "but in my experience, if it looks like a turd, and smells like a turd..."

"It's the Kremlin."

"Exactly."

"All right," Laurel said. "I think we leave things to the RSO for now, see what else comes out of the woodwork. In the meantime, get some sleep. We've got a ream of other things to deal with tomorrow. The White House has been breathing down Roth's neck over the Ukraine situation. It's making everyone in the Pentagon jumpy as a jackrabbit."

"Aye, aye," Tatyana said and put down the phone. She looked out the window at the passing city. The bars were letting out. "I guess I missed the last call," she said to the driver. She'd had him quite regularly of late and often got him to drop her off at a local bar rather than take her all the way home.

"I know a few places that'll still be going," he said and then added, "off the record, of course."

"That's okay," Tatyana said. "Just take me home. I've had enough fun for one day."

She put her head against the glass and shut her eyes. When she opened them, she caught the driver watching her in the mirror. He looked away.

"You live around here?" she said.

"I live in Bethesda."

"Alone?"

"I have a roommate."

They arrived on her street, and he slowed down. "Your roommate," Tatyana said, "wouldn't happen to be your wife, would she?"

"No wife."

"No girlfriend?"

"Are you propositioning me?"

She shrugged. "I was wondering if you wanted to come up."

"I'm expected back at Langley in an hour."

"An hour?" Tatyana said. "I think we can make that work."

8

L ance Spector sat on a stool in a dingy East London bar and sipped his beer.

"Everything all right?" the bartender said to him, leaning on the counter and almost daring him to voice a complaint.

"It's great," Lance said. "Real good."

The bartender nodded, as if his question had been answered correctly, and moved on to a group of guys in cheap polyester business suits across the bar. They looked like they'd just come from a used car salesman convention and were definitely happy about something, slapping each other on the back and making toasts.

"A pint for our friend there," one of them said to the bartender, indicating Lance.

"Not necessary," Lance said, but the bartender pulled the pint anyway and put it down in front of Lance next to the other one.

Lance nodded to the car salesmen and contemplated the glass unenthusiastically before picking it up and taking a sip. He rolled the tepid liquid in his mouth as if trying to place it, then swallowed. He couldn't see how the British stomached the stuff.

He'd been planning on leaving the city. The time had come to move on. Staying now only risked drawing attention to the people he wanted to keep safe. But something was holding him back, sapping his momentum. He felt like he was wading through mud. He told himself he was making sure the dust really had settled, but the truth was, he had nowhere to go and no one to go to. He'd mentioned his feeling to Roth, who'd taken the opportunity to give him a little chore to take care of.

"It's your kind of thing," Roth had said.

"What does that mean?" Lance asked, but Roth only said that he'd see for himself. And that was why Lance was in this bar now, waiting for someone he'd never laid eyes on before to show up. He picked up one of the beer glasses and held it at an angle, letting the light shine through it.

"You sure that beer's all right for you?" the bartender said again.

"It's fine," Lance said, and added unconvincingly, "I like it."

He felt a cold draft and turned to look over his shoulder. A woman walked in, tottering on six-inch heels, a skimpy black dress stretched over her ample hips. She appeared to subscribe to the Kim Kardashian school of fashion, with gaudy inch-long eyelashes and curves that would have put an anaconda to shame.

Behind her was an older guy, muscular, mid-forties with dark stubble and a musky look, like he hadn't bathed in a few days. He probably had fifty pounds on Lance and moved like someone who knew how to handle himself. He had a tattoo of a bulldog on his right forearm.

"Hurry up, would you?" he said to the woman as they made their way to the booth nearest Lance.

One of the salesmen must have said something funny because he slammed a hand on the bar, and the others all laughed uproariously.

"All right, love," another of them said to the woman tauntingly. "What's a fiver get me?"

The woman looked to the man she was with for support, but he said nothing, then she picked up a menu and pretended to read it.

"Hey, how about another round over here?" one of the salesmen said to the bartender. "Come on. Chop, chop."

The bartender poured them more drinks, and Lance took a modest sip of his own, wincing as he swallowed. He was listening to the conversation between the man and woman at the booth, trying to be discreet about it.

"Look at yourself," the man was saying. "You're a disgrace."

"I'm sorry," the woman said, her accent as thick as any Lance had heard.

"You *ever* embarrass me like that again," the man went on, leaving the sentence to dangle unfinished.

"I'm sorry," the woman said again.

"Oi, bartender," the man called. "How about some bloody service?"

The bartender went over and took the order. She wanted a gin and tonic, and he ordered the same abominable substance Lance was drinking.

"I ought to knock your teeth out," the man said when the bartender left.

"You all right?" the bartender said to Lance as he passed.

"Fine," Lance said agitatedly. "I'm fine."

The bartender brought the drinks to the booth, and the woman thanked him. "This is nice," she said to the man quietly.

"Shut it," the man said, "or I'll shut it for you."

Lance glanced over his shoulder at them. The woman caught his eye and looked away instantly. Lance turned back to his beer and took another sip. He grimaced, then downed the entire pint. Whatever its other merits, it was better than the bile in his stomach.

His mother had made all the same mistakes this woman was making. She'd married a real son of a bitch. Not Lance's father. His stepfather. A guy from Cheboygan, Michigan, named Sandor Grey, who once beat him so hard he knocked him unconscious. Lance had to be taken to hospital in an ambulance. He woke up in the hospital bed, eight years old, and standing above him was Sandor, his wispy mustache making him look like Burt Reynolds in *Smokey and the Bandit*.

"You breathe one word," Sandor said, "one fucking word, and I'll take it out on your mother and sister."

The threat worked. Lance never spoke. Child Protection Services conducted four interviews and couldn't get a word out of him. But his mother and sister paid the price anyway. Sandor wasn't just violent. He was deviant. Lance never understood it at the time, but his mother and sister did.

His sister was his twin, and not long after the hospital admission incident, Sandor took them all on 'vacation' to El Paso, Texas. No one who'd ever been to El Paso, Texas, would have mistaken the place for a family vacation destination, but Lance's mother didn't know any better. She had no idea what to expect when they got there and, in any case, probably couldn't have said no to the offer even if she'd wanted to.

To this day, Lance had no idea what had happened. And not for want of trying. He'd trawled through old police records, gone to El Paso to speak to the men of the city's seedy underbelly, the ones involved in prostitution and human trafficking. He'd looked up the CIA's intel on sex slavery on both sides of the border during those years. None of it yielded a thing. Thirty years later, he was no closer to uncovering the truth than he had been as a small boy.

It kept him up at nights. He knew he'd never let it rest. He'd spend the rest of his life searching for the truth. That kind of crime, that kind of pain, it didn't die. It didn't fade away. For all he knew, his mother and sister were still alive, still living that abysmal hell they'd been pulled down into.

What he did know was that after one night in a cheap roadside motel on the outskirts of town, a place called The Lucky Cowboy with a neon sign of a cowboy swinging his leg and waving, he never set eyes on his sister and mother again. His sister had been eight, same as him. His mother, twenty-three. He kept a mental tally in his mind at all times of the ages they would be today, what they might look like.

Listening now to this guy in the booth behind him, threatening his woman like he owned her, like she was his property, Sandor Grey's mustache came into Lance's mind so vividly it was like being back at the Lucky Cowboy again. He didn't realize how tightly he was clenching his glass until it shattered in his hand.

Everyone in the bar turned to look at him. Shards of

glass flew everywhere, his lap, the floor beneath his stool, and blood was flowing from his hand.

"Sorry," Lance said to the room at large. "I don't know what happened."

"Don't worry about it," the bartender said, clearing up the larger pieces of glass from the bar.

Lance looked at his hand. It was bleeding badly. He got down from the stool and went to the men's room to wash it. He wrapped paper towel around the cut and, as he was leaving, almost bumped into the woman from the booth. They were in the narrow hallway that led to the washrooms, and she squeezed by him awkwardly to get to the women's.

Lance looked down the hallway to make sure he couldn't be seen, then knocked on the women's door. No one answered, and he pushed it open. The woman was inside, staring at herself in the mirror. She was pretty. Beautiful even. She wasn't crying. Lance could tell she was practiced in holding in the tears, putting on the brave face. He knew that look when he saw it.

Behind her were three stalls, and he nodded toward them. "Anyone in there?"

She turned and looked at him, looked at his hand. "What are you doing in here?"

"I'll take care of him if you like," Lance said bluntly.

Her eyes widened. "What?"

"Your man."

"You'll..." she said, shaking her head.

"Just say the word, and I'll take care of him."

"You're stark raving mad."

"Maybe," Lance said, "but I mean what I say."

"Get away from me. You can't speak like that. He's my man."

"I know what he is, and if you ever decide you've had enough of him, you give me a call, all right? Day or night. I'll come." He took a business card from his pocket, it was for a Sri Lankan minicab company on Durward Street, and handed it to her. "Call that number, order a cab, ask for Clint."

The woman looked at him like he'd just appeared from another planet. She had absolutely no idea what to make of this. But Lance didn't need her to know. She could think about it, process it in her own time. When she was ready to take him up on the offer, she'd know how to get hold of him.

"He *told* me to wear this dress," she said suddenly. "I didn't want to wear it. I know what I look like."

"You look ... fine," Lance said, eyeing her up and down.

She looked at the card, turned it over in her hand. "Durward Street," she said to herself.

Lance nodded.

"First victim of Jack the Ripper was on Durward Street."

"I didn't know that," Lance said.

"Polly."

"What's that?"

"Her name was Polly, or, at least, that's what she went by."

"I see," Lance said.

He was about to leave when she said, "I call this number, ask for you...." She raised an eyebrow questioningly.

"And I show up."

"Simple as that?"

"If I can, I'll come."

"And if you can't?"

He shrugged. "Maybe they send a cab."

She looked him in the eye defiantly, then ripped the card in half and threw the two pieces to the ground.

Lance sighed. He went back to his seat and put some money on the bar—enough for his drinks and the broken glass. Then he left, walking right by the man in the booth.

Outside it was dark, quiet. It was a night when the air was so still and clear it seemed to be frozen in place. The street was cobbled. It had wrought iron lamp posts every fifty yards or so that gave it an old-time feel, like a scene from a Dickens novel. He walked a few yards in the direction of the river and lit a cigarette. When it was done, he went back into the bar, walked straight to the booth, grabbed the man by the back of the head, and slammed his face hard on the table in front of him. The man hadn't seen him coming, didn't know what hit him, and Lance pulled his head up by the hair and slammed it down again. The glasses on the table crashed to the floor. The woman had a look of absolute horror on her face. The man grabbed Lance around the waist, but Lance simply slammed his face a third time against the table.

The woman got to her feet. She threw herself at Lance, yelling, screaming at him to stop, pulling his arm and sinking her long fingernails into his skin.

Lance let go of the man. The woman took a step back, staring at him, at her man, as if only now realizing what had happened.

The man looked up, dazed. Blood poured from his nose down over his chin, making the neck of his white shirt red.

"I'm watching you," Lance said, then walked out.

9

Valentina took a cab to Arabella Bradwell's neighborhood and got out a few blocks from the apartment. The street lamps were just beginning to come on, and they lit up the snow around them, revealing strong flurries. She was dressed in the same black catsuit and jacket she'd worn the night before and was armed with the same two weapons.

The street was similar to Yvette's, in the slightly less expensive neighborhood of Bubeneč a few blocks to the north. It was busy enough, with pedestrians scurrying home from work and the evening traffic flowing north from the city center.

Valentina got to the building and entered a café across the street. She took a seat by the window, where she would be able to watch Arabella on the street as she got home. Arabella was still at work, probably would be for another hour, and when the waiter came over in his black tie and shirt, Valentina allowed herself the luxury of ordering a Dubonnet. The waiter brought her drink and some olives and asked if he could take her jacket for her. She declined.

She looked at her watch. The research said Arabella usually stayed late at work, like Yvette, but where they differed was in what they liked to do afterward. Unlike Yvette, Arabella wasn't a recluse. She frequently stopped in at one of the bars or restaurants on the way home. The research wasn't detailed, it had been compiled hastily and was yet another sign to Valentina that this target wasn't someone the GRU had ever expected to need a file on, but by the looks of things, Arabella was quite the socialite.

Valentina took a sip of her drink and got the waiter's attention.

"Another?" he said.

"A coffee. Espresso."

"And anything to eat?" he said when he brought the coffee.

She hadn't looked at the menu, but there were some specials on a board behind the bar. "The soup and dumplings," she said.

"They're chicken liver."

"What are?"

"The dumplings."

She nodded. "That's fine."

She'd ordered out of obligation, so as not to stand out, but when the soup arrived with a basket of fresh bread and salted butter, she realized how hungry she was. She ate heartily, and when she'd finished the meal, almost an hour had passed since her arrival. She watched the street and saw a slender woman matching Arabella's description approaching. She was wearing a long green coat that Valentina thought looked quite stylish, and as she got closer, she saw that it was indeed Arabella. She entered the building.

Valentina waved over the waiter and asked for the check. When he returned, she paid and asked for directions to a nearby hotel. She didn't need the directions, but her asking would plant the idea in his subconscious that that was where she was going. When the police came around later, he wouldn't think of her.

She rarely found it difficult to avoid suspicion after a job. It was one of the perks of being a female assassin, and the main reason the GRU hired them. She could walk in and out of a building with a certain demeanor, a certain aloof quality, and men especially would trip over themselves to eliminate her from the suspect list. The soup, the Dubonnet, it was all intentional, what a grandmother might order, carefully calculated to reduce the chance anyone would think of her as a killer.

She left the café and crossed the street, lighting a cigarette that she could pretend to be finishing while she loitered outside the door of the building. She leaned against the wall and waited, and when the next person exited the building, she grabbed the door before it shut again. "Thank you," she said to the man who'd come out, and let herself into a small lobby. The building was old, and a staircase with a wooden banister wrapped around the atrium. There was also an old-style caged elevator shaft, its cables and pulleys visible like the parts of a clock.

Arabella's apartment was on the fourth floor, and as Valentina climbed the stairs, someone came out of one of the apartments. Valentina paused, listened, and realized it was Arabella. She ducked into the third-floor landing, head down, her hand obscuring her face, and kept her back to the staircase as Arabella passed.

There was a window on the landing overlooking the street, and she waited there for Arabella to exit. She watched her head off on foot toward the Československé Armády Boulevard, then hurried down the stairs after her. She followed on the street at a distance of about a hundred yards. Arabella kept a steady pace until the Armády, then turned onto a narrow side street. Valentina stopped at the corner and waited. She peered carefully around the corner. Midway down the street, Arabella stopped and entered a building.

Valentina followed. As she got closer, she saw that the door was for a quaint wine bar, its front window spilling warm light onto the street. She didn't stop, but glanced through the window as she passed. Arabella was sitting at the bar alone, talking to a bartender who was slicing lemons. The bar was small, with room for about six to sit. Behind the stools, a few hightop tables were lined against the wall with seating for another few couples. Three tables were occupied.

Valentina walked all the way to the next corner and lit another cigarette. She watched the street casually, making sure Arabella didn't leave. A taxi turned onto the alley and stopped right by the bar. A man and woman stepped out and entered the bar. Valentina threw away her cigarette and followed them.

When she got inside, Arabella was still at the bar, her face lit by the glow of a single candle. The bartender was serving some other customers, and Arabella was gazing absently at her wine glass. It didn't look like she was waiting for anyone. Valentina stood in the doorway a little awkwardly. She wasn't sure what she was doing. This was a breach of protocol, someone would be able to connect her now to Arabella, but she couldn't help herself. She knew something was off about these missions, and she needed to get to the bottom of it.

"Good evening," the bartender said.

Valentina nodded.

"Reservation?"

"No. Just killing some time. Can I take a seat at the bar?" She spoke without an accent, wouldn't draw attention for being Russian, but if a police investigation ever led to this bar, this guy would remember her for sure.

"Of course," he said. He was young, hip, heavily tattooed, and dressed in a stylish nautical sweater and leather apron. He was about Valentina's age and eyed her provocatively as she took her seat.

She took a seat three away from Arabella and examined the menu. The place specialized in Moravian wines, good ones, and when the waiter came over, she asked what he recommended.

"Something late harvest," he said. "I can bring some samples."

"No," Valentina said. "What she's having looks good." She nodded toward Arabella, who was just taking a sip from her glass, and their eyes met.

The space was intimate, romantic, with dozens of candles scattered about the room. The people were close. She could have reached behind her and touched the couple at the nearest table. The music was from the eighties, everything trendy, Depeche Mode, Kraftwerk, New Order. She glanced again at Arabella as the bartender went through his spiel for the wine.

"Enjoy," he said when he was finished.

Valentina took a sip. It was excellent.

She took off her jacket and tried to look relaxed. It was

her kind of place. The bartender ran the show, working alone to prepare and serve everything himself. He worked deftly, making up simple plates on a narrow counter, cured meats and cheese, a green salad, a bowl of black olives that he fished from an enormous jar on the bar with a set of wooden tongs. There was an ordinary household refrigerator behind the bar that he opened periodically to get what he needed. When he did, its fluorescent light briefly invaded the room. About half the customers were speaking English.

"Nice place," Valentina said when she managed to catch Arabella's eye again. It wasn't difficult. Arabella kept looking her way, pretending not to. "I thought there'd be more men here," she added.

Arabella shrugged. "There never is," she said back in her passable Czech. "Too many candles."

Valentina smiled. "I suppose that's better for keeping out of trouble."

Arabella took a sip of her wine, and Valentina thought she saw something mischievous in her eyes. She'd been trying to read Arabella and was definitely picking up on something. Nothing overt, nothing obvious, and for some reason it hadn't ever been mentioned in the research, but she got the distinct impression that men were not what Arabella was in search of.

"Depends on your definition of trouble," Arabella said.

Valentina smiled, sipped her drink. She let a few minutes pass before speaking again, letting Arabella's curiosity rise a little.

"I'm afraid trouble is not something I've had a lot of experience with," she said.

Arabella shook her head. "That's no way to be."

"No," Valentina said, "but some things are..." she let her words fade out.

Arabella leaned a little closer. "Some things are what?"

They were speaking more quietly now, having graduated from casual pleasantries to something more intimate.

"Some things are *difficult*," Valentina said.

Arabella was less shy than Valentina had anticipated. She was forward, in fact. Flirtatious. Eager to converse. "What things?" she said.

Valentina hesitated, then said, "First steps." She watched Arabella for a reaction. "Taking the first step is difficult."

There was another long pause. They listened to the chatter of the room, the babbling of the men and their dates. At one of the tables, two well-dressed women sat talking. One of them was worried about her job. She didn't get along with her boss. He was a pig, she kept saying. *Prase* was the word in Czech. She rolled the 'r' when she said it, turning the word into two syllables. It wasn't at all like the Russian word, Valentina thought. *Svin'ya.* The boss sounded familiar enough, though.

Arabella turned to them suddenly, surprising them with the bluntness of her remark. "Next time he makes a move, kick him in the balls." The women stared, stunned, just for a second, then laughed out loud. One of them spit wine. "Right in the gonads," Arabella said. "Make it hurt."

Other people in the room laughed. Valentina raised her glass in a toast.

"They've gotten away with too much, for too long," Arabella said, leaning forward to clink glasses with Valentina.

The wine flowed freely after that. Valentina found it

very easy to make conversation with Arabella and allowed herself a little more wine than perhaps she should have. As she spoke to Arabella, she found herself probing constantly for any clue of what Shipenko was up to. He wanted this woman dead, but for the life of her, Valentina couldn't figure out why. It just didn't add up.

Valentina had developed an instinct about her targets, a sort of sixth sense, an ability to read them and see what it was that had led to a kill order being issued. Ordinary people wouldn't have thought of it, but to be an assassin was to play a very intimate role in the life of the target. It created a closeness, like the closeness that was created between a prostitute and her client, or a nurse and her patient. There were certain jobs, often jobs performed by women for men, that created an uncanny ability in the woman to read the intentions of a client. What he wanted. What he thought. What he was hiding. Valentina knew there were hookers on the streets of Moscow who could read a mark more precisely, and with more speed, than any psychiatrist or interrogator in the Lubyanka ever could. They knew things about their marks their own wives would have shuddered to learn. Theirs was a perspective, a level of insight, that could not be replicated. They knew what no one else ever would.

Being an assassin was like that. At least, for Valentina, it was. For her, it was the only profession that could claim to get as up close and personal as a prostitute, or to give as clear a view into the soul of the mark.

She remembered the face of every person she'd ever killed. There wasn't a day that passed when she did not picture each of them. On her death bed, it would be those faces, not the faces of her loved ones, that would usher her across the divide. Hers was not a mindless task. Every time she went on a job, she knew exactly what she was doing. She knew it was a sin. A crime against God. She'd learned to overcome the guilt, to push through it. She could pull a trigger or slit a throat, even though she knew it was evil, even though every fiber of her soul was screaming at her not to. She'd learned to act in spite of it, but she'd never learned to numb it. She felt the pain of the guilt, and she saw the people she was killing for who, and what, they were.

And that was why, when she looked at Arabella, she wasn't just forming a hunch. It wasn't even just a professional opinion. It was a feeling from deep within her, an emotion, a knot in her throat. She knew it the way a lamb knew a wolf. The way a wolf knew a lamb.

And what she knew, unless Arabella had learned to mask her nature so expertly that there wasn't a trace of it left to find, was that Shipenko had no legitimate reason to want this woman dead. He was targeting women, unwitting embassy staffers with no access to sensitive data, with no ability to influence the interests of the Kremlin, women whose only crime was being in the wrong city at the wrong time.

He was playing some sort of game.

As the night went on, Valentina learned more about Arabella than she'd perhaps learned about any previous target. The information kept coming. Arabella made zero attempt at evasion. Her family, her political background, where she'd grown up, her job at the embassy, nothing was off-limits. She was open, unguarded.

She was innocent.

And as the night drew to a close and the bartender began wiping down the tables with the rag he'd kept hanging from his back pocket all night, Arabella turned to Valentina and said, "Walk me home.

Valentina was feeling the wine at that point. Her muscles felt heavy, like lead was flowing through her veins, and her words were beginning to slur. She had to make an effort not to let her Russian accent poke through when she spoke.

"Walk you home?" she said.

She wasn't sure how she felt about that. She wasn't sure how she felt about any of this. She'd gotten close to targets before, but only for genuine tactical reasons. And they were always men. Here, it wasn't necessary. None of this was. She could have performed this job easily, ten times over, once Arabella got home. And maybe it was the wine, or the candlelight, or the music, but she was beginning to feel like maybe a line had been crossed.

Killing. She'd tried for years to detach herself from it. To do what needed to be done. She was a survivor, a she-wolf. She took every job they sent her, and she finished it. She'd built a reputation. Some people inside the GRU said openly that she killed for pleasure. And when they said it, they believed it. Valentina had cultivated that myth. She'd built it up purposefully. She'd attacked rivals in the GRU. In the academy, she'd tried to kill another candidate. Another female. She'd put her own survival before everything else.

But what she was beginning to realize, looking at Arabella as she put on her stylish green coat, was that she wasn't as detached, as mechanical, as inhuman, as she pretended.

"I'll walk you as far as the villa," she said.

Arabella smiled. "The villa?"

"The big house. On Ronald Reagan." The Czechs had a habit of naming their streets after American presidents.

"Perfect," Arabella said, slipping the coat over her shoulders.

They stumbled out of the bar together, and within a few yards, Valentina was surprised to find they'd linked arms. They leaned on each other as they walked, and by the time they'd made it to the corner of the Armády, Arabella had pulled her into the doorway of a kitchen appliance store and put her mouth on hers.

Valentina didn't resist. It wasn't the wine. It wasn't the job. She kissed Arabella back as passionately as she'd ever kissed anyone. She felt a thrill of electricity. She pressed her body against Arabella's.

"I've never done this," she whispered.

"I'll teach you," Arabella said, and Valentina bit her lip hard as Arabella's hand found its way to the zip at the back of her suit.

"It's strange, you wearing this," Arabella said.

"Just open it," Valentina gasped.

Arabella pulled the zip down slowly, all the way, then reached inside the catsuit until her fingers found Valentina's panties.

"Yes," Valentina moaned as Arabella's fingers pulled the underwear to one side.

"By the time I'm done with you," Arabella said, "you're going to be begging me not to stop."

She pulled her hand out of Valentina's pants as soon as she'd said the words, and Valentina was about to protest when she saw that a cab was approaching. Arabella pulled her from the doorway and raised her hand at the cab. Valentina fixed herself as best she could, pulling her jacket tight over the half-open catsuit as the cab stopped.

They stumbled into the back seat, Arabella gave the driver her address, then her tongue instantly found Valentina's ear.

"Behave," Valentina said, but her own hand was inside Arabella's blouse, pulling at the gold clasp at the front of the bra.

"Hey," the driver snapped, his voice thunderously deep.

The two women were sitting up straight in an instant. Valentina opened her window and let the cold air wash over her. It was only then that she realized how easily Arabella might have found the knife and pistol hidden in her jacket pockets.

The ride only took a minute, and the cab came to a stop in front of the café Valentina had eaten in earlier. It was closed now, the lights were out, and the street felt very different. It had stopped snowing, and the wind had died down. The moon was very bright, and a deathly silence had fallen over everything.

"Come on," Arabella said, crossing the street. "I'm going to make you scream my name."

They entered the building and took the elevator to the fourth floor.

"We had a lift like this in my building when I was a child," Valentina said.

"And where was that?" Arabella said as she fumbled with her key at the apartment door.

Valentina waited until they were both inside before answering. It almost pained her to do it. She knew the effect her words were going to have. She knew it would mean they wouldn't be consummating their little tryst.

But what choice did she have? She wasn't going to make love to this woman and then kill her.

And, as much as she might have liked otherwise, she wasn't going to disobey a Prime Directorate kill order.

She was a GRU assassin. She had a job to do. Any failure, any refusal, even the hint of resistance or hesitance, would be dealt with swiftly and harshly.

"It was Saint Petersburg," she said, her voice suddenly taking on a harshness that she hadn't quite intended.

Arabella looked at her, suddenly sober.

"What's wrong?" Valentina said. "You don't like Russian girls?"

"It's not that," Arabella said.

"Yes, it is."

"I'm surprised, is all."

"You thought I was Czech?"

"I work at the US embassy," Arabella said. "I'll have to declare this."

"Do you have a security clearance?"

"What?"

"Answer me," Valentina said, and the look on Arabella's face, the sudden change in the trajectory of the evening, the slow realization that something very bad was about to happen, was heartbreaking.

"No," she said.

"No, you don't have a clearance?"

"Of course I don't have a clearance. I'm practically a receptionist."

"You work for the CIA."

"What?"

"You work for the Central Intelligence Agency."

"What is this?" Arabella said, taking a step backward into the apartment. "What's going on?"

Valentina stood between her and the door, blocking any hope of escape, in complete control of the situation. "I needed to get you back here," she said.

"No," Arabella said, shaking her head. "You and I.... There was something there. We were...."

"Why would the Prime Directorate of the GRU be interested in you?" Valentina said.

"The Prime Directorate?" Arabella said helplessly.

"What do they want?"

"I have no idea."

Valentina became aware of the open zip on the back of her suit. The clasp of her bra had been undone. She felt a pang of regret for what the evening might have been, for what she and Arabella might have been doing at that very moment. She reached behind her back and redid the clasps and zip, then reached into her jacket pocket and pulled out the stubbly little PSS.

"What are you doing?" Arabella gasped, her gaze fixed on the weapon.

"You know what I'm doing."

Arabella looked straight into her eyes. "This..." she stammered. "This...."

"Doesn't make sense?"

"There has to be some mistake."

Valentina shook her head and, for the second time in twenty-four hours, found herself repeating the same hollow words. "The Prime Directorate doesn't make mistakes."

She watched as Arabella put together what pieces of the puzzle she was aware of. Her eyes widened, and she said softly, "You killed Yvette."

Valentina nodded.

"Why?"

Valentina made to speak but, to her surprise, found a knot of emotion choking the words. She had to swallow before saying, "I don't know."

"How can you do this?"

Valentina shook her head. She didn't know the answer to that either. But one thing she did know, and she knew it with a certainty. Neither Arabella nor Yvette had the slightest clue why the GRU was coming for them.

She pulled the trigger. Arabella's body crumpled like a puppet whose strings had just been cut. She fell heavily to the floor, not backward, but straight down, like a building.

Valentina walked over to her.

The bullet had found its mark. Blood seeped through the white silk blouse at Arabella's chest, but too slowly. She was still alive. The underpowered PSS had proved its inadequacy again.

Arabella looked up at her. "Why are you doing this?" she gasped.

Valentina clenched her jaw and cursed the little gun, then drew the firing knife and, in a fluid motion, took Arabella's face in her hand, tenderly, as if she was going to kiss her again, angled her head backward, and ran the blade across her neck.

An impossible amount of blood suddenly gushed from the wound, spilling into a puddle on the floor that grew so quickly Valentina had to step back to avoid getting it on her shoes.

"Why?" she said then, to herself alone, "I wish to God I knew."

10

Osip Shipenko stood in front of the large, oak sideboard in the corner of his office and leaned toward the mirror. He had a pair of tweezers in his hand, and he inserted them carefully into his nostril, plucking an errant bristle.

"Better," he muttered, pursing his upper lip to get a better view.

Were it not for the cruelties of fate, he might have been a vain man. As it stood, no one could accuse him of that particular vice. His appearance was the most hideous, grotesque thing most people he came across would ever see in their lives, and he never for a second forgot it. In times gone by, he would have been forced into the circus, or a freak show. People would have paid good money to stare at him in a cage, to taunt him, to throw food.

When he joined the KGB forty years ago, one of the instructors at the academy inserted the following hand-written note into his file.

Recruit has a gristly complexion, like hashed meat,
or dog food. Fieldwork, and certainly anything
requiring cover, will never be possible. Termination
recommended. Or, as a mercy, transfer to custodial
services.

The description was accurate—his face truly did look
like a half-eaten bowl of wet dog food—and when the
note was discovered by the other recruits, they instantly
took to calling him Dog Face, or Meat Face,
or *Tushonka,* after a popular brand of canned meat that
was available at state-owned food stores.

For his part, Shipenko kept his head down, shrugged
off the indignity, and focused on excelling at every task
the academy set for him. He got through the initial assessment phase at the top of his class and thereby avoided
being demoted, as the note had recommended, to the role
of janitor.

Shipenko's deformity was undoubtedly a handicap,
something that should have stunted his progression up
the ranks of the GRU, but in his hands, the crutch became
a cudgel, and he learned to wield it mercilessly. He'd risen
to the very top of the Kremlin's security apparatus, the
pinnacle of power and privilege, the president's own Dead
Hand organization. He'd done so not through connections, not through luck, but by sheer force of will and an
iron determination.

And yet, for all that, he'd never quite managed to
shake off the nickname. *Tushonka,* Meat Face, the words
still followed him around like a bad smell. They were
whispered the moment his back was turned by subordi-

nates and superiors alike. He'd seen official memos from the Kremlin and the Prime Directorate referring to him as such, and the transcripts of Dead Hand meetings were littered with even worse.

It was his own fault. Indeed, it was an outcome he'd engineered. Back in his Main Directorate days, upon making the rank of director but before he'd become a personal consort of the president, his first order of business had been to find the note from the bowels of the academy archive. That was no small task, given that the entire archive had been transferred years earlier to the basement of the GAZ-30 plant. The note was eventually found, dusted off, and, under Shipenko's personal direction, framed and hung in a prominent position in the Main Directorate's eighth-floor lobby, facing the elevators. It was impossible for anyone to arrive on the floor without seeing it, and, over the years, it became something of a curiosity, a conversation piece that was pointed out to new directors and official visitors who toured the facility.

Shipenko took a certain pride in the whole thing, or, if not quite pride, he at least recognized the power it held. It was a branding tool, a publicity stunt within the agency that allowed him to carve out a niche for himself and use it to advance his career. He was the man people whispered about. Everyone knew his name. It didn't take long for him to get noticed, and then invited up to the top floor.

He should have been grateful to the academy instructor who'd written it, but instead, once he'd risen sufficiently in stature to be able to have his way with people, he had the poor fellow tracked down. Evaluation notes of that kind were supposed to be anonymous, but it didn't take long for a name to be supplied.

Shipenko looked him up on the database. His name

was Tyukavin. He was old by then, retired, but still alive, with his generous GRU pension and a nice apartment near Leningradsky Prospekt. Shipenko remembered him and learned that in the intervening decades, the man had kept his nose clean, stayed out of politics, and, according to his medical file, was beginning to show the early signs of dementia. His wife was dead. He had some family in the Moscow area, but his main companion, as far as Shipenko could tell, was a fine black Chornyi Terrier named Lubov.

Tyukavin liked to garden and had a small allotment near his apartment where he grew vegetables. His routine in the warmer seasons was to walk to the allotment in the morning with his dog, spend a few hours gardening, get his dinner at an inexpensive restaurant on the Prospekt, and then go home for the evening. He kept to this routine six days a week and went swimming or occasionally saw his grandchildren on Sunday.

It wasn't a bad life. Perhaps a little lonely, but Shipenko had certainly seen worse. After reading the surveillance file, he'd had his driver take him out to the allotment, where he sat in the back seat of the car and watched Tyukavin digging in a raised bed of cabbages. Tyukavin noticed the car—you didn't work for thirty-nine years in the GRU and fail to notice a black Mercedes S-Class with tinted windows—but if it scared him, he showed no sign of it.

A week later, the dog went missing. A few days after that, a box showed up at Tyukavin's apartment. The note on the lid read, "Courtesy of your old friend, Dog Face," and inside, it contained Lubov's head, preserved by a taxidermist and mounted to a wooden plaque. A week after that, Tyukavin's pension was delayed, then canceled.

Then, the lease on his apartment was terminated. His family members were paid visits and, in no uncertain terms, told to cut off all ties to him.

Shipenko kept tabs on what followed. The reports provided some light entertainment, like the magazine stories of his childhood before soap operas took over. There were ups and downs, petty victories and reversals, a few surprises, but ultimately, the story was a tragedy. After three years, Tyukavin died of hypothermia at a homeless shelter in Chertanovo. His body was never claimed.

For all that, the note itself had been perfectly accurate. There'd been nothing malicious in it. Shipenko's appearance really was disturbing. Even shocking. It drew a visceral response from colleagues and prevented him from performing ordinary daily tasks in public.

Shipenko was accustomed to it. It was a part of him— had been for almost as far back as he could remember. It had been given to him, like so many things in the communist Russia of his childhood, courtesy of the Soviet state.

He'd been born in Moscow, the only son of two top biochemists at the prestigious Ivanovskii Institute of Virology. His parents were dedicated party members, educated workers in a high-priority field, and Shipenko's early childhood was spent enjoying all the privileges such a position entailed. He attended a special school for the children of elites, had a governess, spent his summers at a Black Sea resort. He lived with his parents in an enormous, pre-revolution apartment near the Tretyakov Gallery that had ten-foot ceilings and balconies overlooking the Moskva River. It didn't last, but he took pride in having lived it at all.

The change came when he was six. One of his parents must have said the wrong thing or upset the wrong person. Shipenko never got to the bottom of it—by the time he had the power to open the files, everyone involved was dead—but such things were common in those days. People went into exile for laughing at a joke, or reading a certain book, or for doing nothing at all.

In any case, a week after his sixth birthday, Shipenko's parents were both transferred from the plush confines of the virology institute to one of the least hospitable scientific outposts in the entire Soviet Union, a top-secret bioweapons facility known as Aralsk-7.

The facility was located on what was then Vozrozhdeniya Island and was now part of the ever-expanding Aralkum Desert—the Aral Sea having completely dried up in the intervening decades. It was a wonder to Shipenko, a symbol of the relentless enormity of Soviet industrial mismanagement, that a sea covering twenty-five thousand square miles could simply disappear. But disappear it had, and what had once been a seabed submerged beneath a hundred feet of water was now part of the bone-dry expanse of desert and salt flats that stretched for hundreds of miles along the Kazakh and Uzbek borders. The steel frames of old boats, fishing trawlers, even old US Coast Guard vessels that had been sold to the Soviets after the war and shipped in on trains from Saint Petersburg sat rusting in sand hundreds of miles from the nearest coastline. They were, to Shipenko, a surreal reminder of a sea that had dried up, and a childhood on its shores that had been lost just as irrevocably.

The town the military built on the island was called Kantubek. It was a godforsaken collection of three-story concrete apartment blocks in neat rows with bunkers beneath them as deep as the buildings were tall. The buildings stood to this day, as did the administrative office at the center of town, its typewriters and steel filing cabinets sitting exactly as they had the day the town was abandoned. There was also a school, a commissary, and a cinema with an iron hammer and sickle above the entrance and an enormous glass chandelier in the lobby. In front of the cinema was a rusted children's playground with a rusted metal statue of Stalin at its center. All of it was lashed constantly by the desert winds, which whipped up so much sand that the military could no longer use the runway at the airfield and could only fly in by chopper. This they did, from time to time, to supervise and monitor the international weapons inspectors and clean-up crews that were periodically granted access to the site.

Four miles south of the village, the Aralsk-7 Bioweapons Research Complex rose from the sand like the set of a high-budget science fiction movie. It had been abandoned with the town, its documents burned in pyres in the parking lot, and its equipment and processing facilities hastily dismantled. *Trashed* would be the more apt term. Chemistry apparatus, lab equipment, even old mainframe computers and monitors sat where they'd been the day the plant was shut down, some smashed with crowbars, others completely intact. It didn't take the weapons inspectors long to figure out what had been going on. The evidence was everywhere. The attempt to conceal it had been so half-hearted and rushed that even the biohazard signs on the lab doors hadn't been removed. Outside the complex, cattle barns, sheep pens, fenced pastures, even vats and heavy industrial equipment, had been left in place to rot.

As for the weapons stockpiles, they'd been dumped in pits that had been intended for burning livestock carcasses, with no containment measures at all in place other than a few feet of soil and sand. Not so much as a fence or a warning sign had been erected.

All of it was abundantly visible to the US spy planes and satellites that had zeroed in on the site years earlier after being alerted to its presence by Soviet defectors. Those reports were confirmed when inspectors were permitted on the island in the nineties. Some modest clean-up attempts were then made, until the spirit of cooperation petered out and President Molotov ascended the throne.

The whole island was a monument to the scale of the Soviet bioweapons program. At its peak, almost two thousand people—microbiologists, virologists, biochemists, military personnel, and their families—lived there. The facility was beyond remote, accessible only by a fourteen-hour military flight from Moscow with a compulsory stopover at the 12th Independent Air Defense Army airfield in Tashkent, six hundred miles away. And that remoteness was, of course, the point. It wasn't just research and development, not just lab work in a controlled environment, that took place at the facility. The Soviets didn't only want the science necessary to develop the weapons, they wanted to know if they were battlefield-ready. For that, they needed a program of large-scale, open-air testing in circumstances likely to resemble battlefield conditions.

They had long ago decided that one of the most feasible ways to deliver bioweapons was by low-altitude crop duster flyovers. Such planes were cheap, readily available, easy to replace, and a single flight could let loose enough payload to wipe out any enemy.

And so, just twenty miles further south, in the open

pastures that had initially so confused US satellite analysts—there was no earthly reason why anyone would want to farm animals at a location that remote—crop dusters sprayed weaponized strains of anthrax, smallpox, plague, brucellosis, and tularemia over thousands of cows, sheep, pigs, chickens, even horses and chimps, and then monitored the results.

It was a strange place now, one of those scars on the surface of former Soviet territory like the exclusion zone around Chernobyl, or the yellow clouds visible from space over the ore smelters in Nizhny Tagil, or the black snow over the Siberian coal-mining city of Anzhero-Sudzhensk. Shipenko didn't think of it that way, though. He still remembered playing outside the school with the other children, or eating stroganoff with his parents in their three-room apartment, or going to the airfield with his father to watch the supply planes coming in.

He certainly remembered the hot summer afternoon fifty years ago, according to weather records the temperature was over forty-five degrees Celsius that day, when his governess brought him to the beach to swim. There were beautiful beaches on the island in those days, white sand dunes interspersed with patches of tall, spindly grass native to the area.

Shipenko was seven. His governess, Anya, was seventeen. Governess was a grand term for her. She was really just a local schoolgirl, the daughter of one of the commissary cooks, who'd taken on the job for the summer as a means of making extra pocket money. Shipenko's parents never failed to refer to her as the governess, though, as if the word somehow brought them nearer to their previous life in Moscow.

He'd received binoculars a few weeks earlier for his

seventh birthday, and Anya let him bring them along. He remembered using them to watch the sea birds. He remembered the waves lapping the sand on the beach. He remembered the persimmon orange bathing suit Anya wore, her red hair in a single long braid, her yellow-rimmed sunglasses. He also remembered raising the binoculars to the sky and shouting, "Anya! Look!".

What he'd seen was an Antonov An-2 crop duster, and what it dropped was a weaponized payload of variola virus intended for a flock of sheep seventeen miles away. How the plane got so lost, no one ever found out. What they did find out, very quickly, was that Shipenko and Anya were among the last people in the Soviet Union ever to contract smallpox. Variola was its causative virus, and it was by that time well on its way to being eradicated in nature.

The particular strain Shipenko and Anya contracted had been lab-altered to take on the most aggressive hemorrhagic characteristics ever measured by the Russian military. In its weaponized form, it was projected to cause a near-one-hundred-percent fatality rate. Added to all the familiar scourges of naturally occurring small-pox, this strain also caused profuse bleeding from all mucous membranes, including the gastrointestinal tract and viscera. The bleeding started within a few hours of exposure and didn't stop. Blood poured from every orifice —mouth, nose, eyes, even ears.

Shipenko and Anya coughed blood, cried blood, pissed and shat blood. Their beds looked like butchers' tables. Around their abdomens, there was so much subcu-taneous bleeding that they both turned black from neck to waist, and their torsos distended as if from severe cirrhosis.

They were sealed in the Aralsk-7 isolation unit, a pressurized steel chamber that was normally used for monitoring the livestock after an exposure test. Shipenko still remembered the straw on the tiled floor, the zinc feeding trough, and the almost unbearable stench. He and Anya raged against their confinement, bashed their fists against the maritime-grade steel door with its round, reinforced window and submarine-style locking mechanism. They threw themselves against it like caged, frenzied animals.

When their temperatures climbed to 108, and they'd vomited so much blood that they were in danger of dying from dehydration, sprayers in the walls and ceiling that had been designed for washing contaminated livestock in chlorine were turned on, filling the room with powerful jets of cold water that smelled like the bleach used to wash the corridors of Shipenko's school.

There was no escape. They'd been sealed in what was at that time the most secure human isolation pod on the planet. Nothing in the West came anywhere near its level of containment. Nothing in the West needed to.

When Shipenko finally emerged, he was not the person he'd been when he entered. In fact, he was hardly a person at all.

He was something else.

11

Gilhofer was splayed on his sofa in front of the television, a bowl of cold popcorn on his lap, the butter long since congealed, and a beer somewhere within arm's reach. He was barely keeping his eyes open and kept dozing off, only to wake himself with one of his own snores every few minutes. Then he'd open his eyes and stare at the TV screen for a few seconds until the whole process started again.

He should have been in bed. He'd been up almost twenty hours, and the Bunting investigation had hit a wall. Langley was watching him, the station chief had cut her trip short—it was a lot of pressure. But instead of sleeping, he was on the ratty sofa in his living room, the curtains wide open so that anyone outside would see the blue glow of his seventy-inch screen filling the room.

He was a Red Wings fan, had been since he was a boy even though he'd grown up in Chicago, and the TV was showing the second period of a live game between them and the Bruins. It was being played in Boston, which meant its seven o'clock start time was one a.m. in Prague.

He could have recorded it, that would have been more comfortable, but instead, he would be on the sofa with his beer and his popcorn, snoozing fitfully until the bitter end.

When the phone rang, it startled him. He knocked over the popcorn and flailed blindly in the cracks of the sofa for his phone.

"Hello," he said hoarsely when he found it, brushing popcorn off his lap.

Klára's voice greeted him. "Gilhofer, it's me."

There were precious few reasons for her to call at that hour, and none of them involved good news. "What's happened?"

"There's been another one."

"Another murder?"

"Afraid so."

"One of ours?"

"Yes, one of yours."

He felt a rush of adrenaline in his veins. "Who?"

"I'm on my way to the scene now. They didn't give me a name, but I'm forwarding you the address. You can meet me there."

"What time is it?"

"Am I interfering with your beauty sleep?"

He glanced at the television, Detroit were down by three with four minutes to go. "No, I'm on my way," he said. "Just give me a minute to put on some pants."

"It's in Bubeneč. Not far from the last one."

"I'll be there in ten," he said, hanging up the phone.

He felt the vibration of the message coming in and pulled up the address on a map. Who did he know, he thought, that lived in Bubeneč?

He wiped the popcorn from his shirt and pulled on

the pants he'd worn the day before. His keys, sidearm, and wallet were by the door, and he grabbed them on his way out. Bubeneč wasn't far from where he lived. The area was popular enough with the embassy's younger staff. The prices were lower than in Malá Strana, but it still had all of the character and almost as many restaurants and bars. As he made his way along the deserted nighttime streets, he went over in his mind the people from the embassy who lived in the area. The embassy had far more personnel than he could keep track of personally, and it was really only the most senior people, the heads of department and the ambassador's immediate staff, whose addresses were familiar to him. Those people received protection details from time to time, drive-bys, and the like. Everyone else was more or less on their own, other than a brief security audit when they first moved into a new apartment. Off the top of his head, he estimated there were two or three dozen junior staffers living in Bubeneč at the least.

He was approaching the street Klára had given him, and even before turning onto it, he could see the blue and red lights of the police cruisers reflected on the wet asphalt. He pulled up behind them and flashed his credentials to one of the officers. There was a café across the street, shut for the night, but the interior was brightly lit. Was it familiar? Had he eaten there with someone? They all looked so similar. He looked at the entrance of the building, and while still not triggering any specific memory, he began to feel a strange sense of dread, a sort of foreshadowing of what he was about to see.

He opened the car door, and a sudden gust of wind caught him, sending a chill through his body. He got out and kicked the door shut behind him, then hurried to the entrance of the building.

"Americký," he said to the officer at the door.

The man waved him past, and he entered a grand lobby with an old-fashioned elevator surrounded by a staircase. He took the stairs to the fourth floor, where another police officer stood in front of an open apartment door. Yellow police tape spanned the doorway.

"Klára Issová? Is she inside?" Gilhofer said in his halting Czech.

"Right in here," Klára said from inside.

As Gilhofer approached, he saw Klára standing just inside the door, and by her feet, a blood-soaked corpse.

"Oh God," Gilhofer gasped, his voice catching in his throat.

"Are you all right?" Klára said. "You look like you just saw a ghost."

"Not a ghost," he said quietly, his gaze fixed on the body. The corpse was young, female, her white blouse so drenched in blood it looked crimson. A body that size contained, at most, a gallon-and-a-half of blood. The pool on the floor looked like it had taken every drop of that.

"You know her," Klára said. It wasn't a question. She could tell from the look on his face.

Arabella Bradwell was lying face up, her throat slit so deeply it had cut clean through her esophagus and trachea, the two openings clearly visible through the wound. Her face was obscured by hair, matted with blood, but there was no mistaking who it was.

He'd spoken to her not six hours before. She'd been sitting at her desk, twirling a ballpoint pen between her thumb and forefinger, talking about having to return some new coat she'd bought because it didn't fit. "Her name's Arabella Bradwell," he said, and, against his will, a quiver ran through the muscles in his mouth and lip. "I worked with her at the embassy."

"You were close?"

"Not so close."

"You worked with her."

"It's a small team," he said, shaking his head. "Prague's a small station."

"I'm very sorry."

"It's okay."

"If you need—"

"I'm good," he said. "Just tell me what we've got. This looks to me like the same MO as last night."

"It's about as close as you could get. Bullet wound to the chest. Slit throat."

"Same gun?"

"We'll have to wait for confirmation from the lab, but it sure looks like it."

"Two killings, two nights," Gilhofer said, more to himself than Klára. "What the hell is going on?"

"We need to figure that out," Klára said, "or something tells me this is just the beginning."

"We've got to stop it."

Klára nodded. "Yvette Bunting, Arabella Bradwell," she said. "What were they working on? What did they have in common? Were they involved in something sensitive?"

Gilhofer let out a long sigh. He suddenly felt very heavy, like just standing up took more effort than he could muster. He leaned on the kitchen counter and tried to clear his head. Wherever his mind was now, it wasn't thinking straight. He couldn't make sense of this. He knew the kind of work Arabella and Yvette were involved in. Or he thought he did. Had he been wrong in his assumptions? Had they been working on something special for Langley? If they were, he couldn't imagine it. He certainly knew what Arabella spent her time on. A lot of her workload came directly from him, or was sent to her in communications from Langley that he had access to. There was precious little he'd ever seen that was sensitive about it—certainly nothing that could have been even remotely interesting to the Russians.

He looked up at Klára. "I don't know what we're looking at," he said. "I really don't."

"If there's something you're holding back," she said, "it's only going to bite us both in the ass."

He shook his head. "I don't see it," he said. "It makes no sense."

"It makes sense to someone," she said. "There's a thread that connects these women. We know they're American. We know they worked at the embassy. What we need to figure out is what else connected them. Something big enough to explain the Russians sending in killers."

"Whatever it is, it's not something I was ever let in on."

"Aren't you above them?"

"I work for the State Department."

"You said you worked with Arabella," Klára said, stooping down to get a closer look at the wound on her neck.

"She was the CI."

"CI?"

"Counter-intelligence liaison. She coordinated between my department, which deals with embassy security, and the CIA, which deals with... you know."

"Intelligence."

"Right."

"You worked with her closely?"

"Yes, but if Langley was sending her private communications, there was no way I'd have known."

"From what you saw, what was she involved in?"

"Ordinary things," Gilhofer said. "Mundane things. She was responsible for getting the new station chief a dedicated parking spot. I remember it because it ruffled feathers. She ended up taking one of ours. "

"Yours?"

"State Department's. We had the largest assignment."

"So," Klára said, "she's somehow gone from handling parking spots to being assassinated by the GRU."

Gilhofer shook his head. "It certainly looks that way, doesn't it?"

"Did you notice any change in her demeanor lately? Or in Yvette's?"

"No, but, I mean...."

"You didn't pay attention."

"I didn't know they were going to be murdered."

"We need to find out what the Russians know."

Gilhofer got up and walked to the door. "The lock's not broken," he said.

"Yeah, I noticed that."

"Do you think she knew the killer?"

"It crossed my mind."

"I need to call my contact at Langley," Gilhofer said. "Whatever they're holding back, they need to start talking."

"Tell them they need to let us in or be prepared to see this keep happening."

"What about the apartment?" Gilhofer said. "Anything taken? Any sign of a search?"

"Nothing, near as I can tell."

Gilhofer looked around the living room. Nothing seemed out of place. It was tidy but not pristine. He opened a few drawers and pulled up the cushions on the sofa. He found some change. "Someone wants us to know it's the GRU," he said.

"The bullets?"

"I don't think that's a coincidence."

"Doesn't mean it's definitely the GRU," Klára said. "We shouldn't be too sure of ourselves."

He nodded.

Klára was searching Arabella's pockets and pulled out a scrap of crumpled paper. It looked like a receipt. "Unless," she said, "they're not being targeted for who they are, but for what they represent."

"What they represent?"

"They're young. They're female. They're beautiful."

"They're American."

"CIA."

"Who would target young, female CIA agents?"

Klára shrugged. "Who would target anyone? You said yourself they weren't working on anything sensitive."

"As far as I know."

"But you think it's unlikely."

"I mean, they're young. This was their first overseas appointment. I wouldn't describe them as battle-hardened spies."

"Someone doesn't like women."

"It can't be that."

Klára raised an eyebrow.

"What?" Gilhofer said.

"You'd be surprised."

"I mean, I know there are freaks out there."

"There are a lot of men who don't like women," Klára said flatly. "Men who hate women, in fact. Trust me."

He nodded. He wasn't going to get into an argument about that, not with a dead woman lying at his feet. "What's that?" he said, indicating the piece of paper Klára had taken from Arabella's pocket.

She read it, and he could tell from her face it was significant.

"What does it say?"

"She was at a bar."

"When?"

Klára's eyebrow arched. She looked at her watch. "Just a few hours ago."

"What bar?"

"Come on," she said. "It's not far."

"It won't be open now."

"No, but I want to set eyes on the place. Maybe they have cameras."

"If she picked someone up at that bar, it would explain why the lock wasn't broken."

"And around here, a girl like that, American, every guy in the place will remember her."

12

For a long time, none of the scientists dared enter the chamber where Shipenko and Anya were being held. And then, when they finally did, they brought electric cattle prods, waving them menacingly at the patients to keep them back. Two men entered the first time, both wearing industrial hazmat suits with purpose-built, pressurized head-coverings that connected via rubber tubes to oxygen tanks on their backs. They looked like apocalyptic invaders from another world and, to this day, visited Shipenko in his nightmares.

Shipenko never learned how long he and Anya were kept in the chamber. All he knew was that, by some miracle that the scientists were incapable of explaining, he survived the ordeal. His fever eventually subsided, the bleeding stopped, and, after what felt like an eternity, he was taken from the disgusting containment chamber to a real human bed at the Kantubek medical clinic.

Anya hadn't been so lucky. She'd died days earlier in a paroxysm of hemorrhaging that left over a gallon of blood on the chamber floor and so terrified Shipenko that he'd knocked himself unconscious against the wall while it was happening.

He woke in the clinic delirious, and when he realized Anya wasn't in the room, he became distraught. At that point, she was the only thing that could have consoled him, the only person he still cared about. He hadn't seen his parents in weeks but never once asked for them. It was as if his time in the chamber had obliterated all memory of what had been before.

Anya never came, of course, but his father did. It was not long after the transfer to the clinic, and according to the visitor record, it was just the one time. Shipenko had not yet regained consciousness, so he didn't know what transpired during the visit. What he did know was that his father never came back. Instead, he got on the first flight to Moscow, and even though he still lived in the city today, Shipenko had never once attempted to contact him.

His mother took longer to make her visit, and when she did, it was more tentative. She didn't enter the room. She didn't try to communicate. She didn't cry. She remained in the corridor, watching him through a small observation window, her eyes squinted as if afraid of what she might see.

She came more than once, and the visits were strange, upsetting affairs for Shipenko. In his dimly lit room, he could see when the curtain was pulled back. He could see her standing there. She never said anything, or if she did, he didn't hear it. He said nothing either. He didn't understand why she wasn't coming into the room, nurses and doctors did so all the time, and when he'd raised a hand in greeting the first time he saw her, she didn't respond. She just stood there, watching, passive, taking in her son with the cold, detached gaze of a scientist examining a specimen.

It was around the time of her visits that one of the nurses left a surgical scalpel on the table beside his bed.

"To do the right thing," she said to him, and when he stared back at her blankly, she added, "For your poor mother's sake."

It sat next to his bed for three days, during which time it dawned on his seven-year-old mind what it was he was expected to do with it. Others must have seen it there, the doctors and other nurses. None raised an objection. But he couldn't do it. He couldn't even touch it. That wasn't because of any will to live, any instinct of self-preservation. He was simply too scared. Every time the nurse came in and saw it still there, she gave him a look of such disdain, such scorn, that he began to hide from her beneath the bedsheets. Eventually, someone took it away.

Maybe she gave it to his mother.

Because her visits stopped. Shipenko never asked why. After a few weeks, he heard she'd killed herself. He'd always imagined her using the scalpel the nurse had left him, but she'd in fact used his father's Makarov pistol from his time in the army. Shipenko remembered having held it. His father had taken it out and showed him a few times. It had a star etched in the grip.

It wasn't long before the Ministry of Defence realized it had stumbled across a bonanza, a veritable trove of data that would enable them to tweak and perfect that strain of variola for maximum military value. Shipenko spent a number of months at the clinic in Kantubek, where a specialized team was assembled to monitor his condition and the long-term effects of his exposure.

The findings proved so important that the Kremlin

authorized an entirely new facility to be built, the All-Union Research Institute of Experimental Virology, which focused solely on hardening the variola strain Shipenko had been infected by. Shipenko was transferred to the facility, located in Pokrov, close to Moscow, where he spent the next eight years being poked and prodded and examined like a lab rat. For the young boy, those years were an unending parade of agonies, indignities, and horrors, and, not surprisingly, they altered him permanently.

The maculopapular scarring that covered over ninety percent of his body was never going to heal. The fluid-filled pustules that had so tormented him and Anya in the isolation chamber, and which the doctors had expected to fade over time to the unsightly pitted pockmarks more typically found on smallpox survivors, never behaved as expected. Instead of forming scar tissue, they hardened to a callous-like scab that became a permanent scaly crust over his skin. This crust frequently cracked, leading to constant bleeding that was so unsightly it once caused a nurse with twelve years experience to vomit on the spot in revulsion. The damage to his skin was found to have much in common with severe burn victims, who simply could not heal without the aid of skin grafts, and at one point, the Soviet Union's premier specialist in the field was brought in to take a look.

That man's name was Alibekov, and he'd studied and treated all of the most horrendous skin conditions known to medical science. One of the nurses told Shipenko he was coming, she even built up the doctor's reputation and allowed the boy's hopes to rise that some relief was coming.

The man walked into the room, took one look at Shipenko, and simply could not believe his eyes.

"My God," he said quietly to the scientists accompanying him. "What in the devil's name have you done?"

Shipenko was twelve by that time and remembered it all.

"Can you help him?" the lead scientist said coldly, his voice flat, monotone.

"This is not natural," Alibek said.

"No, it's not."

"What happened to him? What did you do?"

"We did nothing. He was in an accident."

Those were the days before the Chernobyl disaster, but Alibek immediately said, "Radiation?"

"We can't say," the scientist said.

"Space?" Alibek said. The Vostok space program was big news across the Soviet Union at that time. Just a few years earlier, it had made Yuri Gargarin the first man in space, and new achievements were being announced regularly.

"You know what we do here," the scientist said. "It's not space. It's not radiation. Can you help the boy?"

To his credit, Alibek did everything that could possibly have been expected of him. He tried treatments that were years ahead of their time, experimental therapies that weren't even being used in the West. But talented as he was, he was not a magician, and there was only so far he could go.

He couldn't get rid of the scabbing. He couldn't change the fact that the pigmentation would be permanent. He couldn't help with the distension and bloating of Shipenko's torso.

The pigmentation particularly bothered the boy. It gave his torso, hands, and face a strangely artificial hue, as if he'd been rubbed with a deep, crimson ink.

He later saw one of Alibek's notes—one of many precursors to the note that would be written by Tyukavin at the academy years after.

Patient resembles a badly burned python after a brush fire, bloated from having swallowed a goat whole.

13

Tatyana arrived back at the office before dawn after just a couple of hours sleep—her tryst the night before with the driver had been over sooner than she'd hoped—and was immediately irritated to see Laurel already there, sitting at a new desk she'd set up right next to hers, her seat close enough to enjoy the same view over the Potomac. "Oh," she said. "I didn't expect—"

"I wanted an early start," Laurel said casually, as if being there at that time was the most normal thing in the world. "I've made coffee."

"I see," Tatyana said, squeezing by Laurel's chair to get to her own. "I see you got your desk set up."

Laurel nodded but said nothing. Tatyana stared at her for a moment and then sighed. There was nothing she could say. Laurel called the shots.

She logged into her computer and performed a database query for every CIA record since 1989 that made any reference at all to SP-4 or SP-16 ammunition.

She'd just gotten up to pour some coffee when her

phone started to ring. "It's Gilhofer," she said to Laurel as she answered. Then to Gilhofer, she said, "What have you got for us?"

"It's not good," he said. "Another body."

"What?" Tatyana said, connecting the phone to the conference room speaker so Laurel could hear. "What the hell's going on over there?"

"We've got a second dead agent," Gilhofer said. "That's what's going on."

Tatyana turned to Laurel.

"Two dead agents?" Laurel mouthed, careful not to be picked up by the phone.

"Who found the body?" Tatyana said.

"Czech police. The victim's neighbor called it in when she saw blood seeping into the corridor from under the door."

"Jeez."

"Yeah."

"This is the same detective you've been working with?"

"That's right. Klára Issová. She caught both cases."

"And she's good? She's still cooperating?"

"She called me as soon as she found out. Gave me the heads-up. She could have waited until morning."

"Okay, that's good."

"She's on our side," Gilhofer said.

"As much as she can be."

"Right."

"Don't take her for granted," Tatyana said.

"Sure."

Tatyana detected the same air of defiance she'd heard earlier. He didn't appreciate their interference, giving directions from four thousand miles away like annoying backseat drivers. "Was this the same MO as the other killing?" she said.

"Same MO," he said. "Same weapons, same style, same everything."

"Slit throat?"

"This is the same in every way."

"Was the SP-4 ammo used?

"Waiting for lab confirmation, but yes, it looks like it."

"So, the same killer?"

"You don't need to be Sherlock Holmes to make the connection."

"Right," she said.

Laurel had been looking at something on her computer, and she leaned into Tatyana's ear and whispered, "He knew the victim." Tatyana looked at her, and she nodded. "They were close."

"Who's the victim?" Tatyana said. "A friend of yours?"

Laurel rolled her eyes.

"What?" Tatyana mouthed, but Laurel just shook her head.

Gilhofer cleared his throat. "She was our counter-intelligence liaison."

"Arabella Bradwell," Tatyana said, "another female."

"That's correct."

"That's two."

"You can count," Gilhofer said.

Tatyana looked at Laurel again. She could tell she wasn't getting the most out of Gilhofer. Something about her was irritating him. Laurel could see it too.

"Gilhofer," Laurel said, breaking her silence, "we need to—"

"Who's that?" Gilhofer said, interrupting her. "I thought this was a closed line."

"It's all right," Tatyana said. "She's with me."

"With you?"

"Yes, at Langley."

Gilhofer sighed. He wasn't happy. "I don't know what kind of circus you people are running over there—"

"Us people?" Tatyana said.

"You're not even American," Gilhofer said.

"No," Tatyana said, "but we're on the same side."

"Sure we are."

"You need to check your tone," Laurel said.

"Do I?" Gilhofer said. "I don't even know who the hell I'm talking to. I have no idea what's going on over there. I have no clue what's happening here. All I know is that my colleagues are being picked off, one by one."

"My name is Laurel Everlane," Laurel said. "I'm head of a special CIA unit that reports directly to Roth."

"Roth?"

"CIA Director Levi Roth?"

"That Roth."

"Yes, that Roth."

"Well, *la-di-da*," Gilhofer said.

"You need to listen up," Laurel said. "We've got two dead agents in two nights on your watch, so unless you've got something—"

"My watch? Do you even know what a counter-intelligence liaison is?"

"Of course I do."

"She's CIA," Gilhofer said, his voice rising. "She's one of yours. Your agent. Your personnel. You're the ones who are supposed to be protecting these people."

"Actually," Tatyana said, "it's *your* job to protect embassy personnel in-country."

"Which is impossible to do when you don't tell me what the hell you're up to."

"We're not up to anything."

"Two CIA agents, their heads practically severed from their necks, GRU written all over it, and you expect me to believe you're not up to anything?"

"You have to believe us," Laurel said. "We're not keeping anything from you. If these agents were up to something, we don't know what it was."

"If that's really true," Gilhofer said, "then you need to start talking to your friends on the top floor."

Tatyana wanted to tell him they were on the top floor, she wanted to wring his neck for him too, but she held her tongue and turned to Laurel. From the way Laurel's jaw was set, she could tell they both knew Gilhofer had a point. *Something* was certainly going on. The fact none of them knew what it was didn't change the fact.

"We'll look into it on our end," Laurel said. "Clearly there's more here than what we see."

"No kidding," Gilhofer said.

"In the meantime," Tatyana said, "what did you find at the scene?"

"No sign of a break-in," Gilhofer said. "No sign of struggle prior to the killing. No sign of anything taken or even a search."

"Are you at the scene now?"

"I'm a few blocks away. Klára found a receipt in Arabella's pocket for a wine bar. She was here last night before she went home."

Tatyana looked at her watch. "Did you manage to speak to the bartender?"

"We got him on the phone. He's on his way here as we speak."

"What did he tell you?"

"He said he remembered Arabella. She was regular enough."

"That it?"

"No. He said she was hitting on someone."

"At the bar?"

"Yes."

"Did he get a good look at the guy?"

"She wasn't hitting on a guy."

"Oh."

"It was a woman. A Russian woman, he thought, from the accent."

"That's our assassin."

"You think?"

"Did he give a description?" Tatyana said. "Was there a camera in the bar? Or in the street?"

"No camera in the bar," Gilhofer said, "but he said she was hot, blonde, late-twenties or early-thirties. He said she was like what's her name, in that movie."

"What movie?"

"The one with the female assassin."

Laurel shook her head and looked at Tatyana. "I don't know which one he's talking about."

"There are a lot of movies like that," Tatyana said.

"Anyway," Gilhofer said, "you two know better than I do where all this leads."

"And where's that?"

"Come on!" Gilhofer said. "This goes straight to the Russian embassy, and if you think me and some Czech detective are going to be allowed anywhere near that place, you've got another thing coming."

Tatyana and Laurel both knew that was true. They

were going to need to get their own boots on the ground, and soon.

"Just keep following the leads," Laurel said. "Get as much as you can."

"Right," Gilhofer said unenthusiastically. "Just leave it to me."

"Is that a problem?" Tatyana said. Laurel put a hand on her shoulder, but Tatyana shrugged it off. "You sound irritated, Gilhofer."

"Irritated? Are you kidding me?"

"I get that you're upset."

"*Upset*? Two people I worked with on a daily basis, good agents, just had their throats slit on my watch, and you won't give up the slightest inkling of what's going on."

"We've already been over—"

"And it's obvious it's the Russians, but you're pretending me and Klára aren't going to be outgunned once we catch up to the killer."

"He's right," Laurel said.

"It doesn't mean he gets to whine about it like a baby," Tatyana said.

"I've got to get back to work," Gilhofer said. "You two have fun in your ivory tower."

The line went dead. Tatyana looked at Laurel. "Well, that was nice."

"You need to get over there," Laurel said. "He's right. If he does track down the killer, he's in a lot more danger than she is."

"I'll go now," Tatyana said.

"I'll see if we have a plane for you, but first, we need to call this in to Roth."

14

As Osip Shipenko grew older, he learned certain hard truths about the human condition—truths he would not have come to terms with were it not for the scalpels and microscopes of the doctors at the institute. They were the things civilized people preferred not to think of—preferred not to believe possible. They were the things that made it possible for soldiers to toss living babies into bonfires using pitchforks, the things that lurked in the recesses of deranged minds, the things that made the Kremlin such a terrifying foe for all other nations, no matter how advanced they became or how safe they told themselves they were.

Shipenko knew that men could be forced into molds—could be altered to act in certain ways. They could be made into dogs. They could be made to take on the mentality of a pack. Their minds could be warped. They could be made to become as cruel and obsequious and brutish as any animal that ever lumbered across the face of the earth.

In short, Osip Shipenko knew that monsters were real. And he knew that he was one of them.

That was the thing the Americans could never understand. Unless they learned to see the world as he did, as it truly was, as a tottering balance between the absolute poles of victory and annihilation, they would never understand their enemy, and an enemy they couldn't understand was an enemy they couldn't defeat. All the trade sanctions and diplomatic concessions in the world wouldn't change that.

Shipenko and Molotov and the rest of their ilk fought America tooth and nail, and they did not care if they destroyed Russia in the process. That was what made them such bitter opponents. It was the source of their strength. What they understood, what they knew right down to their very bones, was that no matter how bad war got, it could never come close to the horrors they had already inflicted on themselves.

Shipenko had a cigarette in his hand, and it had burned down to the filter. Two inches of ash had accumulated precariously on the end of it, and with a flick of his wrist, the ash fell to the floor. He lit a fresh one and went over to his enormous desk, sat down, and dialed the president's number.

He had a direct line—no operators, no intermediaries. The president's office would route the call through an authenticator, which would take about a minute, but other than that, there would be no delay.

While he waited, he looked at the framed picture of the president on the wall across the room. He hadn't put it there, it was there when he inherited the office, but he was smart enough to leave it where it was.

He knew Molotov, had met him when they were both

fresh GRU recruits. They'd each been drawn into its sprawling, decrepit bureaucracy for the same reason—in the immediate aftermath of the Soviet collapse, the intelligence service was the clearest path to power in the Kremlin. At least, it was for those who had a certain perspective on what that power needed to look like. Being in the GRU allowed a fledgling autocrat to kill his rivals, silence dissent, shackle the media and civil society, and all while remaining completely hidden.

Molotov and Shipenko both saw it. They saw the world for the system of levers and pulleys it was. They had that particular type of mind that could see, in the truest sense possible, how to work the system.

But it was Molotov who moved first, seizing the top spot while Shipenko was still in the shadows of the GRU, contemplating his strategy, motionless as a lizard, watching his country decline into despotism. He'd always known democracy was a delicate thing, like rotten fruit, soft, corruptible, easily devoured if you had the stomach for it.

He was content to watch and wait. He had a peculiar relationship with Molotov, even back then, and he knew it was something he could take advantage of. Molotov could never be accused of picking favorites, everyone's head was on the block, and he liked them to know it. Even his own family members weren't immune to his suspicions. But for some reason, Shipenko seemed to be something of an exception. Others noticed it. When Shipenko was around, the president was just a little less guarded, a little freer with his words, a little quicker to salivate at the prospect of a new plan. For all Shipenko's physical flaws, his crusty skin, and distended, discolored torso, the president seemed almost attracted to him.

And that was no small feat because, like Stalin and other Soviet leaders before him, Molotov guarded his power with such intense jealousy that Moscow was in constant danger of being enveloped in a wave of political murders. Like a true paranoiac, Molotov cast a wide net, spying danger behind every corner, killing or exiling thousands of rivals, purging the military, and, at times, decimating his own ability to govern effectively.

But Shipenko always slipped through the net. He was the cuckoo's egg in Molotov's nest. By some trick of nature, Shipenko didn't trigger in Molotov whatever mechanisms he'd evolved to protect himself. Shipenko knew more than most about animal mimicry. He'd examined in detail the ways different species tricked and deceived each other, camouflaged their natures, hid their intentions. He was a man who looked like a monster, and that necessitated a certain ability to alter perceptions. He knew that when people saw him, as the nurse at the Kantubek medical clinic had, something within them recoiled in horror—to the point they wanted him dead. For him, therefore, finding ways to worm his way into people's confidence was a matter of life and death. And, in acquiring that skill, he'd also somehow pulled off the impossible. He'd managed to convince Molotov that he belonged in his nest, right in his inner circle next to all his most precious, loyal eggs.

And there, Shipenko was content to bide his time. He watched Molotov the way a snake watched a mouse. He saw that everything Molotov's regime had achieved, the concentration of power, the dismantling of constitutional checks, the evisceration of parliament and the judiciary, the eradication of term limits, the build-up of armaments to the point the Americans hesitated before any confrontation, all paved the way for his own rise to power.

And when that day came, God help the world, for it would burn. It would lament. Nations would wail in agony. Mothers would cry in terror. Death would reign. If the world thought Molotov was cruel, then God help them. God help them all.

For the difference between the two was as stark as the difference between night and day.

President Molotov, for all his flaws, still loved Russia. At least in a way. It was a corrupt love, rotten to the core, but his lust for power stemmed from his love of where it came from, and where it came from was the Russian nation. He reveled in the conspicuous displays, the disgusting excess, the champagne and caviar, the lavish palaces, the jets and automobiles, the strippers and models, the cocaine and opium, the gold bullion, the oil spoils, the three-day binges, and legendary penthouse parties, the pillaged art troves, the extravagant military parades, the uniforms, the monuments and statues and edifices being erected all across the nation. He wanted it all, and he wanted more. He wanted the way a Tsar wanted, as if the entire nation and all its people were his personal property, there for him, for his pleasure, for his glory. His greed, his lust, his desire for more would never be satisfied, his hunger never satiated. And as difficult as that may have been for his populace to bear, it at least guaranteed them a position in Molotov's Russia. They were there to please him.

Shipenko, if he ever ascended the throne, would mold a very different society. A Mordor, an Armageddon, a hell.

He wanted and needed none of the glory, none of the wealth. In any ordinary sense of the word, he had no ambition at all. He had no desire, no greed, no envy, no aspiration. Whereas Molotov spent vast sums erecting monuments to his regime, constantly fortifying his legacy, keeping an eye on the history books as he stole territory from neighbors, modernized the military, and announced vast new infrastructure projects, Shipenko would do none of it. Where Molotov built, Shipenko would tear down. He cared not a jot for history, for legacy. If his name was forgotten the day he died, or if it was never known at all, and he could pull the strings and assert his malignant will completely from the shadows, he would do so.

The only thing more dangerous for a country than a tyrant at the helm was a nihilist. For something else had to take the place of the tyrant's greed, and for Shipenko, that something, and this he had in such great abundance that it threatened to overwhelm his mind with every waking moment, was a rabid, ferocious hatred of all men.

He was a man who knew hell, he knew pain, he knew what it was to have the insides of his eyelids bleed. He hated everything, and he hated everyone. If ever there was a man who wished to see the world burn, and who might actually grasp the power to make that happen, it was Osip Shipenko.

And the world wouldn't see it coming.

"*Tushonka*," the president bellowed when he picked up the phone. "What the hell is going on over there? I gave you Prague to create a diversion. Not to spark off a war."

Shipenko exhaled smoke luxuriantly before speaking. "War's an overstatement, wouldn't you say?"

"Roth's got that new bitch at the helm. She's twitchy as a whore on her first trick."

"She's not going to do anything."

"You're poking her, though? You're seeing how far she'll bend."

"You told me you wanted Roth distracted."

"If killing agents is all that took, I'd have hired a gang of thugs."

"You did hire a gang of thugs."

"I hired *you*," Molotov snapped, "because I thought you were capable of at least a modicum of subtlety."

"Who told you that?"

"Enough games, Osip. I'm getting reports from all over that someone's kicking the hornet's nest."

"I'm not kicking the nest, sir. I'm setting a trap."

"You're shitting the bed," the president said with a sigh. "That's what you're doing."

"Well," Shipenko said, "we like traps, don't we?"

"It depends on the kind."

"Do you remember how they taught us to lure out a sniper?" Shipenko said.

"I remember."

"I'm picking off the easy targets, sir."

"From what I can see, the people you're picking off aren't targets at all."

"They're not, but the Americans don't know that, and they'll send someone valuable to take a look soon enough."

"And who do you think they're going to send?"

"A lineup of dead women?" Shipenko said with a laugh. "You know who'll they send."

"I want you to say it."

"I'm going to bring you his head on a plate, sir."

"You're sure it's wise to get him involved?"

"We don't know where he is. The last thing we need is him getting on a plane to Kyiv without our knowledge.

Better to keep as much attention on Prague as possible. That's what you asked for, and that's what you're getting."

"You're playing with fire, Osip."

"You want him dead, though, don't you? Think of Roth's face when it happens."

"If I thought you could pull it off."

"It's the same with all prey, sir, no matter how dangerous. You lure them out of their hole with bait, something they can't resist. You let them get up real close, get a real good sniff."

"And then?"

"And then you pull the trigger."

15

"Yes! What is it? I'm here?" Roth said gruffly, almost falling from the bed in his haste to answer the phone.

Laurel's voice greeted him. "Sorry, boss. I know it's early."

"It's fine. I was already up," he lied, turning on the lamp on the bedside table.

"There's news from Prague."

"I'm guessing it's not good."

"Another murder."

Roth sighed. "Just what we need. How many is that now?"

"That's two."

"Both CIA?"

"Yes, sir. The first was a junior analyst named Yvette Bunting. Now this one. The CI liaison. Bradwell. I'm sending the file now."

"Who'd want to kill a CI liaison?"

"Well, sir," Laurel said hesitantly.

"Come on," Roth said impatiently. "Out with it."

"We were hoping you'd be able to tell us that."

"Is that how it works now? You call me in the middle of the night, and I explain to you what's going on?"

"Sir, we...."

"Who's we? Is Tatyana with you?"

"I'm here, Levi," Tatyana said.

"Is anyone else on the line?"

"No," Laurel said. "Just us. I should have said."

Roth heaved himself out of the bed and slipped on his night robe. He looked at the clock. It was scarcely four in the morning. "Two agents dead in as many days," he grumbled. "What are the bastards up to?"

"We were thinking," Tatyana said, "that if these agents were working on something ... off the book."

"What do you mean, off the book?"

"Is there something we can't see on the group database?"

"You don't expect me to know what every agent in every station in the world is up to."

"Of course not, sir," Tatyana said. "But if there's something high-level going on in Prague, something sensitive that we're unaware of, it could go a long way toward explaining this."

"I'll look into it," Roth said, "but as far as I'm aware—"

"Anything at all," Tatyana said, butting in. "Because from where we're standing, this doesn't add up."

"I was going to say," Roth said, putting a cup beneath the nozzle of his coffee machine and pushing the button, "that as far as I'm aware, there's nothing at all being run out of Prague right now."

"Really nothing?"

"Yes, really," Roth said impatiently. "Nothing worth mentioning. All eyes are on Kyiv. You know that."

"Okay," Laurel said with a sigh. "We'd appreciate if you ordered an audit all the same. We need to know everything that's happened at Prague station over the last six months. Every agent, every source, every contact, every meeting. We need the transcripts, incident reports, media files, the works."

"That's going to be a lot of paperwork," Roth said. "Have you requested audits on the two victims?"

"Yes, sir, but they're very thin files. Completely run of the mill. There's got to be more to this."

"All right, I'll run the audit, but like I said—"

Tatyana butted in again. She was jumpy, Roth thought. "Laurel will pull Russian embassy comms patterns," she said.

"Have we got a tap on them? I wasn't aware of that."

"No," Tatyana said, "but apparently the RSO's contact has an in with the Czech telecoms regulator. There's enough there to run a traffic analysis."

"That's good," Roth said. "Just eyeballing this whole thing, it's clearly got GRU written all over it."

"You haven't heard the half of it," Laurel said. "GRU ammo was found at both scenes."

"What GRU ammo?"

"SP-4."

"SP-4," Roth said quietly. That was a blast from the past. He remembered it being all the rage in the eighties, briefly, before everyone realized it was as likely to get the assassin killed as the target. "Why would they be using that now?"

"We have no idea, sir. And that's not all. The victim's throats were slit."

"Both times?"

"Yes, sir."

Roth took a sip of his coffee. "Was that necessary?" he said. "I mean to get the job done?" He'd seen assassins take things further than required before. There would always be those who took the opportunity to let loose, release some pent-up rage, but it was rare, especially with the Russians. He'd have been less surprised if it was in the Middle East. The GRU was disciplined. They were clean. They got in and out. If they left behind a mess, it was generally because they were sending a message.

"Not really," Tatyana said. "SP-4 has a bad reputation, but a gun's a gun. Why bring a knife unless you intended to use it?"

"Or were ordered to," Roth said.

"Maybe."

Roth thought for a second, then said, "Right. Is either of you planning on getting over there? I think this warrant's getting someone on the ground."

"There's a plane fueling at Andrews as we speak," Laurel said. "Tatyana's leaving for it right after this call."

"Good," Roth said, "and if the investigation ends up leading to the Russian embassy—"

"Which it will," Tatyana said.

"Well," Roth said, "there's a very limited number of GRU assassins who could be behind it."

"Extremely limited," Tatyana said.

"And we all know the rules."

"We do," Laurel said.

"An eye for an eye," Tatyana said.

Roth swallowed coffee. "An eye for an eye," he repeated. An assassin was like a dog. Once they got a taste for blood they had to be destroyed. He couldn't have Russians thinking they could do this to his people and get away with it.

"I'm already narrowing it down," Tatyana said. "If I put out a bulletin, I could confirm she hasn't been seen else-where, but I'm pretty certain—"

Roth spat out his coffee. "What?"

"Sir?"

"What did you just say?"

"I'd put out a bulletin, but I don't want her to know we're looking—"

"Her?" Roth said.

"We've acquired a suspect," Laurel said. "A female."

"I didn't know that."

"So far, it's just a description from a bartender."

"A woman?"

"Blonde, late-twenties—"

"Tatyana!" Roth said. "Do you know who it is?"

"I think so."

He was wiping the spilled coffee from his robe and caught a glimpse of himself in the mirror. He'd aged. He rubbed the white stubble on his chin and went to the window. "Well?"

"I need to make sure," Tatyana said, "but if it is who I think it is...."

"Then she must die," Roth said. "No two ways about it." He could see outside that it had snowed again. It was turning into one of the bitterest winters in memory.

"She will," Tatyana said.

"You have no loyalties to her?"

"Why? Because she's a woman?"

He said nothing, sipped his coffee, waited for her to answer.

"The truth," she said after a few moments, "is that this woman, if it's her, is a real bitch."

Roth smiled and again caught his reflection in the

mirror by the coffee machine. He looked away. "Nothing you can't handle."

"Oh, I'll handle her," Tatyana said. "I'll handle her real well."

"We still need visual confirmation," Laurel said. "Some surveillance, CCTV, something on satellite."

"We'll get it," Roth said, entering the bathroom. He turned on the water for a bath, then went back to the bedroom.

"These women will be avenged," Tatyana said.

"Women?" Roth said, taken by surprise for the second time in as many minutes.

"Bunting and Bradwell," Laurel said.

"You never said both victims were women."

"Arabella Bradwell," Laurel said. "Thirty-one years old. Born in Wichita, Kansas. She's been CI liaison with the State Department in Prague for less than a year."

"I didn't realize."

"Sorry, sir. I assumed you'd looked at the file."

"I've been on the phone with you."

"Yes, sir."

"So we're looking at a female assassin who's killed two female staffers...."

"That's why we've asked for the audit. We can't make sense of it."

"Is this coincidence?"

"We can't rule that out," Tatyana said, "but it doesn't feel like one."

"No," Roth said. "No, it doesn't."

"If there's an explanation—"

Roth shook his head. "I think the explanation is staring us in the face."

"What do you mean?" Laurel said.

"You know what I mean." There was a moment of silence on the line. He finished his coffee and went back into the bathroom. Two women in two nights, and the suspect was a woman too. "You don't suppose they were fighting over a man," he said.

"That's not funny," Tatyana said.

"No," Roth said. "Quite right."

"Not funny at all."

"I apologize."

"This whole thing," she said. "It's not right."

"We'll get to the bottom of it," Laurel said.

"It's nasty," Tatyana said. "It's very nasty."

"Agreed," Roth said, taking off his robe and hanging it on the hook next to the bath.

"I worked with these people," Tatyana said. "I know them. There are some real sons of bitches in that building."

Roth wrapped floss around his two middle fingers and leaned into the mirror. "Are you thinking of someone in particular?" he said before putting the floss into his mouth.

"There are a few names," she said. "A few...."

"A few what?"

"Faces," she said quietly.

Roth got a piece of last night's dinner from between his molars that had been bothering him. "In the meantime," he said, "we need to take steps to minimize any further damage."

"Such as?" Laurel said.

"How many other female staff do we have at the Prague embassy?"

"It doesn't make sense that they're targeting them because they're women," Laurel said.

Roth wiped his hand on his robe and said, "I know it doesn't, but since when do they only do things that make sense?"

"I agree," Tatyana said. "We shouldn't rule anything out. Until we find something interesting about these two women, the biggest thing holding them together, other than the fact they worked for us, is that they were women."

"I don't know," Laurel said. She was hesitant to draw that conclusion, and Roth understood why. "What is there to gain? They might not do things the way we would, but one thing you can usually be certain of is that they act in their own interest. How does this serve them?"

Roth sighed. "I'm sorry to say this," he said, "but it really could be as simple as Tatyana said. It could just be that it's nasty. A nasty piece of work."

"What do they think we're going to do?" Laurel said. "Do they want us to come after them?"

"They don't care," Tatyana said. "They know we'll hunt down the assassin, but the men in the Kremlin, back in their tower watching it all play out, what do they really care?"

"We won't know until we get to the bottom of it," Roth said, "but in the meantime, I really do need to know how many female personnel we have currently stationed in Prague."

Laurel sighed. "CIA? Or total?" she said.

"CIA."

"Excluding support staff, just the station chief."

"Of course," Roth said. "Carmen Linder." He knew her well—had just seen her in fact, a few days earlier at a Select Committee briefing on Capitol Hill. "She's in Washington," he said. "Been at the senate all week explaining the Ukraine situation."

He heard typing, then Laurel said, "She was scheduled to fly back earlier this morning."

"You mean she's left?"

"She's landing in Prague as we speak."

"For heaven's sake," Roth said. "Get her on the line."

He waited, then Tatyana said, "No answer."

"She's on the ground," Laurel said. "Her plane's taxiing."

"Get a message to the pilot," Roth said. "Get them back in the air immediately."

"She flew commercial," Laurel said.

"Get hold of the embassy," Roth said. "Get them to call the airport. I don't want her off that plane until there's a detail ready to protect her."

"Tatyana's getting hold of the RSO," Laurel said. "But we need to decide what we're going to do about other female personnel."

"You said Carmen was the only one."

"She's the only direct CIA employee, but there are others."

"Who?"

"I can see we've got a SIGINT specialist and a translator, both contracted from the Air Force."

"Both female?"

"Both female, both American, both answerable to the station chief, but their personnel codes aren't CIA."

"Better have them all brought in for protection," Roth said. "I don't want to risk any more deaths until this thing blows over."

"And what about non-CIA? There are over two dozen females employed by consular. And that's just US citizens.

If we include local support staff, secretarial, custodial, it's over fifty."

"Any of them could be targeted," Roth said.

"It's possible," Laurel said. "But at that point, I mean, we need to put limits around the threat. We can't protect everyone."

"We don't know what those limits are yet," Roth said.

"Fifty-two women, all told," Laurel said. "I'm looking at the list now."

"That's everyone? Cleaning ladies, secretaries, receptionists?"

"They do more than that," Laurel said, "but yes, that should cover all the women who work for the United States government in Prague."

"Has Tatyana gotten a hold of Carmen yet?"

"She's speaking to the security office at the airport."

Roth sighed. The last thing he wanted was to raise alarm, and he didn't want to play into the Russians' hands either. Panic might be exactly what they were aiming for. "Bring them in," he said.

"Bring them?"

"All of them. All female personnel. Issue the directive. I want all fifty-two of them in protective custody. See if you can get me the ambassador on the line too. I want embassy security doubled."

"The ambassador's going to—"

"I don't care about the disruption. Get them in safely. Two bodies is a pattern. I don't want to wait for a third."

"The embassy's not equipped—"

"Bring in cots. Set up tents. I don't care how you do it, Laurel. Do what they do in a hurricane. Put them in the gymnasium."

"There isn't a gymnasium—"

"Just get them to safety, Laurel. And get Carmen to safety too." He hung up the phone, then leaned over the sink and spat into it. What was the world coming to? He'd seen his share of low blows but targeting female personnel as an intimidation tactic? Slitting their throats? It would have been unthinkable a few years earlier.

He took his phone to the bath and lowered himself into it slowly. It was very hot, just how he liked it, almost painful. Once he'd adapted to the temperature, he picked up the phone and dialed his chief of staff. It took her a minute to pick up, then he said, "Kathleen, it's me."

"Levi? What's the matter?"

"You'll see soon enough. Do you remember the signal we set up for the asset in London?"

"The minicabs?"

Kathleen was British—she knew all about minicabs. "Yes," Roth said. "I need you to make contact."

"Again?"

"Yes," Roth said, then lowered his head beneath the surface of the water.

16

L ance was asleep when the phone rang. It was the taxi company on Durward Street.

The arrangement he'd made there was straightforward.

He'd noticed that the place was open twenty-four-seven, three hundred sixty-five days a year, and was family-owned. He went inside and liked what he saw—a TV in the corner playing an Indian soap opera, a few landline telephones on a desk behind a counter, a protective plexiglass screen. On the desk, there was an ashtray the size of a dog dish, close to overflowing. Next to it was a thick, tattered ledger with numbers scrawled by hand in columns. Behind the plexiglass, a girl of about twenty in a pink Mickey Mouse t-shirt sat, scrolling on her cell phone.

"What's your name?" Lance said to her through the circular holes in the screen.

She took a look at him and, in an accent that couldn't have been found anywhere on earth but the office of a Sri Lankan, East London minicab company, said, "Not interested, mate."

"You don't know what I was going to say."

"I know you don't need my name to order a cab."

"True," he said.

"And you don't need to come in, neither. You do it on the phone."

"I was passing by."

"Sure you were."

He reached into his pocket for his wallet and counted out a hundred pounds in twenties.

"I told you, I'm not interested," she said again.

He put the money on the counter and slid it under the screen. She looked at it, then back at him. "Take it away, or I call the cops."

"It's nothing illegal."

"You're American."

He nodded.

She thought for a second. His accent seemed to have changed her opinion of the situation. "What are you after?"

"A favor."

"I don't want nothing to do with drugs."

"It's not that."

"Nothing to do with sex neither. No girls."

"Nothing like that."

"What is it then?"

He took a burner cell phone and charger from his pocket and slid them under the screen with the money. "Just keep this plugged in under the desk."

"That's it?"

"You work here with your sisters, don't you?"

She nodded hesitantly. He'd been watching the store —she and her two sisters kept the desk manned at all times. She didn't like that he knew that.

"Listen," he said, writing another cell number on a piece of paper. "All I want is for you or your sisters to answer that phone if it rings."

"And do what?"

"Take a message."

"We don't have time to be taking messages—"

"I don't get a lot of calls."

"If this is going to cause trouble."

"It's really not. Just write down the message, then call me on this other number and read it to me."

"It sounds dodgy as hell."

"It's like being a secretary."

"It's not like being a secretary."

"I'll come by once a week with a hundred pounds for each of you."

"I don't know."

"Why don't you try it for a week, see how easy it is? If you don't like it when I come next week, I'll take it away." He gave her the sweetest smile he could muster.

She looked at him doubtfully. "That's really all it is?"

"That's it."

"No trouble?"

"Swear to god."

She picked up the money and counted it. "You'll have to pay upfront for the week."

"I just did."

"For my sisters too."

He counted another ten bills and gave them to her.

"I have three sisters."

"Three?"

She showed him the screen of her cell phone. The wallpaper was a picture of her and the two sisters Lance had seen. They were on a beach somewhere in bathing suits. In front of them was a fourth girl, about eleven or twelve years old, who Lance had never seen anywhere near the store.

Lance counted out another five bills and slid them under the screen. "That's a nice picture," he said.

She nodded, and he turned to leave. "You live around here?" she said as he reached for the door.

He looked back. "For now."

She shrugged, then said, "It's Pooja, by the way."

"What's that?" Lance said.

"You asked my name."

"Ah."

"And yours?"

"Mine?"

"If I'm going to be taking your messages—"

"My name's Clint."

"Clint?"

He nodded.

"Clint what?"

"Eastwood," he said, leaving the office before she had time to ask any more questions.

That had been a few weeks ago. It allowed him to provide Roth with a contact number without giving him the ability to track every call and movement he made. Roth had used the number already once to get him to look into the situation with the woman at the bar. Her name was Isabelle, and her husband was some British special forces guy named Ritter who was doing work for Roth. Lance expected the call to be from her.

"Hello?" he said, getting out of his bed.

"This is Pooja."

He went to the front door of the apartment and looked

out through the peephole. There was no one in the corridor.

"Pooja," he said. "How nice to hear your voice."

"You got another message," she said.

He opened the door and checked the corridor to make sure. Everything was still, silent.

"What's the message? Did someone ask for a cab?"

"No. They asked that you call home."

"Call home?"

"They said it was urgent."

"Okay," Lance said, looking out the balcony. It was another miserable morning, the snow flitting around so quickly it was like static on a TV screen. "Is that it?"

"It was a woman. She just said to call home."

"All right," he said and hung up. He put the kettle on the stove, then sat at the kitchen counter and waited for it to boil. He tapped the leg of his stool with his foot. A second call from Langley. Something had happened. Lance still knew how to get into the Group's backchannels, but he hadn't been monitoring them. All he knew was what everyone knew—that the Russians were spoiling for war—but that was nothing new.

The whistling of the kettle brought his mind back to the present. He made some coffee, then took his time drinking a big mug of it at the counter. He stared aimlessly out the window. When he was done, he dressed and left the apartment. There were some old payphones outside his building, vandalized, covered in graffiti, and he passed them in favor of the ones at the Whitechapel tube station. When he got there, he entered the main concourse and dialed the routing code Roth had given him.

It was Roth's new chief of staff, Kathleen Kingsbury, who answered.

"Lance Spector?" she said in her British accent. She sounded like a member of the English gentry, but Lance had seen her birth record. She'd been born in Old Greenwich, Connecticut. It was an expensive English boarding school, Cheltenham Ladies College to be precise, that had given her the accent.

"Roth said this was a direct line."

"It's a direct line to me," she said, her voice as firm as a Victorian schoolmistress.

"I see."

"Roth will be here in a minute. I thought the nonsense with the cab company would take longer than it did." Roth had complained when Lance set it up. He'd have preferred a direct line.

"Next time, I'll make you wait longer."

Lance had spoken to Kathleen before but never met her in person. He pictured a cross between Mary Poppins and Cruella de Vil. He was in the station's main concourse, already busy with morning commuters, and kept a close watch of his surroundings. "I take it you didn't call to make pleasantries."

"I've just been notified Roth's in the building. If you'll be good enough to sit tight one more minute."

"Maybe when he gets up, you could remind him that I no longer work for him."

"Oh, he's well aware of that fact, Mr. Spector. Believe me."

Lance wasn't sure how connected operationally Kathleen was. She seemed to know what was going on and had been hired with a view to becoming Laurel's replacement one day, now that Laurel was too important to be at Roth's beck and call twenty-four-seven. Presumably that meant Roth trusted her, but it didn't mean Lance had to. "Did he happen to tell you the reason for this call?"

"He's in the elevator right now, Mr. Spector. I think it's best he tells you himself."

"I could save us both some time and just tell you now I'm not interested."

"But then you'd never find out what it was."

Lance rapped his fingers impatiently on the side of the phone. A man in a long black coat had bought a coffee at a stall across the concourse and was standing at a bar table while he drank it, facing Lance. Lance eyed him suspiciously.

A few more seconds passed, then Kathleen said, "And here he is. I'm transferring you over."

It was always the same song and dance with Roth. Every time Lance tried to leave, Roth found something to pull him right back in.

"Lance!" Roth boomed into the receiver, "There's a situation in—" his words were cut off by a serious bout of coughing, then he continued. "There's a situation going down in—"

"You sound like you're about to die," Lance said.

"It's my coffee. Went down the wrong way."

"Maybe you should call a doctor."

"I'm fine. Let me tell you why I called."

"If you can spit it out."

"Okay," Roth said, clearing his throat. "Tell me what you make of this. Last night, a twenty-seven-year-old junior analyst working out of the Prague embassy showed up dead in her apartment."

"A woman?"

"That's right. Her throat was slit, and there was a 7.62x41mm bullet lodged in her chest."

"7.62x41mm? That's the SP-4."

"Correct."

"So this is a Russian kill. Only the Kremlin uses that ammo."

"Right."

"But I'm guessing from your tone," Lance said, "that's not the end of it."

"Not quite."

"Okay."

"So, we have the RSO in Prague looking into it, working the case with local police, trying to confirm it was a GRU hit. Then I get a call this morning that there's been a second murder."

"Another one?" Lance said, clamping the phone between his chin and shoulder so he could warm his hands in his pockets.

"Another female, again in her apartment not two miles from the first."

"What was her position?"

"CI Liaison."

"Not exactly a high priority."

"No, it's not."

"So two low-priority targets, both female. Were they working on anything special?"

"That's just it. They must have been, right? I mean, no one would go about killing our people for no reason."

"Not if they play by the rules."

"Well," Roth said, "my office pulled every record out of Prague Station from the past six months. We're talking full audit."

"And there's nothing there?"

"Not a thing."

"Not even fishing expeditions?"

"Not one," Roth said. "Not a single thing."

"You need to look again."

"I will look again, but I already know we're not going to find anything. Not on the books anyway."

"You don't get smoke without fire, Levi. You know that better than anyone."

"I'm just worried that by the time I find this fire, it will be too late."

"There's a logic here," Lance said. "Just because you don't see it doesn't mean it's not there."

"The RSO has a suspect. Could be a GRU assassin."

"What do Laurel and Tatyana say?"

"Laurel's working the satellite, seeing if she can confirm the GRU connection. Tatyana's on her way to the airport. She'll be in Prague in a matter of hours."

Lance sighed. "I don't know what to tell you. The GRU is brutal, but we both know they're not in the business of killing people for no reason."

"We hope they're not."

"Levi. We know they're not."

"Slit throats," Roth said. "That wasn't necessary. The whole thing's... I don't know... gratuitous."

"You could be dealing with a dog gone bad?"

"I don't know. Maybe. The ammo's another thing that doesn't stack up."

"It's assassins' ammo."

"It's an odd choice. And you couldn't pick a clearer GRU signature if you tried."

"So you think someone's stirring up trouble? Making it look like the Russians when it isn't?"

"I don't know. It's possible. There's no shortage of

players who wouldn't benefit from a fresh spat between us and Moscow."

"Well, either it is the Russians, or it's someone trying to make it look like them. Either way, this is intended to get your attention."

"They're rubbing it in my face," Roth said, his voice getting angrier. "They're toying with me."

"They're distracting you. It's smoke for smoke's sake."

"And targeting women," Roth said. "That just makes it worse, doesn't it?"

Lance sighed. He took his hands from his pockets and rubbed them together. "Yeah," he said. "Yeah, it does."

"And the clock's ticking. Two bodies so far, and I know there'll be a third."

"Have you taken steps?"

"There are fifty-two female personnel at the Prague embassy. Only one of them is directly CIA, Carmen Linder, the station chief, but I've told the ambassador to call them all in for protection."

"At the embassy?"

"Yes."

"That won't stop an assassin."

"Security's being beefed up.

"Even still."

"God damn it, Lance. That's why I'm calling you."

Lance sighed. "I had a feeling you were going—"

"The RSO's outgunned, and you know it. Even with Tatyana's help."

"And what about the other thing? The Isabelle Ritter situation? I made contact like you asked."

"Forget that. She can take care of herself. That whole thing's her own fault."

"There's no one else you can call?"

"Of course there is, but I'm not calling them, I'm calling you."

Lance said nothing. He reached into his pocket for his cigarettes.

"You still there?" Roth said.

Lance put a cigarette in his mouth and shielded it from the wind while he lit it.

"What do you say? I haven't got all day."

Lance sucked hard on the cigarette. He looked at his watch. The station was getting busier, and he'd been there too long already. The man with the coffee was gone, but there were others—a man with a newspaper, a woman with a dog on a leash.

"I've got to go," he said and hung up the phone.

17

Valentina stared at her reflection in the mirror, then cupped her hands under the faucet and splashed cold water on her face. It was almost dawn, she'd managed to snatch a few hours of fitful sleep at her hotel, but it was time to move on.

She hadn't been much worried about Czech police finding her—she could handle them with both arms tied behind her back—but the CIA was more worrying. She'd researched the local embassy personnel. There wasn't anyone there she was afraid of, but now, with two dead agents in as many nights and Shipenko forcing her to leave behind a signature, she was afraid Langley was going to send in someone more formidable—a fixer or cleaner of some kind.

She aimed to be well clear before they arrived.

She took a shower and dressed, then packed the things she'd used in the killings into a large, black garbage bag. In went her clothing, equipment, weapons, even the SP-4 ammo she'd gone to such lengths to acquire. Then she dressed in a fresh black jumpsuit, did a scan of the room to make sure she'd missed nothing, and left.

She felt conspicuous in the hotel lobby with a black garbage bag over her shoulder, but it was early, and the only person who might have seen her, a gray-haired concierge with the two top buttons of his shirt undone, was dozing behind the front desk.

She left the hotel and crossed the Old Town Square on foot, heading toward the Mánesův Bridge. It had started to snow again, and the streets were deathly quiet. When she reached the bridge, she walked out to the center and looked over the rail. Ice extended about twenty feet from each bank, but the middle of the river had yet to freeze. The black water flowed with a strong current.

She looked in both directions, checking that no cars were coming, then tossed the garbage bag over the side. It remained on the surface for a few seconds, then sank.

She waited then, taking shelter in a streetcar stand until she managed to hail a passing cab.

"The train station," she said to the driver when she got in.

With the streets so empty, it took less than ten minutes to get there. He stopped in front of the art nouveau entrance on Wilsonova, and she got out. A canopy over the entrance shielded her from the snow, and she hurried up the steps into the enormous building.

It was all just beginning to come to life. The station received trains from all over Europe at all hours of the night and never really shut. But the cafés and stores did, and their workers were just beginning to arrive and open them up for the coming day. There was a group of cleaners mopping the floor in the central concourse, and two police officers were smoking cigarettes disinterestedly by the gangway that led to the commuter platforms.

Valentina checked the international departures board —in the next hour, there would be departing express services to Berlin, Munich, Vienna, Linz, Cracow, Milan, Bratislava, and Minsk. That gave her no shortage of options, and she went to the ticketing desk and got a business class seat to Berlin. The train was already waiting at the platform, and she went straight to it, carefully watching her surroundings the entire time. She smoked a cigarette on the platform before boarding, then got into the business class carriage and found her seat. There were two other passengers in the car, a man and woman, sitting separately, dressed smartly, both typing on laptops.

She positioned herself so she could watch the platform and see if anyone else boarded. She noticed her foot tapping and stopped it. She was antsy. She wasn't armed, having ditched her weapons, and she felt the absence of a gun. She'd breathe easier when the train started to move.

She looked at her watch—ten minutes to departure. There was no reason to be nervous. No one could have known she'd be on this train. She hadn't known herself until she'd purchased the ticket, but she counted the seconds nonetheless. The concession cart came wheeling by. She bought nothing. She didn't want to be distracted while they sat in the station. No passengers boarded. She breathed a sigh of relief when she felt a vibration of the engines coming online. It was two minutes to departure. The conductor was out on the platform, checking that the doors were all secure. Someone blew a whistle.

And then her phone vibrated.

She pulled it from her pocket and looked at the

screen. Her mouth opened as she read it. It was another kill order.

Identifier: KO_457832

Agency: Prime Directorate

Lead Agent: Osip Shipenko

Assassin: Valentina Brik

Target: Carmen Linder

Target Post: US Embassy, Prague

Target Position: CIA Prague Station Chief

Order: Kill target. Leave at least one 7.62x41mm
bullet at the scene.

Prime Directorate Kill Order

She heard another whistle. The conductor was out on the platform, waving the all-clear to the driver. In her throat, a knot of emotion formed.

She swallowed. She didn't want to disembark. She wanted to stay put, remain in her seat, let the train whisk her away from that city. She didn't know why she felt so emotional, but she did. She hadn't liked the last two jobs, they hadn't felt right, and she was more eager to leave the city than she'd realized. She gripped the phone tightly in her fist, staring at the message. Again, no stated objective, no item retrieval, no interrogation. Just the kill. She punched the seat in front of her and got up.

The train lurched as it began to move. It was an express service but an older train, and she had a few seconds before it gathered serious momentum. She ran to the door and cranked the mechanical mechanism. The door retracted. Cold air rushed in. She stepped off the train and landed hard on the platform, dropping to one knee and steadying herself with a hand on the ground. The train rushed on behind her, rapidly accelerating.

"Hey!" the platform conductor yelled when he saw her.

She rose to her feet and began pacing toward him.

"Hey!" he said again as she passed. "Are you crazy? You could have killed yourself."

"I'm fine," she said without breaking stride.

She went back to the concourse, straight to a bank of pay phones she'd passed on her way in, and began dialing her emergency contact code. She wasn't authorized to use the cell for calls of that type. She dialed a fourteen-digit code, followed by an automated voice-recognition check.

"*Volchitsey,*" she said when asked for her code word. There was a pause, then it asked her to repeat the word. "*Volchitsey,*" she said again, louder, eyeing the other people in the concourse.

There was another pause, and she felt her heart pound as she waited. Then the operator spoke. "Reference?"

Valentina looked at the message she'd received on her cell, then read out, "KO_457832."

"Message?" the operator said.

"Message?" Valentina said. "My message is, what the fuck is going on? This leaves me wide open. My ass is in the wind."

"Message acquired," the operator said and was about to hang up.

"Wait!" Valentina said.

"Yes?" The phone beeped, indicating they'd been on the line for thirty seconds.

"I've got a rate limit of two kills per mission," she said.

Two was already twice the standard rate, and it put her at significant risk whenever it was utilized.

"There's been an override on your rate limit," the operator said.

"Placed by who?"

"Your lead agent."

That was Shipenko. No surprise there. "This makes three kills in as many days," Valentina said. "If I stick around, I'm just asking for trouble."

"I'll add that to your message," the operator said.

Valentina sighed. She knew the operator had no power to alter the order. She was just releasing her frustration. She took a breath. She had to be careful. Shipenko wouldn't take kindly to a temper tantrum. If he'd issued an override, he knew what it meant. He knew the risk he was putting her at and had accepted it. He would still expect the order to be obeyed. The phone beeped again. Sixty seconds.

"The Americans are bringing in backup," Valentina said. "If I remain in the city—"

"Agent Brik," the operator said, "there's a risk override here too."

Valentina made to speak but stopped. She had to clear her throat. A risk override referred to risk of death. *Her* death. "I discarded my weapons," she said quietly.

"Well, no one told you to do that."

"I thought I was on my way out."

The operator said nothing.

Valentina thought for a few seconds. The phone beeped again, twice this time. "Are there any other flags?" she said.

"Yes. Stress, detection, reprisal, all have been overridden."

"Manually?"

"Yes."

"By Shipenko?"

"That's correct."

"That doesn't make sense."

"Ten seconds," the operator said, indicating that they'd reached the maximum allowed duration for a contact of this type.

Valentina took a deep breath. "Cancel this message," she said. "Cancel my protest." She put the receiver down softly but then slammed her fist on it, cursing. She took a few steps away from the phone, then turned back and smacked it again.

She looked around the concourse. No one took any notice. The two cops that had been smoking were gone. She took another breath, then lit a cigarette and inhaled deeply. She looked over the details of the kill order again on her cell.

The data packet had arrived. There was a picture of the target, the Prague Station Chief. She was a fifty-six-year-old, elegant woman with pronounced features and medium-length hair that, in the photo, looked to be a natural gray. According to the packet, she'd just landed at Prague Airport on a commercial flight from Washington.

"God damn it," she muttered, then flicked away the cigarette and made her way toward the exit.

Gilhofer sat in the passenger seat of Klára's car and rolled down his window a crack. "Do you mind if I smoke?" he said, lighting his cigarette before she had a chance to answer.

She shrugged. They'd come straight from the wine bar and were outside the same café they'd been to the day before.

"Are you all right?" Klára said.

"Fine," he snapped.

"You seem—"

"I said, I'm fine." He sucked hard on the cigarette and blew the smoke toward the opening in the window. He was agitated from his call with Langley, but there was no point taking it out on her. "Sorry," he muttered, sucking the cigarette again.

"If it's any consolation," she said, "my bosses are riding me too."

He sighed. "Well, what did you make of what that bartender had to say?"

She opened her window to let in more air. "I'd say he painted a pretty clear picture, wouldn't you?"

Gilhofer let out a short laugh. There was no arguing with that. The bartender seemed to have remembered every last detail, from the minute Arabella arrived, by herself, to when she left a few hours later with a Russian bombshell who looked like she'd come straight from the casting department of a Cold War spy movie. "Do you think he's reliable?"

"I don't see a reason for him not to be."

"So our killer's a sexy blonde Russian *femme fatale*?"

"Maybe she is."

"And maybe our bartender's got an overactive imagination."

"He stood across from Arabella all evening," Klára said. "Given what we know about what happened afterward, I'd say—"

"I know," Gilhofer said. "I know."

"You seem annoyed."

"I don't see why he had to go inserting all those... *insinuations*."

"What insinuations?"

"He said they were practically in each other's pants when they left."

"That's not an insinuation. That's what he saw."

"He said they were dripping wet."

Klára rolled her eyes.

"I don't see why he had to be so vulgar about it," Gilhofer said.

"You'd prefer he went a little easier on your delicate sensibilities?"

"I'm just saying, I knew her pretty well. I sat ten feet away from her, so I think I'd have known—"

"You'd have known what? That she was gay?"

"She was *not* gay."

Klára's mouth dropped. "You've got to be kidding me!"

"One bartender's uncorroborated—"

"Just stop talking."

Gilhofer let out a long sigh. He suddenly felt very old. He knew he was in the wrong. He knew how he sounded —like an out-of-touch, anachronistic old dinosaur.

"If I didn't know better," Klára said, "I'd say you were more upset about this than the fact she was murdered."

"That's ridiculous!"

"Yes," Klára said pointedly. "It is."

He took a long drag from his cigarette.

"You're worse than my father," she said. "You know that?"

"And your father's just unbearable, I suppose. Wrong about everything."

"Not everything."

"Well then," he said, like that somehow redeemed his position.

"There's a restaurant in our village," she said. "It serves pig's feet."

"I don't see how that has any bearing—"

"That's where my father goes," she said.

Gilhofer was about to say something back but stopped himself.

She was tapping her fingers on the steering wheel like a piano player practicing from memory. He could tell there was something more she wanted to say, but she held her peace.

"I just thought..." he said, letting the words trail off.

Klára opened her door. "Come on," she said. "I need to get out of this car before I suffocate."

He followed her across the street, flicking away his cigarette as they entered the café. A bell chimed above the door, and he saw the place was as empty as it had been the day before.

"Be right with you," a waitress said, poking her head out of the kitchen. Gilhofer stamped the snow off his boots. The waitress came out and recognized Klára. "Same table?" she said.

"Please," Klára said.

The waitress brought them to the same booth by the window they'd been at the day before and said, "Same order too?"

"Not for me," Gilhofer said.

Klára slid into the booth and said, "You didn't like the sausage?"

"Do you have bacon?" he said to the waitress, butchering the pronunciation. "Just ordinary bacon."

"Ordinary eggs, too?" she said.

"Yes, and ordinary toast." He took off his jacket and hung it on the rack next to the booth. Just as he was sitting down, his phone vibrated. He looked at the screen.

"I'll take the same as yesterday," Klára said to the waitress.

"And coffee," Gilhofer added, scanning the text on his screen.

"What is it?" Klára said.

"The ambassador just issued a security directive. All female personnel are to report to the embassy."

"All?"

"Fifty-two people," Gilhofer said. "It applies to US citizens and local support staff alike. They're not taking any chances."

"Isn't it the RSO's job to communicate security directives?"

He looked at her. A normal police officer wouldn't usually know the security arrangements of an embassy, but then, he'd already decided she wasn't a normal police officer.

"Does it give a reason?" she said.

He shook his head. "They'll be keeping that under tight wraps for as long as possible. For now, it just says to report."

"Is that a common occurrence?"

"Maybe somewhere like Baghdad," he said, "but here in Prague, no, it's not common." She nodded, and he added, "but then, I think you know that already."

"What does that mean?"

He gave a slight shrug, and the waitress arrived with their coffee. He put two packets of sugar into his and was about to start stirring when his phone started to ring. "What now?" he muttered impatiently.

It was Tatyana, and there was no missing the urgency in her voice. "Gilhofer, we've got a problem."

"If it's the directive—"

"Carmen Linder's plane just landed at Prague Airport, and we can't reach her."

"Her phone's probably dead," Gilhofer said. "She lets it happen all the time."

"You need to get your ass over there immediately. She's at risk of being the next target."

"Has she cleared customs?"

"We have no idea. She's not answering her phone, and no one we've been able to contact knows where she is."

"Get the airport on the line," Gilhofer said, rising to his feet. "Prague has a dedicated customs gate for diplomatic personnel. Don't let them clear her. They need to hold her until I get there."

"We're on the line to the airport—"

"And I should have been notified as soon as her schedule changed," he snapped.

Klára was already ahead of him, throwing money on the table and calling out an apology to the waitress. They ran out to the car, and she fired up the engine, lurching into the street, her tires screeching on the wet cobbles as she put on the siren. She swung the car onto the Legion Bridge, dodging oncoming traffic and passing two street-cars before breaking a set of red lights. "I'll have us there in ten minutes," she said.

As she sped down Evropská at breakneck speed, Gilhofer said, "No one even thought to warn me she was in the air."

"Have they received a specific threat?" Klára said, downshifting as she passed a bus.

"Hell if I know."

"It's probably a precaution."

He nodded. "They said she was *at risk*."

Klára got onto the highway and really put her foot down. She was doing ninety miles per hour when she picked up the radio receiver.

"Let me hold that for you," Gilhofer said, eyeing the road nervously as she rode up onto the shoulder and passed some trucks.

"This is Issová," she said into the radio. "I need a border screen at Prague Airport immediately. Name is Carmen Linder. She's traveling on US diplomatic papers."

"That's our exit," Gilhofer said as she swerved in front of a large semi and crossed three traffic lanes to make the exit. He clutched his door handle so tightly his knuckles were white.

Dispatch came back with a message, but it was so staticky that Gilhofer couldn't make sense of it.

He looked at Klára.

"They haven't seen her," she said.

He nodded. They were approaching the terminal. "Is it normal for a police officer to order a border screen?" he said.

She said nothing but swerved in front of a line of taxis before slamming the brakes. They skidded to a halt right outside the international arrivals entrance, and Klára was out of the car before he was. He had to run to keep up.

"Come on!" she shouted back at him.

He chased her into the terminal. It was busy—people rushing in all directions, passengers, families, luggage carts, cab and limo drivers lined up in front of the gate holding signs. He scanned the crowd and saw Klára ahead, flashing her badge at a security guard as she rushed toward the diplomatic security office. He was chasing after her, dodging a group of school children, stumbling as he almost tripped over a suitcase, when his phone started to ring. It was Langley.

"This is Gilhofer," he panted.

"Gilhofer, this is Tatyana. She's all right. She just made contact."

"Oh my God," he said, putting a hand on his chest. "You're sure?"

"She's in the back of a cab. She's already left the airport."

"Oh my God," he said again, bending down and putting his hands on his knees to help catch his breath.

"You sound like you're having a heart attack," Tatyana said.

He laughed, more out of relief than amusement. "Klára," he called, but she was too far ahead to hear him.

"Her phone was dead," Tatyana continued. "She plugged it in in the cab. She's *en route* to the embassy as we speak. Should be there in twenty minutes."

"Does she know about the situation here?"

"She does now. If I send you her location tracking, do you think you can get your Czech friend to call in a police escort for the cab?"

"I'll ask her," Gilhofer said. "But something tells me she'll be able to arrange it."

19

Valentina was sitting in a cab outside the airport, still unsure what she was going to do about Shipenko's latest kill order, when a tall woman in an elegant, knee-length coat, her hair cut slightly different than the photo in the file, walked straight out of the main arrival's terminal and up to the curb. She was all business, walking briskly with a smart, metal suitcase trailing behind her and a shearling-trimmed purse slung over one shoulder. She wore an orange silk scarf and a pair of oversized, black sunglasses. When she stopped, she took off the sunglasses and looked almost directly at Valentina.

Bingo!

There was no question it was her—Carmen Linder, Prague CIA Station Chief.

"What the hell?" Valentina muttered under her breath.

Carmen was standing there like she didn't have a care in the world, shaking out her hair and letting a few rare rays of winter sun bathe her face in light. She didn't look like someone who'd just spent the last eight hours on a long-haul flight, but more like she was getting ready for a photoshoot for the airline's inflight magazine.

And something was immediately, almost painfully, obvious to Valentina. This woman didn't have the faintest clue of the danger she was in. Valentina did the math quickly in her head—the time the flight took, when it would have taken off, the earliest the CIA could have been aware of Arabella Bradwell's murder. It was possible, but unlikely, that the CIA had dropped the ball and failed to notify the station chief of what was going on. More likely, she thought, that they'd been unable to reach her on the plane. That would be a serious protocol breach, to be sure, but not unheard of. If that was the case, and Carmen was still blissfully unaware that she'd lost a second agent —the second of three who were women—then getting to her now would be as easy as taking candy from a baby.

Carmen leaned her suitcase against a lamp post as she threw a hand in the air with a carefree flick of the wrist. She looked like a lady waving to a passing knight, and a cab stopped for her instantly. She got in, leaving the suitcase where it was, and the driver came scuttling around dutifully to load it into the trunk.

"Follow that car," Valentina said to her driver, counting out a wad of bills just thick enough that the driver wouldn't need to count it. He looked at the money, then at Valentina in his rearview mirror, and put the car in gear. "Not too close," Valentina said. "Just take it nice and easy."

He didn't have any difficulty keeping up—Carmen's driver had no idea he was being followed. He signaled his turns and lane changes, kept to the speed limit, and took no evasive measures of any kind. At the first set of lights he came to a complete stop, and Valentina suddenly realized she could have ended the whole thing right then and there. All she had to do was get out of the cab, walk up to Carmen's car, and knock on the window. It hardly mattered that she didn't have a gun—a jab to the throat, a quick jerk of the neck, and it would be over.

She put her hand on the door handle, but something stopped her from pulling it. She couldn't bring herself to do it. This entire mission, everything that had happened since her arrival in Prague, the order to wipe out the complete female complement of a station, it just didn't sit right. She was no angel, she knew the rules of the world she inhabited, but something about the thought of Shipenko, sitting in his office in Moscow making her do this, it just didn't gel. She remained in her seat as if glued to it, staring at the steam that billowed from the tailpipe of Carmen's cab.

What would she do, she thought. How would she get out of this? It wasn't like she could refuse a job. That wasn't how the Prime Directorate operated. It certainly wasn't how Shipenko operated. The man was a vindictive son of a bitch, if ever there was one. Valentina once watched him use an orderly as a coffee table. The man had offended him in some way and was forced to remain on his hands and knees, with papers, an ashtray, and even drinks balanced on his back, while Shipenko conducted a string of meetings. When Shipenko finally left the building for the night, he placed a vase of flowers on the man's back and said that if they fell, or if anyone dared to help him during the night, they would all pay with their lives. Somehow, the man made it through the night. At one point, he pissed himself, but he never moved. He kept his back as flat as a board.

But that didn't save him. The following morning, Shipenko never showed up for work. He called to let his secretary know that his order still stood and to let him know the instant the vase hit the floor. All that day, the man kept his position. He was trembling, quivering with fatigue, but he didn't budge. It was during the second night that the vase finally dropped.

When the orderly was found the next morning, he was still on his hands and knees. He'd been crying, and all around him on the floor were the shards of glass from the shattered vase.

Without a word, Shipenko walked up to him, placed a pistol at the man's temple, and pulled the trigger.

He was a cruel master. Valentina thought about that. And she thought about the flags he'd placed on her order. Was he telling her that her time had come? You didn't need to be a psychic to see the signs. GRU kill order flags were in place to protect the mission and keep the assassin alive. Shipenko had personally overridden every one of them. The fact she was already exposed, and that she'd discarded her weapon and couldn't fulfill the requirement to use SP-4 ammo, made no difference. The order had been issued, and that was that.

She also thought about the fact that Shipenko hadn't bothered to mask his actions from her. The overrides could have been hidden. The entire nature of the order could have been concealed from her. But instead, almost as if he was adding insult to injury, as if he was trying to tell her she was disposable, the operator had read out the flags to her like the items of a grocery list.

The more she thought about it, the more suspicious she grew of Shipenko's motives. She didn't have to stretch her mind very far to think he might be trying to kill her. She thought over their last few exchanges.

Shipenko wasn't just vindictive, he was painfully quick

to take offense. It was an unfortunate trait for a man of his appearance, and Valentina knew to be on guard against offending him. The trick was to keep her revulsion hidden, and it wasn't easy, given the relentlessness of his sexual advances.

She'd been playing a game of cat and mouse with him ever since she'd entered the agency. She wondered now, had it finally caught up with her? Had she played the game too well, for too long? Had she dodged his advances one too many times? Had she let him see that she despised him?

She'd heard the horror stories from other women in the office—the button under his desk that locked the door on both sides, the soundproofing that had been fitted at his request, his habit of getting subordinates to meet him at his villa near Novo-Ogaryevo. The man was a predator of the highest order, operating in plain sight, and the fact Valentina had escaped his clutches this long said something.

It was a delicate game, and she played it masterfully. Often, she took steps to avoid being in Moscow entirely, setting up her base in Saint Petersburg and avoiding face-to-face contact for months on end. When she was forced back to the capital, she made strenuous efforts never to let herself be compromised. She stayed away from the GRU building, showed up too early or too late for appointments, courted the interest of other men in his orbit, men whose wishes Shipenko couldn't ignore.

She'd had to learn fast. Right after her appointment to the Prime Directorate, before she'd ever seen him with her own eyes and had still only heard the stories that circulated around the academy and the secretarial pool, he'd made his first attempt. She already knew he suffered from grave facial and bodily deformities. She knew it had something to do with botched military experiments. She had no illusions that she was going to work for a man that was anything less than a monster. But knowing it, and seeing it for herself, were two different things.

She was as green as anyone at the GRU could be. She'd been through training at the academy, but her position had yet to be confirmed, and she hadn't reported in person to headquarters. She certainly hadn't performed a live mission. She was highly trained but also naive, innocent, eager to please.

When Shipenko requested she meet him at his villa, she should have known what it meant. At the GRU, a *home visit*, as the directors called it, was practically a rite of passage—a ritual all female recruits were subjected to at one point or another. But Valentina told herself this was different. Shipenko wasn't just grotesque, he was severely compromised medically. He was extremely prone to infection, to the point that even exposure to air posed a risk, and his office in the headquarters building had been retrofitted with the same ventilation and air filtration system used in hospital ICUs. He traveled with a medical team. Even his movements around Moscow were shadowed by ambulances and paramedics. She told herself a man that sick couldn't possibly have designs on her.

But she was apprehensive nonetheless. He was a powerful man, and in the Kremlin, power was without limits, be they legal or moral. If he had the power to order her to kill, he had the power to order her to spread her legs. That went without saying. Added to that were the rumors—the stories of deformity and disfigurement, the fact they called him *Tushonka*, as if his face had been passed through a meat grinder.

When his car came to pick her up, she told herself everything was all right. When it left the city and brought her through two separate security checkpoints, into a forested compound from which escape would have been as difficult as escape from a prison camp, she told herself it was all right. It was only when the car dropped her at a private entrance used only by servants, and two men in butler's uniforms escorted her into a cavernous, underground spa, complete with sauna, steam room, massage tables, and a naturally heated pool, that she admitted to herself she'd made a mistake.

And by then, there was nothing that could be done. She was brought to a tiled changing room, sickly humid from the steam of the pool, and told to undress. The butlers waited by the door, their backs to her, and one of them explained that the entire compound had been built on the site of a natural hot spring so that Shipenko could benefit from its therapeutic properties. When she'd undressed, she put on the black lace outfit that had been laid out for her, it was little more than lingerie, and was taken to the pool. So much steam rose from the water that it looked too hot to enter.

She stood by it nervously and waited. The air was laden with eucalyptus and jojoba. Men in white garments stood watching her. Some were guards, others masseurs. All were servants of one type or another. She must have waited an hour, the nauseating heat almost overcoming her at times, until one of the butlers returned and told her to get dressed. Shipenko wouldn't be joining her.

To this day, Valentina was grateful to him.

She'd known how close she was to being taken advantage of, but she'd also known that she was in Moscow, that that sort of thing was rampant there, and that sooner or

later, she would have to submit to it. What she didn't
know, what she only learned later when she saw Shipenko
for herself, was the full horror of what she'd so narrowly
escaped—his charred skin, his misshapen form, and,
worst of all, his cruel, distorted personality that took pleasure in all the wrong things.

And it was then that she vowed never to let him get
that close to her again. She would accept a lot in her job
as a GRU assassin—fear, danger, pain, torture. She would
compromise herself sexually when it was to her benefit to
do so. She would accept humiliation. She even accepted
that she would, in all likelihood, die performing her job.

But Osip Shipenko was where she drew the line. She
would never let him get his claws on her. She would never
be his plaything.

So she'd played her dangerous game, avoiding his
clutches the way a fish might avoid the tentacles of a
squid. She knew she was racking up a tab, that it couldn't
go on forever, that one day her debt would fall due. Sitting
now in the cab, following Carmen Linder through the
cobbled streets of Prague's old town, she wondered if that
day had come.

It added up. The entire mission had been suspect from
start to finish. It was the kind of thing they schooled them
against at the academy. It was bad for everyone. There
were rules to the game they played, an equilibrium that
had been painstakingly calibrated during decades of Cold
War tit for tat, an order that was understood by everyone
in the Kremlin and everyone in Washington. This
mission, picking off innocents, going after women without
an objective, it flew in the face of everything, it broke the
rules, and no one would walk away unscathed.

Shipenko wanted to see the world burn, and this

was his opening gambit. She'd always known there was that side to him. He'd flirted with disaster many times, amassing troops on NATO's doorstep, assassinating questionable targets, sending messages to adversaries that flaunted the international status quo. The final decisions lay with the president, of course, but it was Shipenko that was always whispering in his ear. "More troops," he would say. "More force. More pressure." He'd called up nuclear weapons during multiple crises. He'd ordered tests that hadn't been contemplated since the darkest days of the Soviets. He pushed the envelope.

This entire mission had been designed to taunt the Americans. The ammo, the women targets, it was tailor-made to provoke a response.

And then there were the flags on her order.

She'd seen a rate-limit override before. She'd been in Madrid doing a job for Shipenko when some lackey in the Prime Directorate gave her three Spanish tax officials to hit in a single night.

She'd known that job hadn't been right. Russian national security did not depend on the killing of Spanish tax inspectors. She was taking care of a personal matter for someone, and she knew it. She even interrogated the targets about it before killing them. She asked them what connection they had to Russia, to the oligarchy in Moscow, to President Molotov. The first two didn't have the slightest idea why they were being killed. They went to their graves knowing nothing and telling her nothing. It was only the third, the most senior of the three, who could make the connection for her.

"André Suvorov," the man had said. "It's his boat."

"His boat?" Valentina said. She'd never met André

Suvorov, but she recognized the name. He was one of the president's big dogs, like Shipenko was.

"We impounded a yacht at the harbor in Barcelona. Four million euros owing. It was owned by a shell company."

"A boat?" she said again, almost in disbelief. She let out a hollow laugh.

"No one knew it was connected to the Kremlin until after we issued the legal papers."

"You impounded the wrong man's boat," Valentina said, and she looked away as she pulled the trigger. The blood came back on her, landing on her hand, her cheek, and it seemed harder to wash off for knowing why it had been shed.

Three hits, she'd thought. Three lives on her conscience. And for what? Some man's tax bill.

Suvorov was dead now, gunned down like the dog he was by a rogue American asset if the rumors were to be believed, but it didn't make Valentina sleep any better at night.

She remembered now there'd been another flag on that job. A detection flag. It being Spain and reprisals not being a major concern, Suvorov had flagged the detection override too. That meant he didn't care if the Spanish authorities traced the murders back to Moscow.

Two flags on that job. This one had so many she'd lost count. Shipenko didn't care about anything—detection, reprisals, risk of assassin death. He literally didn't care if she succeeded or not.

How could that be anything but a message?

They entered the Dejvický Tunnel, and the driver looked back at her.

"Keep following," she said.

He let a little distance open up, keeping two or three cars between them and the other cab, and as the traffic grew heavier, it became easier to conceal the fact they were following. Near the end of the tunnel, two police cruisers sped by, their lights flashing and sirens blaring.

"Where are *they* going?" the driver said, and Valentina sat forward to get a better view. The police cars pulled into the lane Carmen's taxi was in, one in front of her and one behind, and they began a close escort of her cab.

The penny had dropped. The Americans had realized the danger Carmen was in. For his part, Carmen's driver seemed to be handling the situation in stride, maintaining a perfect speed between the two police cruisers as they took the Hradčany exit out of the tunnel and into the castle district.

"Keep following them," Valentina said, sensing her driver's apprehension.

"Now, look here," he said over his shoulder. "I'm not looking for any trouble with the law."

"It's too late for that," Valentina said, making no effort now to conceal her Russian accent. "You took the money. Now you drive."

They exited the tunnel by the Diplomat Hotel in time to see Carmen's taxi speed through a set of red traffic lights. Valentina's driver seemed to waver for a second between following and not before slamming the brakes at the last second. They screeched to a halt, and Valentina watched Carmen speed off in the direction of the castle.

"I'm sorry," the driver said. "I had to."

"It's all right," Valentina said. He'd made the right call. The Americans still had no idea what was going on. The escort for Carmen was a precaution, nothing more.

Valentina would be doing herself no favors if she alerted them to the fact the threat was real.

"Take me to the US embassy," she said.

He gave her a worried look.

"Don't worry," she said. "I'm not going to get you in trouble."

He didn't look convinced, but when the lights turned green, he proceeded in the direction of the embassy. When they got onto Vlašská Street, he slowed down.

The US Embassy in Prague wasn't one of those expansive, campus-style compounds found in some cities. It occupied a stately sixteenth-century Hapsburg palace, and the chancery, which was on the ground floor, fronted directly onto Vlašská Street. The windows were barred, there were security cameras and a guarded gate for vehicles, and internal security was provided by armed agents of the US Diplomatic Security Service. In front of the building, six uniformed Czech police stood guard. Inside the gates, guards from a private security contractor were also visible.

Valentina glanced into the courtyard as they passed the gates. Immediately inside, she saw Carmen's taxi flanked by the two police cruisers, their lights still flashing.

"Stop here," she said as soon as they'd passed the gate. "Right here. That spot."

He pulled up to the curb and put on his hazard lights. "They're going to move us along."

"Just sit here a minute," Valentina said, collecting her thoughts. She still didn't know what she was going to do. She looked out the rear window, but her view of the embassy entrance was blocked by the other parked vehicles.

"How much money did I give you?" she said to the driver as she lit a cigarette.

"You can't—" he said but stopped when she opened the door.

"How much?" she said again, stepping onto the sidewalk.

He reached into his pocket.

"I'll give you that much again," she said without waiting for him to count it, "if you pick me back up at the corner in five minutes."

"The corner?"

"Back there," she said, nodding in the direction they'd come from. "By the clock."

"In five minutes?"

She shut the door and began walking purposefully back toward the embassy gates. As she approached, a police officer stepped into the sidewalk and raised a hand. She sucked carelessly on her cigarette, acting unperturbed.

"Just a moment," he said to her as the gates opened electronically and a white minivan came down the street, escorted by a police car. The van entered the courtyard and the gates shut again behind it.

"Something going on this morning?" she said to the police officer.

"No idea," he said briskly, adjusting the strap of his rifle.

She looked past him into the courtyard and saw the passengers, all female, exiting the van and being escorted hurriedly into a side entrance of the chancery. It looked like the Americans had come to the same conclusion she had. They were bringing in all female personnel. In addition to the police officers on the street, she counted six armed security guards in the courtyard. She knew there would be at least a dozen more inside the building.

"Okay, keep moving," the cop said.

She flicked away her cigarette and moved on. As she did, she felt her phone vibrate. She continued along the street, walking briskly toward the spot she'd arranged to meet the cab. The phone vibrated again, and she pulled it out of her pocket. It was an update to the kill order.

Confirm Activity

She reached the corner and looked around for the cab. It wasn't there. The phone vibrated again. She crossed the street and began walking down the steep, narrow street in the direction of the bridge. Her phone was vibrating constantly.

She looked around for a cab. There were none. Her phone vibrated again. In frustration, she pulled it out of her pocket and looked at the screen.

Confirm Activity
    Confirm Activity
    Confirm Activity
    Confirm Activity
    Confirm Activity

20

Constantin Antonescu did not appear naked on the earth. He was not born fully formed, as was once believed of eels, from mud and rainwater. He was not a clean slate, a blank page, without precedent and antecedent.

He was a man, and he had a father. And his father had a father. And the things that would come to shape his life, that would dictate the contours of his existence, the boundaries of his soul, had been etched in stone long before he was born.

Simple things, accidents of fate, decades before the birth even of his father, influenced every detail of his life —the food he ate, the money he earned, his sexual preferences, his politics. He didn't feel their presence, didn't appreciate their operation, didn't know where they began and his own free will ended.

All he knew, all anyone knew, was that his life was what it was, that it had been a certain way when he was born, and that it could only deviate so far from that origin before being pulled back. He was born in Pitești, Romania, in 1981. That fact alone decided much of what followed—his nationality, his preference for authoritarianism, his willingness to get his hands dirty. It meant fermented cabbage, minced pork, dill, and a certain brand of condensed milk reminded him of his grandmother. It meant his biggest secrets, what he would come to view as the defining events of his life, happened long before he was born.

He was sitting in the driver's seat of a black Mercedes G-Class SUV with tinted windows, parked with his back to the embassy. Through a discreet rear-facing camera built into the back of the vehicle, he had a clear view of the embassy entrance.

He and his team had been watching Valentina Brik all morning, ever since she'd left her hotel. They'd seen her dump her equipment in the river, a decision that was premature. They'd followed her to the train station, where she'd boarded an express service to Berlin, also premature. They'd observed her call from the train station and had been able to make out some of the argument she'd had with her operator. And now, they were observing what it was they'd been waiting for. She was disobeying a direct order. It was no longer a question. She was going rogue, and the time had come to call it in.

The GRU was very unforgiving of defiance. Constantin knew it better than anyone. He was the one they called when it happened. He was the cleaner. The fixer. That was his reward for being a non-Russian. He killed their people for them when they displeased the Kremlin.

He tapped his phone against the steering wheel. He had a direct number for Shipenko, but a call in the clear like this was not preferred. It was permitted when necessary, when there was a *situation*, as Shipenko liked to refer to them, but even then, encrypted messages were preferred.

He could still see Valentina, but he would have to move soon if he was to keep eyes on her.

"She's on the move," one of his men, Stăn, said over the radio.

Stăn was in another vehicle at the far end of the street. Two other men, Vasile Boc and Alexandru Badea, were at a nearby hotel operating drones. Between the four of them, they were able to keep eyes on her pretty much constantly.

Constantin tapped an error code into the phone and hit send. Shipenko would receive the update. He would decide what was to be done.

Not that there was much doubt. When Shipenko was the lead agent, deviation always spelled death. There were no exceptions. Constantin and his crew had been through the process so many times it was becoming second nature. Shipenko would order them to watch an agent, they would find something the agent had done wrong, there was always something when you wanted to find it, they would notify Shipenko and, an hour later, would be cleaning the blood of a highly-trained assassin from their hands. They were the killers of killers, the hunters of hunters. And Constantin was their leader.

It wasn't anything he'd ever wanted to be, not something he'd aspired to or consciously decided to become. Like so many other things, it was simply a matter of fate.

Constantin had a Romanian's view of fate. He was superstitious. He went to gypsies and had his cards read. It wasn't a game to him. It wasn't fun. It was real, and things they told him were impossible to fake.

Like the time a very old gypsy woman held his hand, looked him in the eye, and said the words, Călărași Express. He hadn't known their significance then, but he looked into it, dug into the records of the Căile Ferate Române, the Romanian national railway company, and he found out.

His paternal grandfather, a man named Mihai Antonescu, was a towerman for the company. He came from a village called Bălilești, not far from Pitești, a place where the Romanian government had located one of the largest rail shunting yards in the country. Shunting, as Constantin learned, was the process of separating and sorting freight cars, unhitching them from one train, hitching them to another. It wasn't complicated, but in practice, moving tens of tons of unpowered steel around a set of sloped parallel tracks and getting them where you wanted without ever moving them back uphill was a delicate art.

Bălilești was strategically placed between the Danube, the slopes of the Transylvanian Alps, and the capital. Hundreds of laden livestock cars rolled through it every day on their way to Bucharest's enormous slaughter yards.

It was hard work, but Constantin saw from his grandfather's file that he took to it. Pushing the cars onto the lead track, uncoupling them as they crested the hump, and then stopping them by throwing chocks on the tracks in front of them, all came naturally to him. He had a knack for running in front of the lumbering cars as they rolled down the slope and dropping the wedges in front of the wheels at the very last moment. He was personally credited with saving the company the expense of installing automatic retarders.

It was dangerous work—boys died running in front of

the brakeless, driverless cars all the time. If they were too slow, if they tripped, if their foot got caught in the tracks, no one could stop the rolling cars. But Mihai survived those early years and rose up the ranks. Most importantly, he took no part in the strikes and worker agitations that plagued Romania in those years prior to the outbreak of World War II.

Communists were everywhere in those days, and Mihai's bosses rewarded loyalty above all else. When the National Legionary State was formed in 1940, Mihai signed up for the Iron Guard. Reading the record, Constantin could only conclude that it was to please his employers. Mihai himself showed no love of violence. He had no discernible political leanings. He was a company man and nothing more. A railway man. If he'd been born in the United States, he would have given his life to General Motors, or Standard Oil, or General Electric. He would have worked quietly, cashed his paycheck, drank at the Christmas party, and retired on his sixty-fifth birthday. That was the kind of man he was.

But he wasn't born in the United States, he was born in Romania, and during the six years he worked at the Bălilești shunting yard, he did not once miss a shift, call in sick, or even show up late. In fact, he frequently took extra work and covered for other men. It paid off, and by his twenty-fourth birthday, he'd been promoted to the rank of train driver, a position of almost unimaginable prestige to a boy of his birth. The story could have ended there. He could have run out his years driving his train, taking sheep and cattle to the stockyards in Pitești and Bucharest, and everything would have been different. He was a simple man, and his ambitions rose no further than that.

But the story did not end there. The meaning of the

gypsy's words did not end there. Events far outside Mihai's conception—Hitler's invasion of Poland, the Fall of France, the repudiation of the Molotov-Ribbentrop Pact, meant that by June of 1941, Romania was at war. And not just at war, but part of the largest land invasion in the history of human warfare, marching east with the Axis powers as the second-largest contributor of troops to Operation Barbarossa. Within weeks, Romanian soldiers were fighting alongside Germans in the Ukraine, Bessarabia, eventually even in Stalingrad.

Everyone in a position of power, from the government in Bucharest, to the local politicians in Pitești, to the bosses at the train company, was in the grip of an anti-bolshevik, anti-semitic frenzy. Romania had done the unthinkable. It had marched on Russia, it had punched the bear in the face, and it was terrified the gamble wouldn't pay off. The Red Army was the largest on earth, and everyone knew in their bones that the day would come when it exacted its revenge.

And that was the environment in which Mihai was awarded the Iași run, moving livestock to the capital from the farthest eastern reaches of the country, areas close to the borders of Bessarabia, Northern Bukovina, and Moldavia. Iași had once been Romania's capital, but when Mihai got there, it was directly in the path the Red Army would take when its eventual counteroffensive came. And everyone knew it would. Even the train company records showed steps to be taken to protect locomotives and rolling stock from the invaders.

Mihai arrived in a city where the populace feared the Russians, despised the Jews, and, if not loved, certainly hoped to gain from the Germans. Those sentiments could be found everywhere in the country, but in Iași, because of its position facing down the Russians, they were amplified.

It was not fear, however, that Mihai recorded in his company journal when he got there. It was the German Abwehr's interference with timetables, which caused him to roll into the city six hours later than scheduled. Six hours was a significant delay when moving sensitive live-stock in Romania's summer heat. It would mean wastage, dead animals. But no one cared about the delay. He was immediately called into the station master's office, where an agent of the Serviciul Special de Informații, the Romanian secret service, told him that his train was being commandeered by the military. They showed him a docu-ment signed by the train company's board of governors in Bucharest, which to Mihai had the same authority as an edict from the Pope.

The station master's report said Mihai raised a hand to his forehead in salute and said, "I am ready to serve my country as the company orders." Then he saluted the two Abwehr officers present and said, "Sieg Heil! Sieg Heil!" without apparently knowing what the words meant.

Mihai's journal made it clear he regarded the order as the same, regardless of whether it originated with the local station master, the company headquarters in Bucharest, or the Reich Chancellery in Berlin. He was a driver, and he would drive where he was told to.

His precise orders weren't expected until the next day, and he was told to wait at the station, on the ready. They gave him three meal tokens for the station canteen, as well as a pass for the company dormitory, where a bunk with coarse blankets and an outdoor shower were at his disposal. It was no five-star hotel but better than sleeping

in the locomotive, where the engine would be kept at a
steady hum all night.

In the staff canteen, which was also being used by the
military, he noted that the Abwehr officers had the run of
the place. They stooped over large maps of the rail
network, barked orders at the Romanian officials, and sent
a steady stream of telegrams to Bucharest and Berlin.
Mihai didn't see their contents, but he spent hours in the
canteen, killing time, smoking cigarettes and drinking the
watery coffee the company provided. During that time,
Iași and Bessarabia police officers, as well as the
gendarmerie, were also given orders. The Romanian intelligence officers did their best to be discreet, but the
Germans were less subtle. Mihai realized that what was
being coordinated was a roundup of the city's entire
Jewish population.

He recorded it in his journal impartially, and if it gave
him pause, he made no mention of it. He knew the
journal was the property of the company, and that may
have made him reticent. Constantin also knew that by that
time, he would have been no stranger to the general
strokes of Nazi ideology. He'd sat through enough Iron
Guard speeches, all of which denounced Bolsheviks,
communists, Jews, labor leaders, and other traitors as fit
for nothing but the gallows.

He certainly voiced no protest to the station master or
other officials present at Iași. He spent the day at the
station, slept that night in the dormitory, and recorded
only that the building, with its brick walls and metal roof,
was too hot for sleeping.

He did later record what he saw the following morning. It was not by choice then, and not in the company
journal. It came years later, during an inquiry by the

communist government into the events that had, by that time, come to be known as the Iași Pogrom. He testified that he rose before dawn and left the bunkhouse, passing the station master who was dozing on the platform. Constantin would have liked to doubt the record. Given how many years that had passed, and the willingness of the communists to alter facts when it suited them, that would have been natural. But the more he read—the inclusion of detail such as the pile of ash at the station master's feet where he'd been tipping his cigarettes, and the fact the government had more to lose than gain from the testimony in the report—the more he knew it was true.

Mihai recorded walking down the street from the station toward the center of town. In the distance, he thought he saw the first glimmers of sunrise, but he quickly realized it was not the sun but the glow of a building on fire. Then he smelled the smoke. When he reached the square, he saw a group of men in black boots running in unison, marching like soldiers. It was a militia of Iron Guard men, thirty or forty strong. The men saw him across the square, and for a split second, he realized there was nothing between him and their guns other than the train company uniform he wore and the Iron Guard membership card in his pocket.

They marched on, ignoring him. It was then that he heard the screaming of a woman. Without thinking, he ran toward the sound. In one of the buildings facing the square, right in the hallway where they could be seen from the street, another gang of men was pounding a young woman with bats, boots, fists. Mihai watched in horror as a knife was pulled, and the woman was stabbed twice in the gut.

The men exulted in what they'd done as the woman's blood spattered on their faces, on their white shirts.

"Who are you?" one of the men snarled at Mihai.

"No one," Mihai said. "A train driver."

"A jew?"

"No," he said. "One of you."

The men looked him over, then told him to get lost. Mihai turned and ran back toward the station. He must have taken a wrong turn somewhere because he came to another square, where a gang of ordinary civilians, without uniforms but armed with tools and implements, had corralled a group of about fifty people. The people had their backs to a wall and looked like they were going to rush the mob who was holding them. The standoff lasted about a minute, until two Abwehr officers showed up and opened fire with submachine guns. The people fell to the ground like blades of wheat mown down by a scythe.

"What's going on?" Mihai said to a member of the mob.

"What do you think?" the man said back to him. "Their time has come."

Mihai backed away. He continued toward the station. He was disoriented, confused, and made another wrong turn. He wandered the streets, at one point passing a synagogue where dead bodies had been piled up against the door like a macabre delivery. There were men, women, children, even a baby among the dead, and a gang of local boys was picking among them, rifling for valuables.

When eventually he got back to the station, he was in such a state that the server at the canteen made him sit down and drink tea with sugar. She was agitated herself.

She'd been at the station the whole time, but reports were already coming in of what was going on. Blood was running in the streets.

He was still in the canteen, sipping tea and smoking a cigarette, numb with shock, when the station master came over and handed him a telegram containing his order. He didn't read it immediately but could see from the header that it had been sent by Section II of the Serviciul Special de Informații. He had no idea what that meant.

Outside on the platform, hundreds of people huddled in groups, hounded by guards and attack dogs, beaten or shot if they tried to run. They'd been rounded up all over the city, and more kept arriving. It later transpired that over five thousand were rounded up and brought to the station that day.

Mihai watched one of them try to escape. He was a young man, and he was caught by an Iron Guard man who proceeded to beat him with a shovel. The steel blade of the shovel caught the man at a bad angle. Blood spurted from his neck ten feet into the air as the man flailed around wildly, searching desperately for the source of the blood like a man trying to plug a leaking lifeboat. His mother, it must have been his mother, ran to him and begged for help. She screamed a shrill, blood-curdling cry until a German officer walked over and shot them both in the head with a pistol.

When it seemed like everyone had been rounded up, the guards forced the people into lines, and the Germans set up tables and chairs and hauled out thick, leather-bound ledgers. They then took down the names, addresses, and other details of the people before they were forced onto the cattle cars.

People were crying and screaming everywhere.

Mothers were separated from children, husbands from wives, siblings from each other. They were pushed and shoved toward the trains, whipped and beaten until they'd crammed themselves so tightly into the wagons that each thirty-foot car, designed to carry a maximum of forty full-grown cows, contained hundreds of people. All five thousand had been swallowed up by just twenty cattle wagons.

The morning wore on, and Mihai read and reread his order. He couldn't make sense of it.

Iron Guard men walked back and forth along the length of the platform, making sure no one escaped the train. Some of them got to work hammering wooden planks over the windows. On the doors, heavy chains were placed around the handles to prevent their opening. As the full heat of the sun began to beat down on the train, the people started to beg for water. The station master brought out the hose used to water livestock, but the Abwehr men took it from him, laughing at his stupidity. Instead of water, the guards stuffed barbed wire into any remaining openings in the slats and bolted any remaining hatches and doors.

Mihai watched it all from the canteen, then went out to the platform and told an Abwehr officer what his order said. The people were crying and wailing in the wagons— all the planks and wire in the world couldn't keep in that wretched sound—and for three hours, the train remained motionless in the station while the Germans and Section II officers argued about where the train should be sent. There was talk of going west, out of Romanian territory completely and on toward the Reich, a prospect that terrified Mihai. Eventually, a German came over and told Mihai his final destination. The man mispronounced it so badly that Mihai needed him to repeat it a number of times before finally getting him to point it out on a map. He pointed to Călăraşi, a Romanian city three hundred miles away to the south.

Mihai gave testimony that the voice of the German officer barking the order, speaking his schoolboy Italian in a diabolical Saxon accent, haunted him for the rest of his life. "Vai! Vai!" he'd shouted in Mihai's ear and then, in a jumble of Italian and German and Romanian, bellowed, "Schnell! Schnell! Veloce! Rapido!"

Mihai drove, but no sooner had he left the confines of the city than he was radioed by the station master. "What the hell do you think you're doing?" he yelled. "Slow the hell down."

"The German told me '*rapido*'," Mihai said. "He said, '*Veloce! Veloce!*'."

"I don't care what he said. Slow the hell down or face a military tribunal when you arrive in Călăraşi."

"How slow do you want me to go?" Mihai asked.

"If there's no one on the track behind you, I don't want you to move at all. Just sit in the sun. Let them bake."

"Let them bake?"

"If you were to never arrive in Călăraşi at all, if your cargo was simply to disappear, that would be fine by them."

Mihai had no idea what to make of that. He was a driver. To not arrive simply made no sense to him. The station master sensed his confusion. "Both our lives depend on you getting this right," he said.

As Mihai made his slow, circuitous way through the towns of Mirceşti, Roman, Săbăoani, and Inoteşti, taking every side route and detour imaginable, stretching a journey of a few hours into days and days, and eventually into more than a week, he began to realize the grim purpose of his mission.

At first, the passengers, if that was what they could be called, were loud. They screamed and cried and banged on the walls of the wagons so hard that he could hear them over the idling engine every time he stopped the train. That first night, pulled in at a siding, he was tormented by the cries—especially those of the children and babies, of which there were many.

He didn't sleep a wink. He paced up and down the siding, chain-smoking and trying not to look at the clawing fingers between the slats, the staring eyes as they caught and reflected the moonlight.

By morning, the cries had grown weaker, and he was ordered into the station at Mircești, where he entered a long warehouse. There were soldiers there who opened the doors of the wagons for the first time since they'd been sealed shut. The stench when the doors were pulled back was almost incomprehensible. The people in the wagons cried and wailed, and the soldiers barked at them, telling them to push out the dead. Dozens had perished. They were pushed out of the wagons and fell to the concrete floor like bags of sand. Produce trucks were brought up, and some of the prisoners were made to load the bodies into the backs of the trucks. They worked silently, bewildered—just the day before, they'd been in their own homes, a thousand miles from the borders of the Third Reich. Now, Hitler's Reich had come to them.

The soldiers resealed the wagons while the men were working and realized too late their mistake. Rather than pull off the boards and redo the work, they shot the men where they stood, then loaded them into the backs of the trucks on top of the bodies they themselves had just loaded.

The next day, at a remote siding in a forest outside Roman, the doors were opened again, and over a hundred bodies were pushed out. Mostly children. The next day, in some corn fields outside Săbăoani, hundreds more, and in Inotești, over a thousand. By the time the train pulled into Călărași, eight days after leaving Iași, less than six hundred people out of five thousand were still alive. Mihai had no godly idea how they had made it. Many of them couldn't walk. They lay in the corners of the wagons, unrecognizable, covered in filth and excrement, their hair matted like wild animals. They didn't speak, and when the soldiers yelled at them, they didn't respond. They'd lost the ability. Like ghosts, like phantoms, they were shoved and beaten and pushed out of the wagons by soldiers and dogs—always the dogs—into waiting trucks. The trucks took them away, and Mihai never found out where they went.

He watched the trucks drive away, then got back in the train. He was ordered from Călărași to a stockyard some miles away, where the cattle balked and refused to be loaded into the wagons. The same cattle that lined up in an orderly manner for their own slaughter refused to go into these wagons until they were hosed down and washed of the blood and filth and stench of death.

But the stench of death couldn't be washed so easily from a man. His mind held onto it. His soul did. It seeped into every crack and crevice of his being, and no amount of water and soap, no amount of wailing and gnashing and hand-wringing, could ever rid him of it. It was a stench he would take to his grave, but not before passing it on to his descendent. That was what Constantin believed. That was how he interpreted the words of the gypsy.

Mihai never spoke of what happened. He got married, and the wife knew there was something dark in his past, but in those days, everyone who had survived the war had something dark in their past. When it came out during the inquiry, she refused to believe it. The subject was forbidden in the home. The world had changed. It had moved on. No one cared for such talk. Mihai didn't speak of it to his son, but that didn't save him. It didn't save Constantin.

What Mihai did tell his son, and what the son in his turn told his own son, was that the men in their family were cursed. Mihai had known it. Constantin's father had known it. And Constantin now knew it. He'd seen the proof.

He pulled the Mercedes out of its parking spot and did a U-turn, following Valentina to the corner of the street.

"In pursuit," he said into his radio.

"Copy that," Stăn said.

Whatever happened next, Constantin thought, he would be visiting his curse on this Valentina Brik soon enough.

21

L ance called Laurel from a payphone at the airport. He'd booked the first flight out of Heathrow and was waiting to board.

"It's me," he said when she picked up.

"Lance!"

"You sound surprised."

"I *am* surprised. Last time we spoke, you made it pretty clear that you wanted to be—"

"Left alone?"

"Yes."

"Well," he said, "maybe I missed you."

"You're calling about Prague."

"Roth filled me in on the whole thing. Two dead agents and no sign of what provoked it."

"We're working the angles, but so far—"

"You have no idea what's going on."

"If you want to be blunt about it," she said.

"What about the station chief. He said she was next on the list."

"We don't know that," Laurel said. "She landed thirty minutes ago, and she's already safely at the embassy."

"In one piece?"

"We couldn't reach her. I thought for sure something was up. She didn't make contact until she was in the back of a regular cab from the airport. She was way out in the open."

"And no one attacked?"

"Not a peep."

"That's something."

"We're still not sure what's behind the two murders we've seen."

"Two women," Lance said.

"It's too early to say that's the pattern."

Lance knew that was technically correct, but he doubted even she believed it. "The station chief is our last female agent in the city, correct?"

"Official CIA, yes, but across the embassy."

"Fifty-two people," Lance said.

"That's right," Laurel said, surprised he knew the number.

"Roth filled me in on all of it."

"Did he tell you Tatyana was already on her way?"

"He did. When does she arrive?"

"She should be landing as we speak."

"Okay, that's good. It improves our position on the ground."

"Roth's also bringing every female staff member into the embassy for protection?"

"He told me."

"You don't sound like you like it."

"Is it wise to corral them all in one confined place?"

"We don't have the resources to protect them any other way."

"We could fly them out of the country entirely. Keep everyone out of harm's way until the dust settles."

"Roth's never going to agree to pull out of a station because of two casualties. Neither is the Pentagon."

"But if this is just the beginning, if there's a chance of more murders...."

"Pulling out is not what we do."

"We wouldn't be abandoning the post," Lance said. "It's just a—".

"Tactical withdrawal?"

"Exactly."

"And where would we fly them?"

"Ramstein," he said. "They could be accommodated there."Ramstein, in Germany, was one of the largest and best-equipped military installations on the planet, with over fifty-thousand permanent US service personnel and enough resources to support over a hundred separate units across the globe. It could provide everything needed to keep fifty-two women safe until they figured out what was going on in Prague.

"I can see the logic in it," Laurel said.

"It's obvious."

"I think you're right."

"Will you be able to convince Roth?"

"You know him better than I do."

"Just tell him that bottling fifty-two potential targets in one lightly-defended diplomatic building is a recipe for disaster. He'll see it."

"He'll say it's too soon. We don't even know what the motivation for the first two attacks was."

"Just because Carmen wasn't attacked doesn't mean they're not—"

"He'll say we don't know enough. He'll say the Pentagon won't want to show weakness."

"But he's willing to bring them all into the embassy?"

"It's not the same as flying them out of the country, Lance. The United States doesn't just give up positions—"

"It's a single flight, Laurel. No one will even notice. We can set up a training session or something at Ramstein and say that's why they're there."

"That's why our local cleaning women were flown to an airbase in another country?"

"If they're worried about appearing weak, ask them how it will look when another one of our women is murdered in her apartment. And another. And another."

"I see your point. I'll talk to him."

"You can convince him. He listens to you."

"I don't know about that."

"You've got him wrapped around your finger. And once the women are in Ramstein, we can get to work on the rest."

"I'll try," Laurel said. "If I can convince him that no one would know it had happened...."

"He'll buy it, Laurel."

"Maybe."

"They're calling my flight," he said. "I've got to go."

He hung up the phone and made his way to his gate. Getting the women out of Prague was the right move. He was sure Roth would see that. And that meant he and Tatyana would have the time they needed to figure things out without the threat of more casualties over their head. He grabbed a coffee and sandwich from a kiosk and waited to board.

He could see the plane outside in the gray morning drizzle. He opened the sandwich and was about to take a bite when his cell started to vibrate. He looked at the screen.

"Pooja?"

"No, it's Pooja's sister."

"Is something wrong?"

"You got a message."

"I think your sister already gave it to me."

"This is a new message. I just took the call."

"Who's it from?" Lance said, expecting another message from Roth.

"It was a woman ordering a taxi."

"A woman?"

"She left an address."

"Did she give her name?"

"Isabelle Ritter. It sounded like she was crying. She said to send Clint."

"She said, Clint?"

"Yes, she did."

Lance looked at the line of people boarding the flight. They would be in Prague in less than an hour, and he would be too unless he didn't board. He looked at his watch. "Hold on one second," he said into the phone. Then he went up to the ticket desk and asked the flight attendant if there was another flight to Prague.

"There's one later this afternoon," she said.

"Can I change my ticket for a seat on that flight?"

She typed something on her computer and nodded. "I've got some open seats. There'll be a change fee."

"That's fine," Lance said, handing her his boarding card. "Put me on the next flight." Then, into the phone, he said, "What was the address she gave you?"

22

Shipenko shifted in his seat uncomfortably. It was one of those folding director's chairs with a canvas back and was ill-suited to his needs. He was also cold, despite being wrapped in a heavy twill coat and scarf, and he pulled the coat closer around himself.

He was in a large, dark warehouse at a private film studio east of Moscow and tolerated the discomfort because of what was being filmed. He'd gone to a lot of trouble to make it happen. It wasn't the kind of place that rented its facilities to just anyone. He'd had to pull strings, lean on the Kremlin's close ties to MediaMost and Gazprom-Media, to get access not just to a fully production-ready soundstage but also to a professional film crew and all of their attendant equipment and services. The result was that Shipenko had everything at his disposal now to recreate anything he could imagine in the most exquisite detail theatrically possible.

The crew was busy putting the final touches on the set, shoveling the white sand he'd imported from the Baltic into mounds twenty feet high, setting up fans to make the long grass sway realistically in the breeze, applying a few final details to the sky and waves on the painted backdrop. There was a botanist that he'd hired from a university in Uzbekistan who was responsible for the grass, and the backdrop painter had worked for all of the high-budget productions at the Bolshoi and Stanislavski. He'd seen preview shots, but only now, if they ever turned on the powerful lights that were pointed at the stage, would he see the final set in all its glory.

He picked up the electric bullhorn that was attached to the arm of his chair and fumbled with the button. "Is this on?" he said, and no one heard him. He flicked the switch a few times and said, "Testing, testing." His voice bellowed from the speaker, and every crew member on the set stopped what they were doing. They turned in his direction but couldn't see him in the darkness. "Are we almost ready to get started?" he said. "It's freezing in here."

"We're almost ready to go now," the director said. He snapped his fingers at one of the many underlings running around the set. "Get Mr. Shipenko a propane heater." He climbed up onto the set for a final inspection, then said, "All right, everyone, I think we're officially ready for lights."

Shipenko straightened himself in his seat. He'd waited a long time for this moment and sensed that he would know instantly if the whole thing, the months of effort, had been worth it.

"Are you ready, Mr. Shipenko?"

He was seated behind the line of lights, right at the center point of the set. "Do it," he said into the bullhorn.

"Clear the set," the director said, and everyone went scuttling in a dozen directions. "Cue the fans," he said. "Cue the mist. Cue sound."

It was the first time Shipenko had heard the sound-track, the typical ambient noises one would have heard on the Vozrozheniya Island beaches of his youth. The wind in the grass, the waves on the sand, some gulls in the distance.

"Lights!" the director announced with a flourish.

The lights came on, one at a time, with an audible snap of electrical power, and the whole scene lit up with thousands of watts of incandescent light. The result was startling. The whole set, previously lit by dingy overhead warehouse lights, suddenly glistened as if under the full glare of the summer sun. Every detail came to life. The water, the grass, even the backdrop seemed real. Shipenko shut his eyes and breathed in as if expecting to inhale the salty Aral air he remembered so clearly. Behind him, somewhere, gulls seemed to be approaching. He opened his eyes and almost couldn't see for all the tears.

He reached into his breast pocket for his sunglasses and put them on.

"What do you think, sir?" the director said, squinting into the light in his direction.

"Good," Shipenko said, clearing his throat. The bull-horn was off, and he flicked the switch and tried again. "Good. Very good."

"Lighting is okay? Sound?"

"It's all perfect," he said. "I'm very impressed."

"Well, then," the director said hesitantly. "If it's all perfect, then we can...."

"Begin?"

"Exactly, sir. The cameras are rolling. They'll keep going until someone stops them. The sound is on a loop."

Shipenko had ordered them to set things up so that he could direct the scene without any of the crew being present. It was necessary for what he had in mind. They wouldn't be far, they'd still be on the lot, still getting paid for their time, but they wouldn't know what he was doing.

"Clear the set, then," he said. "I'm eager to start."

"If you need anything, sir, all you have to do is call on the radio. We'll be right outside."

"Very good," Shipenko said. "Now, leave me. I want everyone out."

"Other than the...."

"Girl."

"...actress," the director said, finishing his sentence quietly.

"Go on, then," Shipenko said. "Get out. Fuck off. All of you."

"You heard the man," the director said. "Clear the set. That means everyone."

As the crew departed, Shipenko felt his phone vibrate. "What now?" he muttered as he looked at it. It was a System Error Response—an automated message that something had gone wrong with one of his missions. He opened the message and glanced over it.

Identifier: KO_457832

Assassin: Valentina Brik

Target: Carmen Linder

Order: Kill target. Leave at least one 7.62x41mm bullet at the scene.

Overrides: Rate-Limit, Risk, Stress, Detection, Reprisal

Override Placement: Manual - Osip Shipenko

Error: Order Not Carried Out

Error: Assassin Failure to Respond

Prime Directorate System Error Response

Order not carried out. Assassin failure to respond. He raised an eyebrow. Two kills, and already she was beginning to lose her nerve. This would teach her a lesson.

He'd known for some time what her game was—avoiding his calls, dodging his summonses, refusing to come to his office or villa. There was a part of him that enjoyed the chase—some women ran harder than others, some did everything they could think of to avoid falling into his grip. It didn't bother him. He knew they didn't want him. No woman in her right mind wanted to be cornered in a bedroom with a creature like him. He was a predator, they were prey. It was as simple as that.

But only up to a point. Eventually, they had to succumb. Otherwise, there was no point to it. His plan with Valentina had been to wear her down slowly, to give her female targets, innocents, maybe even some children. They would be interspersed with legitimate targets, of course—he did have a job to do—but slowly, over time, she would realize the price she was paying for her intransigence. Killing evil men took a toll. Killing innocent women and children took an infinitely higher one. It was a special torture that only an assassin would ever understand, and he knew there was only so much of it Valentina would be able to endure. Eventually, she would crack. Maybe she would come begging for mercy, and when she did, he would make her pay for it with her mouth, her lips, her body. Or maybe she would crack, in which case, killing her would be just as sweet.

He'd guessed it would take five, maybe even ten kills, before any of that happened. It seemed now he'd overestimated her. Just two kills, two low-level American staffers in Prague, and she was already beginning to cave in.

He thought about calling Constantin and finding out the details. He still needed Carmen Linder killed—it would take more than two murders to keep NATO's attention from the Ukraine situation—but his thoughts were interrupted by the sound of someone coming out of the dressing room. It was a girl in a persimmon orange bathing suit, her red hair tied back in a long braid just like he remembered, and a pair of yellow-rimmed plastic sunglasses on her face.

She removed the sunglasses and squinted in his direction. In the darkness behind the array of set lights, she couldn't see him.

"Come on," he bellowed into the bullhorn. "Out with you. No one's going to bite."

She walked slowly, tentatively, as if afraid she might step on glass, covering herself with her arms in the coldness of the warehouse.

"It's warmer on the set," Shipenko said. "Come on. Don't tarry."

She stepped up into the spotlights, and he got his first good look at her. She stood perfectly still, and the sight of her there, the light, the breeze of the fans, the ambient noise, the entirety of the effect hit him with its full force, and it took his breath away.

"Hello?" she said timidly into the darkness.

"Yes," he said. "Yes, yes. What age are you?"

"They told me there would be a film crew."

"The cameras are running," Shipenko said. "You're on."

"On?"

"Yes."

"Is this an audition. I was told—".

"This is it. This is the job. The thing with the photographer. That was the audition."

She said nothing—just stood there uncomfortably, perhaps trembling, her breath billowing a little in the cold.

"Put your arms down," he said.

She lowered her arms, revealing a pale, slender body, her nipples as visible as two grapes beneath the thin fabric of the bathing suit.

"What age are you?"

"Eighteen."

"I told them I wanted seventeen."

"I was seventeen when they took the photos."

He sighed. It wasn't an issue, he told himself. That had been about three weeks earlier. It was close enough. The casting agency wasn't exactly overrun with redheaded seventeen-year-olds. He was lucky to get this one. And what a fine specimen she was, he thought, wiping his mouth with the back of his sleeve.

"Can you play seventeen?" he said. He'd stopped using the bullhorn. She could hear him without it.

"Play seventeen?" she said.

"Imagine you're that age."

She nodded uncertainly.

"The girl I was with, the girl you're playing, she was seventeen."

"I can play seventeen," she said. She glanced around the space. There was very little she could see with the lights shining in her eyes. She looked in the direction of the changing room she'd come from.

"Looking for something?"

"Are we the only people here?"

"It's just you and me. More *intimate* that way. You'll be able to perform more freely."

She nodded again. Around his neck was a pair of binoculars that were an exact replica of the pair he'd had with him the day of the accident. He raised them to his eyes to get a better look at her. She was perfect, shivering from the cold and the fear, the goosebumps on her skin visible even from that distance. She was still glancing around, still looking for a way out, but she wouldn't run. He didn't think so, at least. And if she did, well, that would be the beginning of a whole new game for him. And a whole new nightmare for her.

"What is it that...." Her words trailed off.

"That I want you to do?" he said, relishing every second. "For now, maybe just move around a little. Walk up one of the dunes. Pretend you're walking on the beach."

She walked across the set, then turned around and walked back in the other direction.

"Pretend," he said, "that there's someone with you. Out of sight."

"Who?" she said.

"A little boy."

His phone vibrated again, but he ignored it, transfixed by the performance. Over the next few minutes, he directed her as he wanted, and she performed perfectly, acting like the nanny he remembered, chiding a little boy for running too far ahead, telling him to stay away from the water. He could feel the arousal building in him like the pressure of a river behind a dam.

"I want you to let one of the straps fall over your shoulder," he said.

"Excuse me?"

"Loosen the bikini. Let a strap fall loose."

She slid a finger under her strap and unhooked it from her shoulder. The whole thing seemed to loosen, bringing her breasts that little bit closer to spilling out.

"Good," he said, wiping his mouth again.

He eyed her through the binoculars as she climbed the sand dune. There was a look of grit on her face. A look of determination. Would she resist him, he wondered. Would she put up a fight? Looking at her now, her jaw clenched, her gaze fixed at some indiscernible spot in the distance, it was hard to imagine that she wouldn't. But then, women, as he was only too aware, could be very disappointing when it came to it. Take Valentina. She'd seemed so certain of herself, so strong, so sure of what she wanted. Now, two kills in, and she was unraveling. By the end of the week, she'd be in his bed, eating from his hands, supplicating herself to him, or she would be dead.

The phone vibrated again, and he wondered if something serious was happening. He was about to pull it from his pocket when the girl slipped. She'd been making her way down the dune, and she fell, face-first into the sand. She let out a cry, more of surprise than pain, but the sharp yelp brought a throb of longing to his groin.

"Get up," he said. "Come on."

She was still on the ground, her back to him, and it seemed like maybe she was crying.

"Turn around," he said.

She ignored him, but from her heaving shoulders, he knew she was crying. He picked up the bullhorn and turned it on. It whistled loudly with feedback, and the sound startled her.

"Get up," he snapped. "Come on. Turn around. Let me see those tears."

She turned around slowly.

"To your feet," he said. "Come on."

She rose up and stood looking at him. There was sand on her chest, her stomach.

"I think…" she said, too afraid to finish the sentence.

"I want the other strap from the bathing suit off," he said.

She didn't move. A thin smile crept across his face. This was his favorite part, the moment when she finally realized what it was that she'd let herself in for. The mind could only deny it for so long. Sooner or later, reality kicked in for everyone and obliterated all kinder thoughts to the contrary. "Do it," he bellowed, and the sound shocked her into compliance.

"I wasn't told…" she said, still crying.

"You took the money quick enough," he said. "Who did you think was paying that much for a few hours of your talents?" He laughed, and her eyes darted around the space once more. "You still haven't realized, have you? The doors are locked. No one's coming. And you're not leaving."

Again, the phone vibrated. "God damn it," he snapped in irritation, pulling the phone from his pocket. He was about to turn it off completely when he saw that it wasn't a system response this time but a call from Prague. "Constantin," he growled into the receiver, "this is a very bad time."

"I'm sorry, sir, but you need to hear this."

"What is it, then? Make it quick."

"It's Valentina. She's going off the script."

"I saw the notification. Give her a few more hours."

"She threw away her phone."

"You think she's going to run?"

"You know what I think."

"You've got eyes on her right now?"

"I'm watching her from a car, Stăn's in another, and we've got two drones in the air. She's in the square in front of St. Nicholas. She's looking for a taxi."

"No idea where she's headed?"

"Too soon to say."

"Call a spade a spade," Shipenko snapped, losing his patience. The girl in the bikini was growing increasingly uncomfortable. If he let her hear much more, he'd have to kill her when he was done. It would be a shame to waste such a talent.

"All right, sir. I think she's going to cut and run."

"That little cunt."

"The cell is assembled, sir. We're ready to strike."

"I was hoping to keep your guys under wraps a little longer."

"I can go after her alone," Constantin said. "It won't be quiet, but it will look like it was done by one guy."

"It will look like we don't have our house in order."

"Which could work to our advantage."

Shipenko sighed. Constantin didn't know the whole plan, but he did know that the point of Valentina's mission was to draw an American target out of the shadows. He got out of his seat and stepped toward the girl. It was a done deal now. He couldn't let her go. She'd heard too much of his conversation. "I don't know," he said.

"We can go after Carmen Linder as well," Constantin said.

The girl was backing away from him as he approached.

"Let's not get ahead of ourselves. Stay on Valentina. As soon as you know what she's up to, call me back."

"Yes, sir."

"And if it turns out she's trying to run, do what's necessary."

"Of course."

"But keep it tidy, as you said. Do it yourself."

"Yes, sir."

"And Constantin?"

"Sir?"

"Only kill her if you have to. I had some plans that will be frustrated if...."

"If she's dead?"

"Yes," he said, hanging up the phone. He stepped forward, and for the first time, he was in front of the powerful set lights. The girl was still backing away, and she stared at him like a deer in headlights. She didn't understand what she was looking at.

Shipenko had seen the reaction so many times he should have been bored of it, but he wasn't. Every time it was a thrill. The look on the girl's face, confused, struggling to figure out what she was seeing, making sense of the sluggish posture, the scaly skin. He kept walking toward her. A second passed, and another, and then the loud, shrill screaming of an eighteen-year-old girl in utter, abject terror.

23

L ance caught a cab from Heathrow back to the city. The address Pooja's sister had given him was in Tower Hamlets, and he got out on Hackney Road outside a grocer's store that advertised selling 'Everything and More'. Quite the claim, he thought as he entered the store.

"Can I help you?" the clerk said. He looked to be about fifty and had gray stubble and a Sikh turban.

"There's a flat in this building," Lance said.

"There are two upstairs," the man said slowly.

"Don't worry. I'm not an inspector."

"No, no, of course," the man said. "I didn't think you were."

"Just looking for the entrance. I didn't see one on the street."

"The entrance is at the side. By the alley."

"Thanks," Lance said and went back outside. He went to the side of the building and found a door with two buttons for buzzers marked 'A' and 'B'. He pressed the first, and there was no answer. Then he pressed the second and heard the click of someone picking up.

"Hello?" he said. There was no response. "You called for a minicab?"

It took a second, then the woman's voice answered. "I called for a specific driver."

"Clint," Lance said. She said nothing, and he said, "It's all right. I just want to make sure you're okay."

She buzzed him up, and the electrical lock retracted with a clank. He had to push the door hard to open it, then climbed a narrow staircase to the first floor, where a small landing led to two doors. There were boots and shoes on rubber mats. He rapped on the door marked 'B'. The door opened a few inches, still on a chain, and the woman he'd seen at the bar the night before looked out at him through the crack.

"I didn't think anyone would come," she said in her slightly raspy voice.

"I said I would."

"So you did," she said.

He nodded. "Well, here I am.

She looked like she'd been crying. "You're alone?" she said.

"Who would I bring?"

"I don't know," she said. "I don't know who *you* are."

"I'm the guy who came when you called," Lance said. "Why don't we leave it at that."

She hesitated a moment, then shut the door, uncaught the chain, and opened it again.

"Is he here?" Lance said, scanning the apartment behind her.

"Of course he's not here," she said, making room for him to enter.

Lance looked around. The place wasn't bad, nicer than it might have been, with a decent kitchen separated from the living area by a Formica counter and a balcony at the back overlooking the parking lot of a high-rise council block.

"Hi," Lance said to a girl of about thirteen or fourteen who was sitting on the sofa in the living room. She looked over for a second, acknowledged him with a slight nod of her head, then turned back to the TV. "Your daughter?" he said to the woman.

She nodded. "I guess you're wondering why I called."

He shook his head. "None of my business."

"Really?"

He shrugged. He'd seen enough to know what she wanted him for—a little moral support, a little backup—nothing that would cost him more than a few hours of his life. There was a dustpan on the floor, and he could see some broken glass in it. The woman saw him look at it.

"It's been a bit of a hectic morning," she said.

"Anyone get hurt?"

She shook her head. He looked over at the girl on the sofa, and the woman said, "No one got hurt."

"All right."

"Turn that down a bit, would you?" she said to the girl. "We've got company."

The girl turned the TV down very slightly, and the woman said, "No manners whatsoever."

"It's fine," Lance said.

She led him to the counter, and he sat on one of the stools. She went into the kitchen and began making tea.

"Got any coffee?" he said.

"Right," the woman said, nodding. "I forgot."

"Forgot what?"

"Americans."

He nodded.

She reached up to a cupboard and brought down a jar of Nescafé instant coffee. "One spoon enough?"

"Sure."

"Milk?"

"No milk."

She stirred his coffee for him and made herself a mug of thick black tea. "Sue? Tea?"

The girl didn't answer.

The woman sighed. Lance watched her closely. She was getting calmer. She came over and sat two stools away from him at the counter. "He'd throw an absolute fit if he came home and saw you here."

Lance nodded but said nothing. He knew how this went. He'd seen it enough times. The less he said, the less he advised, the better. There was an empty cereal bowl on the counter, a spoon next to it, and he put his finger on the tip of the spoon, raising the handle. Neither of them said anything for a minute. He looked around the kitchen. There was a forty-ounce bottle of cheap vodka by the stove, about two-thirds empty. Next to it in the sink were some dirty dishes.

The woman fidgeted with her hands, picking at the skin around her cuticles so hard Lance thought she might make them bleed. When she finally broke the silence, she said, "So, Clint, why don't you tell me what you're really doing here."

"I'm not doing anything," he said. "I'm a man without an agenda."

She let out a scoff. "Right, because there are so many of those around."

"Why did you call me?" he said.

"I don't know why I called you."

Lance sipped his coffee. It was vile stuff, distinctly British. He'd been to third-world countries without power or running water that would have balked at it. "Well," he said, "if that's true, then maybe I shouldn't be here." He got to his feet.

"No!" she said.

He sat back down.

She narrowed her eyes. "This is all just fun and games to you, isn't it?"

"It's not fun and games."

"You're here to see what you can get, same as the rest of them. Don't think I can't smell it off you."

He shrugged. "Well, if that's what you think, then you need to make up your mind. Either you roll the dice on me, see where it leads, or you tell me to get out."

"Simple as that?"

"Just say the word, and, swear to god, you'll never set eyes on me again."

She shook her head. "So sure of yourself, aren't you? So easy."

He said nothing. She looked at him very intently, then she said, "You never should have interfered last night."

He nodded. "You're right."

"You could get a woman killed, interfering like that. Butting in where you're not wanted."

"I know," he said. "You're right."

"You could have gotten me killed."

"I'm sorry."

"Or...." She looked toward her daughter.

"I'm sorry," Lance said again. "I know I shouldn't have interfered."

"But you did anyway."

He nodded, showed her his hands, nothing to hide.

"He could have...."

"Did he hurt you?"

"He could have done *anything*."

"Or your daughter?"

She let out a long sigh. Shook her head. "He was too shaken up. He didn't pick a fight. He threw some things around, broke some plates, but didn't pick a fight."

"I didn't think he would."

She looked at him skeptically. "You're an expert on my man, now?"

"I know men like him."

"Oh, you do? Mr. Psychologist."

"I know what a mean man looks like."

She was going to say something but stopped herself. She looked over at her daughter, then, lowering her voice, said, "It's not for myself that I called."

Lance followed her gaze to the girl, still watching TV on the sofa. "Is she his daughter?" he said.

The woman shook her head. "God, no. Her father died in Afghanistan. He was a soldier."

"I see."

"Kabul."

Lance nodded. "So you're worried...."

The woman nodded. "About her," she said.

"Has he ever—"

"He's never touched her," she said. "I'd know if he did."

"But you think...."

"I know him. I know what he's like. The way he looks at her. The way he speaks to her. It's only a matter of time."

Lance took another sip of the coffee. "Well then," he

said, "I recommend you lower your guard. Trust me. Let me help."

She shook her head in disbelief.

"I take it you've got some sort of plan," Lance said.

"Plan?"

"You didn't call me here just to talk."

"I already told you. I don't know why I called."

"You called because you need a way out."

She looked worried. She was picking at her fingernails again.

"It's all right," he said. "I'm going to make sure it's all right."

"Do you have any idea what that sounds like? You coming in here and saying a thing like that?"

"I know you're suspicious."

"You sound like a serial killer, driving around offering sweeties to kids."

"I'm not a serial killer."

"That's what you would say, isn't it?"

Lance shook his head. He was supposed to help this woman without telling her who he was or why he was there, but he could see now that wasn't going to work out.

It was then that the girl spoke up. "Come on, then," she said, challenging Lance. "What's your angle? Why are you here talking to her? Putting ideas in our heads? What are you hoping to get out of it?"

Lance didn't know what to tell them. "Maybe I should leave," he said.

"That's it?" the girl said. "Stir all this up, then walk away?"

Lance walked toward the door, and the girl said, "That's right, coward."

He stopped. Turned back. Looked at them. He could

tell they were scared. It wasn't that they didn't want his help. They did. They wanted to accept whatever it was he'd come to offer. They just needed him to give them a reason to trust him.

"Go on," the girl said.

"Go on?"

"You want to say something."

He looked from her to the mother, then said, "I was sent here."

"By who?" the woman said.

"You really don't want to know."

"We *really* do," the girl said.

"Someone," he said, "who is grateful to your...."

The woman's eyes widened then. The penny had finally dropped. "Craig!" she said softly.

"I didn't know him," Lance said. "Never met him."

The woman was shaking her head, as if her mind couldn't take in the meaning of what he was telling them. "The government..."

"Let's just say someone feels they owe him a debt of gratitude. I don't know why. I don't know what he did. All I know is they sent me."

"To look out for us?" the girl said, looking at her mother rather than Lance for an answer.

She couldn't answer, though. There were too many tears in her eyes. All she could do was shake her head. Lance stood there and let the information sink in for a minute before saying to the woman, "I take it you have some sort of plan?"

She looked at him then, as if seeing him for the first time, then said, "Yes, yes. I have a sister."

"Where?"

"Bristol. It's an hour or two away."

"I know it. Is she expecting you?"

"She's told me before that if I ever needed her...."

"She has a house?"

"A flat?"

"A man?"

The woman shook her head.

"Call her," Lance said. "Tell her you're coming."

The woman looked at her tea. Her phone was already on the counter, but she made no move for it. Instead, she said, "If I do this, if I start, I have to go through with it."

"That's right," Lance said.

"Because once he knows what I'm thinking...."

Lance nodded. "It gets harder."

"You're going to help me get to my sister's?"

"I'm going to call you a cab."

"That's it?"

Lance shrugged. "You want me to escort you there?"

"I want to know that nothing bad's going to happen."

"Nothing bad's going to happen."

"That's easy for you to say."

"You're going to go to your sister's. I'm going to wait here for your man to come home, and when he gets here, I'm going to explain things to him."

"And you think he'll listen?"

"He'll listen."

She nodded.

"Call your sister then," Lance said. "She needs to know you're coming."

The woman left the kitchen and went down the corridor to her bedroom. Lance could hear her talking but couldn't make out the words. The girl was still staring at him. She looked like she wanted to say something.

"What is it?" he said.

"Did you really not know him?"

Lance nodded. "I really didn't."

The girl sighed. "Do you think she'll go through with it this time?"

"She's tried before?"

"She's tried, but we always come back."

"Do you think she'll go through with it?" he said.

"Maybe. If no one comes after us."

"No one will come after you," Lance said.

The mother came out of the bedroom, and from the look on her face, it seemed the call hadn't gone too badly. "You ready to do this then?" he said. "You ready to leave everything here behind? Go to your sister's and stay there?"

"Yes."

"You're sure? Because like you said, once you start, you have to go all the way."

The woman looked at her daughter and said, "There's nothing here we care about. This is his flat. We're not married. If he leaves us alone, we'll make a go of it in Bristol."

"He'll leave you alone," Lance said. "I'll see to that."

"You won't hurt him," the woman said.

"Would you care if I did?"

"Of course I'd care."

"I'll only hurt him if I have to."

"You're sure?"

"Leave it to me. You go pack. I'll call the cab."

"I don't know if I can afford the cab."

"I'll take care of it," Lance said, reaching into his pocket. He counted out some bills and said, "This will help you get settled."

"I can't take that."

"Sure you can. It's not like it's mine."

She stuffed the money into her purse, then said, "Sue, come on. Let's get packed."

Lance watched them go down the hallway to their respective bedrooms, then picked up his phone and called Pooja's minicab company. "It's me. Clint," he said.

"Clint *Eastwood*," the girl said.

"Listen, I need a car," he said. "To Bristol."

"Bristol's way outside our range."

"What does that mean?"

"You'll have to pay the fare both ways."

"Fine."

"It will be thirty minutes."

Lance looked at his watch. "Tell him to make it fifteen, and I'll tip an extra fifty." He hung up and then waited a few minutes while the ladies packed. He finished his coffee, which only grew less appetizing as it got colder, then went down the hall.

"Just about done," the woman said.

Sue came into the corridor with an old-style suitcase, small enough that she could carry it in one hand. The mother hadn't managed to pack so lightly and had two much larger cases on wheels. "Will you be here when he gets home?" she said to Lance.

"I'll be here."

"You'll make sure he doesn't come after us."

"He'll get the message."

She nodded, and he helped them get the bags down to the street. Then they waited in front of the grocer's for the cab. As the minutes ticked by, the woman got increasingly nervous. "He's going to be home any minute," she said. "He's going to see us standing here with you, and he's going to blow a fuse."

"It will be all right," Lance said, looking up and down the street.

It was another five minutes before the cab finally arrived. It pulled up next to them, and the driver got out and loaded the bags.

"How much do I owe you?" Lance said as the woman and daughter got into the car.

"It will be five or six hours roundtrip," he said.

"To Bristol?"

"Easily. Look at the traffic."

Lance counted out six bills and handed them to him. "This should cover it," he said. The driver took the money, and Lance went to the woman's window. "Everything all right then?" he said. "You got everything?"

"If we forgot anything, we won't be coming back for it."

"Good," he said, then to the girl, "you okay?"

"We'll have to wait and see, won't we?" she said.

Lance smiled. He tapped the roof of the cab twice, and the driver pulled away. Lance watched until they were out of view. "God speed," he said to himself.

24

Constantin watched as Valentina climbed into the back seat of a cab, then followed her south through Malá Strana. "Crossing the Legion Bridge," he said into his radio as they crossed toward Národní. The traffic got heavier near the national museum, and he had no difficulty keeping up. "Passing the Wenceslas statue," he reported.

"I'm guessing she's on her way back to the train station," Boc said. He and Badea were watching from two separate drones.

"Agreed," Constantin said. The station was still a few blocks away, and there was definitely some sort of delay ahead. A set of traffic lights was out, and a policeman was directing traffic manually. "Stăn, you park and go ahead on foot. You'll be at the station before we are."

"You thinking an international service?" Stăn said.

"We saw how eager she was to get out of town this morning. Get yourself an express ticket for anywhere out of the country. That will get you onto the international platform. If she gets on a train, you'll have to go after her alone."

"Understood," Stăn said.

Valentina was a dangerous target, there was no getting around that, but Stăn would be able to handle her on a train. They knew she was unarmed--they'd watched her ditch her weapons earlier. Her guard was down. There was no way she'd expect Shipenko to have someone waiting for her on a train she'd only bought the ticket for a few moments before. "Keep it simple," Constantin said. "Make sure she doesn't see you coming. Put a bullet in her gut. That's all you need to do. No fancy business."

"I won't be looking to make up points for style," Stăn said. "Not on this job."

Constantin thought about calling it in to Shipenko, giving him a chance to countermand his order. He'd mentioned having unfinished business with her and, judging by her appearance, Constantin could well imagine what that business might be. He wouldn't have minded having some of his own with her, for that matter.

"If you get on a train," he said into the radio, "let me reconfirm the order with Shipenko before you do anything. He only wants us to kill her if we have to."

"Fine by me," Stăn said.

A man crossed the street, and Constantin glanced at him, then did a double-take. A shiver ran down his spine. The resemblance was uncanny. The man looked exactly like his father. "Fuck me," he muttered.

"What was that, boss?" Stăn said.

"Nothing," he said, shaking his head. It was stupid. But then, he wondered, was it? The man was exactly the age his father would be, and he was wearing the same ridiculous trilby hat his father made a habit of. He looked exactly the way he remembered him, and he knew his father had been in Prague at one point. That was why he'd been thinking about him. He knew he might still be there, in that city, alive, and that there was a chance of running into him. Not that he wanted to. His father was nothing but a bad memory to him, and if the man who'd just crossed the street was indeed him, then that was nothing but an ill omen for their job.

"Everyone good?" he said into the radio, suddenly feeling like all wasn't going to go as smoothly as expected.

"All good," Stăn said.

"Good on our end," Boc said on behalf of himself and Badea.

Every time Constantin thought of his father, it made him faintly sick. He couldn't believe that such misfortune had struck the same family, the same bloodline, not once but twice. First his grandfather. Then his father. What did that bode for him? What was lurking in his path, coiled like a snake, waiting to strike?

When Constantin was young, Pitești was embroiled in a scandal that gripped the attention of the entire nation and forced the communist regime in Bucharest to look at the true nature of the people's revolution in ways no one wanted to. It was a shock to a country that had seen such misery, such depravity at the hands of state officials, that shock was not something anyone thought still possible. But it was, and right at the center of it, just like in the inquiry into the Călărași Express, was another antecedent of Constantin—his father.

Constantin's father had not gone into the train company but instead worked for the State Prison Service. He was hired straight from high school. In those days of a centrally planned economy, it was not unusual for an entire graduating class to be recruited by a single state enterprise, and so it was in this case. Seventeen boys were taken into the Prison Service from that one class, all to work as guards at an important correctional facility located in the city.

They arrived together, trained together, were indoctrinated together, and made to sign a confidentiality agreement that held a maximum sentence of seventy-five years imprisonment if it was ever breached. What they learned during their training was that the majority of the inmates were boys just like them, and they weren't criminals at all, at least not in the ordinary sense. They were political prisoners—young men who'd spoken out against the one-party, Marxist-Leninist state that was known officially as the Republica Socialistă România. Tens of thousands of them were eventually to perish at the hands of that state, and it was at Pitești Prison that the worst of the oppression took place.

The program, or *reeducation experiment* as it was more accurately called, was designed to rid the inmates not just of their political beliefs but of their entire personalities, their memories, their familial and religious loyalties, their very souls. Romania, after the war, subscribed to a theory of state atheism, and members of countless *undesirable* groups—Jews, Catholics, anti-communists, gypsies—were rounded up and put through a program of *reeducation* designed to make them absolutely loyal to the regime of Nicolae Ceaușescu.

This was to be done not by instilling in them a new faith in the regime but rather by seeking to remove their ability to believe in anything at all. It was a pseudoscientific theory, fully fleshed out in academic and scientific journals funded by the government. The premise was purely sadistic. Rather than force the men to recant their beliefs or face execution, they were subjected to a program of torture and humiliation that had no goal other than to erase them as individuals. Once that was achieved, it was argued, their support or opposition to the regime became moot. It no longer mattered.

What emerged was a program universally acknowledged, by international organizations, humanitarian organizations, and the Romanian government itself, as a black mark in the annals of political history. Methods of brainwashing, starvation, physical and psychological torture, humiliation, and sensory deprivation were developed that led to complete mental collapse in the subjects. The men simply lost their minds. Whether that proved the scientific theories or not, and whether it was useful for the government to do it, was never debated. The program was maintained as a weapon of terror. It was argued that its very existence, just by the rumors it gave rise to, would silence dissent.

More than two thousand inmates were processed while Constantin's father worked at Pitești Prison, and he admitted in court to doing things that he could not, no matter how hard he tried, ever purge from his memory. Sometimes, in the middle of the day, when he was sure no one was watching, he would break down and cry, fall to his knees, pounding his fists into the ground for the things he had done.

He and his colleagues tortured men to a point that almost defied imagination, forcing them to do things that were without precedent in the history of man's depravity to man. In Room 4 of the prison infirmary, he and his fellow guards hung weights of forty kilos from the backs of the inmates and made them bear it for five or six hours.

They brought in hundred-watt light bulbs and lit them in front of the men's eyes, forcing them to stare at them until their retinas burned. They pulled out their hair, crushed their fingers and toes, dripped cold water on their heads or faces for up to twenty hours at a time. They induced complete psychotic breaks. They made men fight like rams, knocking their heads together until they lost consciousness. They made them eat over-salted food, or extremely hot food, on the floor like animals. Priests were baptized in excrement, rabbis were castrated with rusted scissors, intellectuals were submerged in raw sewage until they were within an inch of drowning. Men were prevented from washing and sleeping for weeks at a time. They were forced to stand facing a wall for days. They were made to bear the weight of fifteen other inmates standing on them.

And when it was done, they were forced to denounce their families and loved ones and know that the same tortures would be visited on them.

The atrocities eventually came to light. The regime changed, and the new government wanted to scapegoat the old. Trials were held. Dozens of inmates, who'd been forced to take part in the torture, were sentenced to death. They were sent to Jilava Prison, located in a fortress near the capital, and shot.

But no guards, and certainly no administrators or politicians, ever faced punishment. The guards were forced to endure the trial. They were humiliated. But they all walked free. That wasn't to say they didn't pay a price. Some things couldn't be forgotten, couldn't be left behind. Terror, horror, had a habit of spilling over from the intended victim to the perpetrator. Constantin's father drank to numb the voices in his head. He took it out on his wife, on his son. Eventually, he left the country. Constantin didn't know if he was still alive, but he had traced him as far as Prague, where the trail went cold. There was a chance he was still there.

"There's a subway station coming up on the left," Boc said.

"Damn it," Constantin said. "If I have to leave my vehicle, Stăn come back for it."

"Aye, aye," Stăn said.

"Let's hope it doesn't come to that," Constantin said. "Boc, pull up a subway map just in case. I want to be ready."

With two of them on the streets and two drones in the air, they could pretty much tail Valentina through anything. Subways were the weak spot, though. And Valentina would know it. If she suspected for a second that she was being followed, that was the first place she'd run.

"Hold positions," Constantin said. "The train station's still the most likely destination."

He drummed his fingers on the steering wheel nervously. Undid his seatbelt. Checked his pistol.

He'd caught his father crying once. It was in the patch of yellow grass behind their apartment block where the women hung laundry. It was late at night. He was coming down the stairwell and saw him from a window. His father was on his knees, his back to the building, but the moment Constantin stopped, he turned, as if he sensed him, and looked right at him. The two of them stared at each other for about ten seconds. Constantin couldn't have been more than fifteen years old. Slowly, his father rose to his feet, then chased Constantin down. The boy ran up the stairs toward the apartment, but his mother locked the door. He was trapped in the hallway. His father came out of the stairwell breathless, panting. He looked much older than he was. He looked frail, like he couldn't hurt a fly, but he rounded on his son with the ferocity of a rabid dog, uncontrolled, unrestrained, and beat him so mercilessly Constantin lost consciousness. He then spent thirteen days in the intensive care unit of Pitești Hospital Number Three.

When he got out, his father was gone. The two had never spoken about the part his father played in what had by that time become known as *the experiment*. Constantin never asked him what he'd known, what he'd witnessed with his own eyes, what he'd taken part in. When he read the trial transcripts, the descriptions made his stomach turn. Names had been redacted, but all the details that had never been made public were there. And they were shocking. Men had been forced to do things that should not rightly ever have occurred under the sun. There were accounts worse than anything Constantin had ever found in literature or in film. The truth was worse than fiction. And he never knew exactly what part in it his father had played, which rooms he'd been in during certain accounts, which tortures had been administered by his hand.

He didn't know if he'd enjoyed any of it. He didn't know if there'd been a part of his father that had savored the metallic, mineral taste of another man's blood.

"Oh, shit," Badea said through the radio. "Her door's opening. She's going for the subway."

25

Lance went back up to the apartment and sat down on the easy chair by the TV. He turned the chair so it faced the door, then leaned back and put his feet up. He lit a cigarette, looked at his watch. He would miss the afternoon flight to Prague, so he called the airline to rebook for a second time. There was an evening flight that they agreed to put him on. Then he got up and went to the window. No sign of the man.

He boiled water and made more of the instant coffee the woman had served him earlier, then brought it back to the window. Someone was walking down the street. As he got closer, Lance saw it was the man he was waiting for.

He went back to the seat, put his feet up again on the coffee table, and lit another cigarette. When the door opened, the man didn't immediately realize he was there. "What's for lunch?" he called, taking off his coat. "And what the hell did I say about smoking inside?" It was only when he went to hang the coat on the hook by the door that Lance spoke up.

"I don't know," he said. "What did you say?"

The man looked, and his eyes almost popped out of his head. He dropped the coat and was about to reach for the inside pocket of his blazer.

"I wouldn't do that," Lance said.

The man glanced around the room furtively, panic in his eyes.

"Who are you looking for? There's no one here."

"Where's Isabelle?"

"Isabelle?"

"And Suzie?"

"Don't worry about them."

"What have you done with them?"

"I haven't done anything with them."

The man looked back at the door.

"You try to run, I'll shoot you where you stand," Lance said.

Lance wasn't holding a gun. The man looked him over, trying to assess whether or not he had one, assessing his chances if it came to a fight. "What is this?" he said. "What's going on?"

"You remember me from last night, don't you?"

"Of course I remember you. You broke my nose, you son of a—"

"Hopefully, we don't have to do anything like that today," Lance said. "I really don't want to get blood all over these nice carpets." The man had his back to the door, and Lance beckoned him to come closer. "I'm not going to bite you."

"What the hell is this?" the man said again. "Where's my woman? Where's the girl?"

"She's not your woman," Lance said.

"The hell she isn't."

"That's what I'm here to explain."

"Oh no," the man said, shaking his head. "You don't think that just because you got the better of me last night, you can waltz in here and take her for yourself."

"I'm not taking her for myself."

"Then what the hell are you doing?"

"You might not think it to look at her," Lance said, "but your girlfriend has some very powerful friends."

The man scoffed. "Yeah, right."

"It's true," Lance said. "You can take my word for it, or you can ignore what I tell you today and pay the price later."

"Is that supposed to be some sort of threat?"

"I'm not threatening you," Lance said. "I'm just saying, you need to listen to me very carefully, or you're going to be six feet underground."

The man laughed again, but he was worried. It was clear from his face. "That sounds like a threat," he said.

Lance shrugged. "You're right. Now that I say it aloud, it kind of does."

The man looked closely at Lance, again trying to assess how he'd fare in a fight. "You don't even have a gun, do you?" he said.

Lance smiled. He still had the cigarette in his hand, and he sucked the last of it and flicked it across the room. "You want to make a move, big guy? You feeling lucky?"

"You expect me to just accept that she's gone? Disappeared? Like a puff of smoke?"

"I didn't sit here for the last half hour because I like the view," Lance said. "That's exactly what I expect you to accept. And I'm telling you right now, you go within ten miles of that woman again, you so much as send her a text message, or drive your car by her house, and someone's going to come for you."

"Her house? What house?"

"If you were to go looking for her, you'd find her," Lance said. "What I'm saying is, don't do it. Don't look for her. And don't go near her. Leave her alone. Forget you knew her. Forget all of it."

"I can't forget something like that."

"Then me, or someone very like me, is going to kill you."

The man couldn't believe what Lance was saying to him. He literally couldn't believe his ears. He'd been living his life, going about his business, and now, out of nowhere, this was happening. Lance knew it would take a little time for the information to settle in, but in the end, he felt this guy would have the good sense to act in his own best interest.

"Believe me," Lance said. "You don't want to be on the wrong side of the men who sent me."

"The men who sent you? What men?"

Lance stood, and the man visibly flinched. He was a big guy, but he knew instinctively that this wasn't the time to act tough.

"The men who sent me," Lance said, "were in Afghanistan when Craig Ritter died."

"Craig?"

"Surely you asked about him."

"I knew he was a soldier," the man said. "I knew he died in Afghanistan."

"He was with the Special Reconnaissance Regiment. They were on an operation in Helmand Province to detain some Taliban in the Sangin Valley. Some big guys."

"What's any of that got to do with me?"

"It's got everything to do with you. It's the reason your nose was broken last night. It's the reason you're standing there now talking to me rather than eating your lunch."

The man shook his head. He didn't know exactly what kind of situation he'd gotten himself into, but he knew he had no way out of it. "I don't see what you expect—"

"Right," Lance said.

The man said nothing, but he was hearing what Lance was saying.

"Don't test this," Lance said. "They owe Ritter a debt, and they're not the kind of guys to leave a debt unpaid."

The man still hadn't made up his mind what to think, and Lance thought it was best to leave before he had time to come to the wrong conclusion. "So we're clear?" he said. "No calls. No visits. Just forget you ever knew her."

The man said nothing for a moment, then muttered something inaudible under his breath.

"What's that?" Lance said. "I didn't catch it."

"Nothing," the man said.

"It was something."

"We're clear," the man said. "I won't go after her."

26

Constantin and his crew were the killers of killers. They took out the Kremlin's trash. It was a dangerous job and not one they had completely taken on by choice. The job had found them, so to speak, and once it had, it wasn't an easy one to get out of.

They'd known each other since boyhood and went to prison together on a charge of grand larceny when they were still in high school. It was the same prison Constantin's father had worked in, though the man was no longer there, of course. The atrocities of those years were also a thing of the past.

But it was still a cruel place, and it was there that they learned how to kill. Constantin did it first—it was self-defense—but he told the others it wasn't difficult. It was like nothing at all, he said, like wringing a chicken's neck. His hands didn't shake afterward. He didn't taste bile. He did what he had to, and before long, he was doing it even when he didn't have to. He was doing it to get ahead, doing it for others, trading it the way other men traded packets of cigarettes and bags of fermented pruno. He could kill a man, do it with his bare hands or with a shiv, and as long as he wasn't caught, he could sleep like a baby afterward.

The reason he could do it was because of what he learned in the prison, where a full archive had been preserved of both the Pitești Prison trials, and the Iași Pogrom inquiry. Reading those old government reports, he learned that killing was a part of him. It was a curse carried down from grandfather to father to son. It was in his blood, in his DNA.

Boc, Badea, and Stănescu were the same age as Constantin, from the same background, and had grown up in the same city. They'd gone to school together. All of them were the sons of Pitești prison guards, and, most importantly, all found that they had that same ability to keep their cool in the face of bloodshed. None of them was a monster. They didn't relish the violence. They were professionals. They did it because it was a job, their job, and it paid. Their clients valued them for their discretion, their ability to pull off a job without leaving a trail, and, most of all, their willingness to go after dangerous targets.

In the years after they got out of prison—the years leading up to Romania's accession to NATO and the European Union—there was easy money to be made in the capital. The country, which for years had been in the iron grip of an absolute dictator, suddenly became a free-for-all. Fortunes were made, dynasties raised and toppled, and in every corner of the pervasive kleptocracy, politically motivated killings skyrocketed.

Constantin's cell, known among those who purchased its services only as the Splinter, terrorized the Bucharest elite. It got its name after a serial killer from the city of

Craiova in the southwest of the country. The original Splinter was credited with thirty-two kills, and he was never caught. And the thing that made him so terrifying was that he seemed to go after anyone. He'd killed a three-year-old girl, a bus driver, a high court judge, and the mayor of the city. And so it was with Constantin's cell. No one was safe, not even their own clients. If your name came up, if the fee was paid, you died. It was a certainty, a relationship of true cause and effect. There were no exceptions.

No one knew who the cell's members were. No one knew if they had enemies of their own, or an agenda of their own. But what they did know, almost as if they'd learned it by osmosis, was how to hire them. Everyone in the elite, the nation's political and business leaders, its richest and most powerful people, knew how it worked. The system was as simple as it was notorious. It terrorized the terrorizers. And the reason it did so was because everyone knew when a hit had been ordered, but that was all they knew. Someone was going to die. Maybe them. Maybe not.

As soon as he got out of prison, Constantin bought an encryption algorithm. It was nothing special, an off-the-shelf hashing algorithm that any number of security companies could have provided. He purchased his anonymously and then set up a form on the dark web where anyone could enter a message and get back a two-hundred-fifty-six character string of apparently random gibberish, divided into three parts by periods.

Everyone in Bucharest knew that if you wanted someone killed, all you had to do was hash a message on the form, transfer a hundred thousand dollars to a numbered, untraceable Swiss bank account, and then have the hashed character string published in the personal advertisement section of the *Jurnalul Național* newspaper. It was an open secret that the cryptic ads were kill instructions, and the newspaper itself had attempted to stop printing them. They reversed course when a letter was hand-delivered to the editor's home explaining what would happen if he made trouble.

The entire capital, therefore, knew when a new kill order had been placed. But only Constantin and his crew could decrypt it and read what it said. In ninety-nine percent of jobs, the four men worked together, scoping the target and carefully planning the strike. They were meticulous, careful, avoided unnecessary risks, and always completed the job.

The arrangement worked. They made money. They stayed alive. Some started families. All had plans for the future. They had a walkaway number, an amount of money each man felt he needed before he could turn his back on the work for good and live out his life in peace.

And then Shipenko came into their lives. Constantin would always remember the exact moment. He had been sipping coffee in the Hotel Capitol on Victory Avenue, relaxing, happy, when he flipped open the classifieds and saw there was a message. He notified Stăn who would decrypt it, and not thirty seconds later, his phone started to ring.

"Stăn. What is it?"

"You're not going to like this, boss."

"Like what?"

"I decrypted the job from today's paper."

"And? What is it? A hard target?"

"You could say that."

"What's going on, Stăn? I have a very lovely, very

expensive young lady coming down from my hotel room in a few minutes, and I'd rather not be stuck on the phone with you when she does."

"It says the target is Constantin Antonescu."

Constantin was caught off guard. He'd just taken a sip of coffee and had to cough when it went down the wrong way.

"Are you all right, boss?"

"What sort of bullshit is this?"

"I have no idea."

"What did it say?"

"Nothing. Just your name and a confirmation code from the bank."

"We received payment?"

"Yes, we did. I checked the account."

"Someone just paid a hundred thousand dollars to have me killed?"

"It looks that way."

Constantin hung up the phone. He looked at the print on the newspaper, the random characters, and for the first time, felt the fear that Bucharest's elite had been feeling for years. The only difference was that while they feared someone might have paid to have them killed, he knew someone had.

The question was, who?

He wasn't going to run. He'd seen that happen too often. There'd been times, when tensions were particularly high in the capital, and the people involved took to fleeing the city every time they saw a message in the classifieds. It never did any good. There was no hiding. The only defense was attack. You had to find out who wanted you dead, and you had to get to them before they got to you.

The girl he'd been waiting for, a thousand-dollar-a-night hooker who'd told him her name was Leonida, entered the café. She looked stunning in a tan cashmere blazer and extremely short skirt. Every man in the room noticed her. She sat down across from Constantin and began elegantly unfolding her cloth napkin.

"You need to go back up to the room," Constantin said coldly.

She was surprised. She'd just come from there. They'd been in there since the night before, and if anyone had ever earned a decent breakfast, it was her.

"Tell me what you want," he said. "I'll have them send it up."

"What? Why?"

"Don't ask questions," he said, then beckoned a waiter. "Go on," he said to Leonida. "Order what you want." Then to the waiter, "She'll be eating in our room. It's the suite."

"Very good, sir," the waiter said.

The girl wasn't happy. She'd been looking forward to sitting in the café and being seen in her fancy outfit. Constantin had been looking forward to it too. He waited for her to order, then waved her off to the elevators. "Go on, I'll be up soon, and don't pout. It makes you look like a fish."

The girl left reluctantly. Constantin watched her go, then picked up his phone. The first call he made was to his bank in Switzerland. They confirmed the payment and told him there was no way of tracing it, which was what he'd expected to hear. Next, he called the company he'd purchased the algorithm from. They said it was one-way anonymous. Anyone with an internet connection could create a message. There was no way of knowing who. It was also what he'd expected to hear. The third call he made was to Stăn. He told him to pay a visit to the Casa Presei Libere, where the offices of the newspaper's advertising department were located, and find out what record they kept, if any, regarding the placement of advertisements. He didn't expect it to lead to anything, but he had to cover the bases.

He left the hotel without bothering to tell the girl, she'd figure it out for herself soon enough, and took a cab to his office on the Piața Constituției, directly facing the Romanian Palace of Parliament. Constantin was a believer in hiding in plain sight. His office occupied some of the most expensive real estate in the city, within view of the seat of government. When he arrived, Boc and Badea were already there, sitting at the sleek glass conference table sipping espressos.

"I take it you've heard?" Constantin said, lighting a cigarette and taking his seat. The table was round, and for no reason in particular, each man always sat in the same seat.

"Stăn told us," Boc said. "He'll be here in a few minutes."

"I think we wait for him," Constantin said.

Boc went to the coffee machine and made a shot for Constantin, putting sugar in it the way he liked. He put it on the table in front of him and gave his shoulder a squeeze in support. Constantin nodded but said nothing. The office was well-appointed, very luxurious. The building housed law firms, financial brokers, but mostly lobbyists. Secrecy and security were well provided for, and the cell had been operating out of the space for years, taking advantage of the air of legitimacy its location afforded. All four men played the part of legitimate occupants, dressing in expensive business suits, living in fancy apartments, driving expensive cars. It was the perfect cover.

When Stăn arrived, his shirt sleeves were rolled up, and he was carrying a briefcase. He placed the briefcase on the table and clicked it open.

"What happened?" Constantin said.

"I found out who placed the ad."

"You didn't make a scene?"

"I didn't have to. The ad wasn't placed anonymously."

"What do you mean?"

"The newspaper keeps a record of advertisers. By law, they're required to make it public. All I had to do was ask to see it."

"But people can put anything there. They can write Mickey Mouse or Elvis Presley in the form." Constantin was familiar with the rules. No one ever used their real name when placing one of his messages.

Stăn pulled a sheet of paper from the briefcase and slid it across the table to Constantin. Constantin's face went white when he saw what it said.

"Advertisement placed by the office of the Prime Intelligence Directorate of the General Staff of the Armed Forces of the Russian Federation."

It was followed by the address of the public relations department of the GRU headquarters in Moscow, and a phone number, including a five-digit extension code.

"What does this mean?" Stăn said. "Why would they leave a calling card like this?"

"Because it's a joke," Badea said.

"Or they don't care that we know," Boc said.

"It means," Constantin said, pulling his phone from his pocket, "that someone wants to talk."

Stăn looked at each man in turn before saying, "You're going to call them?"

"I think so," Constantin said.

"The GRU?"

"You don't ignore a summons from the Kremlin," Constantin said. "Not if you want to stay alive."

"I think we need to talk about this," Stăn said. "We know nothing of the Kremlin."

"We know enough," Constantin said. "What's there to talk about? My name's on the message."

"It might be your name," Stăn said, "but it's all our necks if something goes wrong."

"I don't know when this group became a democracy," Constantin said. "I must have missed the memo."

"Constantin," Stăn said, "this is big. Someone knows who you are."

"Someone knows who all of us are," Constantin said. He got up from the table and went to the window. Seven floors below them was the Unirii Boulevard, where the dictator in Communist times had held the most extravagant military parades in the nation's history. The processional route stretched right below them, from the enormous Bucharest Fountains all the way to the palace. He looked across the semicircular park at the enormous palace. It was one of the largest buildings on the planet. He'd heard it contained more rock than the Great Pyramid of Giza. It weighed so much, over four million tons, that the entire thing had been sinking at a rate of a quarter of an inch per year since its completion. It had been commissioned by Nicolae Ceaușescu after a visit to

North Korea. He'd seen there that the people were being induced to worship their dictator, Kim Il-Sung, as a god. He had the idea he might persuade the Romanians to do the same to him.

"I need to call them," Constantin said. "Whoever this is from, they want to talk."

He picked up the phone and dialed the number on the sheet before anyone objected further. Some sort of operator, speaking Russian, answered.

"I don't understand," Constantin said to her in English. "Who am I speaking to?"

"This is the operator of the Prime Directorate. How did you get this number?"

"Someone contacted me," Constantin said. "They left an extension." He gave her the extension number, and she put him on hold. The anthem of the Russian Federation chimed out in dial tones. It was a surreal moment, then a strange male voice came on the line. "Constantin Antonescu," it said. There was something wrong with the voice, like the speaker's vocal cords had been damaged in a fire or something.

"Who is this?" Constantin said.

"You don't need to know who I am," the man said. "But I have a job for you."

That had been many years ago, and the Splinter had been working for Shipenko ever since. And he kept them busy. It turned out he was a very vindictive man, even by the extraordinarily vindictive standards of the GRU. He seemed to have taken it upon himself to keep Molotov's house clean. He took out the president's trash. He instigated and carried out the frequent purges ordered by the Kremlin. And that was why he needed a foreign crew, outsiders, a group of killers who would have no loyalty to anyone in the Russian apparatus other than him. He made it worth their while. He paid handsomely for the work he required. And Constantin and his men, for their part, did everything in their power to keep him happy. They knew what would happen if they didn't.

That was all in the past. What was in the present was this mission with Valentina Brik, and it had started normally enough. Two days earlier, Constantin had gone to his secure mailbox at the Patria Bank branch located in Bucharest's old Jewish quarter. The Jews were gone now, of course, almost to the last man—there had been one-hundred-fifty thousand of them at one time—but their buildings remained. Empty synagogues and temples and graveyards. Echoes. Constantin wouldn't have chosen the location, but it was how Shipenko wanted it.

Shipenko liked to do things the old-fashioned way. He kept things simple. He had no interest in using newspaper classifieds and hashing algorithms to send his instructions. He'd heard of Chinese and American quantum computers that could decrypt anything, and instead sent his messages to Constantin using the same techniques the Russian ambassador had used during the Cold War. A runner from the Russian embassy in Bucharest would hand-deliver a note to Constantin's mailbox at the bank.

Constantin, as he always did, waited outside the vault of the bank for the customer ahead of him to finish. There was a flag outside the chamber. If it was up, someone was inside. A man in a black suit came out and marked it as unoccupied by removing the flag.

"I'll take that," Constantin said.

Constantin put the flag back in its sconce and passed through the velvet privacy curtain that concealed the mailboxes. It was a simple system for guaranteeing privacy, and that was why Shipenko liked it. No one, not even the bank employees, knew which box he was accessing or whether he was putting something in or taking something out. And, simple though it was, there was no computer on earth capable of outsmarting the thick curtain that shielded him from view.

Constantin opened his box and found a typed card of the kind formerly used in Romanian government offices. So many of the typewriters had been used that they were still readily available from antique dealers throughout the city, completely untraceable.

He opened the envelope and read the card.

Identifier: KO_457826
    Agency: Prime Directorate
    Lead Agent: Osip Shipenko
    Assassin: The Splinter
    Target: Lance Spector
    Target Position: CIA Special Operations Group
    Order: Follow GRU Assassin Valentina Brik.
Target will come after her.
    Prime Directorate Kill Order

And, knowing nothing more than that, Constantin and his crew had boarded a flight from Bucharest to Prague. They'd landed a few hours earlier and had been tailing Valentina since.

This wasn't the first time they'd been ordered to tail one of Shipenko's own assets, but, as far as Constantin was aware, it was the first time Shipenko had used one as actual bait for a higher value target. Shipenko had given him access to Valentina's personnel file before he left, and Constantin was in no doubt as to the risk involved in this mission. He never took for granted that any job wouldn't be his last, but that applied doubly here. He knew what Valentina was capable of. He knew she was dangerous. And she was just one of the sharks in the water—the one he could see. If Shipenko's plan worked out, there would be another one in the water soon. One he couldn't see. And that was a problem.

27

Valentina felt a sudden shiver run down her spine, a strange premonition, like she'd just crossed paths with a ghost, but when she turned around, there was only an old man in a trilby hat crossing behind her car. She glanced around the street but saw nothing out of the ordinary. There were people dashing about in the slow traffic, making their way between the cars and cabs that were pulling up outside the subway station. Women walked tentatively in the slush, trying to keep their shoes from being ruined. A streetcar stopped, and a load of passengers got off and hurried into the station. Valentina decided then to change plans. She handed some cash to the driver and opened the door of the cab. A moment later, she was out in the street among the crowd of commuters, letting herself be swept into the metro station toward the escalators.

When she reached the turnstile, she hopped it and kept going. Above the escalator was a sheet metal wall that acted like a mirror, and she watched the reflection in it like a hawk as she descended. If anyone hopped the turnstile behind her, she'd see.

And then she did see. She couldn't make out the details, but a figure in a black jacket definitely hopped the gate. She began making her way down the escalator more quickly, squeezing between the people in front of her to get past. She could see in the steel wall that the man behind her was doing the same, though making less effort to be discreet. She made the mistake of looking over her shoulder, and they instantly locked eyes. They'd each seen each other. The chase was on.

"Out of my way," she said, shoving off the escalator and out onto the platform. It was an open concourse with tracks on either side. Large columns blocked the sightlines.

There were a lot of people on the platform, and she crouched slightly, keeping her head below the level of the crowd. When she reached the nearest of the thick columns, she ducked in behind it and took off her jacket. It wasn't the best of disguises, the shirt beneath was black too, but she rolled up her sleeves and tied the jacket around her waist to at least give herself a different silhouette. She also tied back her hair and put on the sunglasses she'd had in her pocket. There was a vending machine next to the column, and she peered around it cautiously.

Her heart froze when she saw his face. It was the Romanian from the cell Shipenko used when he didn't want to dip his pen in the company ink, so to speak. The cell was supposed to be a secret, but in the GRU, rumors of a foreign cleanup crew spread fast. Valentina had seen this man in video footage that she wasn't supposed to have seen.

She'd known something wasn't kosher about this job.

Now she had proof, and she could see she was in a lot more trouble than she'd realized. The Romanian cell was used for one thing—to clean up a mess. If they were here, that meant she was the mess.

She stepped back behind the vending machine as the man—people knew him as the Splinter, but she'd heard him referred to as Constantin once—passed the column. She retreated to the other side of the column before he saw her. He was looking up and down the platform, desperately trying to lay eyes on her before the next train came into the station. And that wouldn't be long. She could already hear its approach, the change in the air pressure of the tunnel. At the far end of the platform was a second set of escalators leading back out of the station. He would be watching those too.

She stayed put, avoiding drawing any attention from the crowd. As the train rushed into the station, she knew it would take Constantin's attention to make sure she wasn't among those boarding it. Its doors opened, and people flooded out onto the platform. Valentina joined them, letting the crowd take her back toward the escalator she'd just come down. She tried to stay low, but for the entire time she was on the escalator, which felt like the longest thirty seconds of her life, she resisted the urge to look back and check if he'd seen her. There was no steel wall to view reflections in this time. He could have been right behind her, his gun pointed at the back of her head, but she remained motionless, eyes forward, and didn't push past the other people or hurry.

When she reached the upper level, she breathed such a sigh of relief she almost cried. Then she went straight out to the street and hailed the first passing cab.

"Where to?" the driver said as she climbed in.

She had no idea where to go. Shipenko had turned on her. She couldn't believe how fast it had happened. She'd failed to carry out one order, hesitated just one time, and already the Romanians had been set loose. It made her wonder if he'd been planning for it to happen all along.

"Drive!"

"Where to, lady? I can't just—"

She reached into her pocket and flung some crumpled bills at him. "Just drive," she snapped. "Get us out of here. Now!"

The driver pulled into the lane, which seemed to have opened up a little, and they crossed the intersection where the cop was directing traffic. She kept low in her seat. They passed the opera house. Her heart pounded in her chest. She was on the outside now. She was in the cold. She'd been a predator. Now she was prey. She glanced back through the rear windshield. Nothing.

"I'm really going to need some direction," the driver said as he approached the towers of a suspended bridge.

She still didn't know what to say. She needed to catch her breath. "Keep going," she said. "Cross the river." She looked back through the rear windshield again. It was still clear. She untied the jacket at her waist and put it on. Removed the sunglasses. She needed to get her act together, and she needed to do it fast.

"Where's this road taking us?" she said.

"This is the Hlávka Bridge," the driver said. "Across the river is Holešovice." She knew that. She'd memorized the plan of every major city in Europe. She forced herself to concentrate. It was one of the major bridges over the Vltava.

"Okay," she said. "Keep going."

"This better not be some sort of—"

"It's not anything," she said. "Just drive."

She couldn't afford to make any mistakes. Shipenko was after her. It was like having a knife to her throat. One wrong move, and it would be her last. She was on her own now. Every asset, resource, apartment, weapon stash, and bank account she'd been trained to use in an emergency could potentially kill her. Every person she'd ever crossed paths with was a potential threat. She eyed the driver, then shook the thought from her mind. She was getting paranoid.

He was looking in his rearview mirror, and she said, "What is it? What are you looking at?"

"Nothing."

"Don't lie to me," she said, looking back to see for herself.

There was a black Mercedes SUV about three cars back, weaving in and out of traffic to catch up. She might have seen it earlier, she thought, outside the embassy.

"Drive!" she cried. "Go, go, go."

The driver put his foot down, but his skills were no match for whoever was pursuing them. The bridge was wide, with three lanes of traffic in each direction, separated by a set of tram lines. The SUV ramped up over the curb and onto the tram lines, accelerating past the cars that still separated them.

"You need to go faster," Valentina said.

"I don't know what's going on," the driver cried, beginning to panic.

They'd crossed the river and were just coming off the bridge when Valentina saw an exit.

"There," she said, leaning forward. "Get us off there."

The driver swerved through the other lane, ignoring a chorus of honking horns and almost colliding with the car he'd cut off. Then they were careening down the spiraled ramp to street level. The SUV had to ramp back over the curb from the tramlines and then cut through three traffic lanes to follow them. Valentina watched through the rear windshield, expecting to see it any second, but it didn't appear.

"There!" she said, pointing the driver down a side street. If he followed her directions exactly, they could lose the pursuer, but just as she said the word, the driver jammed on his brakes, bringing the cab to an abrupt halt.

"What are you doing?" she gasped desperately. "You need to keep going. You need to drive."

"You need to get out of my cab," he said.

Valentina looked at him. There was no time to argue. She glanced back through the rear windshield, then opened the door of the car and began running flat out toward a narrow alleyway across the street.

She could see a church spire beyond the end of the alley and figured it must be the Anthony of Padua. Four tram lines intersected in the square in front of that church. She needed to get on one of those trains.

There was a screech of rubber from the end of the alley behind her. She looked back and saw her pursuers, two men, looking at her through the windshield of the black SUV. The vehicle was too wide to follow her down the alley, and she kept running.

Two shots rang out in the air.

They missed, but not by much, ricocheting off the sides of the buildings, sending chips of stone into the air. Valentina reached instinctively for her own gun before remembering it wasn't there.

The vehicle sped off with another screech of rubber. She knew it was rounding the block to intercept her before she got to the church. She could have turned back the way she'd come, but the streetcars were her only hope. She was in an all-out sprint, sucking cold air into her lungs, flying over the snow-strewn street at full speed. She broke out of the alley and into the church square and didn't even turn to look at the SUV that she already knew was flying toward her.

The street ran along one side of the square, but a row of stone barriers stopped vehicles from ramping up onto the square itself. She ran between two of them and kept sprinting while the SUV sped along the street. Two more shots were fired. She braced for the biting pain of impact, but it never came. Up ahead, directly in front of the church, a streetcar was coming to a halt. She had to make it before it pulled away.

She gasped as she kept running. A hundred yards. Fifty. Twenty. Five.

Then another shot, ringing out over the square like the crack of a whip. She braced, and then she stumbled, the cobbles of the square coming up toward her. Ahead, the streetcar began to pull out of its stop, the driver no doubt alarmed by the gunfire. She wasn't going to make it. She knew it. She was falling. But then, somehow, miraculously, she managed to stay on her feet, stumbling forward as another gunshot flew by, missing her by mere inches and hitting the side of the streetcar. The streetcar was gaining speed, but she reached out and grabbed the steel rail of the rear door with both hands and pulled herself up to the step. The doors were sealed shut, but it didn't matter. She could hold on and ride on the step. Through the window, the passengers stared at her like some sort of feral animal. She held on as they gained speed.

Across the square, Constantin watched her accelerate

away. He remained motionless, as if accepting her escape, but only for a second. Then he began to run, not toward her but back toward the SUV. He wouldn't be able to follow her directly, the tramline ran behind the church and back toward the bridge on a raised section of the street that the SUV wouldn't be able to mount, but Valentina knew that protection didn't last long. It would emerge on the Hlávka Bridge, heading back toward the center of the city, and there was nothing but a few inches of concrete there between the tram tracks and the car lanes. If Constantin got there in time, she'd be a sitting duck.

The streetcar got up to about forty miles per hour. She couldn't see the SUV behind her but knew it was close. There was a set of lights ahead where the tramline rejoined the regular traffic, and she prayed they didn't change. A stop there would be the end of her. She watched the little white signal lights as they approached. To her relief, the driver coasted through the intersection and onto the bridge without slowing down. No sooner were they on the bridge than she heard the crash of breaking glass behind her. She looked back to see the SUV slam into the curb separating the tramline from the car lanes. The SUV had tried to mount the raised concrete level of the tramlines, but it was too high, and the vehicle almost buckled as it hit the barrier. Its passenger-side windows shattered from the impact. One of the front wheels was knocked off balance, but the vehicle managed to limp along, rolling through the red lights of the intersection and only narrowly missing a direct collision with cross-traffic. But then a bus entered the intersection, speeding down the slope from the bridge, horn blaring, brakes screeching, and it clipped the rear corner of the SUV, sending it into a full three-sixty spin.

Valentina couldn't believe it. She was saved. She dared to breathe a sigh of relief, and then, almost like some sort of killing machine from a horror movie, Constantin emerged from the smoking wreck of the car and began sprinting after her. He was bloodied, injured, his gait lopsided, but that didn't slow him down.

She reached to the back of her shoulder and looked at her hand. Blood. She'd been hit after all and hadn't even realized. Constantin was still giving chase. He wasn't gaining on her, he was definitely hurt, but the streetcar was slowing down. He'd catch her at the next stop, just across the bridge. He was armed, and she wasn't. She had no choice. She watched the ground beneath, tried to judge the moment when the vehicle's speed was slower than her running speed, then dropped to the ground.

She landed hard, rolled painfully, struck her elbow on the curb, then stumbled to her feet and kept running. She veered to her left into the three lanes of oncoming traffic, the cars swerving, horns blaring as they narrowly avoided hitting her. Somehow, she was still alive at the other side. As she reached the sidewalk, she heard another bullet. It seemed further away this time.

But the pain didn't. That was real close. She reached out with both hands to break her fall as she hit the ground.

This was it, she thought. This was how she met her end, gunned down in the street of a foreign city like a dog. She struggled to get to her feet, reaching for the concrete wall at the side of the bridge. There were people on the bridge, pedestrians, but they were backing away from her in alarm. The traffic was still flowing, but cars were slowing down to see what the commotion was.

And then Constantin arrived, still running on the tram line, gun in hand. He slowed as he approached, catching his breath. "Give it up," he called out from across the lanes of traffic.

She didn't have a choice. He'd beaten her. She'd broken the one rule GRU assassins lived by. She'd made a run for it. And there was only one penalty. Death. She knew it as well as he did.

He raised his gun. "This is the end of the line, Valentina."

"Go ahead," she said, not loud enough that he would hear. It was a command to herself alone. A challenge to fate. She was ready. "Do it," she whispered. "Pull the trigger."

onstantin eyed Valentina cautiously from across the street. He'd placed the shots carefully so as to only clip her. The shoulder and the thigh. She was an injured bird now. Winged. She would live, but she wouldn't fly.

And she was unarmed.

He was surprised at that. He'd expected more. How had she allowed herself to get caught so completely exposed? He was almost disappointed.

The traffic slowed as people tried to see what was going on, and he crossed the three lanes easily, approaching her with his gun drawn. He remained cautious, at the ready. She was down, but he knew she was still dangerous, even now. She looked at him, and he saw the fierceness in her eyes, like a caged tiger. And he knew it was real. One wrong move and she'd be on him. He'd seen it before. These female GRU assassins, if anything, were even more lethal than their male counterparts. They were trained more harshly. More was expected of them. If he dropped his guard for a second, this close, within reach, he'd have a snapped neck before he knew what was happening.

"Look at you now," he said, holding the gun firmly in front of him. "The famous she-wolf, the Volchitsey, down in the muck like a snarling, snared, worthless piece of—"

"That's right," Valentina spat, "look while you can because I give you my word you're going to pay for this."

He laughed. She had balls. He'd give her that much. "Really?" he said. "Forgive me if I'm not quaking in my boots."

He was laughing, but he did not forget the risk he was in. She was practically snarling, like a predator ready to pounce. They called her the she-wolf, but looking at her now, he thought there was something distinctly feline about her. She was wounded, her energy was spent, she was losing blood, breathless, the cold air billowing in front of her mouth as she gasped for breath. And even still, he knew she was as dangerous a person as he would ever get this close to.

The only thing between them was his gun, and in the heat of the chase, he'd failed to count his bullets. He'd have liked to check now, but that would be a grave mistake. Any hint of doubt, any sign of weakness, and Valentina would capitalize on it. It was too late. He had to give himself the benefit of the doubt.

Shipenko had told him to bring her in alive if possible, and he knew that was what she would be expecting. He would have killed her by now otherwise. She knew what was in store for her in Moscow. There would be the grueling interrogation, the punishments in the Lubyanka, the torture. And there would be other things too. Unofficial acts. The things Shipenko did to women when he had them strung up by the wrists. If Constantin had heard the rumors, Valentina certainly had. She would escape now or die trying. But still, he had to try to take her in.

"So, what is this?" she spat, a gloved hand covering the bullet wound in the back of her thigh, slowing the blood loss.

"You know what it is."

"But why were you there? Why were you watching me?"

Constantin wasn't normally one for chitchat, he preferred to get a job over with, but they each had their reasons for wanting to stall. She had no choice. He wanted his backup to arrive before he tried to restrain her.

"Four minutes," Badea said in the receiver in Constantin's ear.

Constantin would have liked to look back and see if Stăn was coming—he didn't know how badly he'd been hurt in the crash—but he didn't dare take his eyes from Valentina.

"What did I do wrong?" Valentina said. "You can tell me that much, surely."

"You wouldn't like it if I told you."

"I know how Shipenko operates," she said. "You wouldn't be here unless there was a mess to clean up."

"And what would you call this?"

"You were here before this."

"You ran."

"You were already watching me."

He let out a mirthless laugh. "Perhaps he knew you'd run."

"Because that's what he wanted me to do. He was forcing me to make a mistake."

"I'm sure he'll explain it all to you himself."

"He won't get the chance," she said.

Constantin smiled.

"Three minutes," Badea said in the earpiece.

"You want to know why this is happening?" Valentina said. "It's because I wouldn't sleep with him. I'm going to be strung up and tortured, then raped, then killed, because of that."

"I see," Constantin said, only half-listening. He was gauging the time. If the police arrived before Badea, he would have to kill her.

"That doesn't bother you?" she spat.

He said nothing.

She shook her head. "No," she said. "Of course it doesn't. You're his dog, aren't you? You do his bidding, his dirty work. You do the jobs that are unfit for Russian hands."

"If only it were so straightforward," Constantin said. In the distance, he could already hear the wail of police sirens. They would be there before Badea.

Valentina could hear them too. He looked at her, her hunter's mind cranking through the permutations. Her instincts, just beneath the surface, scouring him for weakness, for a means of escape. If she'd thought for a second his gun was out of ammo, she'd have struck already.

"Two minutes," Badea said in the earpiece.

Constantin needed to keep her talking. "Shipenko was using you as bait," he said.

"Bait?"

He nodded.

"For who?"

"Some American," Constantin said with a shrug. "Someone high value."

"An asset?"

"I assume so."

Valentina nodded, her lizard brain calculating the implications. "That's why I was killing those women."

"Make sense now?"

She gave him a rueful nod.

"You're upset."

"Yes, I'm upset."

"You don't like killing people?"

"Not this time."

"One minute," Badea said.

"Police are incoming," Boc said, watching from above.

"He's a vindictive son of a bitch," Valentina said. "You'll see it for yourself one day. Your turn will come."

He looked at her closely. He knew she was right. He'd seen it already. She was about to say something else but stopped herself.

"What is it?" he said. The sirens were almost on them.

"Why haven't you pulled the trigger?"

"Thirty seconds, boss," Badea said.

Constantin smiled. They were cutting it close. Moving his free hand slowly to his back, he reached for his tactical knife and gripped the handle. "I'm to bring you in alive."

She shook her head. "That's not going to happen."

"Maybe not."

"Have you ever seen Shipenko?" she said.

"Not face to face."

"You're lucky then."

He nodded. "But I do know what monsters are. Believe me."

With one hand, he put his finger on the trigger. With the other, he clenched his knife. If it clicked empty, he'd put the dagger in her gut before she realized what was happening.

The first police car came over the rise on the north

end of the bridge and screeched to a halt about a hundred yards away. It was on the other side of the road, a full six traffic lanes, as well as the tramline, blocking the police's ability to take a clean shot at him.

"You're out of time," Valentina said, every muscle in her body taut. She was a cat ready to pounce.

Across the bridge, the cop fired a warning shot into the air. He was shielded behind the door of his car, and another police car was pulling up behind him. "Drop the gun," he cried out in Czech. "Drop the gun now."

"I see you," Badea said over the radio.

Constantin saw him too, speeding toward him from the bridge's south end in a BMW sedan. But it was too late. Valentina wouldn't let it happen now that the police were on the scene. She'd force him to kill her.

He looked at her one last time, her eyes, so beautiful, so young. It was a crime. A grimace crossed his face as he pulled the trigger.

The next second was a blur. She moved so fast it defied belief. If he'd seen a recording of it, he wouldn't have believed it was real. His gun clicked empty, and she grabbed his wrist, twisting it back so hard he dropped it. Simultaneously, she swung a leg beneath him and swept him off his feet. Before he knew what was happening, he was flat on his back, looking at the sky. Above him, the gyre of falling snowflakes came down, and faster than his senses could react, the black figure of Valentina vaulted above him and over the side of the bridge. Badea fired three times from the car, but his bullets hit the concrete rail, sending chips of stone into the air. Constantin leaped to his feet and leaned over the rail, looking down at the frozen river at the same moment that Valentina's body crashed through the thin layer of ice on the water's surface. Before he knew what he was doing, he was on the side of the rail, ready to follow her. It was only Badea who stopped him.

"You're mad," Badea said.

Constantin stared at the ice, at the spot Valentina had broken through, and waited for her to resurface. But she didn't. Badea was firing off shots at the police, still on the far side of the bridge, not caring at all who or what he hit. More sirens were approaching, and Boc said on the radio, "You need to go, now."

"Do you see her?" Constantin cried, but Badea wasn't looking. He was still holding back the police.

Constantin watched the surface of the ice for five seconds, ten, twenty, thirty.

"Come on," Badea said, firing blindly at the cops.

Constantin looked at the ice one last time. Still no sign, no break in the ice other than the one she'd made in the fall. She had to be dead.

Badea got in the car. "Constantin!" he yelled through the open window, gunning the engine. "We really have to go."

Constantin pulled himself from the wall and got into the passenger seat as two shots from the police struck the car. He hadn't even shut his door when the car leaped forward, skidding and burning rubber as it accelerated over the bridge, flying by four more police cars on the opposite side of the tramline.

"We got a tail?" Badea said, shifting gears.

The road seemed to be made of flashing blue and red lights. There must have been eight squad cars speeding after them.

"We've got a tail," Constantin said, taking Badea's gun from him and firing once to clear the rear windshield.

Badea was a good driver, and he expertly used the hand-brake to skid one-hundred-eighty degrees, downshift, and then gun it down an onramp in the wrong direction. As they did, Constantin fired, not at the police cars that were still too far back to be in range, but at the ordinary cars on the road, sending them skidding and crashing and blocking the lanes.

"Any choppers?" Badea cried, swerving wildly to avoid a car coming up the ramp.

"No choppers," Constantin said. "Not yet."

29

Badea pulled the car under the overpass and jammed to a halt between two dumpsters. They were shielded from view while maintaining their own ability to see any cars that came down the ramp.

"What are you doing?" Constantin said.

"Trust me," Badea said calmly. He had the engine running and his hands on the wheel, ready to move.

Six police cars came down the ramp in a convoy, lights and sirens blazing, before splitting into two groups and heading down the riverside highway in both directions.

"We can't stay here," Constantin said.

Badea said nothing, and four more police cars came down the ramp, this time dispersing among the local surface streets. He watched until they were all out of sight, then pulled slowly out of his spot. Driving like a night prowler searching for prey, they rolled along the street at a walking pace, the car's powerful engine humming. He took them past the enormous European Satellite Agency building and then down a narrow cobbled street that ran alongside the highway. The height of the highway gave them some cover, and they followed it as far as the major northbound rail line out of the city. As the highway veered around the tracks, the street was blocked by a chainlink fence and turned ninety degrees northward. Beyond the fence, train tracks and freight cars stretched as far as they could see.

Badea followed the fence for a few hundred yards until they got to a crossing point for a spur line. There was a disused station house by the track and a series of old-style railway crossings.

"If they get a bird in the air, they'll spot you in a second," Boc said over the radio.

Badea glanced skyward but kept going, crossing the tracks into an old industrial area. There was a railway marker for Holešovice station, but they couldn't get to it by car.

"Stăn?" Constantin said into his radio. "Do you read?"

There was no reply.

"He hasn't made contact," Boc said, "but he got away. I saw him get on a tram."

"Was he hurt?"

"He was on his feet, but I'm guessing his radio's broken."

They drove slowly on a potholed road between two brick warehouses, and Badea turned to Constantin. "What are you going to tell our friend?" he said, referring to Shipenko.

Constantin sighed. He checked the glove box and pulled out a pack of cigarettes. "Want a smoke?"

Badea shook his head.

Constantin lit one and opened his window. "I'm going to tell him she's dead."

"*Is* she, though?"

Constantin looked at him for a second before answering. "She better be," he said. "For all our sakes."

"I know that," Badea said.

"Good, because if he thinks for a second that we failed...."

"He's going to ask to see a body."

"There'll be a body," Constantin said. "The police will find it."

"And if they don't?"

"They will," he said and sucked hard on the cigarette. Badea was worried. It was clear from the look on his face. Constantin sighed. "Come on," he said. "You saw the river. If she came back to the surface, we'd have seen her break the ice."

Badea spread his hands. "You're the boss," he said. "I just hope our friend understands."

Constantin flicked away his cigarette and took out his phone. No notifications. "We need to ditch this car," he said. "Get back to the hotel."

"Local police will have your face."

Constantin sighed, then, reluctantly, he dialed the access code for Shipenko.

"Is it done?" Shipenko said the moment he came on the line.

"It's done," Constantin said.

"I'm getting the satellite feed now. She went in the river?"

"She did."

"So she tried to escape?"

"She did," Constantin said again. "I chased."

"I wanted her alive."

"I know you wanted her alive," Constantin said, trying to hide the frustration in his voice.

"And you're sure she's dead?"

Constantin lit another cigarette. Badea, who could hear the conversation, took the pack from him and lit one of his own. "I'll be surer when the police find the body."

"You don't know for certain then," Shipenko said. It wasn't a question.

"You'll see for yourself when you get the footage," Constantin said. "She went through the ice. She never came back up. There's no way she survived."

"She's slippery, Constantin. Slippery as an eel. And she likes water."

"Not this water."

Shipenko said nothing for a moment.

Constantin added, "I know we should wait for the body to be recovered, but my face is going to be all over local television in a few hours. We need to get out of the country."

Shipenko let out a brief laugh. "Oh, you're not going anywhere, my boy. I wanted a show. I'm going to get a show."

"What show?"

"The president told me to distract the Americans."

"What happened today wasn't a distraction?"

"What we're planning is going to require more than a few stray bullets, Constantin."

Constantin eyed Badea nervously. "And what are you planning?" he said, knowing the answer wasn't going to be good news.

"I want you to finish the job Valentina didn't."

"You want us to hit Carmen Linder?"

"I want you to hit the embassy."

"Hit the embassy?"

"Go in, guns blazing," Shipenko said. "Make noise. Leave bodies on the floor."

"What about Linder?"

"Linder, others, it doesn't matter. What matters is that you make your point."

"Our point?"

"Yes."

"And our *point* is?"

"Your point is to spill American blood."

"So we're terrorists now?"

"You are whatever I tell you to be."

"But—"

"But?" Shipenko said, his tone altering. "Is there a problem?"

"No, of course not."

"Because I was under the impression we both understood this relationship."

"We do. For God's sake, of course we do."

"I give orders. You obey them. Like a man and a dog."

"I know," Constantin said, glancing at Badea.

"Good," Shipenko said. "I was beginning to worry for you. For your family."

"You don't need to worry."

"You're sure?"

Constantin sighed. "When you say American blood," he said, "how much blood were you talking?"

"Well, the Americans have pulled all female personnel into the embassy. That's not just CIA personnel. It's females in all departments."

"Okay," Constantin said slowly.

"So why don't you stop pretending to be a bitch, and go kill them for me."

Constantin swallowed. He'd always understood that

Shipenko was deranged, but this was a whole new level of depravity. "How many of them?" he said weakly.

"As many as you can."

"Do I understand correctly?"

"I think you do, Constantin."

"It's just—"

"Don't tell me you're losing your nerve. You, the Splinter of Bucharest, the man descended from killers and torturers."

"Don't talk about what I'm descended from."

"Don't question my orders." The line went dead.

Constantin looked at Badea.

Badea sucked his cigarette and said nothing. He brought the car into a large storage barn and killed the engine. Pigeons cooed from a beam beneath the roof.

"Boc," Constantin said into the radio.

"I heard it," Boc said.

Badea eyed Constantin again. There was nothing to say. They were all in the same pot. Constantin had no more power than the rest of them to alter the facts.

"We're ditching the car," Constantin said to Boc. "Any sign of Stăn?"

"Nothing," Boc said.

"We're going to need all hands on deck for this," Constantin said. "If we're to pull off an...." He didn't finish the sentence.

"There's a passenger station less than a mile from where you are," Boc said. "Leave the barn and go south."

Badea had taken a screwdriver from the glovebox and was in the process of removing the license plates from the car. "This will spark a war," he muttered.

"What do we care if it does?" Constantin said.

Badea laughed mirthlessly. "What did Gavrilo Princip care?"

"We get paid either way."

"Getting *paid* won't help us," Badea said, "because we're not going to be alive to spend the money. You know that, Constantin."

"I know we're dead men if we don't do what he says."

"He wants us to kill women."

"It's what we do."

"Not like this."

"We kill men. We kill women. It's all the same."

"This is going to be a massacre," Badea said.

Constantin wanted to throw up, but he didn't dare show weakness now. If he let the others know he doubted the order, they would mutiny. And if that happened, they would all die. Of that, he was certain. "All jobs are the same," he said again. "Now, let's get the hell out of here."

He went over to the car and opened the fuel tank. Badea found some old burlap in the corner of the barn and shoved it into the mouth of the fuel tank. They gave it some time to soak up the fuel like the wick of a candle.

Badea said, "All jobs are not the same, though, are they? This is a building full of innocent women. Cleaning ladies and secretaries and such. It's a massacre."

Constantin swung around suddenly and grabbed Badea by the throat. "You stop saying that word."

Badea was caught aback. The men argued from time to time, they fought, but Constantin didn't. He didn't lose his temper. He reached up slowly to Constantin's wrist and released himself from his grip.

None of them ever talked of the things their fathers had done as prison guards. Not in the darkness of their cells for all those years, not in the bars of Ferentari, blind drunk. They never spoke of the experiment, though all had read the report. Constantin hadn't told them about his grandfather either. He didn't speak of the Călăraşi Express. But there wasn't a day that went by that he didn't feel cursed. "I'm sorry," he said.

Badea raised his hands. "Hey," he said, "for the record, I know you're right. I know we have no other choice."

"If we did—"

"We don't."

Constantin looked at him and nodded. "We're going to plan this job," he said. "We're going to do it. And then we're going to get as far away from this place as possible."

Badea nodded.

"Boc," Constantin said. "Start pulling the schematics for the US embassy. Whatever you can find. It's an old building, a former palace. There's bound to be something in the public domain."

"I'm on it," Boc said.

"And start monitoring the police frequencies. The second they find Valentina's body, I want to know."

"Yes, boss."

"If we play our cards right," he said, "we might be able to swing this one in our favor."

"How so?" Boc said.

"Once we do this job, we're damaged goods," he said. "We won't be able to travel. The whole world will be after us. We'll be on every database, every Most Wanted list on the planet. We'll be done for."

"And that's a good thing?"

"It means we'll be retiring early," Constantin said. "Shipenko will cough up the money. I'll see to it." He lit another cigarette, then held it to the burlap until it caught flame.

"Let's go," he said.

Badea followed him, scanning the sky for choppers before leaving the barn. They'd walked about ten yards when a fireball, three yards wide, rose up to the rafters of the barn, sending hundreds of pigeons into the air in a cacophony of wings and feathers.

30

Tatyana cleared customs at Prague airport using CIA credentials and went straight to the arrival hall. She'd been told Gilhofer would be there to meet her, and she scanned the line of limo and cab drivers standing by the gate. None of them was Gilhofer.

She sat down on a bench overlooking the concourse and called Laurel on her cell. "It's me," she said when Laurel picked up. "I'm in Prague."

"Gilhofer's on his way," Laurel said.

"I can get a cab."

"No, give him another minute. He'll be there. They've had a hectic morning."

"What happened?"

"A shootout in central Prague. It looks like our suspect was the target."

"Who was involved?"

"Russian on Russian, near as we can tell. The target matches the description of the woman seen with Arabella."

"And the shooter?"

"*Shooters*," Laurel said. "At least three men were involved."

"Did we get facials?"

"I'm still waiting for the Czech CCTV data. One of the men followed her into a subway station. There are multiple cameras in the station, so we should be able to get something."

"What about satellite?"

"Some partials. The satellite was almost directly over-head at the time, so the angle is bad. I've run what we got against our GRU database but so far, nothing."

"So we think it was Russian on Russian because—"

"Because it wasn't us," Laurel said. "Who else would have the balls to go after a GRU assassin?"

"I see," Tatyana said. "So you're thinking—"

"I'm thinking someone in Moscow is cleaning house. This assassin has done something wrong. She's made someone angry."

"Do you think she could have gone rogue?"

"Maybe," Laurel said. "Whatever it is, her handler isn't happy."

"Maybe these hits weren't authorized at all," Tatyana said.

"That would certainly explain a few things," Laurel said. "In any case, we'll know more when we see the CCTV footage. If the woman's who you think she is, that will be a start."

"It is who I think it is," Tatyana said.

Laurel let out a quick laugh. "Yeah, well, let's see. I'm going to hang up and send through the data now."

Tatyana waited for the transfer to complete, then opened the file. It was Keyhole satellite footage, very high definition, but as Laurel had said, the angle made it almost impossible to see faces. The footage showed a blonde woman dressed in black sprinting after a streetcar while an SUV gave chase. A man got out of the SUV and took some shots. Tatyana thought she saw one of the bullets hit the mark, but the woman kept running. She made it onto the back of the streetcar and must have been unarmed because she never returned fire. The streetcar picked up speed and rounded the back of the church. The streetcar disappeared from view, blocked by the church, and reemerged on the wide bridge crossing the river. The SUV had to take another route to the bridge and was just beginning to gain on the streetcar when it was struck by a bus crossing an intersection. The SUV spun, windows shattered, but when it stopped, a man got out of the passenger door and continued giving chase. The woman dropped off the streetcar and kept running, but the man fired more shots. One of them got her. She stumbled and fell. She'd been hit twice, she was down, but she hadn't given up. She struggled to get to her feet, but the shooter walked up to her slowly. He could have killed her, but he didn't. The GRU would have wanted her taken alive.

It looked like one of them had something to say because they spoke for about a minute. No doubt they were both stalling, but Tatyana wondered if they knew each other. She looked closely at the woman. It had to be her.

The police arrived then. More shots were fired, but the police were on the wrong side of the bridge. Then the assailant's getaway car arrived. He made to grab the woman, and that was when she struck. She moved fast, with precision. Even injured, she executed perfectly. She knocked the man to the ground and was over the side of the bridge in an instant. She broke through the ice and disappeared.

Tatyana paused the footage. The man had fallen on his back. He was looking straight up at the sky. She zoomed in on his face. Bingo. It was a face she would never forget. The Splinter. Constantin. Head of a Romanian kill squad the Prime Directorate sometimes used. If he was in Prague, it meant something very serious was going on.

Constantin got to his feet and watched the ice for about half a minute, waiting to see if the woman came back up, but she did not. Whoever was directing the satellite knew to keep the focus on the ice. Even as the Romanians made their getaway, the Keyhole lens remained on the stretch of water downriver from the bridge. It stayed for a minute, two, three. No one came up to the surface.

Tatyana typed a quick message to Laurel.

The assailants are a Prime Directorate kill squad.
They're used by the Kremlin to kill rogue agents.
This was a hit ordered by the Kremlin.

She hit send and looked around the concourse for her ride. Her phone vibrated with a response.

So the two women's murders weren't authorized?

She was about to respond when she heard her name. "Tatyana?"

It was a man in a sports coat, approaching somewhat tentatively. "Tatyana Aleksandrova?"

"Yes," she said. This was him, the RSO who'd been bickering with her so stridently on the phone.

"I'm Gilhofer. From the embassy."

"You're late."

"There was a shooting. I'm sure you heard."

"I heard," she said, rising to her feet. "I just watched the footage." She grabbed the handle of her suitcase.

"Please," Gilhofer said, reaching for it. "Allow me." Tatyana let him pull the suitcase as she followed him to the car, a black BMW with diplomatic plates. It was double-parked in front of the entrance. "Klára's in the car," Gilhofer said. "She's on a call."

"Klára?" Tatyana said.

"Issová," he said. "The Czech cop who's been assigned the case."

"I imagine there's a whole lot more Czech cops on the case after what happened this morning," Tatyana said.

He nodded, popping the trunk and loading the suitcase. Then he opened a rear door and held it for Tatyana.

"The royal treatment," she said, getting into the car.

"Just being polite."

"You're a lot politer in person than on the phone."

"About that."

"Never mind," she said. "I'm here now."

Klára was in the front passenger seat, still on the phone, speaking Czech. She looked over her shoulder and gave Tatyana a curt nod. Tatyana nodded back.

"I can take you straight to the embassy," Gilhofer said, firing up the engine. "If you want to check-in."

"Did Linder ask for me?" Tatyana said. As station

chief, Carmen Linder was the most senior CIA official in the country.

"I didn't see her."

"Where are you and Klára headed?"

Klára got off the phone in time to answer. "That was the crime lab. They got good facials from the metro CCTV."

"Let's go then," Tatyana said, pulling a pack of cigarettes from her coat.

"Oh," Gilhofer said awkwardly, watching her in the rearview mirror.

"What?" Tatyana said. "Don't try to tell me you don't smoke in this car. It smells like an ashtray."

"Klára doesn't like it."

Tatyana arched an eyebrow. "Oh," she said, just a hint of sarcasm in her voice. "I'm sorry, Klára."

"It doesn't matter," Klára said.

Tatyana put the cigarette back in its packet deliberately and looked out at the passing city. She knew Prague well, the buildings, the people. She looked at Gilhofer and Klára, sitting up front, staring ahead. There seemed to be something between them—a tension maybe, or an attraction. As she examined Gilhofer, she couldn't imagine a woman like Klára being too interested.

"By the way," Tatyana said, taking her phone from her pocket, "the gunmen were from a Kremlin cleanup crew."

"How do you know that?" Gilhofer said.

"I recognized the shooter."

"So the Kremlin's trying to kill her?"

Tatyana nodded. "I think so."

"Does that mean the killings weren't authorized?" Klára said.

Tatyana shrugged. "It's too early to say that. Clearly, someone wanted them dead."

"But if it wasn't the Kremlin?" Gilhofer said.

"We don't know that," Tatyana said. "Let's wait and see what this footage tells us. If I see the assassin's face, I'll have a better chance of knowing what she was up to." She reopened the file Laurel had sent and watched it again. There'd been multiple passes of the stretch of riverbank downstream of the bridge. The ice gave way to open water where the river narrowed, and there were areas where the banks were under tree cover. There was no sign of anyone in the water, though, and certainly no breaks in the ice immediately downriver of the bridge. She chewed her lip, trying to think how someone could have gone through that ice and survived.

Gilhofer watched his side mirror as he exited the highway. Klára was giving him directions to the crime lab. It wasn't far from the old Petrin radio tower. They got onto a sidestreet and pulled into a gated parking lot. It was surrounded by a chainlink fence, barbed wire, and security cameras. Klára flashed her credentials to the guard at the gate. It was a police facility, but when he saw her badge, his demeanor changed instantly. Tatyana hadn't gotten a view of the badge.

"What department did you say you worked for?" she said to Klára as they found a parking spot.

"I didn't," Klára said, stepping out of the car.

They entered a squat, brick government building that smelled of bleach and formaldehyde and reminded Tatyana of her old high school science lab. They signed in at the front desk and then followed Klára down a corridor lit with large fluorescent lights. There was an AV room at the end of the corridor that looked like it had been teleported directly from the nineteen-eighties. Bulky reels of film were stacked on steel shelves, and all the equipment and paraphernalia that would have been used for analyzing and editing analog film was still there, ready for use. The technician they'd come to see was thankfully sitting at a computer, scrubbing through grainy black and white CCTV feeds from various locations around the city.

He looked up from the screen, and Klára showed him her badge. Tatyana saw that the badge was from the BIS, the Czech Intelligence Agency, and not the police as they'd been told initially.

"I believe you've been expecting us," Klára said in Czech.

"I have," the technician said.

"And what have you got?"

He looked at Gilhofer and Tatyana for a second, and Klára said, "They're from the embassy. They're with me."

"All right," he said, pulling up the footage.

Tatyana took a breath. The images came up on the screen, and she felt a sudden shiver run down her spine. It was who she'd expected it to be—that piece of work, plain as day, riding a metro station escalator down to the platform.

Gilhofer and Klára were looking at her.

"Well?" Klára said.

Tatyana nodded. She suddenly felt claustrophobic, like the walls of the room were closing in on her.

"Are you all right?" Gilhofer said. "You look like you just saw a ghost."

"I feel like I did," she said.

"Obviously you know her," Klára said, showing less patience.

"I know her," Tatyana said. "At least I did. It's been a few years."

"She's GRU?"

Tatyana nodded.

"Just like we said from the beginning," Gilhofer said. "The gates of the Russian embassy. That's where this investigation ends."

"Maybe," Tatyana said, "unless we can find her before the Russians do."

"She's dead," Gilhofer said. "We all saw the footage of her going through the ice."

"What else do you know about her?" Klára said, eyeing her carefully.

"I can tell you she's not dead," Tatyana said.

"Why do you think that?"

"Because I know her."

"Do you know her name?"

"Valentina Brik," Tatyana said. She couldn't help feeling challenged by Klára. The two locked eyes for a moment until Gilhofer broke the silence.

"Sounds like you weren't too fond of her," he said.

"You could say that."

"That doesn't explain why you think she's alive," Klára said.

Tatyana sighed. "I trained with her," she said. "We were selected for a special exercise. She's... not dead."

"All right," Klára said, giving Gilhofer a look. "If she's alive, she's on the run. She's desperate. She can't go home. She can't turn to her normal options. She has no allies. She's going to make a mistake."

"And when she does," Gilhofer said, "we'll be there."

"She's dangerous," Tatyana said. "As ruthless a killer as you'll ever find."

"Works for the Prime Directorate?" Klára said.

"Yes, but I don't know who her lead agent is. She didn't have one when I knew her."

"And you knew her well?"

Tatyana shook her head. "I wouldn't say that."

Klára gave Gilhofer that look again, like everything Tatyana said was coming from a questionable source.

"Why didn't you tell us you worked for the BIS?" Tatyana said.

Klára looked from Tatyana to Gilhofer, then said, "You know why."

"Following orders?" Gilhofer said.

"Yes, following orders. My government is terrified of antagonizing Moscow. You would be too in their position."

Tatyana nodded. She understood. No one in the Czech government over a certain age would ever forget the columns of Soviet tanks that rolled down Wenceslas Square during the Prague Spring.

"You know what my boss said to me when Yvette Bunting was found?" Klára said.

Gilhofer shrugged.

"He said to assist you in bringing the culprit to justice, unless—"

"Unless what?" Gilhofer said.

"Unless the culprit was Russian."

"Well," Tatyana said, "I think we can say the culprit most definitely is Russian."

"And if the Prime Directorate is involved," Klára said.

"If the Prime Directorate is involved, then there's more going on here than meets the eye."

"What can you tell us about Valentina Brik?" Klára said.

"I thought you weren't supposed to pursue a Russian."

"If a Kremlin kill squad is after her, I want to know why."

"I don't know if there's anything I know about her that would help," Tatyana said. "She's highly trained. She's dangerous. You already know that."

"Do you think she'll try to make contact?"

"With us?" Tatyana said, taken aback by the very idea of Valentina Brik trying to switch sides.

"It's not so hard to imagine, is it? She's being hunted by her own side."

Tatyana thought for a moment. It was a possibility, she had to admit, even if she would have preferred not to think about it. "If she does," she said, "it's a trap. We can't trust this woman."

"You seem to have a very strong opinion on that."

"I do," Tatyana said. "And if you value your life, you'll listen to me."

"What if we want to listen to *her*?"

"You talk about antagonizing the Kremlin. There's no surer way than reaching out to this...."

"This what?"

"This *bitch*," Tatyana said.

Klára raised an eyebrow, and, whatever the gesture was supposed to mean, it irritated Tatyana acutely. "Do you want to say something?" Tatyana said.

"Ladies," Gilhofer said, stepping between them.

"No," Tatyana protested. "If she has something to say, I want to hear it."

"All right," Klára said. "You tell us not to trust her, not to speak to her, but someone spoke to you, didn't they?"

Tatyana made to speak. She was going to say that her situation was different. She was going to say she'd known Lance, that they'd met much earlier, that they'd understood each other long before she ever asked him to trust her. But she didn't say any of that.

"That's what I thought," Klára said.

Tatyana didn't know what to say. It was hard to argue with what Klára was saying, but it was also hard not to give in to the temptation of punching her lights out. "I'm going to wait by the car," she said, pulling her pack of cigarettes from her pocket. She walked down the corridor and had the cigarette lit before she'd even reached the exit, storming by the front desk before the guard had a chance to tell her it was prohibited.

Images from her time at the academy flashed through her mind. She knew Valentina because they'd both been selected for the same special exercise. *Special exercise* was the name given to a series of tests run by the Prime Directorate in response to criticisms that women weren't up to the job of active assassin. Women had been used for decades as honeytraps, of course, as well as for less risky killings such as poisonings or killing targets in their sleep. A number of Prime Directorate memos referred to them as *Hotel Room Assassins,* or, more crudely, *Pants Down Assassins,* because they only ever killed targets when their pants were down

So, just before they were permitted to enter active service, after years of intense training that would have made even the most elite military programs in the world look like a summer camp, Valentina and Tatyana were flown to a remote military camp on the banks of Siberia's largest and most unforgiving river, the Lena. The river was truly a monster, the Russian Amazon—a raging torrent of near-freezing water, five miles wide at places, that flowed through two-and-a-half thousand miles of the remotest territory on the planet before spilling into the Arctic

Ocean in a delta a hundred miles wide. Its sheer scale, and the ferocity of some of its rapids, almost defied belief. North of Yakutsk, which was to say for the vast majority of its length, there was not a single bridge that crossed it. The only way across was by barge. It was so remote, so untravelled, that there were still creatures swimming in its murky depths that had never been seen before. New species were being discovered all the time.

Tatyana sucked on her cigarette as Klára and Gilhofer came out of the building after her.

"Sorry," Klára said before Tatyana could say anything to her. "I shouldn't have let myself—"

"I get it," Tatyana said. "I'm a Russian. I deserve it."

"No one's saying that," Gilhofer said.

"I apologize," Klára said again. "Really."

Tatyana looked her over, then sighed. "You asked how I knew Valentina."

"I did," Klára said.

"Very well, we trained together. She and I were selected for a special program. They flew us up to Siberia and dropped us from helicopters into the Lena River. It was April, and there were still slabs of ice as large as school buses floating in the water. It made the river we saw this morning look like an inflatable swimming pool."

"All right," Klára said.

"They dropped us over a patch of water so swollen from the spring thaw that entire islands had been swallowed up by the water. They didn't expect us to survive. The river narrowed into a gorge a few miles downriver, and they'd placed netting and a recovery vessel there to fish out our bodies."

"What was the point of it?" Klára said. "Why risk the lives of two highly-trained operatives?"

"The point of it?" Tatyana said. "What is it ever? They wanted to see if we'd die."

"Okay," Klára said.

"They gave us each a hunting knife, a small survival kit, and a compass and told us the challenge was to get to a checkpoint thirty miles farther north."

"Not to state the obvious," Gilhofer said, "but I'm guessing you both survived."

"We survived," Tatyana said, without a hint of irony, "but we shouldn't have. It was a test developed in the eighties during the Afghan War. The war wasn't going well, and the 40th Army needed more and more men for its Alpha and Zenith groups. They were supposed to be highly-trained Spetsnaz units, but the men were dying faster than the academy could replace them."

"So they dropped them in a river?" Klára said incredulously.

"They did," Tatyana said. "Only instead of April, they did it in the summer, and not from two hundred feet like they did with us, but from thirty. The survival rate was shockingly low, but any man who did survive was recruited into the elite 459th Special Forces Company and sent to Afghanistan."

"So they dropped you in the river," Gilhofer said. "What does that tell us about Valentina?"

"That she can swim," Klára said.

She said it sarcastically, but Tatyana ignored the tone. "Exactly," she said.

"I don't see how one test—" Klára said, but Tatyana interrupted her.

"The fall alone should have killed us. It nearly did kill Valentina. I told you there were huge chunks of ice in the water. I don't know if she hit one of them when she landed or if it struck her afterward, but when I got to the surface, she was struggling to stay afloat, and there was so much blood in the water I could see the color of it."

"Did you help her?"

Tatyana shook her head. "I tried to, we were to get to the checkpoint together if possible, but the current was so strong and the water so cold, it was all I could do to keep myself from drowning. I lost sight of her and accepted the inevitable. I was sure she was dead. She *should* have been dead."

"Except she wasn't," Klára said.

"It took everything I had, every ounce of strength, to get to shore. I didn't think I would make it. Even now, I don't know how I survived. I've looked up the temperature records of the river at that time of year, the speed of the current, the sheer size of the river. The chance of anyone surviving is vanishingly small. We were supposed to die in that test. The Prime Directorate didn't want us to pass. The political stuff, the honeytraps, the Kompromat, the easy targets, that was one thing. But active agents? No. They didn't want that. I should have died, and Valentina, injured, struggling, certainly should have."

"Then why didn't she?"

Tatyana shrugged, sucked her cigarette, and flicked it away. "I wish I knew."

"What exactly are you trying to say?" Klára said.

"I'm not *trying* to say anything. You asked what I knew of her. I'm telling you."

"Is that it, then?" Klára said. "Old memories of the academy? Do you know anything else? Anything we can actually use?"

Tatyana sighed. "Well, I dragged myself onto the eastern bank of the river about eight minutes after being thrown from the helicopter. I was close to hypothermic by that point. I looked back at the water, but there was no way I'd have been able to see Valentina. The river was so wide I couldn't even see to the other side. And the landscape was so foreign, so uninhabited, so inhospitable. I might as well have been on the surface of another planet. That far north, it's a world of its own. Everything is different—the plants, the trees, the animals. There are no human settlements. No roads. No powerlines. It's like humanity doesn't exist at all. There are packs of wolves larger than anything seen farther south in a thousand years. There are tigers, actual tigers, larger than anything you could find today in India. There is a leopard subspecies."

"And Valentina?" Klára said impatiently.

"That's what I'm trying to say. I remained on the river-bank for hours. I needed to make a fire to get my body temperature back up. I had to get dry. Anything else would have been suicide."

"Did she show?"

"No. She never came ashore. If she had, she'd have smelled the smoke and would have come to me. She would have needed to warm up too. I was at the fire for four hours, and she never showed. There was no question in my mind she was dead."

"You said you were to get to a waypoint thirty miles away," Klára said.

"Yes, and that's what I did. The terrain wasn't difficult. It was cold, and colder still once dusk struck, but I'd been trained for that. I traveled along the river, and for the last mile or so, I could even see the lights of the military camp around a wide bend in the river."

"It was a big camp?"

"It wasn't huge, but there were boats there. Helicopters. It was easy to spot."

"Okay."

"It was dark by then. I was cold, exhausted, completely drained, mentally and physically. But the end was in sight."

"But something happened?" Gilhofer said.

"I saw the silhouette of a figure cross between my position and the light of the camp."

"A figure?"

"A woman, like me, dressed like me, like Valentina."

"It was her?"

"Yes, and she was moving the same direction I was toward the camp. I was going to call out to her, I couldn't believe she was there, but something stopped me."

"What stopped you?"

"The way she was moving, crouching, skulking maybe. It was like she was stalking prey. There was something animalistic about it."

"You followed her?" Klára said.

"I did. The riverbank got rockier. It rose up steeply on both sides. I was on a narrow ledge. The water was rushing by, about twenty feet below. I could see her ahead, and then she was gone. In the darkness, I'd lost her."

Klára was eyeing her closely. "What then?" she said.

"I grew still. I listened."

"You were scared of her?"

"I drew my knife," Tatyana said.

"You thought she was going to attack you?"

"I don't know what I thought. I crept forward silently. Cautiously. We were so close to the camp. I don't know why we couldn't make it back together."

"You said you didn't call out to her," Klára said. "Maybe she was as scared of you as you were of her."

"Maybe," Tatyana said. "All I can say is that I was acting on instinct. My gut told me not to call out."

"What happened next?"

"The ledge was narrow, like I said. I kept creeping forward. It was the only way I could go. I was practically inching forward."

"And then?"

"I heard something, like the snap of a twig."

"It was her?"

"It was a tripwire. She'd rigged up a trap. A stick swung out from the cliff, fast as an arrow, and Valentina's knife was attached to the end of it."

"It got you?"

Tatyana pulled up her shirt to show a scar, an incision two inches wide, just below her ribcage. "It was a vicious son of a bitch," she said. "Designed to kill. And it almost did. I fell off the cliff into the water, and the current immediately grabbed me."

"But you didn't die," Klára said.

"You sound almost disappointed."

Klára shook her head, but Tatyana wasn't convinced. "The river was practically a gorge at that point," she said. "The banks were so steep, almost vertical. I couldn't get out of the water. I would have drowned for sure if it hadn't been for the recovery nets the military had set up to fish out our bodies. I got caught in the net and somehow managed to pull myself above the water and make enough noise that the soldiers on the barges heard me."

"What did you tell them?" Gilhofer said.

"I didn't tell them anything. What was there to say?"

"They could see you had a knife wound."

"They did see," Tatyana said. "I didn't get the impression it surprised them."

"What did you say to Valentina?" Klára said.

"I never saw her. They took me to the infirmary. When I got out, Valentina had already been flown out."

"Did she know you were alive?"

Tatyana shrugged. "I don't know. I don't know if she even cared. She'd have heard later that I was at the Prime Directorate, but by then, what did it matter?"

"You didn't see her once you started work?"

"I did not. I was assigned a traditional female role. I was a honeytrap. Getting close to targets, sleeping with them, acquiring Kompromat."

"You were a *Pants Down Assassin*," Klára said, a slight smirk on her face.

"I suppose I failed the test," Tatyana said. "Maybe that was why Valentina did what she did."

"To make you fail?" Gilhofer said.

"To show the GRU," Klára said, "that she was up to the job."

"In any case," Tatyana said, "she became as vicious a killer as the Prime Directorate ever knew. They call her the she-wolf."

"And what do they call you?" Klára said, that same defiant challenge in her eyes.

Tatyana looked at her, bit her tongue, said nothing.

31

L evi Roth clipped his cigar and let the nib of tobacco fall on his lap. It was a Nicaraguan Padron, ordinarily one of his favorites, but today he was dreading it. He'd woken up feeling under the weather, and the feeling was only getting worse as the day wore on. Smoking, especially so early in the afternoon, would be the nail in the coffin.

He was in the back of his government-issue, reinforced Cadillac Escalade, escorted by two police cruisers, their lights flashing as they approached the White House security checkpoint on 17th Street. The driver stopped at the checkpoint, lowered the windows, and Roth flashed him his top-level CIA credentials.

"Mr. Director," the guard said curtly, "the President's expecting you in the Eisenhower Building."

Roth gave him a nod, and the driver proceeded down a recessed, reinforced driveway that led to a below-grade service entrance. He put the cigar in his mouth, unlit, and entered the building through steel doors paneled in eighteenth-century oak. The building was an immensely impressive structure, fitting to its original purpose as the headquarters of the War, Navy, and State Departments. It was built in the style of the French Second Empire and contained more than two miles of ornate corridor and hundreds of rooms. As he walked toward the library, he couldn't help but be reminded of the events that had taken place under its roof. It had been the Pentagon of its day, the seat of the American military, the epicenter of its power. It was during its time that the United States rose from colonial backwater to geopolitical hegemon.

He was in the heart of the most powerful nation ever to grace the annals of history, and this was the building where that exceptionalism was born. It was hard not to feel the weight of all that as he approached the doors of the library, where he knew a fire would be burning and the president waiting.

It was the president's preferred meeting place when the need for discretion was paramount, and the two men had spent more than their share of winter evenings by the library fire, sipping scotch or cognac and smoking cigars. Those nights had a cozy, conspiratorial feel. Today was different. They were meeting in broad daylight, for one thing, and while the surroundings were the same, both men knew they had little to feel comfortable about. There was a grave threat lurking over the horizon, and if they didn't respond soon, they were in serious danger of being outmaneuvered. What was coming, Roth feared, was the first major war in Europe since the descent of the Iron Curtain. Molotov was preparing for war.

"In here!" the president bellowed as Roth pushed open the heavy double doors. The secret service man remained in the corridor. That was as far as he came.

Roth saw the president in his customary armchair,

directly below an enormous hundred-bulb chandelier that was suspended on a brass chain from the ceiling four floors above. The chandelier, which must have weighed over a ton, looked like it had been placed above him as a temptation of fate.

"Mr. President," he said.

The president indicated the chair next to his own, and Roth took off his coat and gloves before sitting down. The fire was burning nicely, big round logs that the president had trucked in from the woods at Camp David, sixty miles away.

"Don't be shy," the president said as he lit a fifteen-year aged Gurkha cigar.

Roth lit his own and settled into the chair, holding back a strong urge to cough his lungs out. He could already feel the nausea coming on. There was a crystal bottle of single malt scotch on the table, and Roth did the honors without waiting to be asked, pouring two generous measures.

"You're thirsty," the president said.

Roth ignored the comment and took a large sip.

"Well," the president said, "I suppose I should say you were right all along."

"Those aren't words I hear very often."

"Whatever's going on in Prague is a smokescreen. The Pentagon's confirmed everything your man in Rostov told us."

Roth nodded. The man he was referring to was a former British special forces operative named Craig Ritter. He was in Russia posing as an arms dealer while secretly gathering intelligence for Roth.

"It's the largest massing of Russian armor since Soviet times," the president continued. "Two hundred thousand men. At least fifty battlefield tactical groups. We've never seen the likes of it. They could swallow an entire country before we had time to react."

Roth nodded. It was all information he'd been passing on for weeks. He'd been arguing forcefully for a stronger response, but everyone, from the Pentagon, to the NSA, to the president's own advisors in the White House, had been on the side of caution.

"Ritter tells me the buildup is growing by the day," Roth said. "Ever since Lance Spector foiled their efforts on the Latvian border, they've been searching for a new target. Unless we make a show of force, they're going to cross the border of a neighboring country. It's not a feint, sir. It's not a posture. Prague's the feint."

The president nodded. Roth knew there'd been objections. Not everyone had been willing to see things through Ritter's lens. They didn't trust him. He was a mercenary, a Brit, and the Russians had stepped up military activity in dozens of other districts across thirteen time zones. It was impossible to know what they were up to for certain. Everyone had a theory.

"NSA is saying they need more time to analyze the chatter," the president said. "They're convinced something's coming in Prague."

Roth sighed. "*Something*, sure, but at most, it's a sideshow. We're looking at two dead operatives. Weigh that against two hundred thousand massing troops."

"Not just any operatives," the president said. "Women. Two dead women. That has a way of focusing people's attention."

"Which is why the Russians did it. They know the constraints we're under. The sound bites. The headlines. The six o'clock news. They know that once word gets out of two American women being murdered, once people see the smiling photos, the pretty blonde hair, the entire media machine will go into overdrive. We won't be able to concentrate on anything else."

"Maybe that's their plan," the president said, "but Cutler's shown me the numbers. If more attacks are coming in Prague, I have to respond. I can't be the president who sends American women overseas to get their throats slit."

"Well, far be it from me to argue with *the numbers,*" Roth said, not attempting to conceal his disdain.

"The shootout this morning. A Prime Directorate kill cell. Something's going to happen in Prague, Roth. Don't deny it."

Roth puffed on his cigar and the smoke caught in his throat. He began coughing so hard that the president had to lean forward and slap him on the back.

"Are you all right, man? You don't look well."

"I'm fine."

"Do you want me to call someone?"

"No, I just need a good night's sleep."

"Well, hopefully you get it."

Roth cleared his throat and took another swig of the scotch. "Not likely," he said. "Not while Russia is preparing an attack."

"They're always preparing an attack. They've been preparing an attack since before either of us was born."

"This is different, sir. We should be scrambling. This should be all hands on deck."

"What do you have in mind?"

"We should have US troops on Ukrainian territory as soon as possible. We need to send Moscow the message that if they attack their neighbors, we'll defend them."

"I've got the entire Third Air Force on standby at Ramstein. Surely that sends a message."

"They're hundreds of miles away, sir. It's a message, but not the one I'd prefer."

"And thirty thousand troops ready to deploy with twelve hours notice? What's that?"

"It's not enough, sir."

"The 77th Field Artillery Regiment is ready to move," the president said. "They've got the M270 Multiple Launch Rocket System and the M242 High Mobility Artillery Rocket System ready to go."

Roth sighed. He knew what forces the president had at his disposal in Europe. They were good, battle-hardened units, but they were in Germany, where they could do precious little to dissuade Russian soldiers from crossing the Ukrainian border. "Mr. President," he said, "as long as we can agree that Prague's a sideshow, an attempt to distract our attention—"

"I'm not prepared to say dead American girls are a sideshow, Levi."

"No one's saying abandon the investigation. Tatyana's on the ground. She's got personal knowledge of the assassin. If she didn't die in the river this morning, Tatyana will find her."

"I thought you'd sent Lance Spector."

"Spector handled something else."

"Not another one of his wild goose—"

"No," Roth said. "Something for me. In London."

"What something?"

"Something to do with Ritter. I made assurances when I took him on. I promised to look out for his family. His wife."

"And that required Spector?"

"He was handling this before this situation in Prague arose."

"Our knight in shining armor rides to the rescue again."

"What does that mean?"

"Come on, Levi. You know what it means."

"No, I don't."

"You're going to make me spell it out?"

Roth took another sip of the scotch and reached for the bottle. "You think he's a—"

"It's not a question of what I think," the president said.

Roth sighed. "There's a trauma there. I admit that. There's a wound."

"He's damaged goods, Levi. He's got a huge blindspot. Any time there's a damsel in distress, the one thing you can count on is that he'll show up, like clockwork."

"He was doing a favor for me. I should remind you that he doesn't even work for the CIA."

"But he carries your water."

"Sometimes."

The president sighed, puffed his cigar. "Are we still planning on evacuating our female personnel?"

"From Prague?"

"Of course, Prague. What are we talking about?"

"I'd like to be talking about Ukraine. We've got an ally to shore up. We've got an invasion on the horizon."

"Let's not get ahead of ourselves, Levi. Some troop movement inside his own territory is hardly the most menacing thing President Molotov has ever done."

"It's mobilization, sir."

"I know you think so, Levi. And believe me, I've heard you. Now move on."

Roth knew he had to let it drop. He took another sip of

scotch. He felt it was going to his head, but it was also making him feel better.

"Now," the president said. "Evacuation in Prague. Where do we stand?"

"It's off the table," Roth said. "The threat doesn't justify it. If we pulled out of European capitals with our tails between our legs every time the CIA suffered two casualties—"

"Agreed," the president said. "It's too weak."

"They never even made a move on Carmen Linder," Roth added. "She rode a regular taxi all the way from the airport, and there wasn't a peep."

"So you think the threat there might be over?"

"I wouldn't say that just yet, but if the Kremlin's trying to take out their own assassin, someone's screwed up somewhere."

"Well, tell Tatyana I don't want any more dead women. I want that situation contained before the press gets on it."

Roth puffed his cigar, and a cloud of thick, blue smoke billowed around him. He coughed again and sipped more scotch. The president did the same, and for a brief moment, a silence filled the room.

"You're still thinking about the Ukraine," the president said.

"Sorry," Roth said, "it's just...." He let his words trail off.

"Just what?" the president said.

"I'm tired of having the same argument. We know what Molotov wants. We know he's committed to getting it."

"He wants NATO out of his backyard."

"No," Roth said, more forcefully than he'd intended.

The president looked up from his glass.

"I'm sorry," Roth said, rubbing his temples, "but it's not just about NATO expansion. What he *wants*, what he really wants, is a complete reassertion of Russia's position as a superpower. He wants to reconstitute the Soviet Union. He wants empire."

"We can't be certain—"

"He's said it," Roth said. "He's admitted it. And everything he does proves it. Even objecting to NATO expansion, it requires a certain worldview. A worldview in which our interests and Russia's are the only two that count. Iran doesn't like NATO, North Korea doesn't, China doesn't, but they don't pretend to have a say in whether other countries join. The Kremlin thinks it has a right to dictate anything. To Molotov, Ukraine isn't a sovereign, equal nation. It's a chess piece. It's a pawn, and it's *his* pawn."

"In a game he plays against us," the president said.

"Yes," Roth said, relieved that someone was finally listening.

"I get it, Levi. You're saying Molotov thinks the world is a game with only two players."

"Exactly, but if it is a game, it's not chess. It's dominoes. And if we let Ukraine fall...."

"Then so falls the world," the president said, sipping his drink. He topped up Roth's glass and gave him a slightly bemused look.

"What?" Roth said.

"I'm not disagreeing with you. I know the Soviet Union enjoyed being one pole in a bipolar world. I know Molotov hearkens back to those days. But I think it's a bit dramatic to say we have to redraw our entire defense strategy along Cold War lines."

"Is it dramatic to say that one way or another, sooner

or later, there's going to be a clash between us and the Kremlin?"

"It's a risk—"

"It's a certainty. He's going to expand. If we don't stop him here, he'll do it again and again until we're forced to act. One way or another, this year or next, or ten years from now, there's going to be contact. There has to be."

"And you'd like it sooner, I take it?"

"I'd like it on our terms, for once," Roth said, exasperated. The ache in his head was beginning to throb. He'd have liked to get out of the room and get some air, but he didn't want the president to think they'd quarreled.

"You're saying—"

"I'm saying he's mobilized for war. At the very least, we should do the same."

"The problem with that," the president said, "is that you're forgetting who you're speaking to. I don't have the luxuries that Molotov has. I don't even have the luxuries you have, Levi. I can't ignore the reality of my position in congress, or the fact that less than thirty percent of Americans support military intervention in Europe, or that my own party would eviscerate me in the primaries if I suggested for a second that I was considering sending our boys overseas."

"Your position's complicated," Roth said. "I understand that."

"Complicated? No, Levi, it's simple. It's very simple."

"I'll tell you what's simple, Mr. President. We're headed for war."

"You know what my predecessor told me when he welcomed me into the White House, Levi? He told me the same thing his predecessor told him, and his before him."

"Which was?"

"That the single greatest task of any American president is to keep us out of a full-scale conflict with Russia. That's it. In a nutshell, that's the job. If you do that, and fail at everything else, you've succeeded as a president, and you know why?"

"No," Roth said. He really needed to get out of that room.

"Because at the end, you'll be able to pass on the keys to the next president."

Roth sighed. He raised his hands in defeat. "So, what now then? We let them march in on weaker states? We let them have what they want? We let them pillage and rape and destroy? We let them grow stronger? And then we let them do it again and again until they're on our own border?"

The president shook his head. He knew what Roth was saying. He understood the argument. He just wasn't ready to face the unfaceable, to think the unthinkable. He wasn't ready for a hot war between two nuclear powers. "Let's not lose our heads, Levi."

"Forgive me for saying this, Mr. President, but as head of the CIA, it's my job to tell you things you don't want to hear."

"I suppose I can't tempt you not to?" he said, holding up the cigar box.

Roth shook his head. "I have to advise you, Mr. President, that the steps we're taking are leaving us unprepared, should push come to shove."

The president nodded. He took another cigar from the box and refilled Roth's glass. "I understand you have to do your duty, Levi. As I have to do mine." He cut the cigar and put it in his mouth. He had a habit of wetting the tip like he was sucking a candy. "And my job tells me that I can't allow push to come to shove. It's not going to happen. What you're talking about is preparation for World War Three. That's a war I can't win, because it's a war that can't be won. If Russia invades Ukraine, we're going to piss and moan, we're going to sanction them and take their yachts, but we're not going to start a war. I simply cannot prepare for that, because I cannot allow it to happen."

"They'll sense our hesitance, sir."

"I'm sorry, Levi. Ukraine is in their backyard."

"They won't stop there."

"Maybe you're right."

"You know what my predecessor told me?" Roth said. "When I took on the role?"

"I do not," the president said.

"He told me we don't choose the wars we fight."

"Be that as it may," the president said, "there will be no American boots on Ukrainian soil."

"Please, sir. Let's not play make-believe. If they move, we move. There's no other way. What would we be saying if we let them invade a democratic ally on the border of NATO?"

"Stop calling them an ally."

"What are they?"

"They're..." the president threw up his hands. "I don't know what they are, but if we get sucked into this, if he enters Ukraine and we move against him, there's no coming out ahead. Not for our country. Not for our people. I've seen the projections—the simulations. Even in the best-case scenario, with no nuclear escalation, even if we limited ourselves to airstrikes and left the ground fighting to the Ukrainians, which in all likelihood would not be sufficient, but even then, we'd still walk away the loser. And you know who wins?"

"Not Russia."

"China," the president said. "That's the bottom line. They're the only ones who come out ahead. There's no question. If we lock horns with Russia, we lose our place in the pecking order. We go in number one, and even if we hand the Russians their asses, even if we send them back to the stone age, we come out of the fight number two. We go in number one, and we come out number two. Russia doesn't take our place. China does."

Roth leaned back. He knew what the president was saying. He'd seen the same war games played out. He knew Russia probably would resort to some form of nuclear deterrent when their backs were against the wall, and he knew that even if they didn't, even if they just took their ass-whooping the old fashioned way, by the time the conflict was over, China would have taken possession of Taiwan, it would have pressed its claims on Japan, and it would have cemented its control of the South China Sea.

"Beijing's gains would be permanent," the president said. "We wouldn't be able to roll them back, even if we were willing to get our hands bloody."

"I don't know what to say to that," Roth said. "Except that I believe we need to confront our enemies as we find them. Not as we wish they were. We can't fight Russia while keeping one eye on China. We need to face this."

"You've got your position." the president said, "You've got your reality. I've got mine."

Roth sighed. His cigar had gone out, and he flicked it into the fire. "Well then, let me give you the *tertio optio*," Roth said, referring to the Latin maxim—the third option.

It was for when the two preferred options, diplomacy and military force, were insufficient.

"And what option is that?"

"I can increase the cost of this for the Russians."

"And how do you propose doing that?"

"Ritter's compiling a list of names."

"Names of people you want to kill?"

"I'd rather not say, sir, but one thing I can promise you. It will involve Lance Spector."

32

Lance caught a cab from Hackney Road. If the driver hurried, he might still make his flight to Prague.

They got onto the road known locally as the Highway —the east-west thoroughfare through Limehouse and London's financial district. It was a major artery, two lanes in each direction, but it was anything but a highway. The traffic was heavy, and Lance leaned forward and said to the driver, "Any way you could get me to Heathrow in less than an hour?"

The driver looked at him like he'd just suggested flying to the moon.

"I can pay," Lance said, "if you can step on it."

"You're already paying," the driver said.

Lance took out his wallet and counted six fifty-pound notes. He put them in the yellow tray used for payments and said, "That's yours if you hustle." The result was immediate. The driver pulled into a bus lane, ignoring the cameras, and they cruised past the other traffic. "This is more like it," Lance said, sitting back in his seat. He was just starting to relax when his phone rang. It was Pooja. He got a sinking feeling as he answered.

"Pooja?"

"Message from your dad. He wants you to call home."

"Okay," Lance cried, hanging up. He dialed Roth's number directly. He was going to get rid of the cell soon, so it didn't matter. "It's me," he said when Roth picked up.

"Where are you?"

"On my way to the airport."

"You took care of the issue?"

"I think so. She's gone to her sister's place. He's not going to follow."

"He better not. Ritter keeps tabs on them on social media. The slightest sign things are going badly, and he gets jittery."

"It's his family," Lance said, keeping his voice down so the driver wouldn't hear.

"I know," Roth said. "I just hope his woman gets her act together this time."

They were passing the Tower of London, and Lance looked out at the bridge turrets. "So," he said, "to what do I owe the pleasure of this call?"

"I've got a jet fueling at Farnborough."

"For who?"

"You, and it's going to Russia."

"Why?"

"Another favor," Roth said tentatively.

"I see."

"I wouldn't ask if it wasn't important."

"One of these days, all these favors are going to catch up to you."

"I know," Roth said, "but right now, it's a debt I'm willing to rack up."

Lance sighed. He knew the situation Roth was in. All the other Assets were dead. It would take years to replace them. "So, what happened to Prague?"

"You never went," Roth said, coughing.

"I thought you were going to see a doctor."

"It's nothing. The president made me smoke a cigar."

"I'm sure he didn't have to twist your arm very hard."

"I couldn't refuse," Roth continued, clearing his throat right into the receiver. "Anyway, Prague's under control for now."

"You caught your killer?"

"The killer's probably dead. Killed by her own side. Tatyana's in the country. She knew her. They trained together back in Russia."

"What's her name?"

"The assassin?"

"Yes."

"Why? Do you think you might know her as well?"

"I might if you tell me her name."

"Valentina Brik. Have your paths crossed?"

"I don't think so."

"You'd remember this one if they had."

"I'm sure I would. So Tatyana's got the situation in hand?"

"I hope so. Apparently she had a run-in with Valentina in the past."

"A run-in?"

"Valentina tried to kill Tatyana during a training exercise."

"I see."

"We still don't know what was going on. It may be that Valentina was acting outside her chain of command.

That's the only reason I can see for the GRU to go after her."

"Maybe," Lance said.

"You don't sound convinced."

"I know nothing about it. I never heard of Valentina Brik. She could have been up to anything."

"She might have been planning to reach out to us."

"Well, if she was thinking of defecting, killing our two agents wasn't a good start."

"No," Roth said. He sounded distracted, tired.

"You sure you're okay? You sound like an old man."

"Very funny," Roth said. "The truth is, I'm uneasy. Everything in Prague was a distraction."

"From the troop build-up?"

"The Russians are ready to devour the Ukraine."

"And the president?" Lance said. "What does he say about it?"

"He's got a lot on his plate."

"Don't tell me he's too busy to notice a Russian invasion of Europe."

"Not too busy to notice," Roth said with a sigh. "Just too busy to do anything about it."

"You think he'll let it happen?"

"I think when Molotov holds a victory parade on Kyiv's main boulevard, our president will be in the audience, waving a little Russian flag, keeping the peace."

"He can't shoot at every target they put in front of him."

"Yes, but he should shoot at this one."

"Surely he knows Molotov won't stop at Ukraine."

"He's worried about China."

"If he does nothing, China will only be emboldened. If

they think we've lost our nerve, it's game over in Asia. They'll go after everything."

"He's afraid of fighting them both. He doesn't want a two-front war."

"He's making a mistake. Showing weakness is the last thing he can afford now."

"That's why I need you to go to Russia. There's documentation and equipment on the plane. It will take you as far as Rostov-on-Don. Once you get there, make contact with Ritter. He's compiling a list of targets."

"A list?"

"Yes," Roth said, clearing his throat again.

"I thought we agreed I was done with lists."

"This is a special circumstance."

"All circumstances are special."

"Lance. I'm not doing this to make your life difficult. I need you."

"Levi. We need to talk."

"I know, Lance. I know this isn't what you want to do."

"It's not about what I want."

"Will you at least get on the plane? We can discuss the details once you make contact with Ritter."

"Levi. You're not listening. I don't think I can work a list right now. I don't think...."

"I know, Lance."

"I don't think I can handle it."

"Can I tell Ritter you're on your way?"

Lance sighed. He knew the kind of job Roth had in mind. It would be a killing spree. A list of names that he'd be expected to go through, one at a time, until he reached the end. Lance had done it before. He knew what it felt like, he knew the toll it took, and he wasn't sure he could pay it.

"Lance, I mean it. The president's going to let the Russians have their way with this. And if they have their way once, they're going to get a taste for it. We're the last line of defense. There's no one else."

Lance said nothing. He watched the traffic outside the car. It was getting heavier.

"You there?" Roth said.

Lance didn't answer. He tapped the plastic divider between himself and the driver.

"Yeah?" the driver said, leaning back.

"Change of plan," Lance said. "We're headed for Farnborough now, not Heathrow."

The driver nodded. "Fine by me. Either way, it's the A4."

"Thank you," Roth said.

"Don't thank me," Lance said, hanging up the phone.

The route brought them right down Piccadilly, past Buckingham Palace and Hyde Park Corner. Lance stared out at the famous landmarks. He knew Roth had good reason for wanting him to do this job. He also knew he could pull it off. What he didn't know, what worried him now, was how he would live with himself after it was done. He was about to remove the sim card and battery from the phone, but for some reason, instead of doing that, he found himself dialing Laurel's number.

33

K lára's cat was mewling pitiably at the door when she got home. "You poor thing," she said, bending down to it. She brought it to the kitchen counter and opened a can of food. "There you go," she said, watching the cat eat. "Mommy's here now."

Klára's work kept her away from her apartment for extended periods, and she was beginning to wonder if the cat had been a mistake. She'd bought it a few weeks ago on a whim, but now, even it seemed like too much of a commitment for her non-existent personal life. It didn't bode well for her marriage prospects, but she tried not to think about that. She went to the refrigerator and scoured it for anything remotely edible. There was some leftover takeout she'd picked up the night before, Indian, and she put it in the microwave. Then she went to the bathroom and had a long shower.

As the water washed over her, her mind went to Tatyana. She didn't like her, although she couldn't put her finger on exactly why. Something more than the normal rivalry, in any case. Her mind turned to Gilhofer. She should have liked him even less, but somehow, despite his faults, she didn't. She might even have gone so far as to say he was growing on her. She trusted him, which was not something she could say about very many people. There were officers she'd worked with for years she didn't feel that way about. Something about Gilhofer was different, though. It made her think he was on her side.

She thought about the breakfast they'd shared. It seemed like an eternity ago now, but she'd enjoyed it. Enjoyed the company. She wasn't used to feeling that way.

She got out of the shower and wrapped herself in her robe before going to the microwave to retrieve her dinner. She grabbed a beer from the fridge, too, then went to the sofa and sat down.

The cat jumped up next to her.

"Did you miss me?" she said, feeling faintly ridiculous for speaking to it. She'd never had a cat before, never had a connection to one, and was beginning to realize it was too late to start now. The cat stared back at her blankly, and she said, "thought so," quietly to herself. She wondered if the store accepted returns. She'd only had it a week.

She looked at her watch. It was late, but probably not too late to check-in. Her boss, Poborský, was a chain-smoking, hard-nosed veteran who'd been with the agency since the days of the Soviet Union. He'd given two marriages and a heart attack to the job and seemed to live at his desk. He even took his meals at it.

"You're still there," she said when he picked up the phone.

"Where else would I be?"

"Honestly, I don't know," she said. "At home, maybe?"

He grunted, summing up his view of that option, and

said, "You're the one calling after nine. Shouldn't you be out living your life, as they say?"

"I can't stop thinking about the assassin."

"You saw the footage," he said. "That woman's dead as a dodo."

"Then where's her body?"

"We'll continue the search tomorrow. She's got to show up."

"I'd rest a lot easier if she did."

"I called the divers, but their blasted union doesn't let them go out in the ice."

"I wanted to ask," Klára said, "as well as searching for a body, have we looked for signs on the riverbank of someone climbing out?"

"Climbing out?"

"Of the water."

"Klára!"

"The park," she said, heading off his objection. "The tree cover there. She could have climbed out without being seen."

"She'd have to have been alive to do so."

"And what if she was?"

"In that cold? After being shot twice?"

"Apparently this woman has some pretty specialized talents."

"Well, patrols up and down the river, as well as on Štvanice Island, saw no trace of her."

"We have to check the riverbank on foot," Klára said. "And not just for a body. We need to look for signs of someone getting out of the water. We need to take the possibility she's still alive seriously."

"Very well," Poborský said. "I'll order the search in the morning. It's no use sending them out at night."

"From what Tatyana Aleksandrova told me, it will take a lot more than a dip in some cold water to kill this woman."

"Speaking of Tatyana, what else did she have to say?"

"Other than what I already told you?" Klára said. "I don't know. She identified Valentina Brik. Confirmed that the gunmen were a GRU kill squad."

"She must know more than that."

"Not very much more."

"We've got the superpowers shooting it out on our streets," Poborský said. "Someone knows what triggered it."

"I don't think that someone is Tatyana."

"We'll wait and see," Poborský said. "But keep a very close eye on her."

"I intend to."

"Call me old-fashioned, but something about a defector GRU assassin doesn't exactly fill me with confidence."

"I'll watch her," Klára said. "But you have to watch my back for me too."

"What do you mean?"

"I mean, is there anything you haven't told me yet? Anything our side has picked up?"

"Klára, you know I—"

"I know you play your cards close to your chest, Poborský."

"As I should."

"But if there's anything I need to be aware of—"

"I'd tell you. You know that."

"Don't let me get ambushed," she said. "Don't let me walk onto a minefield without realizing it. Not where the top floor is concerned." She wasn't sure what she was afraid of, but things were sensitive when the Kremlin was involved, and Poborský was privy to the political considerations that were above her pay grade.

"You know I'd never allow that to happen," he said.

"Just make sure you don't."

"I know what you're worried about," he said.

"And what's that?"

"You think they're going to scupper the case."

"Well, are they?"

"Not yet."

"They're not nervous of what I'll find?"

"They're always nervous when the GRU is active."

"But I can pursue this?"

"Yes."

"You're certain?"

"Well," he said, "if you want to know the truth, what they'd really like is for the whole thing to blow over. No one wants Prague to be the place Moscow and Washington settle their scores."

"But in the meantime, I have my green light?"

"You do, Klára. Someone killed two American women on our turf. Washington wants to know who did it, and it's only right that we help. They're our ally. A good ally. They're the relationship that matters."

"Okay."

"That's what you wanted to hear?"

"It is. I was afraid you'd take me off the case."

"Well, it was considered. I won't lie. Once the GRU connection was confirmed, there were a few who got jittery."

"Well, I'm glad the braver voices prevailed."

"It didn't hurt that the assassin seems to have been disavowed," he said. "And the gunmen aren't Russian citizens. So as long as this doesn't bring you into Gestapo HQ, you can do what you need to."

Gestapo HQ was a euphemism, so to speak, for the Russian Embassy. It was located in an extravagant villa north of the river on the edge of Stromovka Park. The villa once belonged to a Jewish banker but was confiscated by the Nazis in 1939. Hitler then turned it into the Prague headquarters of the Gestapo, fortifying it to the hilt and digging an enormous underground compound beneath it. The Gestapo wasn't ousted until the end of the war.

Following that, the Communists took over, and the Russians selected the site for their embassy, one of the largest in the world. They proceeded to expand and upgrade the Gestapo's underground compound, turning it into one of the most important KGB facilities anywhere outside the Soviet Union. It became responsible for coordinating KGB actions across all of Western Europe, including the activities of the First Chief Directorate's Line X section. The Czechs despised the compound, and the BIS expended significant resources every year monitoring and containing its activity.

Klára took a bite of her food. "I don't suppose," she said, "that there's been any communication from the Russians regarding all of this?"

"What do you think?"

She sighed.

"Just stick to your lane, Klára. This is a proxy battle. We're not party to it. Remember that. There's no need for you to get caught in the crossfire."

"That gunfight on the bridge—"

"Klára, listen to me. By some miracle, none of our citizens have been killed in this thing. Let's keep it that way. Help your American friend, but keep your head down."

"He's not *my* friend."

"You're sure of that?"

"Of course I'm sure."

"I thought you two were hitting it off."

"He's not even in my league."

"If you say so."

"He's old enough to be my father."

"Barely."

"Well, he looks it."

"I thought you liked older—"

"Why don't you mind your own business?"

"I was only teasing. It seems I hit a nerve."

"You didn't hit anything."

"Quite right. I apologize."

"The last thing I need is a rumor like that going around."

"It was a joke, Klára."

"Jokes are supposed to be funny."

"I said I was sorry."

"My career can't handle another scandal."

"You're too hard on yourself, Klára. No one would care if you were to...." He let the sentence trail off. He knew he was beat.

She said nothing. The scandal she'd referred to was the single biggest humiliation of her professional life. An affair with a superior—a director at the economic intelligence unit named Formánek. He was older, about Gilhofer's age in fact, and married. He'd promised to leave his wife, and, for some reason she couldn't get her head around, Klára took his word for it. She pinned her hopes on it. Made plans around it. Let her guard down. The affair lasted two years. Everyone knew.

It took longer than promised, but Formánek eventually did leave his wife. Only, by that time, it wasn't for Klára, it was for one of the younger secretaries in her department.

Klára never saw it coming.

"The thing is," Poborský said, his tone becoming more conspiratorial, "there is *something* the top floor was hoping you would help with."

"Why do I get the feeling you're about to say something I won't like?"

"No, it's nothing like that."

"Like what?"

"It's just, they were hoping you might be able to use your *feminine charms*."

"My what?"

"I'm not saying you have to sleep with—"

"Are you kidding me?"

"We've got good reason to believe he'd be *susceptible*—"

"Drop it. Right now. I mean it."

"He's lonely, and if we got ongoing access to the Keyhole satellite surveillance over Prague—"

She hung up the phone, slammed it on the sofa, then punched the cushion next to her as hard as she could. She was livid. She looked at the food in front of her. She'd suddenly lost her appetite.

34

_____

Laurel finished her laps and got out of the pool. She'd been spending more and more time there. It felt like the only place where her mind wasn't constantly racing. She checked her watch--her lap times were getting better--then went to the changing room and took off her swimsuit. The place was quite busy during office hours but was deserted now. She wrapped herself in a towel, then went through to the sauna, turning the heat up to max. As soon as she was in the little cedar room, she felt calmer. It was quiet in there. Dark. Secret. Even when other people joined her, which was rare, something about the space made her feel alone. She lay on the bench and stared at the ceiling. Then she shut her eyes. She must have dozed briefly because she was sweating when she opened them.

She took a long, cool shower, and when she got back to her locker, saw that she had a voicemail. It was from Tatyana, flagged as non-urgent. She listened as she toweled off.

_____

Laurel, I've been able to access the Prime Directorate database. There's no record of anything involving Valentina Brik in there, which makes me think she's been taken aside by someone. Most likely someone important. Possibly Dead Hand. I'll let you know when I find out. Anyway, remember what I said earlier. If she makes contact, do not trust her. She's a real snake. In the meantime, if you need me, I'm at the embassy. All female staff have been asked to spend the night here. That includes me, apparently. I've got a bunk with three translators. It's like summer camp. Okay, well, I should go before I get in trouble for breaking curfew. But make sure, if Valentina makes contact, do not believe a word she says.

Laurel put the phone in her pocket and walked briskly across the quadrangle back to her building. The cool air felt good after the sauna. She passed the security desk and grabbed a coffee from the Starbucks kiosk in the lobby. She'd intended to take it upstairs but found herself sitting down at one of the café tables instead. There was no one waiting for her upstairs, and she'd spent twenty of the last twenty-four hours, basically all of the time that she wasn't in the pool or sauna, either staring at her computer screen or snatching sleep on the sofa in the office.

She glanced at the barista, a guy in his early twenties from Texas or somewhere, and their eyes met. She looked away immediately. They'd been playing that game for days, glancing at each other and looking away, never exchanging more than a handful of words. Laurel hated to think what he must have seen when he looked at her. She was just a few years older than him, they could have bumped into each other in any bar in the city, and it would have been the most natural thing in the world, but there at the office, with all of the formalities of the Agency hanging over them, it felt as if they were two different species.

"Everything all right?" the barista said.

"Yes, of course," she said, hating how stiff her voice sounded. She felt so self-conscious. He was wearing a white t-shirt that revealed thick, tattooed arms. She was in a stern navy blue skirt and blazer that she suddenly felt added ten years to her age.

He shrugged and got back to work, cleaning the blender they used for making shakes and frappés, but she couldn't stop glancing his way. The place was deserted, and, apart from a few security guards at the far end of the lobby, they were alone. He looked her way again, catching her before she could look away. She pulled out her phone for cover, pretending to be suddenly very interested in something on the screen. She glanced at him again without meaning to and instantly regretted it. He was looking right at her, and she could tell he was about to come over and say something.

She took a breath, braced for the awkwardness of it, but at that moment her phone started to ring.

"Lance?"

"Is it a good time? I'm not interrupting—"

"No," she said, flustered, looking from the barista to the cup on the table in front of her. "It's a good time. I was just grabbing a coffee."

"You're not still at the office?"

"Where else would I be?"

"You haven't left since this started, have you?"

"My goldfish is dead, Lance. I have no reason to leave."

"You really need to get some balance in your life."

She supposed it wasn't a good time to tell him she'd been sleeping there. She'd even considered converting part of the sixth floor into an apartment of sorts. She'd already reached out to the building supervisor and maintenance department to see what could be worked out. They hadn't got back to her.

She picked up her coffee and went to the elevator.

"Are you sure it's a good time to talk?" he said. "You sound—"

"I can talk. I'm just getting in the elevator." She waited for the doors to close, then said, "It's not like you to make a personal call."

"Who said this is a personal call?"

"You asked about my goldfish."

"I didn't ask," he said, sounding uncharacteristically playful. "You just brought it up out of the blue."

"Well then," she said, matching his tone, "if this isn't about the fish, what is it about?"

"I felt I should touch base. I spoke to Roth."

The elevator doors opened, and the empty office stretched out in front of her, silent but for the low hum of the ventilation system. She made her way to the conference room and sat on the sofa, her blazer from earlier still draped over the back, badly creased from being used as a blanket.

"For two people who no longer work together," she said, "you two sure do talk a lot."

"We have a lot to talk about."

She leaned back on the sofa and stretched out her legs. She wouldn't have admitted it, but she was enjoying the call. She was glad to have someone to talk to. "Just say it. You miss him."

Lance was quiet for a moment, then said, "Maybe."

That surprised her. He didn't often admit things like that. Even as a joke.

"I miss *something*," he added.

She didn't say anything then, and the silence seemed to keep expanding until she said something to break it. "What did you talk about?"

"He told me not to go to Prague."

"He wants you in Russia."

"Yes. He wants me to connect with his guy there. Ritter."

"Ritter the fixer."

"Is that what he calls him?"

"That's what Tatyana and I call him."

"But he said Tatyana had a history with this assassin in Prague."

"Apparently she was something of a nemesis."

"Roth said she tried to kill her?"

"It's true. And Tatyana has made it very clear she's eager to return the favor."

"It's a vendetta, then?"

"I think it would be fair to say that, yes."

"What do you think of that?" Lance said.

"I think emotion is a bad idea in this business."

"That's what I was thinking."

"Are you saying she might do something stupid?"

"I think, for most people, it's hard enough to kill strangers and not do something stupid."

"Right," Laurel said.

"Killing someone from your past," he said, "from your own life. It's the kind of thing that can linger."

"Linger?" she said, again surprised by his words. He didn't usually talk like this.

"In your head," he said. "You think about it afterward. You dream about it."

"Well," Laurel said, "I think in this case it's not going to be an issue. Valentina Brik is most likely dead."

"Maybe," Lance said.

"You're not convinced?"

"I don't know, but whatever was going on there, we haven't seen the end of it. An assassin doesn't kill for no reason."

"No. I suppose not."

"Whatever was going on, it isn't over, and I don't think Tatyana should be facing it on her own."

Laurel sipped her coffee. She'd been enjoying the call, enjoying the attention, but now that the topic had moved to Tatyana, she had to admit she was starting to feel differently. "You're considering disobeying Roth," she said.

"I've already disobeyed him. I commandeered the plane he sent to take me to Russia. I'll be in Prague in an hour."

"He's going to have you for breakfast."

"He doesn't give me orders. Why do I have to keep reminding everyone of that?"

"Maybe because every time he tells you to jump—"

"I'm worried about Tatyana."

"I can see that."

"Is that a problem?" he said.

A knot of emotion formed in Laurel's chest. She hated

herself for feeling it, for caring, but emotions were wily things, hard to rein in. "Of course not," she said.

"Nothing adds up," he said. "A false alarm, a rogue agent, I'm not buying it. Whatever's going on over there hasn't happened yet, and Tatyana's marching right into it."

"Well," Laurel said, keeping her voice as flat and free of emotion as possible. "She's lucky to have you worrying for her."

"I'm not *worried* for her, exactly."

"Yes, you are," Laurel said.

"Are you all right, Laurel? I feel like I've upset you."

"I should go," she said curtly, then hung up.

She was upset, as much at herself as at him. She felt silly. It made no sense. There was nothing between her and Lance, and there never would be. If he was worried about Tatyana, he had every right to be.

She went to her computer and typed in the coordinates for the embassy in Prague. The view panned over the Eastern European countryside in stunning resolution. If it was daytime, she'd have seen cows in the fields, smoke in the chimneys. The satellite took a moment to align, then zoomed in on the area around the embassy, closer and closer until she could see the individual cobbles in the streets.

What had been the point of it, she thought. The killings. The attack on Valentina. Lance had been right about one thing. It didn't add up.

It was the middle of the night there, but she could see from Tatyana's access logs that she was still awake, still working at her terminal.

She got up and went to the window. There was traffic on the parkway, and beyond it, in the darkness, the

Potomac flowed on. Her phone vibrated, and she saw it was a message from Tatyana.

Valentina definitely connected to the Dead Hand.

The words sent a shiver down Laurel's spine. It was big news. The Dead Hand was the group tasked with maintaining president Molotov's position at all costs. If it was involved, then Prague was no sideshow. Something critical was in play. She should have called Tatyana back immediately, but for some reason, she couldn't bring herself to dial the number. Instead, she just stared at the satellite feed, looking down at the roof of the embassy, the narrow streets around it. If Tatyana had walked out the front door at that moment, Laurel would have seen her.

And Lance, he would be there soon. She felt unsettled. Worked up. She went to the sofa and lay back. It felt like a minute passed, but when she opened her eyes, she realized she'd been dozing. She leaped up from the sofa and went to the screen. Nothing had changed. Still the same view of the roof. The street. She ran the camera through the different wavelengths of the spectrum, everything from infrared to ultraviolet. There was a vehicle outside the embassy that was occupied. The infrared imager was picking up a heat signature.

That was slightly concerning. It was a public street, people came and went, but it was also late at night. She zoomed in on the vehicle, a gray Audi sedan, and scrubbed back in time. She'd had the area in focus for twenty minutes. The car hadn't moved. Whoever was inside had been there the whole time. The engine wasn't running. It would have been cold in the car.

She picked up her phone and, forgetting her earlier hesitance, called Tatyana's cell.

"Laurel? I'm just trying to confirm the connection, but I think—"

"Never mind that," Laurel said. "How near are you to the front of the building?"

"What? Why?"

"There's a gray Audi parked outside. By the entrance to the cultural institute."

Tatyana said nothing for a moment, then said, "I see it. Windows tinted. Is there something wrong?"

"Could be nothing," Laurel said, "but someone's inside. I think they're watching the embassy."

"Valentina," Tatyana gasped.

"We don't know that, but if you get the guards to check it out—"

"When I get my hands on that bitch," Tatyana spat.

"Tatyana," Laurel cried, "don't go out there." But it was too late. Tatyana was no longer listening. The line was open, Laurel could hear her barking orders to guards, but she couldn't stop her.

"You, and you, with me, now," Tatyana was saying.

Laurel kept her eyes glued to the screen. Tatyana and four embassy guards came out of the front entrance, and two more guards came out of the gate by the cultural institute.

Instantly, the Audi's engine fired up, and it pulled out of its spot, almost colliding with a passing cab. It accelerated rapidly down the narrow street. Tatyana sprinted after it, but it was no good. The car was gone.

"Did you see that?" Tatyana panted breathlessly into the phone.

"I'm watching," Laurel said. "That was incredibly stupid. You could have gotten yourself—"

"If that was her, so help me—"

"Tatyana!" Laurel said. "You need to calm down."

"Just track that car," Tatyana said. "Do not lose it."

35

Constantin, Stăn, and Boc stared at the hotel room phone, which was clanging loudly, its tiny metal mallet vibrating between two steel bells like an overexcited pinball machine.

Stăn was on a chair. He'd been hurt in the collision with the bus but not too badly. "Uh oh," he said, eyeing the phone like he expected it to leap up and attack them all any second.

They'd sent Badea out to do recon on the embassy while they went over the embassy schematics before the attack. They were about ready to leave.

"It could be him," Boc said.

"It could be anybody," Stăn said.

Constantin stepped forward and picked up the receiver. "What is it?" he growled, eyeing Stăn and Boc nervously.

It was Badea's voice, frantic, on the other end of the line. "I've been made."

"What?"

"They came out of the embassy and approached me."

"Who did?"

"Guards."

"What did you do?"

"I hightailed it, but Constantin, you're not going to believe who was with them."

"Who?"

"The defector, Tatyana Aleksandrova."

"What's she doing here?"

"I don't know, but it's bad news."

"Don't worry about it now. They'll be tracking you from above."

"I know that. I'm headed south, away from the hotel."

"And your phone? They'll trace it."

"Not fast enough to do anything about it."

"Well, ditch it as soon as I hang up."

Constantin got Stăn and Boc's attention and made a circular movement with his finger. "We're out of here," he said. "Pack up everything." It wouldn't take them more than a couple of minutes to tear down, and they got started immediately.

Constantin opened a laptop and pulled up a map of the city. "Have you passed the railway bridge yet?" he said to Badea. "Three steel arches over the river. You can't miss them."

"I see the bridge. I'm headed toward it."

"Pass it," Constantin said. "You'll see the Palacký bridge right after. You can cross the river there. There's a metro station on the other side. Ditch the car and lose the satellite on the subway. You need to shake them."

"Understood," Badea said. "Cut and run."

"Not cut and run, you dumb fuck," Constantin said. "This is a four man job, and you know it. You're not getting off the hook."

"We're still going through with it?"

"Yes, we're going through with it. Get your ass to the Můstek metro station pronto. Wait for us at the square. We'll pick you up in the van."

"This is going to be a complete shit show."

"Just keep your cool, Badea. We'll get through it, and once it's over, we're going to have real *walk-away* money. You understand me?"

"Yeah," Badea said, not sounding too convinced.

"This is it," Constantin said. "This is *fuck you* money. We'll be set for life."

"Got it," Badea said with a sigh.

"Good. Now throw away your phone and get underground. We'll see you at Můstek in an hour. We're picking up the weapons first."

The line went dead, and Constantin looked at the other two men. "What is it?" he said, sensing their unease.

"Are we sure we want to go through with it?" Stăn said.

"What do you think?"

"I think we need to take a step back."

"A step back? Do I need to remind you who we're in bed with?"

"Of course not."

"Osip fucking Shipenko," Constantin said. "We don't get to take a step back. We don't get to reconsider. We obey orders, and we all know what happens if we don't."

"But this," Stăn said, "this job...."

"This job what?"

"It's different, boss."

"It's not different," Constantin said, knowing his words rang hollow. They all knew exactly how different this job was. It was an order of magnitude more serious than anything they'd ever contemplated before. They weren't taking out a target, they were attacking a US embassy. It was the type of thing that started wars. Even if they walked away, the US government would hunt them down for the rest of their lives. Nothing would ever be the same again.

"The people who do this kind of thing," Stăn said, "are people with a death wish."

"That's their business."

"Suicide bombers, Constantin. Is that what we are? Is that what we want?"

"And what's the alternative?" Constantin said. "Do you want to cross Shipenko? How do you think that ends?"

Stăn threw up his hands. "So we're fucked?"

"That's right, we're fucked," Constantin said. "Unless we get this job done and get our pay."

Stăn looked at Boc. Constantin knew they weren't convinced, but he also knew they weren't disloyal. They were scared. That was all. He was too. And he knew it was a no-win situation.

"All the pay in the world is no good to a dead man," Boc said.

"And Shipenko's already told us that he was using Valentina Brik to lure another target," Stăn added. "We're taking her place as bait, aren't we?"

"So what?" Constantin said. He wanted the conversation to be over. "There's no point wishing it was otherwise. There is no otherwise."

"Don't you see it?" Stăn said. "Tatyana Aleksandrova. That's who he was trying to lure out all along. She's what he wanted, and now he's going to use us as the bait to get her."

Constantin suddenly did see it. That was the play.

That was why he'd been ordering hits on innocent embassy staffers. He'd known Tatyana would step in to stop it. "Well," he said, "it makes no difference to us. We have no choices here. No plays. We need to get out of this hotel before the street outside fills with cops."

"You read the dossier on Tatyana," Stăn said, refusing to drop the subject. "You know how dangerous she is. If we do this job, she's going to come after us."

"What would you prefer?" Constantin said. "That it was Shipenko himself who was after us?" He picked up his bags and made for the door. The others stood for a moment, looking at each other, then followed him. No one said a word in the elevator, but Constantin knew the situation was bad. They were right. This job was far more dangerous than anything they'd done before, and not all of them were going to be alive when it was over. Even if they survived the attack, they'd be hounded by the CIA until the end of their days. The men were close to mutiny. He could feel it. But if they didn't do the job, they were all dead men for certain. "I'd rather be up against Tatyana Aleksandrova than Osip Shipenko," he said as the elevator came to a stop. "That's it. That's what it comes down to."

They got out of the elevator at the hotel's underground parking lot. GRU agents based in the Russian embassy had arranged for a rental car, and he pressed the button on the key to find it.

A white Audi A3 beeped and flashed. "I'll drive," Constantin said.

"Have they placed the equipment?" Stăn said.

"It'll be there," Constantin said, referring to a van that the same GRU agents were supposed to have left for them at a long-term parking lot near the airport. "They dropped off a pickup ticket. The key is with the parking lot attendant."

Stăn nodded, and Constantin drove out of the parking lot onto the street. It was still snowing, and the city was eerily quiet as they made their way toward the airport.

"There's a reward on her head," Boc said.

"What's that?" Constantin said, pulling himself from his thoughts.

"Tatyana Aleksandrova," Boc said. "Shipenko put a reward on her head."

"I know that."

"Well?"

"Well, what?"

"Call him."

"For what?"

"Tell him we want it."

"I don't know if this is the time—"

"You just told Badea we were going to get *fuck you* money. I heard what you wrangled out of Shipenko on the phone."

"It's a good deal."

"Three million each is hardly the retirement we had in mind," Stăn said. "Not now that the entire American military will be hunting us down."

Constantin looked at them. They were deadly serious. If he didn't meet them halfway, he'd be carrying out this operation alone.

"Fine," he said. "I'll call from the van."

"Call now," Stăn said.

Constantin sighed. He handed his phone to Stăn to dial the code. Stăn put it on speaker, holding a finger to his mouth for Boc's benefit.

"Constantin," Shipenko growled when he answered. "Is there a problem? You haven't picked up the weapons."

"We're on our way now. Did they give us everything we asked for?"

"More or less. It was short notice. Is that the only reason you called, because you could have—"

"No," Constantin said, trying to come up with a way to broach the subject.

"Well, I'm all ears, Constantin."

"Tatyana Aleksandrova," he said, "is in the US embassy."

"What?"

"Badea just saw her. He recognized her from your bulletin. She's there."

"You're certain of it?"

"We're certain."

"I see," Shipenko said. He sounded pleased.

"It makes our job significantly more difficult," Constantin said.

"It changes nothing. The embassy was bound to have security."

"Not a GRU-trained assassin."

"She's hardly an assassin, Constantin. Not if you manage to keep your pants on. She's a whore. Nothing more."

"She's dangerous," Constantin said, knowing he couldn't back down.

"What are you telling me, Constantin?"

"The reward."

"What is this? We already negotiated. You want to be paid twice for the same job?"

"Acting as bait for your defectors was never part of our agreement."

"What are you talking about? Bait? Are you mad?"

"You're using us as bait to lure Tatyana."

Shipenko laughed. "You think what you want to think," he said. "But I don't give a rat's ass if you kill Tatyana or not. Just do your fucking job. Kill the whores in the embassy and get away."

Constantin was surprised. Judging from their faces, Boc and Stăn were too. "Look," he said, thinking on his feet, "I need to offer the men something more. They know we're not all going to make it."

"I've given you twelve million."

"Split four ways."

"Split fewer ways if someone dies."

"That's hardly reassuring."

"I'm giving you and your men the keys to the kingdom, Constantin. You've got safe passage."

"I need you to sweeten the pot," Constantin said, eying the other two men. "They're restless."

Shipenko let out a sigh. Constantin knew he understood. It was very difficult to motivate mercenaries when they knew they might not be alive to spend their paychecks.

"Do I need to get ugly?" Shipenko said.

"No, sir."

"I have files on all of them. They know that. I have files on everyone they ever loved. Everyone *you* ever loved, Constantin. I don't take kindly to men who try to weasel out of an agreement."

"Agreement? We never—"

"You said you'd do this. And you said Valentina Brik was dead. If either of those promises is broken, everyone you ever loved—"

"It won't come to that," Constantin said. "We'll finish the job."

"All of it."

"All of it. Yes."

"Because, renegotiating now, at this late hour, going back on an agreement, it might look to a less generous man that you were trying to act in bad faith."

"There's no bad faith here. I was just trying to get the men the best deal I could. You know the position I'm in."

"Sometimes you need to use the stick, as well as the carrot, Constantin."

"I know that, sir, but this job—"

"I'll tell you what. You remind your men of what they're getting. The keys to the kingdom, Constantin. They have my word. I'll bring them into the inner circle. They won't be forgotten. Moscow is a very comfortable place for friends of the Kremlin. They'll never want for anything again."

"And what if—"

"And if that doesn't calm their nerves, remind them what a nasty piece of work I can be when I'm pissed off."

"Very well," Constantin said. "And what about getting out of the country afterward? They need to know there's at least a reasonable chance of getting away after all this is done."

"You keep your promise, Constantin, I'll send you and your men my own personal jet."

The line went dead. Constantin looked at Stăn and Boc, uncertain how they would react. They knew what waited for them in Shipenko's inner circle. Prostitutes, drugs, champagne, caviar. Everything money could buy. Shipenko wasn't lying when he said the Kremlin looked after its own. It paid its bills. "Well?" he said when neither of them spoke up.

"Nothing," Stăn said.

"You're satisfied?"

Stăn shrugged. "Like you said. It's not like there's a choice."

"No, there's not. Everyone we ever loved is on the block if we don't do this."

"I know," Stăn said.

"And you, Boc?"

"I'm with you," Boc said.

"Good," Constantin said. They exited the highway and entered an industrial area near the airport. "The parking lot is around here somewhere."

"There," Boc said, spotting a rusted old sign that said *Worldwide Parking* in English.

There was a small office by the gate with a light on inside. Constantin drove up next to it and got out of the car. He entered and found a shabby attendant with a cigarette hanging from his lip sitting at a grubby desk. The man seemed to be asleep, and Constantin cleared his throat to get his attention.

"Yes, yes," the man said.

Constantin gave him the ticket.

The attendant hauled himself out of his chair to find the key, and Constantin stood and waited. He put a cigarette in his mouth and stared at an old map of Europe on the wall. He knew what he was asking of his men. He knew what he was asking of himself. By the time this night was over, someone would be dead.

The attendant came back with the keys to a Ford Transit van and some paperwork. Constantin scrawled a fake signature and went to the door. Through the little window, he could see Stăn and Boc waiting for him. Stăn was in the driver's seat of the Audi, and Boc was standing outside, smoking.

Constantin took his phone from his pocket and scrolled through his list of contacts. There was a call he needed to make, and he had the feeling that if he didn't make it now, he might not get another chance. He thought of his father, his grandfather, and the curse they'd passed down to him, then scrolled down to the name he needed —Cosmina—and pressed dial.

It took a moment for her to pick up, and when she did, she was worried that something was wrong.

"Nothing's wrong," Constantin said. "I'm sorry I called so late."

"What is it?"

There was little love lost between them, they'd been together only briefly, but it was long enough for Cosmina to become pregnant. She gave birth to a son, and for some reason, named him Mihai, after Constantin's grandfather. Constantin would never have allowed it, but they'd broken up by the time the baby was born, and he didn't find out until it was too late. He'd been distraught when he heard it. The name symbolized everything Constantin feared, everything that had gone wrong in his life, but he couldn't tell Cosmina that, so he told her nothing.

"Can I speak to the boy?" he said.

"He's asleep, Constantin."

"Wake him."

"Call him in the morning if you want to speak to him."

"I have something he needs to hear."

"He's two years old. Please tell me you're not drunk."

"I'm not drunk."

"I'm going to hang up."

"Cosmina," he said, "there's something I need you to tell him for me. When he's older."

"Are you in trouble?"

"Don't worry," he said. "I've made arrangements for you. For both of you."

"What are you talking about?" There was emotion in her voice now. He'd scared her.

"Don't cry."

"I'm not crying."

"You're better off without me. Mihai is too."

"What are you thinking, calling like this?"

"If something happens to me, you're going to get a call."

"What call?"

"From a Russian."

"I want no part of that world."

"Take the call," Constantin said.

"I don't need a payout from those people."

"Take it, for the boy's sake if not your own."

"I won't."

"I need you to tell him something for me, Cosmina. When he's older."

"You're speaking like you're already gone."

"Will you tell him? For me?"

She was crying. He was surprised. "I always thought you'd find your way back to us, Constantin."

"You don't want that."

"You're his father."

"Tell him, when he's older, that he's his own man."

"What does that mean?"

"If he ever learns about me. If he reads about me, about his grandfather, and his great grandfather, tell him he's not bound by it. Our stain doesn't stain him. He's clean. He's not sullied by it all."

"I don't know what you're talking about."

"You'll know if the time comes. Tell him I said it. Tell him it doesn't stain him. It doesn't touch him."

36

Klára leaned over the side of the Hlávka Bridge and looked down at the ice. She'd tried to sleep, but it was impossible. Tatyana's words kept coming back to her. "Don't think for one second she drowned in that river. She's alive." Rather than toss and turn and think about it all night, Klára got out of bed and came back to the spot.

It was dark beneath the bridge, and her breath billowed in the icy air, illuminated by the light of the street lamps. The place where Valentina broke through the ice had frozen back over, but she could see the shape of the hole. If anyone had broken through the ice anywhere, it would have been visible.

It was a few hundred yards downriver, however, where the river narrowed and the current got faster, that she was worried about. There were sections there that hadn't frozen over, and the river flowed through a large, forested park. If Valentina had made it that far, it was conceivable that she could have made it to shore without being seen by the satellite.

She took out her phone and thought about what Poborský had said. She thought about Gilhofer. It wasn't true that he was old enough to be her father. He was older than she was, but by fifteen years tops. She'd tried calling him, but he wasn't picking up. She took out her phone and tried again.

"Klára?"

"Gilhofer," she said, surprised he'd answered. "I was beginning to think you were avoiding me."

"It's been a madhouse here. The ambassador wanted to release the female personnel back to their homes, but then we spotted a vehicle outside that seemed to be spying on the embassy. Tatyana stormed out after it, and it sped off."

"Did she get the license plate?"

"Yes. Your people ran it for us. It's from a rental company known to have done business with the Russian embassy in the past. They put the plate out to Prague police. It seems the car's been abandoned by the Karlovo Náměstí subway station.

"So the Russians are watching the embassy?"

"Yes, but I mean, when are they not?"

"Are you worried?"

"Let's just say none of these women will be leaving the compound any time soon. We've been told in no uncertain terms that we can't have any more casualties."

"Of course," Klára said.

"What about you? What's the reason for the call?"

"I couldn't sleep."

"So you thought you'd...."

"Call you," she said, suddenly feeling awkward.

"I'm not sure what I can do," he said.

He was flustered too. She felt excited, even though she

wasn't sure what she was doing. She wasn't usually a flirt, and Gilhofer certainly didn't seem like the type either. She'd been thinking of Poborský's request, but there was more to it than that when she said, "There's been talk on our end of the possibility of getting access to the Keyhole surveillance from this morning."

"Langley's been poring over it," Gilhofer said. "If they tell me anything, you'll be the first to know."

"The thinking on our end," she said, "is that with our access to the scene, to the riverbank, we would be better positioned to interpret what the satellite picked up."

Gilhofer sighed. "They're pretty protective of that stuff, Klára. I don't know if it will do much good, but I can get Tatyana to pass on the request. I know she won't oppose it."

"She wants to find Valentina even more than we do," Klára said.

Gilhofer let out a worried laugh. "Yeah," he said. "She definitely seems to have a bee in her bonnet."

"Well, if a colleague tried to kill me, I'd hold a grudge too."

"Right," Gilhofer said. "I'll remember that." A streetcar went by on the bridge, and Gilhofer said, "What was that? Are you outside?"

"I'm on the bridge, actually."

"You're not serious!"

"If the satellite found nothing, and the CCTV found nothing, and the police didn't find a body—"

"Klára, you're mad! Have you at least brought backup?"

"I'm looking at the river right now, and I've got to say, whatever Tatyana may think, this water looks pretty darn cold."

"What are you thinking of doing?"

"The stretch downriver, where the trees hang over the riverbank, is the one section that the satellite didn't have a good view of."

"But it's been searched, hasn't it?"

"City police checked it, but BIS personnel didn't. And the police were looking for a body, not signs of someone climbing out."

"Well, can you at least promise me you won't go down there without backup?"

"I'm an intelligence officer. I don't get backup."

"Then wait for me. I'll be there in twenty minutes."

"Just follow my footsteps in the snow when you arrive," she said. "You'll see my car. I won't do anything crazy."

Her car was double-parked on the bridge with its hazard lights flashing. She went back to it and grabbed her flashlight, sidearm, and government-issued coat and boots. She pulled on the boots and went to the concrete wall that separated the bridge from the snow-covered slope on the other side. Then, she climbed onto the wall and dropped down to the other side, sinking two feet into the wet snow.

"Ugh," she said, feeling the snow enter over the tops of the boots.

She turned on her flashlight and shone it around. She couldn't be seen from up on the bridge unless someone leaned over the wall, but Gilhofer would be able to follow her easily enough. The riverbank sloped down toward the water, at the bottom of which was a low concrete wall about a foot high and two feet wide. Downriver, the bank opened onto parkland, where the trees provided overhead cover, and someone might conceivably have climbed out of the water unseen. Looking at it now, it seemed a very long way downriver, at least a hundred yards, and she couldn't picture anyone pulling it off, especially after being shot.

Nevertheless, she had to make sure with her own eyes. She began inching down the slope, the deep snow making her progress difficult, and more than once, she almost lost her balance. She was relieved when she made it to the bottom without falling into the water. She wasn't so far from the spot Valentina had gone through the ice, and she shone her flashlight out at it. She couldn't see much, but she suddenly realized that beneath the bridge, the ice was even thinner than it was in the open. She looked out at it. How had that not been considered? There were even patches where unfrozen water rippled, reflecting the beam of her flashlight. She'd been told that the river current was stronger than people realized, and to swim against it after the ordeal of being shot and falling would have been no small feat, but it had to be considered.

She stepped onto the low wall and began walking under the bridge, careful not to lose her balance. There was less snow beneath the bridge and more of the usual filth of a city—graffitied concrete slabs, bags of garbage, broken bicycles. At the top of the slope, in the sheltered nook where the bridge met the ground, there were some blankets and sleeping bags, even an old tent.

"Who's up there?" she called out, scanning the area with the flashlight.

There were definitely people there. She could see them already rousing themselves and shuffling away, clearly accustomed to being harassed by cops. There was a man, stooped so as not to hit his head on the bridge, shuffling away in a long black coat and wooly hat. There was also a younger guy dressed in what looked to be army fatigues. Everywhere were shopping carts and cardboard boxes and even a ring of stones for a fire pit. There was no fire now, but there was some sort of ventilation grate in the concrete bridge support, and periodic bursts of steam came from it, providing some heat.

"Who's there?" she said again. "I'm not police."

She began climbing the slope and saw that a third man was still on the ground, dressed in a grubby bomber jacket with a mangy-looking dog at his feet. A knot of filthy blankets were wrapped around his legs.

"Is there anyone else here?" Klará said, shining the light at his face.

He raised a hand to shield his eyes, then glanced around, his eyes darting left and right. He raised a hand to point, and Klarà spun around, but she was too late. She felt a hard crack on the back of her head, followed by the sound of smashing glass, and then everything went black.

37

Constantin and Stăn were in the back of the van, going through the ammo and weaponry, while Boc drove. Stăn held up a steel tube, about a yard long and six inches in diameter, and said, "I've got to admit, I didn't think they'd come through for us with these bad boys."

What he was holding was a piece of Soviet-era military hardware known as the RPO-A Shmel rocket-propelled infantry flamethrower. It was introduced during the waning years of the Soviet-Afghan War, when things were going badly for the Russians, and was designed to kill as much infantry as possible with a single shot. It had seen heavy use in Chechnya and eastern Ukraine, and Constantin and Stăn were experienced in its use.

"Two launchers," Constantin said, "and four RPO-Z rockets."

The RPO-Z variant was an incendiary warhead with a blast radius of thirty feet. It would decimate the unarmored guards of the embassy.

"Careful," Stăn said to Boc as he hit a large pothole.

"Sorry," Boc said.

The men's spirits were slightly higher now that Shipenko had come through with the hardware they'd requested. They were beginning to think they might actually survive the assault.

"How do they look?" Constantin said as Stăn checked each of the rockets in turn.

"They'll do," Stăn said. "They'll do nicely."

Each launcher held a single rocket and weighed twenty-four pounds when loaded. They could be carried, brought to firing position, launched, and reloaded by a single man. Stăn finished inspecting them, then packed them with the launchers into two large carryalls.

"This is it," Boc said, bringing the van to a halt. Constantin leaned forward to get a view of Wenceslas Square. It was deserted, and he was aware the van would look conspicuous there at that time of night.

"I don't see him," Boc said, throwing up his hands like he couldn't believe Badea would leave them waiting.

"Kill the engine," Constantin said. "Turn out the lights. We'll give him five minutes. He'll show."

Boc took out a pack of cigarettes, and Stăn said, "Are you mad?"

"Sorry," Boc said, putting them back in his pocket.

"We're literally sitting in a powder keg."

"I said sorry."

"Right," Constantin said, sensing their nerves. "Is everyone clear on the plan?"

"We are," Boc said, "but is Badea?"

"Come on," Constantin said. "Walk me through it. Last time."

"Fine," Stăn said, pulling a street map from his pocket and opening it up. "Boc is going to drop the two of us here." He pointed at Nerudova, the street a block over from Tržiště, where the embassy was located. "We get out with the Shmels and enter the old Liechtenstein Palace here. It won't be locked."

The palace housed the music and dance faculties of the Prague Academy of Performing Arts. It was open to students twenty-four-seven, and security was minimal.

"We take up position at the back of the building," he continued. "There are second-floor windows here and here." He pointed them out. "They have a clear view across Tržiště to the front of the embassy."

"I got all that," Boc said. "What I'm less clear on is how you figure me and Badea are to concentrate the guards around the entrance."

"You two take the van around the block," Constantin said, "and park somewhere along here. Not too close. Embassy security won't tolerate a van out there. Especially after what happened earlier."

"They'll tell us to move on," Boc said.

"Hop the seats and get in the back of the van. They won't be able to see you, but obviously they'll know the van didn't park itself. It's suspicious. They'll bang on the doors, draw their weapons, call it in to the police. More and more guards will come."

Boc looked at his watch. "That's five minutes."

Constantin looked at Stăn. "If Badea doesn't show," he said to Boc, "you'll have to do your part alone."

"Fuck that," Boc said. "This is a four-man job."

"All you have to do is stall the guards," Constantin continued. "Don't wait for the police to come, and don't force them to break into the van. But stall as long as you can. Give them time to muster. To concentrate."

"And then?"

"Then get back into the front of the van and open the door."

"They'll arrest me."

"They can't arrest you. They have no jurisdiction. No one can arrest you except Prague police, so get out before they arrive."

"And what do I say? They won't care if they have jurisdiction or not if they think I'm a threat."

"Just make a scene," Constantin said. "Act drunk. Be rude. You're there to agitate them. They'll get in your face, try to question you, but that's all. And if you start staggering down the street, away from the embassy, they won't stop you."

"They'll just let me go?"

"You're a local drunk. They don't own the street."

Stăn was loading the other weapons into more carryalls. They were for the next stage of the plan. There were four PP-19 Bizon submachine guns loaded with 9mm Makarov bullets. They could fire seven hundred rounds per minute and were light, accurate, and lethal. They also had four RG-6 revolver-style, six-shooter grenade launchers armed with forty millimeter high explosive shells. It was exactly what Constantin had requested, perfect for maximizing casualties.

"Once you're out of the way," Constantin said to Boc, the guards will be gathered at the front of the embassy. There's no way of predicting how many there'll be, but if you do your job right, it should be quite a few of them."

"And that's when we light them up," Stăn said.

"Rockets," Constantin said. "We'll take out dozens of them if you do your job right, Boc."

Boc looked out at the square. "We need to get out of here, boss. He's not coming."

Constantin looked at his watch again. "That piece of shit," he said. "I'll have his neck for this."

"Can we go?" Boc said.

"Go," Constantine said, "but like I said, it's a three-man job now."

"Are you sure about that?" Stăn said.

"What part of the plan requires Badea's sorry ass?"

Stăn gave Boc a worried look and said, "The next part, boss."

Constantin nodded. It was true that the next part of the plan was where the danger lay. If Boc did well, there could be as many as twenty security guards congregated in the street. The rockets would burn them to a cinder. He and Stăn would then fire off their second rockets, either at the guards in the street if they looked like they needed it, or at the embassy directly. Ideally, they'd fire a shot or two through an upper-level window. That was where the female staff were being housed for the night and where maximum casualties could be achieved.

Boc pulled the van away from the square, and Constantin said, "As soon as the rockets are fired, we all get to the van as quickly as possible and take up the other weapons. Stăn and I will try to kill the women with the rockets, but we'll be firing into the building blind. We need to go inside to confirm the casualties."

"A massacre of women," Boc said.

Constantin ignored the comment. None of them liked the job, but it was what it was. "Breaching the entryway is the most dangerous part. Even after the rockets, we might hit some resistance. The entry chamber is overlooked by a second-floor gallery and if there are guards up there, we'll be vulnerable."

"They'll be in tatters," Stăn said. "Disoriented, confused, injured."

"Which is why the risk of a frontal assault is acceptable," Constantin said. "We should have the firepower necessary to brute force our way through the lobby and up to the second floor. There's a wide corridor along the front of the building leading to the consular section. That's where the female personnel are being housed. We get up there, we confirm the job's been done, and we get out."

"The same way we came in?" Boc said.

"Yes, back to the van. If we can't get to the van, we split up and each make our way back to the safe house at Vršovice. We wait at the safe house until dawn. Then we disappear."

"No going home after this one," Stăn said.

"No," Constantin said. "And if anyone wants to make any calls, now's the time. Then we ditch the electronics."

"Did you call Cosmina?"

Constantin nodded. "I did. I said goodbye."

"What about Badea?" Boc said. "He knows about the safe house."

"For his sake, he better not show his face there," Constantin said. He ran a finger along his neck.

The other two nodded. They were all in agreement.

"Not far now," Boc said. "This is Nerudova."

Constantin looked at Stăn. "You ready for this?"

"I'm ready," Stăn said.

"What about you, big man?" he said to Boc.

"No one lives forever," Boc said dryly.

Stăn cleared his throat. "Maybe I will use the phone," he said.

38

L ance cleared customs at the private terminal at Prague airport and went straight to the payphones in the arrival hall. He called the embassy and gave a CIA clearance code. When he got through, he asked for the RSO.

"The RSO is unavailable," he was told by a stern-sounding woman.

"Tatyana Aleksandrova, then."

"Who is this?"

"Tell her it's the Asset."

"What asset?"

"She'll know."

He had to wait a minute for her. When she came on the line, she sounded stressed. "Lance? You're in Prague?"

"I'm at the airport."

"Good. Come straight to the embassy. Gilhofer literally just left the room. He's going back out to the Hlávka bridge."

"Where Valentina fell into the water?"

"Yes. He got a call from Klára Issová. She insisted on

having another look, and apparently he's worried about her going out alone."

"He should be," Lance said. "Valentina could be still out there."

"Right, well, she's somewhere."

"You're not convinced she's dead either?"

"Death is too good for the bitch. She's like a cockroach after a war. Nothing can kill her."

"It doesn't sound like you're too fond of her."

"Laurel told me that's why you came. You think my judgment has been compromised."

"I never said that."

"You're here instead of following Roth's orders and going to Russia."

"I'm here because I know what it's like to be personally connected to a mission. It's a headfuck."

"I can assure you, Lance, I'm thinking very clearly."

"Well, that's a shame," he said. "I hate to think I came all this way for nothing."

She was quiet for a moment, then said. "That's weird."

"What is?"

"A bulletin just came in on Gilhofer's feed. A Prague police unit just called for backup on the Hlávka Bridge."

"Is Gilhofer there yet?"

"He's probably not even out of the building yet."

"Does the bulletin say anything else?"

"Suspicious vehicle," Tatyana said, and then, "Oh, fuck."

"What?"

"Shots fired."

"I'll meet you there," Lance said, hanging up the phone.

He ran through the terminal and straight to one of the

cabs parked out front. "The Hlávka Bridge," he said to the driver in Czech. "How quick can you get there?"

"This time of night? Twenty minutes."

"Step on it," Lance said. "I'll give you a hundred US if you get me there in fifteen."

The streets were deserted, and the driver had him at the bridge scarcely ten minutes later. Lance paid him and said, "I've got another hundred for you if you wait here."

The driver eyed the police cruiser up ahead, its lights flashing. It looked like its windshield had been shot out. "No can do," he said.

Lance scanned the bridge. Two cars—the police cruiser and a sedan that he assumed was Klará Issová's. He wondered what had happened to Gilhofer. He should have been there already, Tatyana too, but he saw no sign of either of them.

He watched his cab do a u-turn, and then, everything was quiet. Lance was unarmed, and there was little scope for cover as he approached the vehicles. He should have waited for backup, but he could see the reflection of light in a pool of liquid near the police cruiser. It was blood, and he didn't know whose.

"Valentina Brik!" he called out, walking cautiously toward the car. He could hear static and garbled messages on the police radio. "Code Red," he heard, then it went back to static. He rounded the cruiser and saw the source of the blood. It was the uniformed patrolman, shot through the skull and lying on the ground.

He raised his hands slowly in the air and waited. "Valentina!" he said again. "I'm not armed."

"Don't move," a female said in Russian.

He couldn't see her, the voice came from behind him, but as he turned slowly, he saw that a back window of the sedan was open. She was inside. "Don't move, or you're a dead man."

"Where's Klára Issová?"

"If you try *anything,* she gets it."

"I'm not going to try anything," he said. It was dark, but he could just about make out her figure in the back seat of the car. There was someone in there with her, unconscious, lying on her lap.

Lance knew where Valentina had been trained. He knew how she'd been trained. One wrong move and things would get bad. Klára would be dead in an instant if she wasn't already.

"I want you to take out your gun slowly and put it on the ground," she said.

"I'm not armed."

"You expect me to believe that?"

"It's the truth."

"You want me to kill your friend?"

Very slowly, Lance lowered his arms and let his jacket fall to the ground. Then he pulled up his shirt so she could see the waist of his pants. He held it up and turned slowly until he'd done a full three-sixty.

"All right," she said. "Get in the car. The driver's seat."

"It's no good trying to run," he said. He could already hear police sirens, but something told him that things weren't quite right. Tatyana had known shots had been fired fifteen minutes ago. An officer had been killed. Where were all the police? Why hadn't they arrived? And where were Tatyana and Gilhofer?

"Hurry up," Valentina said. "Get in."

"It's crazy to run," Lance said, stalling.

"I'm the one with the gun," Valentina said. "I'll decide what's crazy."

"The police will be here any second," he said, glancing back across the bridge, expecting to see the blue and red glow of police lights at any moment. The sirens were getting louder and louder, and Lance prepared to dive for cover. "They're already here," he said when he saw the lights, but then something strange happened. A police car came into view but didn't turn onto the bridge at all. It drove right through the intersection, at full speed, sirens blazing, without so much as slowing down. It was followed by two more police cars. They were headed somewhere else.

The radio in the police cruiser crackled to life again, but the only words Lance made out were, "Code red, code red." He had no idea what it meant.

"What's going on?" he said.

"Come on," Valentina said. "Get in. I don't want this woman's brains all over my lap."

Lance got into the driver's seat of the car and shut the door. It was equipped with a radio, too, and without warning, Valentina pulled the trigger on her gun and fired a shot right into it.

"Whoa," Lance said, raising his hands.

"I didn't want you getting any ideas."

"You could have hit the engine."

"Just drive," she said. "Get us the hell out of here."

He turned the ignition, and the engine fired up. Then he pulled the car carefully away from the body of the dead police officer. They were headed toward Argentinská, and he picked up speed as they approached the main ring road.

"Go south," the woman said. "Highway Three toward Ceske Budejovice."

Lance knew what she was trying to do. The Austrian

border was just two hours away, completely open. Still, he didn't fancy her chances. Laurel would be tracking them by satellite. And whatever was going on with the Czech police, they were bound to get their act together very soon and set up roadblocks. There was no way Valentina was getting out of the country without a fight. And if by some miracle, she did manage to make it to the border, the Russians were hunting her down too. One way or another, her days were numbered, and she had to know it.

He looked at her in the rearview mirror. She'd taken off her shirt and was in a black sports bra. She'd patched up a gunshot wound on her shoulder as best she could, but he could tell just by looking that it was serious. He doubted she'd have been able to remove the bullet. And she'd been shot in the thigh too. Two gunshot wounds would slow anyone down.

He looked at the expression on her face as she checked her makeshift bandage and then pulled her shirt back on. He was looking at a caged animal, desperate, panicked, soon to be dead, and she knew it as well as he did. She was running, but only because that was what she'd been trained to do. If she had any sense, she would surrender to the Czechs. Better to be in a Prague prison than a cell in the basement of the Lubyanka. Her own side had turned against her. She'd killed Americans. She was screwed on both ends.

He saw more flashing lights in the mirror. The police were chasing them. "Better late than never," he said aloud.

"Keep driving," Valentina said, poking him in the back of the head with her pistol. It was a Glock 17, he noticed. He could have tried to snatch it from her, but it would likely lead to a car crash.

"It's over," he said. "You can't outrun them, and even if

you could, your own side is hunting you now. Wouldn't you rather be caught by the Czechs?"

She said nothing. He didn't want to push her too hard. He didn't want her to panic. She was a professional. She would see reason if he let her.

"Speed up," she said.

"We can't outrun them."

The police were moving fast. She glanced over her shoulder and saw for herself.

"They'll set up roadblocks," he said.

The look on her face was not of someone who wanted to die. She knew what she had to do. The game was up.

"Let me bring you in," he said. "You can't survive out in the cold with both the CIA and the GRU after you. No one can."

"I'm fucked," she said.

"They'll take it easy on you," Lance said, removing his foot from the gas.

"I killed a cop," she said.

"They won't kill you for that."

"They'll beat me up, though."

"You don't care about that."

She laughed mirthlessly. "Sure I do."

"The embassy then. I'll bring you to the embassy."

"The American embassy? I just killed two innocent women. They'll never cut me a deal."

"Well, believe me, you don't want to be brought back to Moscow."

"What are you doing?" she said. "Why are you slowing down?"

"You might have a death wish," he said. "But I don't."

"I'm not letting them take me," Valentina said, raising

her gun to her head. "I'll kill myself before I let them take me."

Lance put his foot on the brake, and the car skidded to a halt. Then he turned toward her, and they locked eyes. "Don't do it," he said, holding her gaze. "Let the Czechs take you. It won't be so bad."

"You know what happens to people like me."

He looked at her, looked in her eyes, and knew that in the end, he really didn't care if she killed herself or not. Everything she'd said was true. She'd killed the two staffers. Two women. She'd killed the cop on the bridge. She was an assassin, a killer, just like him, and the world would be better off when all of them were dead.

But then something happened. The police cruisers that had been gaining on them didn't stop. They didn't even slow down. They flew right by, six of them, and kept going.

"What the hell is going on?" Lance said.

The expression on Valentina's face turned. The game wasn't up yet. She put her gun back where it had been, against Klára Issová's head, and said, "Drive. Now."

Lance drove on, wondering what the hell was going on in the city that the police were so preoccupied. The more he drove, the more worried he became. As they passed the exit for the Trojský Bridge, he saw dozens of police cruisers, ambulances, and fire trucks. In the air, two choppers flew low over the river.

"What's happened?" he said.

She shrugged. "Nothing to do with me."

"But you know what it is," he said, looking at the radio she'd put a bullet in.

"No, I don't."

"Why do I find that hard to believe?"

"Believe what you want," she said, "but get in the next lane. Take the tunnel."

She still hadn't given up. In the tunnel, she would switch cars and throw the satellite. Her chances of making it to Austria were still one in a million, but she wasn't giving up.

"Do it," she said again, and he switched lanes.

He brought the car into the Blanka tunnel complex, the longest city tunnel network in Europe, where three separate tunnels extended for miles in multiple directions. There were exits all over the northwest corner of the city. Even without changing cars, Laurel would have had a hard time finding them when they came back out. It would take multiple satellites to keep all the relevant areas in focus, and Laurel only had exclusive access to one.

There was virtually no traffic in the tunnel, and, about a mile after entering it, Valentina said, "Stop the car." Lance turned on his hazards and pulled over. The tunnel had narrowed to two lanes in their direction with no shoulder. Their car blocked the slower of the two lanes.

"Even if you make it to Austria," he said, "what can you possibly hope to—"

"Who said we're going to Austria?"

He shrugged.

"Get out," she said. "Flag down the next car that approaches."

He got out and stood in the live traffic lane. Valentina got out, too, leaving Klára in the car alone. For all Lance knew, she was already dead. Valentina raised her gun and fired two perfectly placed shots at a traffic camera on the ceiling. Then she went to the far side of the car, where she wouldn't be seen by approaching vehicles, and crouched down. She could see Lance and kept her gun pointed at him.

"One wrong move," she said, "and I blow your head off."

A car approached, an old Honda, and just as he was about to stop it, Valentina told him to let it pass. It slowed down, and he waved it on. She said the same for the next two, and he let them pass also. They waited another few minutes for the next vehicle, which was a new, black Mercedes SUV, and Valentina said, "This is the one."

Lance stood in the lane and got the driver to come to a halt.

"What's going on?" the driver said, leaning out his window. "If you've broken down, I don't have time to help."

Valentina crept around the back of the SUV and snuck up behind the driver. Lance realized too late what she had in mind. Before he could do a thing to stop her, she pulled the trigger of her gun. There was a single, loud crack of a gunshot, and the sound ricocheted and echoed in the confined space of the tunnel.

The man's head jerked forward, and blood flew out onto the road. Lance's eyes widened in shock. The man's body slumped down over the side of the door. "What the hell—"

"Shut up," Valentina said, pointing the gun at Lance. "You're no better than me. You've done worse."

"Not for no—"

"Get him out of the car. Come on. Hurry. Throw him behind that wall. If someone gets here before you're done, I'll kill them too."

Lance pulled the man from the car and dragged him

to a drainage gutter that ran behind a low concrete barrier to the right of the traffic lanes.

"Get his wallet," Valentina said.

Lance took the man's wallet, then lifted the body over the barrier and let it fall into the gutter on the other side, where it couldn't be seen.

"Now, get the woman from the car. We're going to need some leverage."

Lance went back to the car and got a clear look at Klára for the first time. She'd been cuffed and gagged and seemed unconscious. He put his hand on her neck to check for a pulse, and she opened her eyes slightly.

Lance eyed Valentina, who was watching from a few yards away. He leaned forward so that the door blocked her view of him and whispered to Klára, "If she realizes you're awake, she'll kill you."

"Hurry up," Valentina said. "I told you what happens to anyone who comes along while we're still here."

"I need to take this tape off her mouth," Lance said.

"Leave it."

"She'll suffocate."

"Just put her in the back of the SUV. Try anything, and she pays the price, you understand?"

Lance lifted Klára in his arms and carried her over to the back of the SUV. Valentina kept her gun on him the whole time.

He was about to put her in the trunk when he stopped and said, "She's a liability. You should leave her here."

"What are you talking about?"

"You'll be across the border in two hours. You don't need leverage with the Czechs. You need leverage with the CIA."

"What do you know about what I need?"

"With the situation you're in, the CIA is the only friend who can do you any good."

"The CIA will never be a friend of mine."

"Well, taking this woman is a mistake. She's not a cop, she's a Czech intelligence officer. She was tasked with finding you, and if you take her, the entire BIS will be after you."

"Stop talking. Put her in the trunk."

"You're guaranteeing they'll put up roadblocks. They'll put choppers in the air. They'll do anything to recover her. I'm not lying. If you want to get out of this country, you need to leave her behind."

Valentina's jaw clenched while she thought about what he was saying.

He watched her think for a moment, then said, "The last thing you need is an extra hostage."

She looked at the gun in her hand and said, "Fine. Fuck it. Put her on the ground."

"No," Lance said. "You can't kill her. If you do, you're as good as dead."

"And what's it to you if I make it or not?"

"Our interests aren't as misaligned as you think," he said.

"Why do I find that hard to believe?"

"I know that you killed those women from the embassy," Lance said. "But what I *want* to know is who ordered it and why. I need you to tell me that."

He watched her mind at work—processing all the angles like an old Turing machine breaking a code. He knew the cold, brutish world she'd come up in, and he knew he could rely on her to act in her own self-interest. What he'd told her made sense.

"You expect me to believe—"

"I expect you to see there's a deal to be made."

"If you try to double-cross me—"

"You'll kill me."

Valentina looked up and down the tunnel as if that might tell her what to do, then sighed. "Okay," she said. "Put her back in the car, then get in the driver's seat and get us the hell out of here."

Lance put Klára back in the car and took the tape from her mouth. There was nothing he could do about the cuffs but it wouldn't be long before she was found. Any cop could get them off her. He didn't know if she was still conscious or not, but he leaned in close to her and whispered, "Highway Three, south toward Austria." Then he went back to the SUV and got into the driver's seat. Valentina sat in the back, behind the passenger seat, where she had a clear view of every move he made. She held the gun in her lap, angled directly at his head.

"What now?" he said, pulling away.

"We're going to the Austrian border."

He drove on, and they exited the tunnel near the Strahov Monastery. Before they entered the next tunnel, he saw an entire fleet of ambulances and other emergency vehicles crossing the bridge above the highway. Something very big was definitely going down.

Valentina watched the vehicles too, and Lance said, "What have you done?"

She eyed him defiantly in the mirror, then said, "Keep driving."

They entered the next tunnel, then left the city southward, following signs for Bratislava and Vienna. They drove for about ten minutes before the road split, and from there, they took Highway Three directly south toward Ceske Budejovice and Linz.

It was quiet in the car. Valentina was lost in thought, and he wasn't surprised. There were precious few options left for her to play, and she had to be going through them all, over and over, searching for a way out of her predicament.

"This isn't going to turn out the way you want," he said.

"You don't know how I want it to turn out."

"Yes, I do."

"Stop talking."

"What's going on with all the police?"

"How would I know? I was fighting off hypothermia underneath a bridge."

"Why did you kill those two women?"

"I'm a tool. I pull the trigger. I don't choose the targets."

"Why is your own side after you?"

She sighed and looked out the window. She was done talking. Lance wondered how much she knew. He wondered if she even knew that Tatyana was in Prague.

"Just shut up and drive," she said.

39

Gilhofer was waiting for the elevator outside the Station Chief's office. She'd stopped him to get an update on the situation, and he'd had to tell her he was in a hurry to get away. His phone started to ring, and he saw on the screen it was Tatyana. He wondered what she wanted so soon after leaving her. "Tatyana?"

Her voice was panicked. "Shots fired on the Hlávka Bridge," she said. His office was so near he could hear her voice carry down the corridor.

"What?"

"It just came in on your police bulletin system. Where are you?"

"I'm still here. I'm standing at the elevator."

"Wait for me," she said as the elevator arrived.

He got in and held the door with his foot. Tatyana came storming down the corridor toward him, already checking her gun.

"Come on," he said. "Come on."

She got in, and he pushed the button for the ground

floor repeatedly as if that would make it go faster. He'd dialed Klára's cell number, but it was going through to voicemail.

"Nothing?" Tatyana said.

He shook his head and shoved the phone into his pocket. "I have a very bad feeling about this," he said.

Tatyana was about to respond when suddenly, the entire elevator shuddered violently. "What the hell was that?" she said.

Neither of them dared say what they were thinking. The elevator jammed to a halt, stuck between two floors. Then the fire alarm came on, its steel bell clanging above their heads with the ferocity of a jackhammer. A second later, it was followed by the sprinklers.

"We need to get out of here," Tatyana said.

Gilhofer nodded, mashing the elevator emergency button over and over. There was no answer.

"That was an explosion," Tatyana said.

He looked at her again, then nodded slowly.

She looked up at the ceiling, then said, "Give me a boost."

He bent down and linked his hands. She stepped up and pushed a steel tile from the ceiling, giving her access to the elevator shaft. He pushed her up, and she slipped through the opening. "We're between the second and third floors," she said. "I can see light."

"Pull me up," Gilhofer said.

She reached down for him and tried to pull him up, but he was too heavy. Then they heard gunfire, rapid, automatic. It was coming from the corridor.

"The building's been breached," Tatyana said, rising to her feet to get a better look around the shaft. "I think I can get out."

"You're not leaving me," Gilhofer said, but she ignored him. She used the main elevator cable to pull herself up to the level above, then disappeared from view.

"You've got to be kidding me!" he said, but if she heard him, she made no reply.

He saw light as she managed to open a door, but immediately the entire shaft filled with the sound of more gunfire. In desperation, he slammed his fist on the control panel. Suddenly, the elevator dropped. He braced for impact as it fell one floor, maybe two, before an emergency cable yanked taut and stopped it from crashing into the concrete foundations two more levels down. The jolt knocked him to the floor, and he hit his head hard. He was dazed, disoriented, and then, as if on cue, the lights went out, leaving him in complete darkness.

"God help me," he whispered, struggling to his feet. No sooner was he standing than the sharp crack of more gunfire filled his ears. The bullets clanged and ricocheted against the metal doors of the elevator, and he dropped again for cover. He was still on the floor when the doors began to shudder open mechanically. They only opened a few inches before getting stuck, and he got up and began to pry them further apart. It took all his strength to move them just a few more inches, but it was enough that he could squeeze through the gap. He tripped on something on his way out and, looking back, realized it was the dead body of an embassy security guard.

A fire was burning somewhere, and the corridor was filling rapidly with thick black smoke. He coughed as he strained to see what lay ahead, then his ears filled with the staccato burst of more gunfire—and then, screaming. A lot of screaming. Agony, terror, desperation. He heard women mostly, injured, burning, begging for mercy, but he couldn't tell from which direction.

He stumbled forward, down a flight of stairs, and found himself in the main lobby at the front of the building. The embassy's entire front entrance had been blown away, and the cold air from outside cleared enough smoke to give him his first view of the devastation. The sight before his eyes defied belief. He'd been in that same lobby not thirty minutes earlier, but it was utterly unrecognizable now.

Everywhere there was carnage. Security guards, military personnel, civilian staff—no one had been spared. Everywhere they lay on the ground, dead or dying, moaning or crying or screaming in terror. It was a scene from a warzone. He saw a woman whose leg had been blown off in the explosion. She was still alive, completely in shock, and he was about to run to her when a security guard staggered into the lobby from the street outside, and, to Gilhofer's horror, the man was on fire. His clothing, his hair, his skin. It was like footage from the Vietnam war.

"What the..." Gilhofer stammered, unable to comprehend what was before him. The man collapsed on the ground, flailing desperately in his death throes, and Gilhofer ran toward him.

As soon as he took the first step, however, Gilhofer dropped to one knee. There was something wrong with his leg. It was hurt. Slowly, through the haze of his confusion, it dawned on him that he'd been shot. His brain had failed to register it. He hadn't heard the shot, hadn't even felt the bullet, but when he looked down, one entire leg of his pants was completely soaked in blood. He reached down and touched it as if he doubted it was real, then looked at the blood on his fingers.

Drawing on some deep resource in his mind, more instinct than conscious thought, he reached into his jacket and pulled out his gun. In the smoke, the chaos, the confusion, he waited, coughing, eyes streaming with tears, and counted. Everything grew silent. He didn't know what he was doing. He scarcely knew where he was. But he raised his hand, shut one eye, and pulled the trigger.

In that instant, a man appeared in the doorway, running, carrying a submachine gun and wearing a balaclava. Gilhofer's bullet struck him right in the chest, and before he even knew what was happening to him, the man was lying on the ground, face-up, staring at the ceiling.

Gilhofer coughed and wiped his eyes and strained to breathe as he staggered forward. The entire front of the building had been destroyed in an explosion. Cold air was coming from outside, and instinctively he moved toward it. Out in the street, the carnage was even worse than inside. There was more screaming, more gore, and everywhere he looked, the mutilated bodies of security personnel littered the ground.

He staggered outside, gasping for breath, as noise and confusion bombarded him from every direction. Snow whorled in the wind, lit by the flames of burning vehicles. The pain in his thigh forced him to one knee, and it was then that he felt a grabbing at his ankle. When he turned, his mind failed to register what his eyes saw. He thought he was having a nightmare. There was a man on the ground, if the creature before him could still be called a man, and he was clutching at Gilhofer's leg, using his dying breaths to beg for mercy. Gilhofer regarded him in horror. Skin was falling from his face, from his charred limbs, and with a voice that scarcely sounded human, he gasped, "Kill me."

Gilhofer leaned down over him. There was no chance of survival. That was clear. The man's nose was gone. His ears were gone. There were only openings where they had been.

"Kill me," the man said again.

Gilhofer no longer knew what he was doing. Tears streamed down his face. He wiped his eyes and put his gun under the man's chin. Then he pulled the trigger. The moaning stopped.

Gilhofer pulled himself to his feet. He staggered away and threw up. Then he looked back at the body. In all that chaos, in all that destruction, he'd noticed a strange detail. The man's socks weren't burned at all. They were untouched, almost clean. They were sports socks, and the logo on them said Tulsa Oilers.

"Pritzker!" Gilhofer gasped, then he let out a long, low wail, like the sound an animal might make. It was a lament from deep inside his soul as he realized the man he'd just killed was a boy, the kid from Pawhuska, Oklahoma, who talked about hockey while he ate his donut.

Gilhofer fell over Pritzker's body, buried his face in his chest, and cried.

And then he heard a voice. "He's dead."

Gilhofer swung around with his gun but whoever was there kicked it from his hand, then kicked him in the chest. He fell backward, knocked his head hard on the ground, and might even have blacked out for a moment. When he opened his eyes, a man was standing above him, silhouetted in the night air against the glow of the flames. And perhaps it was the light, and the whorling snow, and the sulfur and smoke, but in that moment, something looked unnatural about the man. It was his eyes. They were glistening, catching the light from the flames, and they looked red.

"You devil," Gilhofer cried. "You cursed, hellish monster."

The man's expression changed when he heard the words. He put his gun to Gilhofer's forehead. "What did you say?" he said.

"I said, you're cursed," Gilhofer said. "Cursed to hell." And then, all the world was black.

40

Tatyana ran toward the rooms where the female embassy personnel had been setting up their makeshift quarters. She couldn't believe it when she got there. It was a bloodbath. Everyone, from consular and diplomatic personnel to local secretarial and custodial staff, had been slaughtered where they lay. Women lay dead in the military cots they'd been sleeping in. They lay dead in the corridors, shot in the back as they ran for exits. There were bodies crouched in corners, behind furniture, even in bathroom stalls and storage closets where they'd tried to hide from the gunmen.

Tatyana drew her sidearm and burst into the station chief's office, where she saw Carmen Linder, dead at her desk with more than a dozen bullets in her chest.

She heard more gunfire and went to the door. When the shots stopped, she pushed the door open slowly with her foot. There was a man at the far end of the corridor. He was facing the other way, and, without thinking, Tatyana began to charge straight at him. He turned and saw her, and then, almost casually, he raised a grenade launcher to his shoulder and fired off a round. The grenade ricocheted against the ceiling, then bounced off the floor, heading directly toward her.

She dropped to the floor as it bounced over her head, exploding behind her. The shockwave flew down the enclosed space of the corridor and struck her like a wall of water. Everything went black, she couldn't breathe, she couldn't see, and, apart from a high-pitched squeal in her ears, she couldn't hear. She crawled forward, then struggled to her feet, using the wall for support. By the time the smoke cleared, the man was gone.

She staggered down the corridor, stepping over a trail of dead bodies as she followed the path the man had taken back toward the front of the building. When she got to the gallery overlooking the front lobby, she saw embassy security guards everywhere, dead and dying. The attackers had used incendiary rockets to maximize the casualties.

The gunfire seemed to have stopped, and she descended the staircase and rushed out to the street. More bodies, more fire. It had been an all-out military assault. There was a white van backing away at the far end of the street, and she raised her gun in time to let off six shots before it rounded a corner. Its windshield shattered, and it smashed a wing mirror against another vehicle as it disappeared. She sprinted after it. By the time she reached the corner, it was speeding away. She fired more shots but to no avail. All she could do was read the license plate. She knew it would do no good, the van would be ditched in a matter of minutes, but she kept repeating the number to herself, over and over, like a mantra.

She hurried back toward the embassy and saw some-thing she recognized. Gilhofer's blazer. She'd seen it scarcely five minutes earlier when she'd left him in the elevator. The blazer wasn't by itself, it was on a body that lay face up in the snow. As she got closer, she saw that it was him. She crouched down and checked for a pulse. There was none.

Someone approached from behind. Moving as swiftly as a cat, she grabbed a wrist as it reached out to touch her shoulder, then twisted a man's arm backward as she rose up and spun behind him. She bent the arm back hard, and the man gasped, "Ms. Aleksandrova! Please!"

It was only then that she realized it was an embassy security guard. "Sorry," she muttered, releasing him.

He took a step back, eyeing her like a dangerous animal that could pounce at any second. "You're in shock," he said.

The ringing in her ears was so loud she could only just make out what he was saying.

"The RSO," she said, looking at Gilhofer's body.

"I know," the guard said, "but there's something you need to see. He got one of them before he died."

She followed him back toward the embassy and saw a man lying on the ground wearing a balaclava. He'd been shot in the chest, and blood sputtered from his mouth as he struggled to breathe.

She crouched down to get close to him. There wasn't much time. Blood gushed from his chest, and he could lose consciousness any second.

"What's your name?" she said in Russian.

He shook his head, and she grabbed his hand, laid it flat on the ground, and jammed the barrel of her pistol against it.

"Last chance to do it the easy way," she said.

The man looked at her, narrowed his eyes, clenched his jaw. She pulled the trigger. He screamed in pain, and Tatyana, ignoring his cries, grabbed his other hand and spread it on the ground like before.

"Let's keep going," she said. "Your name?"

"Boc," the man gasped. "Vasile Boc."

"You're not Russian."

"I'm Romanian."

"What's a Romanian doing here?"

"I don't know. I follow orders. I'm just a foot soldier."

"Oh, you're more than a foot soldier now, Vasile Boc. What you just did could start a war."

"I work for money. That's all. I swear."

"You work for Constantin Antonescu."

His eyes widened when she said the name. "How do you know—"

"You're the Prime Directorate's dogs, you and your crew."

"I know nothing of the client. Constantin deals with all of that."

"You know who gives the orders, though, don't you?"

"I swear, I know nothing."

Tatyana pressed the gun into his hand hard and said, "You ever want to shuffle a deck of cards again, you better start remembering." She could see in his eyes that he knew he was going to die. The only question was how much pain he would feel before it happened. "I saw some men burn," she said. "You did that. You set them on fire."

"No," he said, shaking his head.

"It only seems fair that you burn too," she said. She turned to the guard and said, "Find me some gasoline. Go, now." The guard ran off, and she turned back to Boc. "Come, now. Who ordered all this? All I need is a name."

He hesitated, just a little too long for her liking, and she pulled the trigger again. He yelped in agony like a stricken dog, a pitiful sound.

"Come on," she said again.

"Shipenko," he said weakly.

Tatyana wasn't sure she'd heard correctly. She leaned closer. "What did you say?"

"Shipenko. Osip Shipenko."

"Shipenko?" she said, touching her cheek. "Shipenko? With the face—"

"Yes."

"Bullshit," she said, emotion suddenly filling her chest.

"Not bullshit. It's true."

She knew who Shipenko was. She'd met him, just once, outside the president's office at the Kremlin. She'd been there with Aralov, and as they were leaving, Shipenko stopped them in the hallway with his walking stick.

"Hey," he said, poking her with the cane as if she was a farm animal to be prodded. "I know you."

She looked up and would never forget the sight that met her. The shock of it. She shuddered every time she thought of it.

"I don't think so," she'd said. Aralov was right behind her, and she turned back to him for support, but he said nothing. That meant the man before her was powerful. She didn't know who he was then, but Igor told her his name after.

She remembered the way he looked at her, like he was

a starving animal and she was a piece of meat he might devour. He raised his cane to her chin to make her tilt her head upward. "Let me look at you," he said. He ran the cane down the side of her leg, then up the inside. She was wearing a knee-length skirt, and he used the cane to raise the hem until he'd revealed her underwear. Tatyana had glanced at Aralov, then at the receptionist. Neither uttered a word.

"No one's going to save you," Shipenko said, letting out a wheezy laugh.

"We need to go," she'd said, but he prodded her, between the legs, with the tip of the cane. "You're not going anywhere. It's my right to have you. I don't need anyone's permission."

She looked back at Igor again, but he refused to meet her eye.

"That's right," Shipenko said. "I can have you. I can own you. No one will stop me."

Tatyana looked at him and tried to imagine what could have happened to disfigure him so terribly. It was like nothing she'd ever seen.

The tip of the cane pushed harder, making her feel extremely vulnerable. Her eyes watered. She didn't know where to turn. She knew what men like him could do. If Igor was afraid of him, there was no one who would stop him.

But then, by some miracle, the one man who could stop him, the president, appeared at the doorway. Tatyana had never thought she'd be glad to see Molotov's face, but at that moment, she could have kissed it.

"Osip!" the president snapped, as if scolding a dog. "Let her be. Leave *something* for the others."

And, just like that, the moment was over. Tatyana and Igor fled, and even though she'd never run into Shipenko again, she never for a second forgot him. She never forgot he was there, somewhere, lurking in the shadows of the Kremlin, and every time she went there, she thought of him.

Afterward, she'd done her research, but there was very little on Shipenko for her to learn, other than that he was close to the president. And there was certainly no way this Romanian mercenary could have known his name if what he was saying wasn't true.

"So, Shipenko's the one who gives you your orders?"

"Yes," the man said. "He sends them to Constantin."

"The Splinter?"

"That's what they call us. Some people."

"So Shipenko also gives Valentina Brik her orders?"

"I don't know about that. I never heard of Valentina Brik until Shipenko ordered us to follow her."

"And why was that?"

"I don't know. He was up to something. How could I know what it was?"

"Why did he want you to attack the embassy?"

"Who knows? It makes no sense."

"And yet, you did it."

"We were told to create carnage. That's what he wanted. He wanted us specifically to target the women who were taking shelter here."

"But why?"

He shook his head. He was losing too much blood. She looked at the wound in his chest. If she got him to an ambulance, there was a chance he would survive. But then, she didn't think there was that much more to be learned from him, and she certainly didn't think it was enough to justify keeping him alive longer than necessary.

She wondered what path he'd taken to end up there that night, lying on the ground before her. Then she raised her pistol to his temple, turned away her face, and pulled the trigger.

41

Stăn did the driving. Constantin watched their tail.

"Anyone?" Stăn said, rounding a corner and getting onto the ring road.

"No one," Constantin said. "Drive carefully. From here on, we stick to the plan."

"Hopefully, no one notices the shot-out windshield."

"Just get us to the safe house. If we make it that far, it will be a miracle."

They drove quietly until Stăn looked at Constantin and said, "We lost Boc."

Constantin nodded. There was a camaraderie that came from risking their lives together, from relying on each other, and losing Boc hurt. It cut close to the bone. Especially so soon after losing Badea. The four men had been through a lot together. This was the end.

They drove on in silence until Stăn said, "If Boc's the only one to pay the price, we got off light."

"You can say that again."

They exited the highway and turned onto a road lined with tall trees and expensive homes. The homes were built into the hillside and had long, private driveways and expansive views of the surrounding farmland.

"Up here," Constantin said. "This is it."

Stăn slowed as they passed the driveway of the safe-house. It had been prepared for them by the GRU, and the plans for getting them out of the country were supposed to be inside. Constantin saw a maroon-colored minivan parked in the carport. Next to it was a large garage where they were to leave the van.

"Looks clear," Constantin said. "I'll open the garage. You drive on and double back."

Stăn nodded. "I just hope there are arrangements for a jet when we get inside."

"He's never let us down so far."

"We never did something that could spark off a war before, either."

It was almost dawn, and the sky was beginning to lighten.

"Okay, let's not linger. Just go on a mile or two, make sure you're not being followed, and turn around."

Constantin got out of the van and made his way up the gravel driveway on foot. He approached cautiously, his hand on the gun in his jacket pocket. About halfway up, he stopped and listened. Everything was quiet. He entered the gap between the house and garage and checked the garage side door. It was open, as he'd been told it would be, and inside, there was a button to open the garage door. He pressed it, and the electronic motor clanged and hummed as the rickety door opened. It seemed painfully loud in the dawn stillness.

He watched the road then, waiting for Stăn. His hand trembled slightly as he lit a cigarette. He'd never killed so many people at once before. By his own count, he'd killed at least a dozen of the guards. Inside, in the women's quarters, it had been worse. Possibly twice as many. How could he come back from that, he wondered? How could he go on? How could a man sink that deep into the underworld and ever hope to reach the surface again? He sucked nervously on the cigarette and then cocked his head. He thought he heard something.

He drew his gun. How had they gotten there so fast, he wondered. It wasn't possible unless someone at the embassy had sold them out.

He scanned the road, the grounds in front of the house. All was as silent as it had been. Then he crept around the back. There was a wide set of glass patio doors leading to a patio. Inside was the kitchen. The lights were out, but he could see there was something there. As he got closer, he realized it was the blue flame of a gas burner. Someone was boiling water on the stove.

He put his hand against the glass patio door and tried to slide it open. It moved, but no sooner had it started than it let out a loud squeak. He froze instantly, readying himself for some coming onslaught. Time seemed to stand still, seconds stretched, and then he heard a familiar voice.

"Constantin?"

It was Badea, who emerged cautiously from behind the kitchen door holding a pistol.

Constantin waited for him to lower his gun before doing the same. "What are you doing here?" he said.

"It was the plan," Badea said. "Meet here if we separated."

They heard the van pulling up the driveway. It entered the garage, followed by the sound of the garage door closing. "That's Stăn," Constantin said.

The two men eyed each other. "You were making coffee," Constantin said to ease the tension.

"Yes," Badea said.

Constantin put his gun back into his jacket. "Go on, then," he said. "We're going to need it."

Badea went to the stove, his gun in his hand by his waist.

Stăn came around the back of the house and appeared at the door. The instant he saw Badea, he drew his gun.

"Stăn!" Badea said. "What are you doing?"

"You've got some nerve, showing your face here," Stăn said.

Badea eyed the pistol nervously. He had a hand on the kettle, and Constantin realized he was near enough to be burned badly if he flung it.

"Boc's dead because of you," Stăn said.

"I had a tail," Badea said. "I was being followed."

"Bullshit," Stăn said.

"I couldn't risk leading them to you. I couldn't compromise the mission."

"Where's this tail now?" Constantin said.

Badea looked at each of them in turn. There was a desperation in his eyes Constantin had never seen before. "I lost them," he said.

"You fucked us," Stăn said, still pointing his gun at Badea.

"Believe me," Badea said. "I know how it looks."

"Then you know the consequence," Stăn said

Badea turned to Constantin. "Please, boss. You have to understand."

"I understand that we were three when we needed to be four," Constantin said. "And I understand that Boc's dead."

"Constantin!"

"This gives me no pleasure, Badea."

"No!" Badea cried, picking up the kettle and flinging it at Constantin.

Constantin dove for cover at the same moment that Stăn pulled the trigger. Badea's head jerked back, a single splash of blood hit the wall behind him, and his body slumped to the floor.

Constantin looked up from the ground. He'd been burned by the water but not badly. Stăn still held out his gun, his jaw clenched so tightly it looked like he would crack his teeth.

"Stăn," Constantin said. "Put down the gun. We did what we had to."

"He gave us no choice," Stăn said, a quiver of emotion in his voice.

Constantin took the gun from him. "Sit down," he said.

Stăn sat, and Constantin picked up the kettle Badea had flung, refilled it, and put it back on the stove. When the water boiled, he made coffee, and then the two men sat at the counter and drank it in silence, Badea's body lying on the floor next to them.

"The van," Stăn said when he'd finished the coffee. "Do you want me to burn it?"

"No," Constantin said.

"It's full of our DNA. Our weapons."

"It doesn't matter now. We'll be in Moscow before they can do anything about it. A fire would only draw attention."

"What about the jet?" Stăn said.

"I'll call Shipenko now."

Constantin got up and, stepping over Badea's body,

went into the living room, where an analog landline had been set up for him to make contact with Moscow. He dialed the access code, his personal identification code, and then Shipenko's recipient code. Stăn stood in the doorway, watching.

Shipenko's voice came on the line. "Well," he said. "It's done."

"You're satisfied, then?" Constantin said dryly.

"You did your job. I'm satisfied with that."

"Good, because it cost us Boc and Badea."

"I'm sorry to hear that."

"Their share goes to me and Stăn."

"Of course."

"Now, what's the plan for getting us out of here? Our faces will be on every news network on the planet within the hour."

"I'm afraid it's not going to be that straightforward," Shipenko said.

"Don't you dare fuck me," Constantin said, eyeing Stăn. "I swear to God—"

"No one's fucking anyone."

"You said there'd be a jet."

"You said you'd finish the job."

"What are you talking about? We did everything you asked. Now we expect you to hold up your end of the—"

"Valentina Brik," Shipenko said.

The name stopped Constantin in his tracks.

"That's right," Shipenko said. "She's not dead."

"That's impossible."

"Tell that to the widow of the Prague city police officer she just killed."

"I saw her go in—"

"She's alive, Constantin, and she's on the run."

"Where did you find her?" Constantin stammered. "Where did she kill this officer?"

"At the last place you saw her."

"The Hlávka Bridge?"

"The one and only. Now she's headed south from the city in a stolen SUV."

"She won't make it more than ten miles before the Czechs—"

"She's got a hostage, Constantin."

"The intelligence officer? The woman?"

"No. Someone else. A bystander, near as I can tell."

Stăn was shaking his head. They both knew what this meant. They weren't going anywhere. Not until the job was finished. "Tell him no," Stăn mouthed. "Tell him we're done."

Constantin couldn't do that. Shipenko was going to hold them to this. If they didn't finish the job, everything they'd done would have been for nothing. "You're tracking her on satellite now?" he said.

There was a picture frame on the wall by the door, and Stăn smacked it with his elbow. The glass shattered.

"I am," Shipenko said. "She stole a car at the bridge and entered the tunnel network. At that point, she had two hostages. In the tunnel, she switched vehicles and left one behind."

"You're certain of that?"

"We would have lost her in the tunnels for sure," Shipenko said, "but I'd requisitioned additional satellites because of your attack on the embassy. We were able to monitor every vehicle coming out of every tunnel and trace them. She's in a black Mercedes SUV headed south for the Austrian border. We're certain of it."

"And you have eyes on that vehicle now?"

"Yes."

"Will we be able to catch her? I see the vehicle you left us here is rather modest."

"It will do," Shipenko said.

Constantin looked at Stăn. He wasn't one bit happy.

"You're sure you want this?" Constantin said. "If we're captured—"

"It's not a question of want, Constantin. She knows too much, and you promised to take care of her. You're going to keep that promise."

Constantin let out a long sigh.

"I've left you a cell phone," Shipenko continued. "You should see it somewhere."

Constantin glanced around and saw it on the coffee table. "I see it."

"Valentina's coordinates will be sent to that phone. You follow them, or you know what happens."

Constantin hung up and turned to Stăn. "We have no choice," he said before Stăn had a chance to protest.

"We're dead men if we don't get out of this country," Stăn said.

"We're dead men if we don't finish this job," Constantin said. "The only home we have now is Moscow. If we show up without finishing this, the only thing waiting for us there will be a bullet."

"He wants us to follow her?"

"He's going to track her for us," Constantin said, nodding.

"We'll need the weaponry from the van."

"Load everything into the minivan."

Stăn left, and Constantin checked the phone. The coordinates were already being pinged. He went out to the garage and helped Stăn take whatever weapons were still useful out of the van.

"We better leave now," he said when they were done. "We've got some catching up to do."

Stăn looked at the minivan with derision. "Is this thing up to the task?"

"You drive," Constantin said, getting into the passenger seat.

Stăn turned the ignition and brought the car down the driveway. Before them, the sky was pink over miles of open farmland.

"We can do this," Constantin said. "She's injured. She's desperate. She's in a stolen vehicle, with no friends, no allies, and nowhere to run. She's going to make a mistake."

Stăn nodded grimly. "She's running blind," he said. "She'll fuck up. The question is, will we?"

42

Tatyana's hand was trembling so badly she could hardly dial the number on her phone. She was in the courtyard next to the embassy. The scene in front of her was chaos. Police and firefighters were everywhere, coordinating the evacuation, and dozens of ambulances were lined up on Tržiště, gathering the dead and injured.

Above her, thick black smoke, billowing from the second floor of the embassy where a fire had broken out, darkened the morning sky. Her eyes stung, and when she saw the medics coming her way, she didn't resist but let them take her into the back of an ambulance and check her for injuries.

"This way," they said in Czech, and only when they put the blanket over her shoulders did she realize how badly she was shivering.

"I need you to help me," she said to one of the medics. "I need you to dial a number for me."

The medic was surprised, but when he saw the look on her face, he took the phone. She told him the number, her voice flat, her mind numb, and he dialed it and handed the phone back.

"Tatyana?" Laurel said as soon as she picked up. "I was so worried you were dead."

"Gilhofer's dead," Tatyana said. "He's dead. Not me."

"I'm sorry," Laurel stammered. "Are you hurt? Do you need medical attention?"

"I'm in an ambulance," Tatyana said. "I think I'm all right."

"I'm watching everything from the satellite," Laurel said, "but the smoke's so thick I can't see much."

"It's a disaster," Tatyana said. "We still don't know how many casualties."

"Roth's on his way to pick me up," Laurel said. "In twenty minutes, we'll be in a room with the president."

"And this?" Tatyana said. "Will it be war?"

"I can't see how it will be anything else."

Tatyana's mind reeled. Two nuclear superpowers. How was war between them even conceivable? She didn't know, and her mind was too shattered to think about it.

Her medic seemed to have concluded his examination. He'd left her alone and was helping some police with a stretcher. They were carrying someone, and Tatyana saw that it was one of the women she'd been slated to share a room with in the embassy.

"Everyone's dead," she said.

"What?"

"The women," Tatyana said. "They were targeting the women."

"But why on earth—"

"Does the name Osip Shipenko mean anything to you?" Tatyana said.

"No," Laurel said.

"That's who ordered the hit."

"Is he Dead Hand?"

"I don't know. Probably. He's close to Molotov. I know that much."

"I'll tell Roth."

"He's...." Tatyana's words trailed off.

"He's what?" Laurel said.

"Laurel, I met him once."

"Where?"

"You'll find very little about him on the database. All I can say is he's close to Molotov. But there's something else."

"What is it?"

"He's a monster, Laurel."

"What does that mean?"

"You'll see. There are pictures of him on file. Physically, there's something wrong with him, I don't know what, but I'm not talking about that. I mean, he's a monster in the true sense of the word."

"Well, clearly, if he ordered this—"

"He ordered Valentina to kill women," Tatyana said. "And this attack, it was targeting women too."

The medics came over with another stretcher, and this time they loaded it into the ambulance next to Tatyana. Tatyana stepped out to give them more space, and as they raised it into the vehicle, the plastic coversheet fell off, and she saw that it was Carmen Linder they were carrying.

"He's a special kind of monster," Tatyana said again. "That's all I can say. Maybe someone at the briefing will have more to say about him."

"Okay," Laurel said, "and, well, this probably isn't what you need to hear right now, but Klára Issová found your old friend."

"Valentina!"

"Yes."

"Alive?"

"Yes, and it seems Valentina got the better of her."

"Is Klára dead?"

"No, thankfully."

"We were supposed to be there," Tatyana said, picturing Gilhofer's dead body as she said the words. "Gilhofer and I, we were on our way out of the embassy when the attack struck. I left him in the elevator."

"Tatyana, none of this is your fault."

"I left him, and now he's dead."

"It's okay, Tatyana."

"Lance," Tatyana said, struggling to keep her thoughts clear. "Lance called me. I sent him to the bridge."

"He went."

"He was too late?"

"No, he got there on time. Valentina took him hostage, it seems."

"What?"

"That's what it looks like from the satellite."

"He let her take him?"

"I think so. It was probably the only way of saving Klára's life."

"Does Valentina know who he is?"

"I don't know what she knows, but maybe Klára can tell us more. Valentina left her in one of the tunnels when she switched cars."

"I can tell you this," Tatyana said. "It's not like Valentina Brik to spare someone."

"Maybe she'd killed enough women for one week."

"I doubt it," Tatyana said. "Where's Klára now?"

"Still at the tunnel, but you need to—"

Tatyana didn't wait to hear more. She hung up the phone and walked up to one of the few embassy guards who hadn't been caught in the attack. "Tatyana Aleksandrova," she said to him, showing him her credentials. "I need a vehicle right now."

The guard wasn't in much shape to offer assistance, but he did point her to the guardhouse by the gate. "Keys to the embassy vehicles are in there," he said.

There was one thought going through her mind as she entered the guardhouse, one thought that was giving her the clarity to go forward. Valentina Brik was alive. And she had Lance.

She grabbed a set of keys from a lockbox and pressed the button, looking around the lot. The lights of Gilhofer's sleek black 7-series BMW flashed.

43

L aurel took the elevator to the ground floor and waited in the lobby. It was snowing outside, and she watched it fall through the glass doors. It had been a long night, and it was only going to get longer. By the time the sun rose, the world might be a very different place. The world might be at war.

The Starbucks kiosk was shut, and the barista was gone, but a security guard at his desk across the lobby was watching her. She gave him a nod.

"I can call you a car if you like," he said.

"Someone's meeting me."

"Oh good," he said. "It's no night to be out alone."

She looked out at the snow, then back over to him. "Hey," she said, "would you mind if I smoked a cigarette?"

He was startled by the question, as if she'd just asked if she could steal the hard drives from the security system, and said, "It's really not my place—"

"Forget it," she said. "I shouldn't have asked."

"It really wouldn't bother me—"

"It's fine. I'll go outside."

He nodded, looking relieved. "Cold night, though," he added as she opened the door.

"Hence the request," she muttered as the icy air hit her.

"What's that?"

She didn't reply. Outside, she leaned into the building for shelter as she lit the cigarette. She felt tense. The situation was bad. The briefing was not going to be pleasant. They'd been completely blindsided. Questions would be asked. Why hadn't they seen this coming? Why hadn't they responded more quickly to the murders? How had they allowed this to happen?

She saw the lights of Roth's Escalade approaching, escorted by two secret service cars, and hurried down the steps to meet it, flicking away her cigarette.

"Laurel," Roth said as she climbed in, "the president's already waiting." He tapped the screen that separated them from the driver, and they moved on.

"This is very bad," Laurel said, eyeing him, trying to get a read on his frame of mind.

"It's not bad," he said. "It's a disaster."

She nodded.

"A real disaster," he repeated.

"Yes, sir."

"The Pentagon, the State Department, the NSA. They're all there, and they're going to eat us alive."

"It's not our job to protect the embassy," Laurel said but instantly regretted it.

"I hope you're not planning on saying that in the briefing."

She shook her head. "Sorry. I've got my back up."

"It was our job to see this coming," Roth said. "No one's going to let us forget that."

"We were doing everything..." Laurel said, before letting the words trail off.

"It's not going to count a damn," Roth said.

They drove on, their police escort speeding through every red light they came to, and Laurel said, "Tatyana spoke to one of the attackers."

"She did?" Roth said, his voice rising. "Please tell me she got something useful out of him."

"It was one of the men from the Romanian kill cell. And she got a name."

"What name?"

"Shipenko," she said, watching him carefully. "Osip Shipenko."

"Osip!" Roth gasped.

"You know him?"

"Not exactly," he said, shaking his head slightly. "But I've...."

"You've what?"

He shook his head again, lost in his own thoughts.

"Is there something I should be aware of?"

"No," Roth said, almost too quickly.

She watched him. She knew him well enough to know when he was holding back. "Tatyana knows him," she said, using the information to see if she could prod him into saying more.

"Knows him?" Roth said.

Laurel shrugged. "Well, she met him."

"What did she say?"

"She said he's some sort of monster."

"Hmm," Roth said, nodding.

"What does that mean?"

"You'll see for yourself soon enough," he said. They were approaching the White House, and Roth pressed the button to speak to the driver. "We're taking the back door, Harry."

"Aye, Aye," Harry said, turning onto H Street. He brought them into a narrow alley next to the Federal Claims Courthouse and came to a halt.

Behind them, a ram-proof vehicle barrier rose from the pavement.

"What's this?" Laurel said.

"You'll see," Roth said, lowering his window.

She saw that there was a discreet window set into the wall of the building. It was tinted, and it descended like the window of a car, revealing two secret service agents. They nodded, recognizing Roth, and Roth said to Laurel, "Follow me."

They got out of the car and walked to the end of the alley. There were cigarette butts and empty takeout coffee cups on the ground, as if the area was used by courthouse staff on smoke breaks, and two identical steel doors led into the building. The first had a sign saying 'Staff Only'. The second said 'No Entry'.

They entered through the second, where more secret service agents were waiting, and Roth said to Laurel, "This is the Treasury Annex," as if that explained everything. They descended a set of steel stairs, and an agent led them down a tunnel beneath Pennsylvania Avenue. The tunnel led directly into the White House basement, and they passed more secret service agents and a series of rooms housing computer servers, audiovisual equipment, and security monitors. To her left, Laurel saw the White House wardroom, and to her right, a service elevator with large doors for accepting deliveries. Directly in front of them was a hotel-style laundry cart full of bedsheets. They waited a moment for the elevator, then took it down to another corridor. This time, the corridor had the feel of a hardened bunker, made of unpainted reinforced concrete. They followed it to a set of steel blast doors, beyond which was a small waiting area and a glass door. Through the door, she saw an ultramodern situation room, complete with all of the usual comms links and facilities.

There was an unsettled feeling in the pit of Laurel's stomach as she entered the room. Before them was a large conference table, and around it, the president's most trusted security advisors—Schultz, Schlesinger, Winnefeld, even Cutler—were seated. Some military advisors and executive branch staffers sat on seats against the walls, and at the far end of the room, an enormous screen displayed the same live satellite feed Laurel had been staring at in her office.

"Gentlemen, ladies," Roth said, taking his seat. Laurel looked for a seat by the wall, but Roth motioned for her to take the one next to him. It put her right next to the sole remaining vacant seat, which she realized was for the president.

Roth looked around the table and said, "Where's NSA?"

Elliot Schlesinger, the Chairman of the Joint Chiefs, looked like he was about to answer when the president entered, and everyone stood.

"Sit down, sit down, for God's sake," the president said in the faintly nautical accent that never failed to remind Laurel of an old production of Moby Dick she'd been forced to watch in high school. "What are we looking at, Levi? It's war, isn't it? Tell me we're not at war."

"It's an attack, sir," Roth said.

"Oh, quit hedging," the president said. "Call a spade a spade."

"It's an attack, sir," Roth said again, holding his ground. "Whether it's war remains to be decided."

"And who is to make that decision?" Cutler, the National Security Advisor, said in his nasal voice, "I mean, the intelligence around this whole situation has been an absolute train wreck."

"That's hardly—" Schlesinger butted in, but Cutler kept going.

"No, really. What the hell's going on over there? The Russians have been picking off CIA personnel in Prague for days, and this is the first we hear of it? You had all that time to identify the threat. To find out who was responsible. To prevent this... this *atrocity*."

"We've been working round the clock to identify—" Roth said before being cut off.

"The GRU has been provoking us," Cutler said. "They've been rubbing what they're doing in our faces, as if they wanted us to know this was coming—"

"They've been trying to divert our attention," Roth said, raising his voice. "This whole thing—"

"Don't tell me for one second this is a diversion," Cutler continued. "Thirty-two dead and counting. Seventeen women. This is the dirtiest, nastiest...."

The view on the screen zoomed in close enough for everyone to see the situation on the ground. Cutler let the sight distract him from what he was saying. Emergency responders were everywhere, covering bodies, hauling them away on stretchers. Ambulances clogged the streets for a block in every direction. Black smoke billowed from the embassy's second floor.

"It's a war zone," the president said quietly. "An utter war zone. How the hell am I supposed to respond?"

"Very carefully," Schlesinger said.

"Agreed," Cutler said. "One wrong move, and we'll be decimated in the polls."

Everyone at the table turned to look at him.

"What?" he said.

"The *polls*?" Roth said, and there couldn't have been more contempt in his voice. "At a moment like this, you bring up polls?"

"Come on," the president said to Roth. "He didn't mean anything. We all work at the pleasure of the people. If we don't calibrate our response in line with public expectations, we might as well all go home now."

"And what is that response going to be?" Schlesinger said.

The president looked at Roth, but no words came out of his mouth. The man was tired, and Laurel wasn't surprised. The pressure on his position, on his administration, on the country and its interests had been relentless for weeks. Moscow wasn't just testing him, she thought, it was trying to break him. There'd been a time, back when Laurel first considered entering the academy, when people spoke of the Cold War as if it were a thing of the past. No one spoke like that anymore. The nation was at war, if not with Russia, then with President Molotov and his cabal of cronies, and everyone in the Montgomery administration knew. They were at war, and their window for gaining the upper hand was closing fast.

"We've been sitting on our hands long enough," the president said. "We need to start hitting back at the enemy, and we need to start hitting back hard."

"This is the third embassy attack in as many weeks," Cutler said. "We need to bring the fight to them."

"So far," Roth said, "our response has been measured. My people have assassinated every person in the Russian chain of command linked to each of the attacks against us."

"Every person other than Molotov," Cutler said.

"Yes," Roth said, "and I hope I don't have to explain to you why that is."

"He's a man like any other," Cutler said. "Does he not bleed?"

"He bleeds," Roth said, looking at the president.

"It seems to me," Cutler said, "that we're willing to go after everyone except the one man we need to go after. If I'm not mistaken, we had an assassin in the same room as him not too long ago. Molotov could have been taken out with a single bullet. But we didn't do it."

"It's complicated, Cutler," the president said.

"With all due respect," Cutler said, "we've let this prick have his way with us for too long. Incident after incident. Attack after attack. He'll never stop until he's pushed us over the edge."

The president turned to Roth, eyeing him carefully. Everyone else followed his gaze, and Laurel knew they all had the same question. How long would the world tolerate Molotov's provocations? How long would the risk calculus dictate they do nothing? What would it take before the danger of removing Molotov from office was outweighed by the cost of allowing him to remain?

It was a question that was easier for them to ask than it was for Roth to answer. Laurel felt for him as he looked around the room, clearing his throat. There was a long pause, then he said, "I'd rather not get drawn into a discussion of hypotheticals."

The statement was followed by more silence, then the president said, "I think, Levi, that we need to hear a bit more about your thinking on that matter. Cutler's right. We just suffered a grievous attack. They went after our women. Some of them were little older than girls. If you say we can't go after Molotov, I need to hear the reasoning."

Roth cleared his throat again, then broke into a bout of coughing.

"Are you all right?" the president said.

Roth raised a hand, then muttered, "I'm fine, I'm fine."

"You're sure?"

"President Vladimir Molotov," Roth said, rising in his seat, "is the *absolute* leader of Russia. He has complete control of the military, the economy, the political institutions. His power rivals that of a Czar, a king. Every button, every lever, every trigger is under his control. There's no corner of the government that isn't in his pocket. Russia doesn't speak of a pyramid of power. They speak of a vertical of power. Every decision flows straight up, and he's at the top."

"He's a dictator," Cutler said. "We get that. So was Saddam."

"Well, Saddam was a piece of work," Roth said. "I'll grant you that, but he wasn't sitting on the largest nuclear arsenal on the planet. Six thousand warheads. Enough to destroy every man, woman, and child that ever lived a thousand times over."

"But the generals—"

"Forget the generals," Roth said, his voice rising

slightly. "If Molotov says launch the nukes, make no mistake, his order will be obeyed."

"But the chances—"

"Zero doubt," Roth said, and then, for emphasis, "*absolute* zero."

The president turned to Schlesinger. "Is that the Pentagon's view also?"

Schlesinger nodded. "I wouldn't go so far as to say my doubt was ever zero, but our assessment of current Kremlin doctrine is that the use of nuclear weapons is warranted in defense of Molotov's personal position."

"They'd destroy the planet to defend against regime change?" Cutler said.

"The threat of them doing so," Schlesinger said, "is regarded by the Pentagon as credible."

"He has nothing to lose," Roth continued. "And if we back him into a corner, there's no knowing what he'll do."

"But surely there are steps we can take," Cutler said, "to contain the threat his nuclear arsenal poses."

Roth let out a hollow, mirthless laugh. "Let me ask you this, Cutler. Have you ever heard of nuclear power politics compared to a game of chess?"

"Of course I have."

"Well, the truth is, it's like a game of chess with a pile of dynamite under the table. And if either player ever feels he's going to lose the game, he has the option to blow the board, and both players, to hell. That's the game we're playing. We can beat the Russians at chess. We know we can."

"But if we do, Molotov might...."

"Kill us all."

Cutler threw his hands up. "So, that's it? Game over. We're powerless."

"We're not powerless."

"It feels that way."

"We're not powerless. We just don't think we can go directly after Molotov."

"If we take him out," Cutler said, "we can neutralize the threat before he ever gives the order to retaliate."

"It doesn't work like that," the president said.

Cutler was getting impatient. "Why not?"

It was then that Laurel chose to speak for the first time. "Because of the Dead Hand," she said.

Everyone at the table turned to her.

"You've heard those words before," she said.

"Of course I have," Cutler said. "A dead hand is a weapon system that retaliates for you even if you're already dead."

"Exactly," Laurel said. "Moscow has utilized dead hand systems for decades. We know that if we ever hit Russia with nukes, even if they never saw us coming and we hit every target, even if we killed every Russian alive, there are automated systems in place, satellites in orbit, hardened unmanned bunkers in the remotest stretches of the Siberian wilderness, submarines deep in the ocean, that would fire back and ensure they took us, and the world, down with them. It's a system that fights back, even if the people who built it are all dead."

"And that's what would happen if we target Molotov?" Cutler said.

"If President Molotov got even a whiff that we were going to go after him personally, the Dead Hand organization, his closely-knit group of staunchest, most loyal men, would unleash weapons more destructive than anything the world has ever seen."

Cutler leaned back in his chair, exasperated. He'd

heard these arguments a dozen times before, which made Laurel wonder why he insisted on rehashing them over and over. They all wanted to hit Molotov. But they knew it wasn't as simple as that.

"I wish," the president said, "that we were in the driver's seat for once."

"We're the stronger power," Frederick Winnefeld, the Navy Chief, said.

"Then why do I feel like Molotov has us on the back foot?" the president said. "Why do I feel like he's calling the shots. Why do I feel like…. I don't know," he said, throwing his hands up.

"Like we're losing?" Roth said.

"Exactly."

"Because we have more to lose," Roth said. "Because we care about the outcome, and the world, and the lives of our citizens. We can't make the threats he makes. We can't threaten oblivion, and he knows it."

"He's the crazy man in the room," Schlesinger said.

"It's like we're in two cars hurtling toward each other," Laurel said, "waiting to see who swerves first. Only everyone knows his car has no steering wheel. He can't swerve. So we either give him the win—"

"Or die," Cutler said.

"That's right," Roth said. "That's the game. That's the situation. He knows we're a rational actor. He knows we'll pursue our objective interest. We don't know the same about him."

"About this Dead Hand," the president said. "What do we know of the actual organization?"

He directed the question to Roth, but Roth turned to Laurel.

"Well," Laurel said, "very little in fact. We know it exists, and we've identified members of it in the past."

"Those men are dead," Roth said.

"We know there are others, though," Laurel said. "And we know there are ironclad procedures in place in the event of a direct attack on Molotov's regime. If we go after Molotov, it's game over. Nukes will launch. Biological weapons will be unleashed. He'll take the world down with him."

"Well, how do you fight something like that?" Cutler said.

Roth looked at the president, and the president gave Cutler the same answer he himself had received from Roth so many times. "Carefully, Cutler. Very carefully."

"There are methods," Laurel said. "We've successfully gone after individual members of the Dead Hand in the past, and those attacks did not provoke a general retaliation from Molotov."

"He'll use his system to protect himself, but not his friends?" Cutler said.

"Yes, and we know we can continue to increase the costs for individual members of his clique by going after them when there's an attack. If they continue to see their number dwindle while Molotov remains unharmed, it will erode his hold on them over time."

"Time is the one thing we don't have," the president said.

"Which is why we've put together a response plan," Laurel said. "We got a name today. It was given to us by one of the embassy attackers before he was killed."

"The name of a Dead Hand member?" the president said.

"If it turns out to be true," Laurel said, "then it's not

just the name of a member, but *the* member who ordered this attack."

"Who is he?" the president said. "For God's sake, who is he?"

Laurel turned to Roth then.

"She'd rather not say," Roth said. "Not yet."

"But you think we can go hit him?" the president said.

"I think so, yes," Laurel said.

"The problem," Roth said, "is that the Dead Hand is like a sea monster. We can keep going after tentacles, but unless we go after the head, which is Molotov himself, the tentacles will keep growing back."

"It's a start, though," the president said. "I'd rather cut off a tentacle than do nothing."

Cutler threw up his hands in frustration. "Please," he said, "please don't tell me that we're going after one single Russian because of this thing."

"We're not going after one Russian," Laurel said. "But knowing the name of the man who ordered the attack, that's something."

"It's a start," the president said.

"So far," Cutler said, "we're looking at thirty-two dead from this attack. That number is still growing, and it doesn't include the murders that took place in Prague before tonight. And you're suggesting our response is to go after one single man in the Kremlin?"

"There's also the cell that carried out the attack," Laurel said. "We're not going to rest until every member of that group is dead. And there's the assassin who killed Yvette Bunting and Arabella Bradwell. One of our operatives, Lance Spector, is already on her tail." She didn't mention that Lance was currently Valentina's captive.

"That means everyone who had a hand in this attack will be dead," the president said.

"Everyone that we know of," Cutler added.

"If there are any other names," Laurel said, "we'll get them. And the Russians know it. They'll see that every time they get sucked into one of these plots, they're the ones who pay with their lives, even if Molotov doesn't."

The president leaned back in his chair. He was shaking his head.

"What is it?" Roth said.

"I don't know," the president said. "It's just...." He looked at Cutler.

"It's not enough," Cutler said. "They kill over thirty people, and we... we what? Apprehend the perpetrators."

"We kill the perpetrators," Roth said.

"But it's not even," Cutler said.

"It's not a soccer game," Roth said. "We're not counting goals here."

"But you know what I mean," Cutler said. "In terms of optics. In terms of the... *political* considerations."

"What do you want me to do?" Roth said. "Find thirty more Russian names to add to the list?"

"You're acting like that's a joke," Cutler said, "but that's exactly what I want you to do. I want to even the score."

"That's not how it works."

"If they kill thirty of ours, and we retaliate by killing four or five of theirs...." Cutler shook his head. "In terms of optics," he said again, then turned to the president. "I'm sorry, sir, it just doesn't play."

"This was an attack," Roth said, "and we're proposing to kill every person directly involved. If that's not enough, I don't know what I can offer you. We're not the KGB. I can't just add names to a list until it... how did you put it?

Until it *plays*? And I can't give you Molotov. The risk of catastrophic retaliation is too high."

"When 9/11 happened," Cutler said, "we didn't just kill those responsible. We didn't just go after the plotters. We didn't limit ourselves. We went to fucking war."

"War?" Roth said. "Is that what you want then?"

"That administration," Cutler continued, "understood the optics. They understood the play. The messaging. They said to the world that if you strike us, if you hit America, we don't just hit back proportionately, we obliterate you."

"We can't go to war every time someone—"

Cutler cut him off. "Molotov has to understand he's not the only crazy man in the room."

"Crazy man?"

"We don't just settle the score," Cutler continued, practically frothing at the mouth. "We come out ahead. Every time. Overwhelmingly. For every one of ours you kill, we'll kill a thousand. After 9/11, we sent our troops, and we kept sending them. For twenty years, we sent them. We didn't give a fuck what it cost."

"And how did that end?" Laurel said.

"It ended the way *we* wanted it to end, when *we* wanted it to end. It ended with our enemies completely vanquished."

Roth looked at the president. "Well," he said, "if that's something the president wants to address with the Pentagon, that's his prerogative, but my understanding of the purpose of this briefing was to outline a proportionate, sane response to this attack, and that's what Laurel Everlane has done. You have my word that within twenty-four hours, every man involved in this attack will have a bullet in his skull. If that's not swift justice, I don't know what is."

The president raised a hand. "Levi," he said, "I don't think anyone's criticizing your response plan, *per se*."

"*Per se*?" Roth said.

"Some men perpetrated an attack, and those men must be brought to justice."

"They'll be brought to the wrong end of a gun," Roth said.

"No one's questioning that," the president continued. "We're just saying, systemically, on a grander scale, there's a problem here that's not being addressed. Molotov gets his lackeys to launch some sort of attack against us. We kill the lackeys. Molotov gets new lackeys and plans another attack. On and on it goes. That's not sustainable."

"Hey," Roth said, "if this administration is ready to start putting more options on the table, if we're in agreement that something has to be done about Molotov and that we're willing to risk the consequences—"

"Hold on," the president said. "We know what those consequences include."

"They include the threat of nuclear war," Roth said. "But if there's appetite for facing risk like that, I can assure you Langley is ready to have that conversation."

"Levi," the president said, trying to calm him down, "we all know you've been hawkish—"

"Hawkish is an understatement, Mr. President. We're ready to take action on Molotov. We're ready to go after him. It's the Pentagon and the White House and Congress who are putting the brakes on it."

"Levi," the president said, eyeing Schultz and Schlesinger, who'd been uncharacteristically quiet, "we know your position on regime change in Moscow. And you know the arguments for our hesitance."

"Well," Roth said, "that being the case, no response we make to this attack is going to be truly satisfying."

"The Pentagon's concerns," Schlesinger said, "are legitimate, and please don't put words in our mouth. We've got more than just Moscow to look at. We're eyeing Pyongyang, Tehran, Beijing. We can't act on one without knowing what we're doing vis-à-vis all of the others."

There was a knock on the door. One of the president's aides popped her head in and said, "Sir, you asked to be notified when the story hit the networks."

The president looked at the faces around the table. "Things are getting heated," he said. "Let's take a step back and see how this mess is playing on TV, shall we?"

Roth looked like he was going to object, but to Laurel's relief, he managed to contain himself.

"Someone bring up the network, please," the president said, and a moment later, the huge screen at the end of the table switched to a cable news network. There was a reporter on the ground in Prague, the US embassy burning in the background.

"How did she get there so quickly?" the president said.

Laurel recognized the reporter. She was a strident critic of the president and a frequent thorn in his side at White House press briefings. Behind her, emergency responders were working flat-out to contain the carnage.

"Turn up the volume," the president said. "What's she saying?"

An aide turned up the volume, and the reporter's voice filled the room.

The scene you see behind me right now is the summation of President Ingram Montgomery's failure as Commander in Chief. He's shown, time and again, that he is unwilling to face up to the threat posed by Molotov. This is the result of that weakness. He failed us in Latvia when Russia blatantly violated the sovereignty of a NATO ally. He failed us in Moscow and Beijing when those embassies were obliterated in attacks linked to the Kremlin. And he's failing us here today.

"Turn her off," the president barked. "I've seen enough."

The aide fumbled with the controls, but the broadcast continued. The news anchor in the studio asked what the attack would mean for the president's re-election chances.

That's what's really going to be telling. American voters will get their say at the polls, and when they add these failures to Montgomery's long list of failures at home, support for his agenda is going to evaporate. We're looking at a one-term president here. I mean, if you're too weak to stand up to a resurgent Moscow, you have no place being the leader of the Free World.

"I said turn her off," the president bellowed. The poor aide was still fumbling with the controls in vain, pushing buttons desperately, but the screen wouldn't go blank.

We're just getting reports that the president was considering pulling all female personnel out of the embassy in Prague just days ago. And as we're already seeing, this attack appears to have targeted women disproportionately. That raises the question, if the president was aware that a threat was imminent, why the hell didn't he do something to stop it? If these reports are accurate, it appears he would have preferred to pull out of the city and run away rather than face the threat head-on. This is a president who can't even keep American women safe while they're overseas serving their country.

The president marched over to the aide and snatched the controller from her as the reporter continued.

This president still acts like we're living in 1990, like the Cold War is over, and we're the winner. He's living in a fantasy. President Molotov has repeatedly demonstrated that the Cold War is not over. He's hell-bent on reconstituting the Soviet Union, on taking back the territory lost after the fall of the Berlin Wall, on regaining the status of Superpower. And Montgomery's letting this catastrophe take place before our eyes. It's a catastrophic failure of gargantuan—

At last, the screen went blank. The room fell silent.

The silence filled the air, growing in weight until the president broke it.

"God damn it. This is a disaster. An unmitigated disaster. It's going to derail my entire agenda. There's no coming back from this."

"Let's not lose our heads," Roth said.

"You heard her," the president snapped. "I need to step up to the plate."

"I don't think we should act rashly," Roth said, giving Schlesinger a worried look.

"Where's your man?" the president said. "Your vigilante. Where is he?"

"I don't know who you're talking about," Roth said.

"Cut the crap, Levi. You know."

"He's speaking of Lance Spector," Laurel said, the tenor of her voice surprising even her.

"Yes. Spector. Where's Spector?"

"He's in Prague, sir," Roth said.

"Well, get him on the line. I want to speak to him."

"He's in the field."

"As soon as he's back, I want to speak to the man myself. Do you hear me?"

"Sir," Cutler said, alarm on his face. "I don't think it's wise for the President of the United States—"

"I don't care," the president yelled furiously. "I don't care what's appropriate. Molotov speaks to his henchmen. He speaks to his assassins. Why can't I?"

"But what are you going to say to him?" Roth said, his face suddenly ashen.

Laurel had never seen the president's face so angry. "What do you think I'm going to say to him? What the hell do you think I'm going to say?"

44

Tatyana gunned the powerful engine of Gilhofer's car and got on the highway, headed for the tunnel where Klára had been found. Morning traffic was beginning to pick up, but she weaved between lanes and was entering the tunnel within minutes. She jammed on the brakes when she saw the lights of a police cruiser ahead. It was blocking the right-hand traffic lane, and, just after it, Klára's car was still parked with its hazards flashing.

"I'm from the American embassy," Tatyana said to the officer. "I need to speak to her." She flashed her credentials, and he waved her on.

She parked in front of Klára's car and walked over. Klára was seated on the back seat, hugging herself beneath a blanket the police officer had given her.

"You're alive," Tatyana said. "Are you all right?"

"He's insisting I wait for an ambulance," Klára said, nodding at the cop leaning on his cruiser. "But there's some delay."

Tatyana nodded, and Klára looked at her closely.

"What is it?" Klára said. "Why are you soaking wet?"

"The Russians attacked the embassy."

Klára's eyes widened. "Oh no!" she gasped.

Tatyana nodded.

"Casualties?" Klára said.

"A lot."

"They went after the women, didn't they?"

"Yes, they did."

Klára shook her head. "Animals," she said quietly.

"Yes," Tatyana said, shining her flashlight into Klára's eyes to check for sign of a concussion. "And now we make them pay."

Klára nodded. She brushed the flashlight away. "I told you I'm all right."

"What happened with Valentina?" Tatyana said.

"She got the better of me. Hit me from behind."

"That sounds like her style."

Klára nodded.

"Did you see the vehicle she left in?"

Klára reached into her pocket and pulled out a piece of paper. "I wrote this down as soon as that cop got me out of the cuffs." It was a license plate number. "They left in a black SUV. She killed the driver."

"Where's the body?"

"Behind the barrier," Klára said, indicating the low wall along the side of the road. "The cop called it in. We put a blanket over it."

"I see," Tatyana said.

"There was an operative," Klára said. "An American."

"His name is Lance Spector," Tatyana said, pulling her phone from her pocket.

"He walked right up to her," Klára said. "Let himself be captured."

She was clearly curious about him, but Tatyana only said, "I see," and began typing a message to Laurel. She sent the license plate and a description of the SUV and hit send. Then she looked at Klára. "Wait here."

She walked over to where the driver's body had been left, and Klára said, "They took his wallet, if that's what you're looking for."

Tatyana came back. "Okay," she said. "Well, I can get you to the hospital. You've got a concussion."

"You don't have time to take me to the hospital. You need to follow Valentina."

"I have to wait for Laurel to find her, if she even can."

"You don't have to wait. I overheard her telling Lance to make for the Austrian border. You need to take Highway Three. Follow the signs for Ceske Budejovice."

Tatyana looked at her in surprise. "You got all that?"

Klára nodded. "Now, get going. You've got a lot of ground to make up. And I need to talk to this cop about getting me out of here. It doesn't sound like there's going to be an ambulance any time soon."

Klára rose to her feet. She was a little wobbly, and Tatyana helped her. Then Tatyana's phone started ringing.

"It's Laurel," she said to Klára.

Klára nodded and made her way toward the police officer, who was directing traffic. Tatyana watched as she answered the phone.

"Did you find Klára?" Laurel said as soon as she picked up.

"Yes. She gave me the license plate number. You need to find that vehicle."

"I'll divert every satellite I can. We'll find it."

"It's possibly heading south on Highway Three toward the Austrian border. Klára overhead Valentina say so."

"That makes my job a lot easier," Laurel said. "I'll get on it as soon as I'm at the office. I'm with Roth right now. We're on our way back from the White House."

"How was the White House?"

"It was... strange," Laurel said. "I'm not sure what the president is thinking."

"Okay," Tatyana said. "Find me that SUV. Gilhofer's car is a beast so I should be able to make up the lost ground." She hung up and looked over at Klára, who was staring at the BMW. She turned to face Tatyana and said, "Where's Gilhofer?"

"He's—" Tatyana said, cutting herself short.

"At the embassy?" Klára said. "I spoke to him just...."

"Klára," Tatyana said. "Slow down. You've been through a lot."

Klára shook her head. "What's going on?" she said. "Why are you driving his car?"

"Gilhofer was caught up in the fighting."

"He's dead, isn't he?"

Tatyana didn't know what to say, but what Klára said next surprised her.

"This is my fault."

"No," Tatyana said. "Of course it isn't."

"I was given the job of finding out who was killing embassy staff. That was three days ago. Now, dozens of people are lying in body bags, including Nate."

"Klára, none of that's your fault."

"Then whose fault is it?"

"It's Molotov's fault," Tatyana said. "He's the one we need to make pay."

Klára sighed. "Hey," she called out to the cop. "I can't wait anymore. I need to get to Stodůlky, and you need to take me." Stodůlky was the location of the Czech intelligence service headquarters.

"I should go too," Tatyana said. She gave Klára a final look, then made for the car.

She was just getting in when Klára called out. "Tatyana, wait."

"What is it?" Tatyana said.

"How did it happen?"

Tatyana cleared her throat. "He was...."

"The truth," Klára said.

Tatyana nodded. "It was in the street in front of the embassy. I wasn't there. I don't know exactly what happened, but he was shot execution-style."

"I see," Klára said.

"It wasn't in vain," Tatyana said. Klára didn't look like she believed that, and Tatyana said, "There was a gunman near him. Injured. Gilhofer got him."

"I see."

"No," Tatyana said. "You don't."

"What are you talking about?"

"I questioned the man. Before I killed him."

"What did he say?"

"Are you really going to help make the Kremlin pay?" Tatyana said.

Klára was quiet for a moment, then nodded her head. "Yes."

"He gave me a name."

"What name?"

"Shipenko. Osip Shipenko."

45

Valentina watched her captive closely as he drove. She'd gathered he was American, and was beginning to suspect he was the asset Shipenko had been trying to lure into the open. If that was true, then she had some questions for him.

She was sitting behind the passenger seat, her gun on her lap, pointed at his head. If he made one wrong move —if he so much as took a curve too sharply, or accelerated too aggressively, she would pull the trigger. She knew all the tricks. As long as they were moving, his life was in her hands, and hers was in his.

"You killed those two staffers," he said, breaking the silence. He didn't look at her. His eyes remained on the road.

She knew his game—seeking to build rapport, gather information, distract her attention.

"You know I did," she said coldly. He intrigued her. She wanted to ask his name. Maybe she'd even heard it before. "You're an assassin too," she said.

"What makes you say that?"

She wasn't sure. All she knew was what Constantin had told her. Shipenko was using her to draw out someone high-value.

"Those women had nothing to do with anything," he said.

She let out a quick laugh. "You're going to have to do better than that."

"Than what?"

"You're fishing."

"Maybe I'm just passing time."

"Sure you are," she said.

He said nothing then, and they drove on in silence. A few minutes passed, and she said, "You know my name, but I don't know yours."

"Do you want to know it?"

She shrugged.

"Lance Spector," he said, "but now I get a question."

"You want to know why they were targeted."

"I know there's probably no point asking you."

She nodded. "That's correct. All I know is Shipenko referred to you as high-value."

There was a pack of cigarettes on the dashboard, and he said, "Mind if I take one?"

She shifted her weight in the seat. Her shoulder hurt. She'd done her best to patch up both bullet wounds, they'd gone through only flesh, but that didn't make them hurt any less. "Give me one too," she said.

He passed her the pack, then cracked open his window to let in air.

"Do you ever think about what we do?" she said to him.

"I don't know what you're asking."

"The people. Do you think about the people?"

"The people I've killed?"

"Yes."

He nodded. "Sure," he said. "I think about them."

"Do some stand out in your memory more than others?"

"Some victims?"

She nodded.

He thought for a moment, then said, "The ones I think about most are the ones I killed on questionable orders."

"Questionable orders?"

"Bad intel. Bad reasoning."

"But you don't know the intel. The reasoning."

"I usually find out, sooner or later."

"Usually later," she said.

He nodded. "Usually later."

"And then you get angry."

He sucked his cigarette. "I don't know what I get."

She was quiet for a moment, then she said, "That's what you think about the women in Prague, isn't it? You think I killed them on bad intel."

He shrugged. "Maybe I'm wrong. I didn't know them. Maybe they deserved to die."

"They didn't deserve to die," she said. "I don't know why I was sent to kill them, but I know that much." It felt strange saying it aloud. She'd never been a person who struggled with guilt. Very early in her life, she'd developed an ability to dissociate from her emotions. It was a skill she'd been forced to develop in order to survive, and it had served her well in the GRU. It allowed her to see things as they were, without the fog of emotion clouding everything. But it gave her no pleasure, and she took no pride in it. It came from a dark place, a time in her past when she'd been powerless to protect herself. It wasn't a strength, it was a weakness, an artifact of her victimhood. It was a scar.

Lance said nothing, and she watched him closely. She knew that everything she felt, he'd felt at some time too. There were no assassins who didn't have regrets. There were no killers who weren't also slowly killing themselves, their own soul, one bullet at a time.

She sucked on her cigarette and blew the smoke toward him. She wanted him to speak, to keep talking. Silence was not a comfort to people like them.

He waved away the smoke and said, "Why haven't you killed me? You know I'm dangerous."

"That remains to be seen."

"You don't need me."

"Do you want me to kill you? Is that what you're saying?"

"No," he said. "It's just...."

"Just what?"

"You didn't kill the intelligence officer in the car either."

"Self-interest," she said. "Like you said, I didn't want the entire Czech intelligence community coming down on me."

"They're already coming down on you. They'll catch you. You know they will. And if not them, the CIA."

"And when they do, you're my bargaining chip."

"I might not be as valuable as you think."

She smiled thinly. She knew he was trying to get inside her head, get her to drop her guard. Every word from his mouth was a manipulation tactic. But one thing he'd said was true. He was dangerous. More dangerous than his value as a hostage justified. She should have killed him, but the truth was, she needed him to drive.

The pain in her shoulder was constant. She didn't think she'd get ten miles without him, but she couldn't let him see that.

"Why would someone in the Prime Directorate want to lure you to Prague?" she said, changing the subject.

"Lure me to Prague?"

"Yes."

"They wouldn't."

"Yes, they would. One of the objectives of my mission was to draw you out of the woodwork. Perhaps it was the only objective."

Lance took a long draw from his cigarette, buying himself time to come up with a response. When he exhaled, he looked like he was going to speak, but he said nothing.

"You don't like that," she said.

"Of course I don't like it."

"It doesn't make you any more complicit," she said.

"Doesn't it?"

"You're a target of the operation, same as everyone else."

"It doesn't feel that way."

"I've made you angry."

"I was angry before this."

"No, you weren't," she said, "but what I'm wondering is how they knew you'd show your face."

"I had no choice. I was sent."

"No," she said, shaking her head. "They knew. The Prime Directorate knew."

"Knew what?"

"They knew that if they killed these women, you'd come. You specifically. Not someone else." He shrugged, but she wasn't letting him off the hook that easily. "How could they be so certain?"

He smoked his cigarette but said nothing. He'd gone silent. "Come on," she said. "Tell me, and I'll tell you who sent me. It's not as if I'm unaffected. I was the one doing it. I was the one killing these innocent women."

He drove on, and she said, "What does it say about you that they could read you so easily?"

She didn't expect an answer, but then he said, "It says they've done their homework."

She looked at him. "I can't imagine you're a man who's easy to do research on."

"I'm not," he said, his voice softer than it had been before.

"But you think they learned something about you?"

"I know what they learned," he said, his face more taut, less playful than it had been.

"And what's that?"

He turned to look at her.

"Eyes forward," she said, raising the gun.

"I thought we were becoming friends."

"Eyes forward or I'll pull this trigger," she said. "Even if it means killing us both."

He looked forward. When he finished his cigarette, he threw it out the crack in his window and immediately lit another.

"Given that one of us probably doesn't have very long to live," she said, "why don't you indulge me and let me in on the secret?"

"What secret?"

"What did my boss find out about you?"

He drew on his cigarette, exhaled, then said, "You said you'd give me his name."

"Always working," she said. "Always looking ahead."

"It's a simple trade," he said.

She opened her window and discarded her cigarette, then closed it. "All right," she said. "Osip Shipenko. Ever heard that name?"

Lance raised his hand slowly to his face. "The one with the...."

"With the skin," Valentina said. "Yes. The lizard skin. Now, your turn."

He reached for the rearview mirror and angled it to see her better.

"Don't touch that," she said. "Put it back how it was."

He fixed the mirror and said, "I had a sister once."

"*Once*?" she said.

"She disappeared when I was eight."

"She was older or younger than you?"

"We were both eight."

"You were twins?"

He nodded.

"I see," she said.

"You see what?"

"Nothing," she said. Then, "What happened?"

"She disappeared. Her and my mother."

"Together?"

"Yes."

"They just disappeared?"

"Not exactly, but I never got to the bottom of it. Not yet."

"You think it's still possible to do so?"

"The trail is cold," he said, "but I'll get to the end of it one day."

"And you think that's what Shipenko found out about you?"

"I know how the Kremlin thinks," he said. "There's a saying in the GRU. 'Know a man's past, and you know his weakness'."

"That's true," she said.

"I always knew that when the Kremlin decided to come after me, when they started to look for weakness, that was where they'd dig."

Valentina nodded. He was right. It was textbook GRU methodology. "They also say," she added, "that if you don't know what a man loves, you can't take it away from him."

They drove on in silence for a while, smoked a few more cigarettes, and at some point, Lance turned on the radio. She didn't stop him, and on every station, the news was the same. There'd been a massive attack on the American embassy in Prague. It was the worst terrorist attack on Czech soil in decades. Over thirty dead and counting.

She watched Lance's reaction. His face showed nothing, but his hands clenched the steering wheel so tightly his knuckles were white. "Did you know that was coming?" he said.

"I swear, I didn't," she said.

"That was more than a ruse to lure me," he said.

She nodded. "I didn't know that was coming. My last order was to kill the Prague station chief. Carmen Linder. I didn't do it, and they came after me."

"Why didn't you do it?"

She was quiet for a moment before saying, "I'm not sure."

"Yes, you are."

"I suppose," she said, "that Shipenko, working for him, it had a way of getting under my skin."

Lance nodded.

She added, "Especially as a...."

"A woman?"

"Yes."

"This will mean war," Lance said.

"Whatever it means, rest assured they've done their calculations. If it's war, it's because war is what they want."

Lance nodded. "Who carried out the attack?"

"I don't know."

"You know."

"It's Shipenko's operation."

"Was he going to give the job to you?"

She thought for a moment, then said, "No. He had another team. A group of mercenaries with the firepower for a job like this. They came after me when I failed to kill Linder, but they were already in the city."

Lance nodded. "Who are they?"

"Romanians," she said. "Contractors. Shipenko calls them the Splinter."

Lance looked at her. "Does he?"

"You've heard of them?"

He said nothing for a few moments.

"They'll be on our trail by now," she said. "Shipenko will know I'm alive, and they were supposed to kill me. Failure is not something he tolerates. He won't let them pull out until I'm dead."

"That's what I'm counting on," Lance said.

She leaned forward and looked at the speedometer. He'd let the speed drop without her noticing. "What are you doing? You want them to catch us."

"You need them dead as much as I do," he said. "Let them catch up, and I'll take care of them."

"That's not a good idea."

"It's a good idea," he said.

"They're not ordinary men. Shipenko uses them for

house cleaning. Their job is to kill GRU assassins. They're very dangerous men."

Lance angled the mirror at her again. "I'm a very dangerous man," he said, looking her in the eye.

"You're mad," she said.

"Maybe."

"You'll get us both killed."

"Not if you do what I tell you."

"I'm not taking orders from you."

"You need to send Moscow a signal. Once they know where we are, the Romanians will follow."

"You can't lure them into a trap. They'll see it coming."

"Not if you sell it well enough."

"Me?"

"Yes."

"I can't sell anything. Shipenko is trying to kill me."

"Oh, you can sell," Lance said. "It's all you've been doing since we met."

46

Laurel was back in her office, back at her desk, alone, struggling not to give in to the temptation to shut her eyes. Roth had dropped her off with strict orders to notify him of even the slightest developments. She'd identified the vehicle that Lance and Valentina were in, the satellite was tracking it as it made its way south toward the Austrian border, but she'd decided to wait before calling Roth. He'd been pretty worked up after the briefing, and she knew he had back-to-back meetings with Pentagon officials through the night.

She'd sent Tatyana a message confirming that she was on the correct road and that she was gaining on them, but that was it. She got up to stretch her legs and went over to the window. Still no sign of dawn on the horizon. She looked at the sofa longingly but didn't dare give in to the temptation to sleep. Not yet. Instead, she went to the coffee machine and put on a fresh pot.

She waited for it to brew, then poured herself a cup and stirred in more sugar than usual. She brought it to the computer and sat down. The SUV wasn't going very fast. Klára had said Lance was driving. Laurel wondered if he'd slowed on purpose. She had to believe he wouldn't have allowed himself to be captured without some sort of plan in mind.

The SUV got even slower, and she looked ahead on the road. There was a highway service station less than a kilometer away. It looked like they were going to stop there.

She picked up the phone and dialed Tatyana's number.

"What's happened?" Tatyana said, answering immediately. " Are you still tracking them?"

"They're about fifteen kilometers ahead of you," Laurel said. "They're slowing down for a service area." She had Tatyana's vehicle on a separate screen and saw her immediately accelerate. "Careful, Tatyana. You'll get pulled over."

"Why are they stopping?" Tatyana said. "Do they need gas?"

"No," Laurel said. She'd hacked into the vehicle's onboard computer and could read its data. "They still have more than half a tank."

"Then why stop?"

"Could be a trap," Laurel said. "You should proceed on that assumption."

"I'm going to proceed on the assumption that Valentina Brik deserves a bullet to the skull."

"Tatyana, go easy. She could be up to anything."

"What if she's pulling over to get rid of Lance?" Tatyana said. "Have you considered that possibility?"

Laurel had considered that possibility. She'd been going over it all night. On the one hand, Lance had value as a hostage. He could be used to trade. On the other, Valentina had to be aware of how dangerous he was. Even without knowing the specifics, she'd have figured out by now that he was CIA. Every second she held him was a risk.

"They've stopped," Laurel said, her eyes glued to the screen. She tapped the keyboard to zoom in closer and leaned forward. "They've pulled up by the convenience store. It doesn't look like they're getting gas. They haven't gone under the canopy that shelters the pumps."

"I have a very bad feeling about this," Tatyana said.

Tatyana's car accelerated. "Easy," Laurel said. "You're going to have an accident."

"She's going to kill him," Tatyana said, and Laurel was concerned by her tone. She was also still picking up speed.

"Take a breath, Tatyana. You're going more than double the speed limit."

"What are they doing?" Tatyana said.

"The driver's door is opening," Laurel said.

"Is it Lance?"

Laurel waited, still as a statue, then saw Lance step out of the vehicle. "It's Lance," she said.

"What's he doing?"

"Taking a few steps away from the vehicle."

"Why?"

"I don't know."

"She's going to shoot him," Tatyana said, her speed edging even higher.

"No," Laurel said. "She'd have done it already. She's waiting for something."

"Waiting for what? The Romanians?"

"I don't know," Laurel said. She pulled up what information she could about the service area. There was the gas station with a small store and some washrooms attached. There was also a building on the far side of the lot with some fast-food restaurants in it. "There's a payphone right next to them," she said. "I think that's why they've stopped."

"A payphone? Why?"

"Hold on," Laurel said, more to herself than Tatyana.

"Hold on?"

"Oh no!"

"Laurel! What is it?"

Lance stopped a few feet from the vehicle, then did something very strange. He looked straight up at the sky, almost as if he was looking at Laurel's satellite.

"What's happening?" Tatyana said.

Laurel looked from Lance's screen to Tatyana's. "Tatyana, you need to slow down, or you're going to crash."

"What are they doing?" Tatyana said, her voice growing increasingly frantic.

"He's looking at the sky."

"Why is he looking at the sky?"

"He's sending a message."

"Oh no!" Tatyana said. "He's not sending a message. Valentina is. She knows Shipenko's watching. He's tracking her the same way we are. She's showing him that she has Lance. She's going to make a deal."

"Shipenko wants her dead. What deal can she be trying to make?"

"She's going to shoot him, Laurel. She's going to shoot him in front of Shipenko."

47

V alentina was still in the car, parked in the service area, looking through her open window at Lance. He was wearing a bright orange construction parka he'd found in the back of the SUV. It was thickly padded with a large hood and was easily big enough for a man twice his size. He looked ridiculous, but she knew not to underestimate him. Shipenko had been willing to risk an awful lot to draw this man out into the open. There had to be a good reason for that.

"I want to make sure Shipenko sees me," Lance had said when he put on the coat.

Valentina knew she needed to be careful. The next few minutes would decide whether she lived or died, and she knew it.

She touched her shoulder. The pain was getting worse by the minute. The wound was definitely becoming infected, which made her even more vulnerable. She couldn't even drive. She'd had no choice but to bring Lance this far, and now that she was there, she had no choice but to betray him.

"You're a mad man," she said through the window. He was standing in the parking lot, about ten yards from the car, staring straight up at the sky like a child who'd never seen snow before.

Russia had dozens of satellites over Europe capable of resolving a face, especially at that angle. What Valentina didn't forget for a second was that the United States also did. Lance said he was sending a message to Moscow. That was true. But you couldn't send a message to Moscow without also sending one to Langley.

"How long are you going to do that?" she said.

"That should be enough," he said, looking at her.

She'd just touched the wound at her shoulder, and he saw her wince.

"That's getting worse, isn't it?" he said.

"It's not me you need to worry about," she said. She still had the gun pointed at him. They both know if he tried anything, she wouldn't miss. Even if she was delirious with septicemia, she wouldn't miss at that range. He was putting his life in her hands, and what was troubling her was that she still couldn't figure out why.

"But I am worried," he said. "You're my bait. I need you."

She nodded slowly. "It seems I'm everyone's bait these days." She moved across the seat toward the door and winced again from the pain. The thigh wasn't so bad, but the shoulder was burning. She was loath to do it, but she turned her face in toward it and sniffed, like someone checking themself for body odor.

"You need to do something about that," Lance said.

"Is that your plan? Get me to waste time while the CIA homes in on our position?"

"If that was my plan, I wouldn't have let you take me," he said.

"So, you think you *let* me take you?"

"Didn't I?"

She didn't know. She supposed he had, which should have worried her, but in the situation she was in, she didn't think she'd even have made it this far without him.

"I just need a minute," she said, reaching for the cigarettes. She put one in her mouth and lit it. It gave her some slight relief.

Lance was still out in the lot, and she put the lighter inside the box and threw it to him. She almost wanted him to make a move. She could have pulled the trigger and ended it all. But he didn't run. He caught the packet and put a cigarette in his mouth as if he didn't have a care in the world. She looked at his face and tried to read his mind. It was a tricky situation. For her, she needed him. She was dead without him. She had no doubt the Romanians were on their tail. If they hadn't been before, they certainly were now. For him, it was more complicated. He was her prisoner, but it didn't feel that way. He wanted to kill her. The only reason he hadn't tried to do so already was that he wanted to kill the Romanians even more.

"Okay," she said, forcing herself to get out of the car. Her legs were weak, and she held the door for support. "That's enough time for the satellites. I need to call Shipenko."

Lance hadn't moved, but he was watching her hold on to the door and said, "You need to check that wound. You're white as a ghost." He nodded toward the gas station's washroom, a single, unisex stall with a door facing the lot. "You need to look at it now. Once you make the call, the Romanians will swoop in like a homing missile. There won't be time."

She knew he was stalling, manipulating the situation. Every second that passed was another chance for something to go wrong. But he was right, she needed to check it. And he wouldn't try anything until after the Romanians had been killed.

"Go check the door," she said, keeping her gun on him.

He opened it and stepped aside to show her the interior. It was basic—a sink, toilet, some paper towel, a garbage can, an electric hand dryer.

"Get back," she said, then limped inside. It didn't exactly smell like a rose garden, but it would do. At least it looked like it had been cleaned recently.

"Stand by the door," she said. "Keep your back to me."

He did as she said, keeping the door open with his foot. It was another opportunity for him to escape. If he ran then, his chances would have been at least even, but he didn't.

"You really want these Romanians," she said as she took off her top.

"If I don't get them now, they'll disappear into the woodwork. I've seen it happen before. It could take years to track them down."

"And that's worth risking your life?"

"Am I risking my life?"

She said nothing, watching him in the mirror above the washbasin. She didn't hurry but moved methodically, waiting for the water to heat up before removing the bandage. She'd used a strip of fabric from her undershirt for it, and she winced when she saw what was beneath. The wound was tinged yellow around the edge, and the stitches she'd given herself on the bridge with the cop's first aid kit didn't look like they were going to hold. She'd taken an antiseptic cream from the cop but what she really needed was antibiotics.

"You don't happen to have any first aid supplies, do you?" she said.

"What am I, a pharmacist?"

She put her hands under the running water and washed them thoroughly. Lance hadn't moved a muscle. It was tempting to think she might win him over, that she might convince him to help her, but she knew it was impossible. They were friends only for as long as the Romanians were still out there. Once they were dead, he'd turn on her in a second.

Suddenly, she pulled her hands back from the water. She hadn't realized how hot it was until it had practically scalded her. "Damn it!" she said.

"You okay?"

"I'm fine. Stay where you are."

She washed the wound as best she could and applied more of the cream. Then she tore another strip from her undershirt and bandaged it back up. She washed her hands again, and, looking at them in the sink, realized they were shaking. She stood there for a moment staring at them, staring at her reflection in the mirror. The situation was beyond desperate. She was in no state to pull it off. Lance knew it. She could tell by how calm he was. He would kill her the moment she'd served her purpose.

Unless she got him first.

"You about done?" he said, pulling her from her thoughts.

"Just about," she said, putting her shirt back on. He

backed away from the door, and she said, "Wait here while I make the call."

"I won't be able to hear you," he said.

"You need to be visible. If Shipenko doesn't see you, there's no way he'll believe I'm the one calling the shots."

Lance knew she was right.

"Very well," he said, "but promise me one thing."

She looked at him. "You know there can be no promises between us."

"Just don't do anything rash until the Romanians are dead."

"You care more about killing them than about surviving this, don't you?"

He shrugged. "I care only about killing them."

She nodded. She knew that was true. What she was worried about was what he'd care about after it was done. "Put your hands on your head," she said. "It will look more convincing for Shipenko."

48

Shipenko slipped on the blue hospital gown and lay back on the examination table. Above him, a bright light similar to a dentist's shone down on his face. He was at the exclusive Tsar Nicholas II medical laboratory, an exclusive clinic not far from the Kremlin that was frequented by some of the country's richest and most secretive oligarchs.

Shipenko, despite his years spent at the mercy of scientists and doctors, had never given up hope that something might be done for his condition, and he was at the clinic now for yet another expert opinion.

His doctor, flanked by over a dozen assistants, interns, and nurses, entered the room, and Shipenko prepared himself for the usual reaction. It was one of the nurses, a girl scarcely old enough to be out of high school, who responded first. These people were supposedly professionals, and they'd been warned in advance of what to expect, but exposed as he was under the bright light, Shipenko's face was too much for her. She threw a hand over her mouth and vomited.

"Darya!" the doctor exclaimed in horror. "Control yourself. Someone, clean up this mess."

Another nurse ran out for a mop, and the doctor proceeded to apologize profusely to Shipenko for the *inconvenience*, as he put it.

"I only wish it was an inconvenience," Shipenko said. "I trust you'll provide my office with the nurse's full name."

The doctor hesitated only a second before saying, "Absolutely, sir. Of course. Whatever you want."

"I think I can *educate* her," Shipenko said in front of the entire team. "I think I can teach her to love what her mind wishes to despise."

"Do you?" the doctor said, his voice trembling.

"I do," Shipenko said, "and if I can't, fuck it. I'll throw her to my dogs."

A silence descended on the medical team then, and Shipenko relished in it. That silence was the evidence of his power, and every person in the room knew it.

It was broken by the sound of his phone ringing. "How irregular," he said, looking at it on the desk next to the examination table. "I gave explicit instructions not to be disturbed."

He looked at the screen, saw where the call was coming from, and waved his hand imperiously. "I must take this," he said to the doctor. "Get out. All of you. I must take this call."

The medical staff hastily retreated, and when the door shut, Shipenko answered, saying, "Well, well, well. If it isn't the long-lost prodigal daughter."

"You tried to kill me," Valentina said.

A smile spread across Shipenko's scab-crusted lips. "Feisty little bitch, aren't you?"

"You have no idea, Shipenko. I'm going to hunt you down and cut off your—"

"Now, now, Valentina. There's no need for that. You've been cast out in the cold. Now you're looking to come back to papa."

"I'm not looking for anything from you."

"Then why did you call me?" Shipenko said. Valentina said nothing for a moment, and Shipenko added, "Exactly. You want back in. That's why you called. You're looking for my mercy."

"Why was I cast out in the first place?"

"Because you disobeyed an order."

"I didn't disobey. I hesitated."

"You ran."

"I ran because you were having me followed."

"No," Shipenko said. "You ran before you knew that. You couldn't go through with your orders, and you wanted out."

"Three women, one after the other—"

"You broke protocol. You broke contact."

"It was a crisis."

"A crisis?"

"Yes."

"Any crisis you had, Valentina, was a crisis of faith. And as you are well aware, that is the one kind of crisis you are not permitted to have."

Valentina said nothing, and Shipenko leaned back on the bed and luxuriated in his moment of triumph. This was all he'd ever wanted from her. Surrender. An admission of his power.

"You were pushing me," she said at last. "Making me kill those women, again and again, you knew what would happen. You wanted me to break."

"And did you?" Shipenko said. "Did you *break*, my dear? Have I made my point?"

"You're a monster."

"Yes, but that's not the point now. The point is, are you ready to give me what I want?"

She was quiet again, struggling with herself. She knew what he wanted. She knew what her life would cost. "I can give you *some* of what you want," she said at last.

"Can you give me yourself, my dear? Can you give me your body? Your soul? Your complete surrender?"

"I can give you Lance Spector," she spat.

Shipenko sat up instantly. That got his attention far more than the sexual submission he'd been seeking from her. "You're lying," he said.

"Am I? Locate the source of this call. It's a Czech landline."

"I'll have to put in the request. I'm not at my desk."

"Do it," she said. "Get them to send you live footage of my position. I'll wait."

Shipenko forwarded the call signature to his office and told them to zero in with the satellite. "Where are you?" he said to Valentina when it was done.

"You'll see soon enough."

The satellite feed came through to his phone, and he switched her to speaker so he could view the screen.

"Czech territory," he said. "A highway service station."

"Do you see the gas station?"

"Yes."

"I'm beneath the canopy, but there's a man in the open, standing near the vehicle."

"I see him."

"Scrub back five minutes."

"Why?"

"Just do it."

He scrubbed back through the last few minutes of the satellite's feed. He saw Valentina come out of the vehicle. Then he saw the man, looking straight up at the sky. He zoomed in on the face. "My gosh!" he exclaimed. "It's him. You got him."

"My gun is pointed at his head right this second."

"But how is that possible? This is the most dangerous man outside of the—"

"He thinks this will lead him to the Splinter. All he cares about is killing them."

"What are you waiting for, Valentina? Kill him. Kill him now."

"Not so fast, Osip."

"What are you talking about?"

"What do you think I'm talking about? I have something you want."

"He's using you, Valentina. Kill him, or this will explode in your face. He'll snap your neck the moment you give him what he wants."

"You see my dilemma, then? I'm trapped between a rock and a hard place."

"You're not trapped."

"Call off your Romanian dogs. Let me come back into the fold."

"Of course. Anything. Just shoot that man right now. I want to see it with my own eyes before we discuss another detail."

"I have your word?"

"You have whatever you want," he cried. "Pull the trigger!"

And then, bang!

49

Tatyana pulled into the service station and jammed on the brakes, sending the powerful car skidding across the open parking lot. She had a gun in one hand and the steering wheel in the other.

Lance was standing in the open, alone, his hands on his head like a prisoner waiting to be shot. Valentina was under the canopy of the gas station, on a payphone, and she had a gun pointed right at him. The bitch was going to shoot him. She was going to shoot him right in front of the satellite and worm her way back into the Kremlin's good graces.

"No!" Tatyana screamed, steering the car right at Lance in some desperate attempt to alter the facts. At that very same moment, a bullet was fired—the crack of it ringing out in the air—and Lance leaped out of the path of the oncoming vehicle.

Tatyana had the door of the car open before it had even come to a halt, and she leaned out and fired off a shot. The bullet missed its mark but shattered the window behind Valentina, inches from her face, and sent shards of glass crashing down around her.

Valentina ducked for cover, and Tatyana fired again, this time hitting the payphone. "Drop it!" she yelled.

Valentina dropped the gun, then looked up at Tatyana.

Tatyana saw the flash of recognition on her face. "That's right," she said. "Remember me?"

Valentina looked toward Lance, who was getting to his feet.

"What are you looking at him for?" Tatyana said. "You were about to shoot him."

"I was not," Valentina said.

Tatyana laughed. "You lying bitch," she said.

In the convenience store, the employee, a boy of about eighteen, was frantically dialing the phone. Lance caught his eye and shook his head. "Go in the back," he called through the shattered window. "Take the customers. No one will get hurt."

Tatyana looked at Lance, then back at Valentina, and couldn't make sense of what she was seeing. They seemed to be working together. "What's going on?" she said.

Lance walked toward her and got her to lower her weapon. "It's not what it looks like," he said.

"What it looks like? She was about to shoot you!"

"I know," Lance said.

"She wanted to kill you."

"I know," Lance said again.

"Then explain to me," Tatyana said, "what the hell is going on here."

Lance's hand grazed Tatyana's. "Don't look down," he said quietly. "Give me your gun."

"What are you up to?" Tatyana said. "You can't work with this woman. You can't trust her."

"I know," Lance said.

She slipped the gun discreetly into the pocket of his enormous coat.

"I saw that," Valentina said.

"It's not you I'm hiding it from," Lance said, glancing upward.

"The satellites?" Tatyana said.

Valentina butted in then, her saccharine voice making Tatyana nauseous. "We've got a plan, Tatyana. You're wrecking it."

"A plan?"

"We need each other, don't we, Lance?" Valentina said, and something about the way she looked at Lance then made Tatyana's blood boil. If she'd still had the gun, she would have shot her right then and there, plans be damned.

"We should kill her right now," Tatyana said to Lance, but Lance only shook his head.

"We can't," he said.

"Why the hell not?"

"Because," Lance said, "if we do, the men who attacked the embassy will disappear."

"Let them disappear," Tatyana said. "They can't hide forever. We'll find them."

"They know what they've done," Lance said. "They know the whole world will be after them. These men will go to ground. They'll disappear. If I don't get them today, while they think they have the advantage, it could be years before they're brought to justice. Do you want to wait years?"

Tatyana looked at Lance and suddenly felt like she was speaking to a stranger. She felt at a disadvantage, like a third wheel, like he and Valentina were the ones in cahoots, and she was in the way. "It won't take years," she said helplessly.

"This cell is disciplined," Lance said. "They're professional. If we let them slip the noose today, they'll go completely dark. My guess is that not even Shipenko will know how to find them. They won't stay in Moscow. They'll drain whatever bank account he pays them in, and they'll go completely off the grid."

"They'll make a mistake."

"They'll be ghosts," Lance said, "living in the dark. And yes, you're right, they might make a mistake, ten or twenty years from now when they think the world has forgotten what they've done."

"Sometimes it takes years," Tatyana said. "Osama bin Laden took years—"

"It took two wars to find Osama bin Laden," Lance said. "Our president can't afford years, and he can't afford two wars."

"All right, bitch," Valentina said. "You heard him. Step off."

"Why don't you just keep your mouth shut," Tatyana said. The image flashed through her mind of clawing Valentina's eyes out.

"We don't have a lot of time," Lance said.

"Lance," Tatyana said. "I know this woman. She's a rattlesnake. I know her—"

"You had your chance," Valentina said, eyeing Tatyana up and down. "He's had a look at the options, and he's made his choice."

Tatyana rounded on Valentina. "Why don't you just shut your dumb—"

"How much more time are we going to waste on this?"

Valentina said to Lance, ignoring Tatyana's words. She bent down to pick up her gun.

"No," Tatyana cried.

"Not so fast," Lance said. He was pointing his gun at her through his jacket pocket.

"You know it needs to look like I'm the one in control," Valentina said, glancing upward. "If Shipenko thinks for one second that I've lost the upper hand, he'll call off the Romanians. Then all of this will have been for nothing."

"I want no part of this," Tatyana said to Lance. "Whatever it is, I want no part."

"No one asked you," Valentina said, bending down to pick up her gun.

"This bitch will stab you in the back the first second she gets. Believe me."

"Tatyana, I have no choice," he said, making for the SUV.

"She's a psychopathic—" Tatyana's words were cut off by the clap of another gunshot. Tatyana didn't move. She was confused. Then she reached for her back. It was wet. "Lance!" she gasped.

Lance was holding his gun beneath his jacket, but Valentina had taken cover inside the store. "That bitch," he said, catching Tatyana with one arm and lowering her gently to the ground.

"I told you she was a cunt," Tatyana said.

"You're going to be all right," Lance said. "Everything's going to be all right."

"Oh, don't be dramatic," Valentina called out from inside the convenience store.

"I should just kill you right this second," Lance spat.

"If you do," Valentina said, "your precious Romanians get away."

"I'm going to be all right," Tatyana said. "It's a flesh wound."

Lance checked her back and nodded. "You'll live," he said.

"I told you she was a cunt, though," Tatyana said.

Lance smiled. "I'll call you an ambulance. You're going to be all right." He looked toward the store. "Valentina," he called out. "Call an ambulance."

They could see Valentina come toward the window, where there was a phone on the cashier's desk. They watched her make the call.

"Don't let her get away," Tatyana said softly.

"I won't," Lance said.

"Promise?"

Valentina appeared above them. Tatyana would have spat at her if she could have.

"Don't look so sour," Valentina said to Tatyana. Then to Lance, "You know I had no choice. Shipenko had to see me regain control, otherwise your plan fails."

Lance rose to his feet, his gun still on Valentina through the jacket pocket, and hers still on him, the two of them bound to each other by the threat of a finger on a trigger.

"Tatyana, I'm sorry," he said.

Tatyana nodded. "Go," she said. "And remember what you promised."

He nodded.

"And for God's sake, watch your back."

50

L ance got into the driver's seat of the SUV and kept his gun on Valentina while she climbed into the back. She shut the door, and he said, "You drive this time."

"What if Shipenko sees?"

"He won't see," Lance said, sliding across to the passenger seat. "Now, climb up."

She remained where she was, looking out her window to where Tatyana still lay, bleeding in the snow. Lance shook his head, then swung out his hand and snatched her gun from her. She barely even resisted.

"Go ahead," she said. "I'm going to die anyway. Shoot me."

"I'll tell you what," he said. "Either you get into the front of this car and drive right now, or I let Tatyana kill you."

She rolled her eyes but did as he said and got into the driver's seat.

"Now, drive," he said. "Nice and easy."

She got back onto the highway. A few miles down the

road, an ambulance and two police cars sped by them in the opposite direction.

"See," Valentina said. "I told you she'd be okay."

"You didn't have to shoot her," Lance said.

"Sure I did. I did it for you."

"You're insane."

"You and Tatyana against me? Shipenko would have called off his dogs. I wanted to help you make sure they paid for what they did."

"Why do I find that hard to believe?" he said, looking at her. She was very pale, very weak. He wondered if she'd be able to drive, and, as if on cue, the car began to veer toward the side of the road. He grabbed the wheel and helped her steer.

"Sorry," she said. "The truth is, I don't think I can keep going."

"So you're going to give up?"

She shut her eyes. He kept his hand on the wheel, but they were slowing down. "Wake up," he said.

"I told you, I can't drive. I'm not playing. I really can't."

He knew she was telling the truth. "Pull off the highway up here," he said. "This exit."

"What's here?"

"Just do it."

She smiled. "Where are we going, Lance? Where are you taking me?"

"I'm not taking you anywhere," Lance said, eyeing the road, keeping one hand on the wheel for her.

They crested a small hill, and she said, "I had to shoot your friend, you know."

"I know," he said. What she'd said was true. Shipenko would have certainly called off the Romanians if she hadn't. "You didn't have to aim for her spine, though," he said.

"I did no such thing."

"I felt the wound. An inch to the left, and she'd have been paralyzed for life."

"That would have been unfortunate," she said.

"You're a piece of work."

She turned to look at him. "Really, Lance, I don't think I can drive much further. It's my shoulder. I can't go on."

"It's not much farther."

They drove another minute, and she said, "You know, there's a history between Tatyana and me."

"I'm sure there is," he said.

"I have my reasons for wanting to hurt her."

"Well, I don't want to hear them."

"Do you still have the cigarettes?" she said.

He lit one and gave it to her.

"We trained together, her and I."

"I told you, I don't want to know."

"Why not? Are you afraid you'll hear something you don't like?"

"I'm afraid I'll hear lies."

"She's not as innocent as you think."

"I never believed she was innocent."

"She's done things, Lance. Things that would make your blood curdle."

Lance lit a cigarette for himself and said, "Slow down."

The road was a windy, single lane with a white line painted on either side. Tall trees hung over it on both sides. It had been a few miles since they'd left the highway, and they'd been in forest the entire time. They'd seen no villages, no buildings, not even a barn.

Valentina dropped the speed slightly and checked her rearview mirror. "You're not curious about her at all?"

"No, I'm not."

"She's no better than me."

He said nothing.

"You're wrong to trust her."

He remained silent, eyes on the road. They approached a fork, and he said, "Turn here. On the right."

She exhaled smoke. "What do I care?" she said. "It's all the same. You believe what you want." She drove on silently, drawing on her cigarette, watching the rearview mirror diligently. "What's our plan?" she said after a minute.

He looked at her, and they locked eyes. "*Our* plan?"

"What you said earlier was right. I can't survive alone. I need to be on *someone's* side. If not the GRU, then the CIA."

"You think you can defect?"

"Do *you* think I could?"

He shrugged. He could have told her, yes, but for some reason, he couldn't bring himself to lie to her. "I don't think so," he said.

"Tatyana did it."

"You're not Tatyana."

"I already told you she's no better than me."

"It doesn't matter."

"It doesn't matter to you?"

He sighed. "To me. Yes."

"Then why don't you pass my offer up the chain? See what the top floor has to say about it?"

"I don't think so."

"You did it for Tatyana."

"Yes."

"But not for me?"

"No."

"You have feelings for her. That's why."

"That's got nothing—"

She looked at him then, her eyes flashing with emotion. "Don't lie to me."

51

Shipenko watched his screen with a mixture of confusion and anger. He couldn't make sense of what he was seeing. He'd had no idea Valentina's hostage was Lance Spector, but now that he knew, he was desperate to offer her whatever she wanted in exchange for his life. Spector would be the crowning achievement of this whole thing, a cherry on top of what had already been an enormously successful operation. President Molotov would be eating out of his hands.

But then Tatyana arrived and ruined everything. She'd gotten a bullet for her trouble, but for some reason, Valentina hadn't killed her. Nor had she killed Spector. From what Shipenko could make out, Valentina was the only one who was still armed at the end of the encounter. She could have killed both of them. The fact that she hadn't meant only one thing. She was keeping her options open, hedging her bets, playing both sides.

Shipenko didn't fancy her chances. The CIA was willing to go quite far when making deals with a devil, but Valentina had just slit the throats of two innocent young staffers. Their bodies were barely cold. That would be a lot to swallow, even for Langley. Perhaps Spector had been planting ideas in her mind, though. Telling her that the embassy attack had altered the landscape, that Langley would do a deal with anyone if it meant getting their hands on the attackers.

Shipenko had no doubt she was being lied to, but that didn't make the prospect any less worrying. When Valentina started talking, it was his name she'd give them first. He wasn't worried about what the CIA would do with the information. His position was assured. He was a member of the Dead Hand, one of President Molotov's closest associates. He was untouchable. Western sanctions, war crimes allegations, asset freezes, the seizure of his yacht off the coast of Malta—it was all a joke. He was a Russian, and nothing the West could ever do to him came close to what the Kremlin could do. He wasn't afraid of Washington, he was afraid of Moscow.

But Valentina could harm him at home. Even without knowing it, she could poison everything he'd been working for. Shipenko had been nursing a plot for years, holding his cards close to his chest, biding his time, and he never took his eye off the prize.

All emperors succumbed eventually. All empires crumbled. Washington knew that. They knew that no matter how many precautions Molotov took, he wouldn't be in power forever. His time would come, as it did for all men, and when it did, they wanted to be in a position to benefit from it. They knew the list of potential successors was small. They also knew that the most likely place the successor came from would be the Dead Hand.

Levi Roth was like a truffle pig. He'd been sniffing around that fact for years, obsessing over every detail that emerged, slavishly snatching every piece of information about the Dead Hand he could get his grubby hands on. And the more he learned, the more he realized that Osip Shipenko was the most likely candidate to succeed Molotov.

Shipenko, for his part, stayed under the radar. He was a creature of the darkness, and would have preferred to remain in darkness for as long as possible. He knew the risks that accompanied a fight for the top spot. In Molotov's Kremlin, the two most dangerous words in the Russian language were 'regime' and 'change'. If Molotov got even a whiff that Langley was eyeing Shipenko as a potential successor, it would be the end of him.

Valentina, of course, knew none of that. But that didn't mean she couldn't scupper the whole thing. Even without realizing it, she could poison every hope Shipenko had dared to cherish about taking the throne. If Roth and the Americans heard even a fraction of what she knew, they would abandon every thought they'd ever had of allowing him to ascend. They didn't control the process. It wasn't with their permission or blessing that the next leader of Russia would take his position. But they were a piece of the puzzle, and what they wanted, what they did, mattered. The Americans spoke of election interference like it was the most egregious crime they'd ever heard of, but Shipenko had seen dozens of instances around the world when the will of the CIA mattered more than the will of the people choosing a new leader.

It was a dangerous situation, and it wouldn't do. He had to make absolutely certain Valentina Brik never made it into a CIA interrogation room.

His phone started to ring, and he saw that it was

Constantin. "You better not be getting cold feet," Shipenko said as he answered.

"No, sir. We're still following the marker. The thing is, it stopped for a few minutes. And a police car just passed us."

"Don't worry about that."

"We're getting nearer the border. I'm worried we're headed right into a police roadblock."

"There's no roadblock," Shipenko said, "but there is new information."

"What information?"

"Her hostage is someone I know."

"I see," Constantin said. "That sounds ominous."

"Tell me, what weaponry did you bring from the safe house?"

"Now you're really making me worried."

"He's dangerous," Shipenko said. "There's no point pretending otherwise. He's a CIA asset. A very valuable one. I know your task is only to kill Valentina, but if you kill him too, I'll triple your pay."

Constantin sighed. Shipenko had no doubt the other man had heard him too. It was just the two of them now, and Shipenko needed them to follow through with this mission more than ever. "You never answered my question," he said.

"What question was that?" Constantin said.

"What weaponry did you bring?"

"We brought everything we had left from the attack."

"That's what I was hoping you'd say."

"It still doesn't mean this will be an easy—"

"It won't be easy, but at least you're prepared for the job. You can attack from a distance. Take them both out before they even know you're there."

"We used all the rockets."

"But you have the grenade launchers?"

"We do. And the submachine guns."

"I'll sweeten the pot," Shipenko said. "You have my word, neither of you will ever want for money again. And I guarantee the Americans won't find you. You'll have plastic surgery, new fingerprints, the works."

"None of it will do us any good if we're dead," Constantin said.

"There's also a jet waiting for you, fueled and on the runway at the airport in Linz. This is no suicide mission." The truth was, he would have sent them to their deaths in a second if he thought it would get him what he wanted. But, right now, he needed them alive. "If there's a way for you to attack from a distance, using the grenades, do it. But if not, just keep your distance, and keep following. They don't know you're coming."

"They've left the highway," Constantin said. "They're on a country road."

"Just keep following, Constantin. I guarantee the reward will be worth the risk."

"And you won't order us in if an attack is... untenable?"

"I can't. I need you alive. Just stay close, and remember this. Valentina's badly wounded. She can barely stand, and all she's got is a pistol."

"It's not Valentina I'm worried about," Constantin said.

The line went dead, and Shipenko got up. He went to the door of the examination room and called for the doctor. The doctor came, and Shipenko said, "I have business to take care of. Someone from my office will call to reschedule."

"Of course," the doctor said, handing him an envelope.

"What's this?" Shipenko said.

"The name of the nurse who... upset you earlier."

"Of course," Shipenko said, tearing it open. "Darya Kovalchuk," he said, reading the name. "Very good. Send her to me. I'll need help dressing."

"Very good, sir."

The doctor left, and Shipenko went back into the examination room. He looked at his phone. The satellite team was still tracking Valentina's vehicle. He wondered what was really going on inside it. What was Valentina thinking? What was she playing at?

He removed his robe and lay back on the examination table, naked. He was nervous. He didn't want Spector to slip through his fingers, but he sensed things were beginning to go off the rails. His thoughts were interrupted by a knock on the door.

"Is that the nurse?" he said.

A voice as tiny as a mouse's answered. "It is, sir."

"Then come in. Don't be shy."

He leaned back on the table, revealing to her the full glory of his naked body. It would be even more shocking than his face had been.

She pushed open the door and peered around it, then gasped.

"Come on," he said. "Come in. Lock the door."

She was crying, and the sight of her filled him with such anticipation that his entire body started to tingle. She remained by the door, paralyzed with fear, and he was about to get up and drag her into the room when his phone beeped.

"Damn it," he muttered, looking at the screen. It was a notification from the satellite team.

Identifier: SI_490521

    Agency: Prime Directorate

    Lead Agent: Osip Shipenko

    Satellite: MKA-V High-Resolution

    Orbit: 330 Kilometers

    Inclination: 96.64 Degrees

    Optical Reconnaissance Target: 49.05 Degrees
North, 14.43 Degrees East

    Russian Identifications: Valentina Brik

    Foreign Identifications: Lance Spector

    Incident: Shot fired. Man down.

    Prime Directorate Satellite Surveillance
Incident

Shipenko read the words, 'Shot fired. Man down,' and almost dropped the phone. "Get out," he barked at the nurse. "Get out, now, and shut the door." She disappeared, and he immediately opened the file attached to the notification.

It was the surveillance footage. He couldn't believe what he was seeing.

52

B y the time the ambulance arrived, Tatyana felt dizzy from blood loss. She was shivering from the cold, and the gas station attendant had put his coat over her. The other people from the convenience store crowded around her.

"Get back, get back," the paramedics said as they approached. "Give her room to breathe."

Tatyana tried to get up, and one of the medics rushed forward. "No, no, no. Don't try to move."

"I'm cold," she said. "Very cold."

He put a silver survival blanket over her while his colleagues brought over a stretcher. The tag on his uniform said his name was Václav.

"Thank you," Tatyana said as three medics lifted her smoothly onto a stretcher and brought her to the ambulance.

She still couldn't believe what had happened. For a second time, she'd allowed Valentina to get the better of her. What had she been thinking, turning her back on her?

She wasn't too happy with Lance for leaving her there, but at the same time, she was praying nothing happened to him.

In the ambulance, the medics rolled her over so that they could examine the bullet wound.

"You were lucky," Václav said.

"I don't feel lucky," she said, but she'd already concluded the same thing. She knew what a life-threatening wound felt like. This wasn't one. It hurt, though, and she swore as the medics bandaged her up.

"I need to make a call," she said when they were done, searching for her phone, which she couldn't seem to find.

"You need to lie still and let us get you to the hospital."

The police had arrived on the scene, she could see them outside the ambulance, and when a cop came over to question her, Václav told him in no uncertain terms that he would have to wait.

"This woman has just been involved in a gunfight," the officer protested. "From the reports, she's the one who fired the first shot."

"It's all right," Tatyana said to the medic. "Let him speak to me."

The cop climbed into the back of the ambulance and took out a notebook. He was young, barely old enough to shave by the look of it, and he chewed the end of his pen.

"Klára Issová," Tatyana said before he had a chance to get started. "She's the one you need to speak to."

"Klára Issová?" he said, jotting down the name.

"She works for the BIS."

"The BIS?" he said, looking up.

"That's right. Give me your notebook. I'll give you the number."

He handed it to her, and she scrawled down Klára's

direct line. "Tell her I want to be taken to the military hospital in Prague."

"Has this got anything to do with what happened at the embassy this morning?" the cop said.

She stared at him for a moment, and he shook his head, dismissing the question.

"Just pass on the message," Tatyana said. "Tell the medics not to move me until you get through to her."

The cop left, and Tatyana sat up on the bed, wincing as she did so.

"You shouldn't be moving," Václav said.

"This isn't the first time I've been shot," she said. "I know what I'm doing."

The cop went back to his car and made a call. Tatyana watched him. It took a minute for him to get through, and it seemed there were quite a few questions, then he came back over to the ambulance.

"Did you reach her?" Tatyana said.

"No, but the BIS agreed you should be taken to the military hospital. We're to escort your ambulance all the way."

"Okay," she said. "I'm also going to need a phone."

He handed her one, and she saw it was her own.

"It was in your car," he said.

"Thank you."

The paramedics made sure she was stable for the journey. When they were done, Václav looked at her curiously and said, "So, who are you?"

"No one you want to know," she said.

"I'm going to ride in the back with you. Keep an eye on you."

"No," Tatyana said. "I need to make some private calls."

"It's standard protocol."

"If I need anything, I can still reach you up front, can't I?"

"Yes," he said, showing her a button. "Press this, and we'll be able to hear you."

"And if I don't press it? Can you hear me then?"

"Only when the light's green."

"Okay," she said. "Leave it red for now."

He took one last look at the bandage, then left and got into the front of the ambulance with the driver. As soon as they got onto the highway, she called Laurel.

Laurel picked up in an instant. "Tatyana! Are you all right?"

"I'll live," Tatyana said. "I just can't believe I let that bitch get the better of me again."

"There was no other choice," Laurel said. "It had to look like she was in control."

"And how's it working out? Any sign of our Romanian friends?"

"Not yet," Laurel said, "although it does look like Lance is leaving the highway."

"I feel nervous," Tatyana said.

"Of course you do. It's a lot to juggle. He's being followed by mercenaries, he's got a GRU assassin in the car with him, and if he tries to do anything to prepare for the fight, if the Russians get one whiff he's trying to set a trap, the Romanians will disappear forever."

"What if something goes wrong?" Tatyana said. "Valentina makes me nervous. If he takes his eyes off her for a single second—"

"Well," Laurel said, "you did everything conceivable to get her away from him. You took a bullet for it. There's nothing more to be done. Just focus on getting back to Prague in one piece."

"I'll get there in one piece," Tatyana said. "I've been given a police escort. They're taking me to the military hospital, but can you get Klára to meet me there when I arrive?"

"You need to focus on getting some rest," Laurel said.

"I need to speak to Klára. I gave her Shipenko's name. She might have found something."

"I don't think she will have."

"She has access to records we don't," Tatyana said.

"I'm afraid she's been taken off the case."

"What?"

"The Czechs are coming down hard on her."

"Why? What has she done wrong?"

"It's the embassy, Tatyana. The biggest terrorist attack on Czech soil in decades. They're saying it was her case."

"That's ridiculous. No one knew this was coming. She was investigating two deaths, and the men who carried out the attack weren't the ones who carried them out. There's no way she could have stopped this."

"I know," Laurel said, "but you know how the top brass is. They're afraid if they don't choose someone to take the fall, then it will come down on them."

"They're scapegoating her."

"In any case," Laurel said, "she's not going to be able to help you when you get to Prague."

Tatyana sighed. She was about to continue arguing the point when Laurel said, "There's a Toyota minivan leaving the highway at the same exit Lance took."

"Is it them?"

"It could be. It's a quiet exit. I'll trace the minivan backward. See if it's come from Prague."

"How far is it behind Lance?"

"A few kilometers. If something's happening, it will be soon."

"Is there any way we can send backup?"

"I can request it. Czech police will respond, but I doubt they'll get there in time to help."

Tatyana took a deep breath. She could tell from Laurel's voice she was worried too. "What does Roth say about all this?"

"Washington's a zoo. The media are tearing the president to shreds over this. Saying it's his fault for being soft on the Kremlin."

"And how's he responding to that?"

"Not well, as I'm sure you can imagine."

"And Roth?"

"Roth's worried."

"About our response?"

"The president has said he wants to speak to Lance as soon as possible."

"Presidents don't usually speak to assets in the field."

"No, they do not."

"And that's why Roth's worried?"

"Well, the president has refused to say what he wants to speak to Lance about."

"If they're calling him weak, he's going to want to hit hard."

"The question is, what's he going to want to hit?"

"Well, we've got more immediate concerns," Tatyana said.

As if on cue, Laurel said, "Hold on, they've stopped."

"Who's stopped."

"Lance and Valentina. They're just outside a little village."

"Is it a defensible position?"

"Not particularly. Just a clearing by the side of the road. By the river."

"Why stop there?"

"Maybe he knows something."

"Maybe something's wrong."

Tatyana waited with bated breath while Laurel watched the satellite feed. "What's happening?" Tatyana said when the suspense became too much.

"The door's opening," Laurel said.

"The car door?"

"Yes. Lance just got out."

"Why is he getting—"

"Oh, God!"

"What?"

"Oh my God!"

"What is it, Laurel?"

"He's been shot. He's down."

"Is it definitely him?"

"It's a headshot, Tatyana."

"What?"

"He's dead."

53

Stăn lit a cigarette and turned to Constantin. "If we ever see that jet, it will be a miracle."

"We'll see it," Constantin said, but he wasn't sure if he even believed the words himself. It had been hours since the embassy attack. Their window for making a getaway was getting smaller by the minute. And now, a high-value CIA target had been added to their list of problems. "This man is the target Shipenko's been trying to draw out all along," he said.

Stăn sucked hard on his cigarette and nodded. "We're like Osama bin Laden after the 9/11 attacks," he said. "The only difference being, he didn't drive around the New York countryside for hours after the World Trade Center came down. He got as far away as possible and then kept his head down."

"The ping's stopped," Constantin said. "Just outside the village up ahead."

"What do we do?"

"You heard Shipenko. We don't have to go after the American."

"But he'll sweeten the pot if we do."

"The pot's sweet enough," Constantin said. "Pull over here, and we'll wait for them to start moving again."

Stăn pulled over at the side of the road and opened his window. "Nice out here," he said.

Constantin nodded.

"What do you think it will be like where we're going?"

"What do you mean?" Constantin said. "We're going to Moscow."

"But it's not like we'll be free to walk around. We'll be spending the rest of our lives in bunkers underground, hiding from everyone, scared to go outside in case a satellite spots us."

"We'll be hiding," Constantin said, "but not underground. The opposite, actually. We'll be in penthouses, Stăn. And we'll be living off the fat of the land."

Stăn sighed. "I don't see it," he said.

"You don't have to see it. You just have to keep moving forward, one step at a time, until this is over."

"How long will he make us follow Valentina?"

"Until he can get more feet on the ground. He won't want her defecting to the American side. Not after what he's done."

"She can name us too."

"Makes no difference," Constantin said. "They already had enough to identify us."

"What about our families?"

"They'll be alive," Constantin said after a long pause. "That's something."

"Maybe we can look after them from Moscow," Stăn said. "Send money."

Constantin nodded. "Maybe."

"Maybe we'll even be able to bring them over one day when everything's cleared."

"Maybe," Constantin said. He thought about what he'd said to Cosmina earlier. He knew she would pass on the message. He'd already decided, if he got through this alive, he would never contact his son again. Not ever. It was the only chance the boy had at leaving behind the curse that Constantin and his forbears had passed on to him.

The phone rang, and he looked at it. "It's him again," he said before answering.

"Well, pick it up," Stăn said.

"What is it?" Constantin said, looking at Stăn.

Shipenko's voice filled the line. "He's dead. She's killed him."

"What?"

"Valentina killed the American."

"You're sure?"

"She shot him in the back of the head. He's lying in snow as we speak. I'm looking at the feed with my own eyes. I can see the blood, Constantin."

"But how is that possible?"

"She had a gun. He didn't. She must have known she couldn't keep running."

"According to the tracker, the vehicle's not moving."

"She's just sitting there," Shipenko said. "The engine's not even running."

"What's she waiting for?"

"You!" Shipenko said.

"But she knows we're trying to kill her."

"No," Shipenko said. "When I spoke to her, I told her I'd take her back if she killed the American."

"But would she trust you? We've been hunting her like wolves."

"She has no choice. She's hurt. She can't keep going. And she knows coming back to me will be better than the deal she'll get from the Americans. She's slit too many throats to go in that direction."

"So," Constantin said, "what do you want us to do?"

"What do you think I want you to do? Kill the bitch."

"Not bring her home?"

"She's exhausted. She's desperate. She's injured. She can barely walk. When she sees you, she'll think you've come as friends. You could walk right up to her, and she wouldn't resist. All you have to do is put a bullet in her head, and your ordeal is over, Constantin. Do you think you can handle that?"

Constantin looked at Stăn. "And that jet is still waiting for us in Linz?"

"Yes. Scarcely thirty minutes from where you are. I've had my team map a route to the airfield for you. You won't have any trouble getting to it, and a few hours after you take off, you'll be in Moscow."

"We'll be flying through NATO airspace," Constantin said. "That won't be an issue?"

"The jet's registered to Bahrain. No one will question it."

"Even after today's attack?"

"Look, Constantin, this is your chance. Finish the job, get on the plane, and you'll never have to worry about another thing as long as you live."

54

L ance and Valentina approached the village. It was a picturesque place in a deep valley of the Vltava River, and he told her to turn down a side road.

They passed stuccoed houses with red tile roofs, and when they rounded the bend, they saw rich forest sloping steeply up from the river. Perched high on top of a rocky outcrop was a white castle. It looked like it had been taken straight from the pages of a child's fairytale.

"Wow," Valentina said.

"Pretty, isn't it?" Lance said.

She nodded. "A pretty place to die."

Lance said nothing, keeping his eye on the road.

Valentina said, "You know what they call me in Moscow?"

He shook his head.

"*Volchitsey.* She-wolf."

He shrugged. "I wonder how you got that name."

"We both know," she said, "but they have a nickname for Tatyana too."

"I don't want to hear it."

"Of course you don't because you don't want to know the truth about her."

"I already know the truth about her."

Valentina let out a wheezy laugh and sucked hard on a cigarette. Her skin was as pale as paper now, and she was growing weaker by the minute.

"Stop here," Lance said.

She pulled off the road in front of a small grotto. There was an alcove for a statue, but the statue was gone. There were some flowers and a wreath in front of where it should have been.

"That used to be for the Virgin Mary," Lance said.

She looked at it. "Not anymore."

"No," he said, taking off the heavy orange construction coat he'd been wearing. "The Communists got to it."

She opened her seatbelt and watched him. He could tell she knew what was coming. He didn't think she had the strength left to resist it.

"I lied to you," she said.

He nodded.

"What they say about me, what Tatyana said about me, it's true."

He handed her the coat. "Put this on."

She was looking out at the river. It was a damp morning, misty, with a chill in the air. Beyond the grotto, the wide river bend was covered in ice. They could see a place by the bank where children had been testing its thickness. There were some hockey goals, but they hadn't put them out yet.

"Let me go out on the ice," she said softly.

He followed her gaze. The view was very picturesque,

very beautiful, with cliffs and forest rising on the far side of the river like a postcard.

"It's not thick enough," he said.

She nodded. She was resigning herself to her fate. Lance lit himself a cigarette.

"It's peaceful out here," she said.

He nodded.

"You've been here before. You know this place."

He looked back across the road. Through the trees, they could see a grand house with balconies overlooking the river and the same red tile roof they'd seen in the village. "Someone I knew lived in that house," he said.

"When?"

He shook his head. He didn't want to get into it. "Those sheds up the road," he said, changing the subject, "the Russians used to store emergency supplies in them. Gas masks. Radiation suits. Geiger counters."

"In case of nuclear war."

He nodded.

She was silent for a moment, then said, "There are things I can offer you. Things you're not aware of."

"I don't want anything from you."

"Tatyana. She has connections you're not aware of. You're wrong to trust her."

"I don't trust her. I don't trust anyone."

"People say that," she said, "but if you look closely, it's never true. There's always someone they trust. Someone they let their guard down for."

"You think I do that for Tatyana?"

"I've seen the footage."

"What footage?"

"I'd been trying to place you," she said. "I knew I'd

seen you before. Then, when we saw Tatyana at the gas station, I remembered where I knew you from."

"Where?"

"There was some footage I saw once. Footage I wasn't supposed to see. It was of Tatyana, tied to a bed, slowly being strangled to death."

Lance nodded but said nothing.

"She would have died," Valentina said. "She very nearly did die. But someone broke in at the last minute and killed the man."

Lance remained silent.

"But then, you already knew that, didn't you, Lance Spector?"

"Stop talking," Lance said. She'd put on the orange coat, and he said, "Do up the zip."

"That footage," she said, "it really got my heart pounding."

"What are you talking about?"

"There was something so...."

"What?"

"*Intense* about it."

"Well, it's in the past."

"It could have been me on that bed," she said. "I did all the same jobs as Tatyana. It could just as easily have been me in that room, dying, praying to be rescued." She put a hand on his leg.

"Don't do this," he said.

"Do you think I'd have been any less loyal to you if I was the one you'd rescued? Do you think I'd have been any different?"

"Pull up the hood," Lance said.

She moved her hand further up his thigh, and he brushed it away.

"Whatever she is to you. That could have been me."

He said nothing. They sat in silence for a minute, then she said, "Well, it got my heart pounding. That's all I wanted to say."

"It's time to go," he said.

"Let me go out on the ice," she said again. "Please. You can give me that much."

"Let's not make this any worse than necessary."

"I can't imagine you find it easy to kill women."

"You imagine wrong."

"Do I?"

He clenched his jaw. His chest felt tight. She was quiet, calm, but he knew she was fighting with every weapon she had. Fighting tooth and nail. She was fighting for her life. She knew that if she could find even an ounce of compassion in him, it might not be too late to save herself. It pained him to watch her. It pained him to know she would never find what she was looking for.

Their eyes locked, and she whispered, "Lance, please."

"Valentina," he said, "you have to get out. It's time."

"I *know* you don't want to kill me."

He leaned over her and pushed open the door.

"You need me. These men Shipenko is sending, they're no joke. They don't make mistakes."

He finished his cigarette and flicked it out the door. Then he said, "Go with God."

She remained where she was. "If you're going to kill me, at least look me in the eye when you do it."

"You asked to go on the ice."

She looked at him, trying to read him. "You're not going to let me go on the ice."

He said nothing, and after a moment, she shook her

head. She pulled up the hood of the coat, turned, and got out of the car.

Lance watched her walk. She was visibly weaker than she'd been at the service station, like the life had already begun to drain away from her. She walked toward the river, and he knew what she was thinking. The water was frozen for about a hundred yards from the bank. Then the ice gave way to open water. She'd survived the ice before, and she was thinking she might do it again.

She was about twenty feet away when he raised the gun. It was Tatyana's gun, or more accurately, a gun he'd once given to her. Before him, it had belonged to Roth, and before Roth, his father. There was a star carved into the handle.

He raised it, aimed at the orange hood of the parka, and pulled the trigger.

55

L ance stared out the window at Valentina's body. He'd aimed for the head to make sure she fell face down. The blood was seeping into the snow around her head like a crimson halo, spreading across a surprisingly large area. She'd deserved it, but that was little consolation to him. He deserved the same himself. He'd done all the things she had. At times, he'd done worse. They may have fought for different sides, but their job was the same.

He wondered, when a man fought in a war, when he did all the things a soldier was supposed to do, would it make any difference in the end which side he fought for? Would that be taken into account in the final reckoning? Was pulling the trigger ever less damnable because of the flag on a man's sleeve?

He didn't know the answer, but what he did know was that it could just as easily have been him lying in the snow and her sitting in the car, holding the gun.

He lit a cigarette and blew the smoke out the window, careful not to let himself be seen by any satellites. It crossed his mind that Laurel would be watching, that she would think the body in the orange coat was his, but that couldn't be helped now. The plan depended on the Russians thinking he was dead. He needed their guard to be down.

He heard a car approaching and flicked away the cigarette. This was it, he thought. The moment he'd been waiting for. It was time to make the men who'd carried out the attack pay for what they'd done.

He looked out at the river one last time. Valentina had wanted to go out on the ice. She was a strange creature. Fewer than one person in a hundred could have survived water like that, but she was one of them.

He checked his gun as a maroon-colored minivan crested a rise in the road. It was moving slowly, and the passenger side window was open. That was his signal. They'd come for Valentina, and they'd come to kill her, not take her back.

He slipped out of the car on the side farther from them and backed away from it, remaining out of sight. He'd be seen by the satellite, of course, but that no longer mattered. The minivan came to a halt less than fifty yards down the road. He kept backing away, remaining out of sight, waiting for them to make their move.

It came in the form of the distinctive whoosh of a grenade launcher. A grenade had been fired, and a second later, it bounced off the roof of his vehicle, flew overhead, and exploded in the air behind him. He felt the heat of it but kept backing away from the car anyway. Some trees had caught fire, and the smoke and flame gave him additional cover.

The minivan remained where it was as a second grenade was launched from the same window. He shielded his face and braced, but this time the grenade found its mark. It struck the SUV's front windshield, lodging in the glass for a brief moment before exploding. Glass flew everywhere, and a thick cloud of black smoke billowed toward the sky.

That was the moment to strike. He rose to his feet and ran directly toward the burning SUV, his pistol in front of him like a bayonet. He rounded the front of the car and, concealed partially by the billowing smoke, dropped to one knee. Through squinted eyes, he peered in the direction of the minivan. The smoke stung, and he had to hold his breath, but the moment he made out its shape through the smoke, he let off four bullets, placed for the driver and front passenger.

He ducked back behind the SUV and waited. He could hear nothing over the noise of the flames. As the smoke cleared, he confirmed the bullets had hit where he'd intended—four holes clustered in two groups in the windshield.

He watched for any sign of movement. There was none. Cautiously, he rounded the SUV and crept forward. As he got closer, he made out two occupants. One, in the driver's seat, had been struck by a bullet in the forehead and was dead. The other was alive. A bullet had gone through his neck, and blood bubbled from the wound like a spring. He was trying desperately to stop the blood with his hands but in vain. The rest of the vehicle was unoccupied.

Lance got closer, watching the man's blood-soaked hands as he tried to stem the bleeding. "You're not going to make it," he said.

The man hadn't noticed Lance, and when he saw him, his eyes widened. He tried to speak, but Lance couldn't make out the words. He got closer, watching the road, the trees, the back of the vehicle.

"What is it?" Lance said as the man gasped desperately for breath, struggling to get some final words out.

It was strange, Lance knew, the things men said at such moments. There was a truth to their final words they rarely found during the rest of their lives. Few people were used to hearing them—doctors, priests, assassins. Lance had heard hundreds. He'd heard prayers, curses, messages for loved ones, pathetic babblings. This man had something to say, and Lance knew better than to let it go to waste.

He reached into the car and put his hand on the man's neck, helping slow the blood loss. The man tried to swallow. He coughed, and Lance could tell there was blood in his lungs. He was literally drowning.

"What is it?" Lance said, applying more pressure to the neck.

"You already know," the man managed to say.

"Know what?" Lance said.

Often, the final words were delusional. They made no sense. When they did make sense, it was almost always something personal, of no value to Lance. But every once in a while, a man said something actionable, something that affected the mission.

"You and me," the man said. "We're the same."

"What do you mean?"

"The same curse hangs over us both. I've never seen it before, but I see it now. You were born from as much blood as I was, and you'll drown in it the same as me."

"I see," Lance said, leaning back. He took his hand away from the man's neck.

"You're as damned as I am," the man continued, spitting blood as he spoke.

Lance looked down the road. It wound along the side of the river, hugging the rocky bank. "We are what we were born to be," he said.

The man grew silent then. Lance stood, watching him die. He lit a cigarette. When the cigarette was finished, the man was dead. Lance searched his pockets. He found a phone and checked it for the last number called. He called it and waited. It rang for a long time without any response. He could hear the analog clicks and buzzes of the GRU's authentication system, and he stepped back from the vehicle and looked skyward.

The line was opened, but no one said anything.

"Osip?" Lance said.

He could hear breathing, but there was still no response.

He looked up again and, knowing the Russian was watching him from his satellite, ran his blood-soaked finger across his neck and said, "I'm coming for you next, you son of a bitch."

56

K lára got out of the shower and toweled off. As she dried herself, she realized that her hands were shaking. She wasn't sure why. Nothing like that had ever happened to her before. She tried to steady them but couldn't. She wasn't all right. It didn't help that every time she closed her eyes, the images she'd seen of the embassy attack victims filled her mind.

Those casualties were her fault. That wasn't just her guilty conscience speaking. It was the official finding of the parliamentary investigation committee, which had been hastily set up to apportion blame for the biggest breach of Czech national security since the collapse of the Soviet Union. It had been less than forty-eight hours since the attack, and the committee had not only found her guilty of gross misconduct, but had revoked her security clearance, suspended her from her position at the BIS, and threatened her with a lengthy prison sentence if she ever breathed a word of it to the press.

"Fuckers," she said to her reflection in the mirror.

She could hear her cat mewling in the bedroom and

went out to it. "Shh," she said. It followed her to the kitchen and got in her way as she tried to feed it. More food ended up on the tiled floor of the kitchen than the cat's bowl, but she didn't care. She watched it eat for a minute, then went back to the bedroom and finished dressing. She got the gun she'd been given and put it into her inside jacket pocket. It was a clunky old thing, heavier than she was used to, but her own weapon had been confiscated by the BIS. She also opened her underwear drawer and dug down beneath the clothes to find the passport she'd hidden there. She looked at it, its unfamiliar red cover, the coat of arms of the Russian Federation.

When she was ready, she went back to the bathroom and took a final look at herself in the mirror. Passable, she thought and went to the kitchen. The cat was done eating and had done such a thorough job that she couldn't even tell where the food had spilled. She put on her coat and picked up the cat. "Come on, sweetie," she said as it struggled to get free. "It's going to be okay."

She brought the cat out of the apartment, down to the ground floor of the building, and out the front entrance. It looked around in the cold air in bewilderment. As she bent down and put it on the sidewalk, she wondered if it had ever felt outdoor air before in its life. It scurried a few feet away to a patch of pavement that wasn't covered with snow and looked back pitifully.

"Go on," Klára said. "We're both on our own now."

It was still dark out, before dawn, and she'd walked almost to the metro station before finding a cab. The cat followed her every step of the way, and she looked out at it from her seat in the car.

"Where to?" the driver said.

"The military hospital," she said, still looking at the cat.

The morning traffic was beginning to fill out, and it took longer than she'd expected to get to the hospital. When she arrived, she entered the lobby and flashed her revoked BIS credentials to the receptionist. She wasn't sure they'd work, but when the receptionist scanned them, no alarms sounded, no red lights flashed, and no guards came rushing toward her with their guns drawn. A green light appeared on the scanner, and the receptionist looked up at her expectantly.

"Tatyana Aleksandrova," Klára said.

The receptionist typed on her computer, then said, "Fourth floor."

Klára passed through security, put her gun through the scanner, and was given it back on the other side. She took the elevator to the fourth floor and asked the attendant at the nurses' station for Tatyana's room. They showed her to a room down one of the corridors with a uniformed policeman sitting on a chair by the door. Klára showed him the same BIS credentials, and he waved her through.

When she entered the room, Tatyana was awake. A television was on, showing cable news coverage of shelled-out buildings in Kyiv. The view then switched to the Ukrainian president, who had sent a recorded statement to the UN Security Council pleading for security assistance. He looked impressive, Klára thought, dressed in khakis with a gun holstered beneath his arm.

Tatyana picked up the controller and hit the mute button. "Klára," she said, "I wasn't expecting you."

"I know," Klára said.

"I'm flying back to Washington today."

"The doctors signed off on that?"

"I forced them to. I can't lie here and do nothing while the entire world burns."

"I know the feeling," Klára said, reaching into her inside jacket pocket. She found the cold steel of the gun and gripped the handle.

"I heard what happened to you," Tatyana said. "The committee's decision was—" She stopped short when she saw Klára's drawn gun.

It was an old Browning pistol, and Klára thought it felt very heavy in her hand.

"Where did you get that gun?" Tatyana said slowly.

"I found it," Klára said.

"You found it?"

"Yes," Klára said, handing it to Tatyana. "And I believe it belongs to you."

Tatyana took the gun hesitantly. "It was a gift," she said.

Klára nodded. It was old enough to have been used in the Second World War and, judging from the star carved into the handle, carried no small amount of sentimental value.

"Lance took it at the service station," Tatyana said. "Right before I was shot by Valentina."

Klára nodded. "I thought you'd want it back."

"But how did you get it? Lance disappeared."

"He did," Klára said, "but the gun didn't."

Tatyana eyed her skeptically. "That's very cryptic."

"It is, but it's all I can say right now."

Tatyana nodded, but the look on her face said she wasn't completely satisfied with the explanation.

Klára glanced at the television. "What a mess," she said.

The US president was giving a live press conference, and Tatyana unmuted it to hear what he was saying.

In response to recent Russian aggression in Prague, in Latvia, in Berlin, and most pressingly of all, in Ukraine, I've taken the unprecedented step of ordering the Pentagon to raise the readiness of the United States nuclear deterrent. This is in addition to the decision yesterday to send a Carrier Strike Group into the Black Sea. This marks the highest state of readiness that US and NATO forces have been at since the end of the Second World War and brings us one step closer to the unthinkable. I want to stress to the world that if war breaks out, it is not between the West and the Russian people. It is a war between the West and President Vladimir Molotov.

The view switched back to the studio, and Tatyana muted it again. "He's not messing around, is he?"

"Do you think it will be war?"

"Who knows?"

"I never thought we'd see this in our lifetime," Klára said. "Armies on the move, invading their neighbors, shelling cities in the middle of Europe. It's like something from our grandparents' time."

"I think we're beginning to realize that less has changed in the intervening decades than we thought," Tatyana said.

"Well," Klára said. "I hope something's changed."

Tatyana nodded. "We'll have to wait and see. You know what we say in Russia about these things."

"What do you say?"

"Whatever happened can happen again."

Klára nodded.

Tatyana had been holding the pistol in her hand. She turned it over and looked at the star on the handle. "I heard they put you on a leave of absence."

"Not a leave," Klára said. "I've been pushed out. It's official."

"I'm sorry."

Klára shrugged. "It's not your fault."

"No, but it doesn't sit well with me."

"I'll land on my feet."

"I'm sure you will," Tatyana said, "but it's not just that. It's the whole thing. The way it happened. I know the attackers are dead. Valentina Brik is dead. But something about it still feels like it all played out exactly how the Kremlin wanted."

"I get that same feeling," Klára said.

Tatyana nodded. "Having worked with the men responsible," she said, "I have the sense that there's very little we can do that doesn't play into their hands, one way or another."

"Well," Klára said, "we just landed Moscow with the biggest package of sanctions in history, and all that's happened is a spike in oil and gas prices."

"They're making more money than ever," Tatyana said.

"And none of the men who are truly behind the attack have been held to account. No one who pulls the strings has been punished. They're all sitting pretty."

"While thousands die and entire cities are shelled to rubble."

Klára nodded. Tatyana was looking at her curiously, and she wondered for a second if she'd guessed what was going on.

"I heard you went to inquire about Gilhofer's body," Tatyana said.

"I did, but it had already been flown back to the States."

"You two were closer than I realized."

"Not so close," Klára said.

"Then why ask to see his body?"

"I was," Klára said, hesitating. "I suppose I was looking for closure."

Tatyana nodded.

Klára waited to see if she would ask about her visit to his apartment, but it appeared that secret was still intact. "What about, Lance?" she said, changing the subject.

"What about him?" Tatyana said.

"Well, he killed Valentina. He killed the last two Romanians."

"And then he disappeared."

"Is that a common pattern?"

Tatyana shrugged, as if she'd never thought about it. "Not so common," she said. "Not like this."

"I see."

"Even Roth doesn't know where he is."

"He never called in?"

"I heard he made one call. The president wanted to speak to him personally."

Klára nodded. She'd heard the same thing. "I guess when the president wants to talk."

"You pick up the phone."

"I don't suppose you know what they talked about."

Tatyana let out a brief laugh. She wouldn't have been

able to say, even if she did. "No one but Lance and the President know what took place on that call," she said.

"Maybe we'll find out," Klára said.

Tatyana shrugged. "I just hope I see him again."

"You sound like you think you might not."

"With a man like Lance Spector, it's hard to know."

Klára looked at her then. "Maybe you're better off."

Tatyana shrugged.

They both looked at each other for a moment, neither saying anything, then Klára said, "Well, I just wanted to give you your gun. I knew you'd want it."

"Thank you," Tatyana said.

Klára was at the door when Tatyana said, "Klára."

"Yes?"

"Whatever you've got planned, good luck."

Klára said nothing. She went down to the lobby and had the receptionist call her a cab. When it arrived, she told the driver to take her to the airport.

She sat back in the seat and wondered about her cat. It was snowing. The poor thing wouldn't like that.

She reached into her pocket for the envelope she'd found at Gilhofer's apartment. Tatyana had been right about one thing. They had grown close.

Klára wasn't sure what exactly had spurred her to go. There hadn't been any concrete reason. She'd wanted closure, she supposed, but what she'd found was the exact opposite. On the mantle by the door, next to the Browning pistol, was an envelope with her name written on the front. At first, she'd thought it was a final note from Gilhofer, but, of course, that made no sense. Gilhofer hadn't known he was going to die that day. Even if he had, she didn't think he'd have been writing goodbye notes to her.

She opened the envelope and almost dropped it when she saw the contents. There was the Russian passport she had with her now—her photo on the page, but a false name. And there was a business card for a London cab company. On the back was written simply, 'Ask for Clint.'

She didn't dare call the number from her cell, but at the Vyšehrad metro station she found a payphone and dialed the number. A woman answered English with an Indian accent and asked if she needed a taxi.

"No," Klára said, "I'm calling for Clint."

"Clint Eastwood?"

"I don't know."

"Leave me your number," the girl said. "He'll call you back."

Klára gave her the payphone number and waited next to it. A few minutes passed, and she was beginning to wonder if the whole thing was a joke when the phone started to ring.

She picked up, looking around the station nervously for anyone who might be watching. "Klára," she said into the receiver.

A man's voice spoke back. "Lance Spector."

"Lance!"

"Remember me?"

"I remember you."

"I take it you found my message."

"I did, but how could you possibly have known I would?"

"I didn't," he said, "but I figured, if she goes back to Gilhofer's apartment, then I want to hear from her."

"And why's that?"

"Because of what it would say about you."

"And what would it say?"

"That your answer would be yes."

"My answer to what?"

"To whether or not you want to finish the job."

"Finish the job?" she said quietly.

"That's right."

"What job?"

"You know what job."

AUTHOR'S NOTE

First off, I want to thank you for reading my book. As a reader, you might not realize how important a person like you is to a person like me.

I've been a writer for fifty years, and despite the upheavals my industry has faced, the ups and downs, the highs and lows, one thing remains constant.

You.

The reader.

And at the end of each book, I like to take a moment to acknowledge that fact.

To thank you.

Not just on my own behalf, but on behalf of all fiction writers.

Because without you, these books simply would not exist.

You're the reason they're written. Your support is what makes them possible. And your reviews and recommendations are what spreads the word.

So, thanks for that. I really do mean it.

While I have your attention, I'd like to give you a little

bit of background into my opinion on the events portrayed in this book.

Writing about politics is not easy, and I hope none of my personal thoughts and opinions managed to find their way into this story. I never intend to raise political points in my writing, and I never intend to take a stand. I'm one of those guys who stays out of politics as much as possible, and I would hate to think that any political ideas raised in my book hampered your ability to enjoy the story or relate to the characters.

Because really, this is your story.

These characters are your characters.

When you read the book, no one knows what the characters look like, what they sound like, or what they truly think and feel, but you. It's your story, written for you, and the experience of it is created by you when you read the words and flip the pages.

I write about people who work for the federal government. The nature of their work brings them up against issues of national security and politics, but apart from that, I truly do try to keep any views I might have to myself. So please, don't let any of my words offend you, and if you spot anything in my writing that you feel is unfair, or biased, or off-color in any way, feel free to let me know.

My email address is below, and if you send a message, while I might not get back to you immediately, I will receive it, and I will read it.

saulherzog@authorcontact.com

Likewise, if you spot simpler errors, like typos and misspellings, let me know about those too. We writers have a saying:

To err is human. To edit, divine.

And we live by it.

I'm going to talk a little about some of the true facts that this book is based on, but before I do, I'd like to ask for a favor.

I know you're a busy person, I know you just finished this book and you're eager to get on to whatever is in store next, but if you could find it in your heart to leave me a review, I'd be truly humbled.

I'm not a rich man. I'm not a powerful man. There's really nothing I can offer you in return for the kindness.

But what I will say is that it is a kindness.

If you leave me a review, it will help my career. It will help my series to flourish and find new readers. It will make a difference to one guy, one stranger you've never met and likely will never meet, and I'll appreciate that fact.

Now that those formalities are out of the way, let's talk about some of the events in this book.

As I write these words, the world watches in shock and horror the war of aggression President Vladimir Putin has unleashed on the Ukraine. These events were on the horizon when I started writing the book, and there is no doubt they influenced my thinking as I developed the plot, but I could scarcely believe my eyes when Russian troops actually crossed the border and started shelling Ukrainian cities. It is a strange feeling for a person in my profession when the events on the nightly news are more dramatic and alarming than the plots of my novels. All I can say is that, like everyone else, I had no idea that Russia was actually going to invade the Ukraine, and my thoughts and prayers are with every person affected by that unjust and illegal conflict. While the plot of the next book will certainly have to take account of the events that are unfolding before our eyes, the true events that were included in this book are more historical in nature.

The first that comes to mind is Valentina's use of the PSS silent pistol and the NRS-2 Scout Firing Knife. Both are real weapons developed by the Soviet Union for use by assassins. The PSS, also known as the MSS "Vul," was developed in the early 1980s for assassinations and reconnaissance and was issued to KGB Spetsnaz units beginning in 1983. It is still in development and was updated in 2011 to use a more powerful silent 7.62x43 mm SP-16 cartridge. Today, elite units from the FSB and MVD in Russia, as well as similar units in Georgia, are known to use the weapon.

The firing mechanism in the PSS was reproduced for use in the NRS-2 Scout Firing Knife, which was manufactured during the 1980s at the Tula Arms Plant. Soviet Spetsnaz units were issued the weapon, and it remains in use today among special law enforcement units in Russia. The knife can be used for stabbing or throwing, and a single shot can be fired with a twenty-five-meter range.

It hardly needs to be said, but any country that commissions weapons for assassins probably has assassins, and probably carries out assassinations. At the very least, it keeps that option on the table.

The depictions of the US and Russian embassies in Prague are accurate, and the history of the Russian embassy, including its use by the Gestapo during the Nazi occupation of the Second World War, is also true. The tunnels that the Gestapo built were indeed used by the Soviets to house KGB Line X officers. Today, the building is widely suspected to be a hub of Russian intelligence activity in Central Europe.

Perhaps the most disturbing thing my research uncovered are the events that took place at the Pitești Prison between 1949 and 1951. Known today as the Pitești Experiment or the Pitești Phenomenon, this chapter is a truly shocking example of the pain and degradation that man can inflict on his fellow man. The words written in the book are no exaggeration, and in fact, I forced myself to hold back and tone down the more disturbing events that I unearthed. For those who are interested, there is ample material available publicly that I will allow you to look up for yourself. Even here, in this author's note, I cannot bring myself to go into it in more detail.

The other incident that is based on history is the Iași Pogrom, in which Romanian government forces under the command of Marshal Ion Antonescu killed 13,266 Jews, a third of the city's Jewish population, during the first week of July 1941.

I draw from such true events for no reason other than to emphasize, as we are being forced again to witness with Putin's invasion of Ukraine, that the truth is often worse than anything that occurs in fiction. It is a sad fact, and one that many people do not realize, but what we read in today's espionage thrillers or see on the silver screen is nothing compared to what has actually happened, and continues to happen.

I am told from time to time that events in my books are unrealistic or far-fetched, and while I wish that were the case, any reading of history tells us otherwise. There is a famous quote from the Roman playwright, Terence.

Homo sum, humani nihil a me alienum puto.

It is translated in English to:

I am a man, and nothing human is alien to me.

While I remain an optimist on the direction the world is taking, and while I believe people are more good than bad, the truth is that terrible things have happened in the world, and we do ourselves no favors in pretending otherwise.

Finally, I'd be remiss if I didn't tell you that Book Four in the Lance Spector series, *The Sleeper,* is now available for pre-order.

So grab your copy now. I promise, if you enjoyed the first three, you're only going to be drawn into these characters more deeply!

God bless and happy reading,

Saul Herzog

Made in the USA
Thornton, CO
04/20/23 20:43:36

b38e3979-b905-49e1-bff3-ffcfa49580bcR01